Moving Out

A.J. WOODS

First edition

ISBN: 979-8-9914136-4-0

Cover art by Spellcast Books

This book was professionally typeset on Reedsy.
Find out more at reedsy.com

To anyone that feels like they are unlovable. You aren't. I promise.

FEBRUARY

Chapter 1

Ashtyn King stares at the man in front of her with a mix of boredom and contempt. She tries to keep her eyes open, but it's getting harder and harder. How she ended up on a first date with a man she barely knows, on Valentine's Day of all days, is beyond her. She leans her head into her hand, her spoon twirling circles in her soup absentmindedly.

"So, do you like being a Kindergarten teacher?" her date, Spencer, asks. He's cute, with black framed glasses and dark, windswept hair that would normally make Ashtyn swoon. But for some reason, she doesn't feel anything towards him. In fact, all she feels is indifference.

"Um, yeah, it's fun," Ashtyn responds. "You never know what's going to come out of a five-year-old's mouth, whether it's the f-word or a spew of vomit."

Spencer wrinkles his nose in disgust and puts his fork full of food back down. "Sounds... interesting."

Ashtyn sighs heavily. "Sorry." She rubs her temples, trying to mitigate the headache she can feel forming behind her eyes. The restaurant is crowded, filled with couples in love that gaze adoringly at one another. She should have never agreed to this date.

"No, it's okay. I want... to hear about your life." He doesn't sound too convincing, but he sure is faking it. She really needs to delete all her dating apps, at this point. This is the first date she's been on in almost a year. She's rusty, out of practice, or maybe she's just tired of it all. Pretending to care about small talk and exchanging pleasantries. It's all just so exhausting. Especially when most of what everyone says ends up being a lie. What's the point of any of it anyway? There isn't one.

She's about to change the subject when her eyes flick upward, and she sees a person enter the restaurant that makes her blood run cold. No, no, no, no. Why is *he* here? He cannot see her here, on a date, looking as incredible as she does right now. And on fucking Valentine's Day of all days. It feels like the universe is playing a cruel joke on her right about now.

"Fuck," Ashtyn whispers under her breath, averting her eyes from the doorway.

Spencer looks up, startled. "Are you okay?"

Ashtyn forces a smile to her face. "Peachy." She's about to make an excuse to run to the bathroom and hide, when Drew sees her, their eyes locking from across the restaurant. Surprise, then something like amusement, crosses his face. Ashtyn clenches her fists and takes a deep breath, preparing herself for the sparring match that's about to occur. Well, at least this would be more interesting than boring conversation with Spencer. Even if it's going to infuriate her senseless.

Drew saunters his way over to them, hand on the lower back of someone Ashtyn can only assume is his date for the evening. She's beautiful, long blonde hair cascading down to her thin waist. Her expression is blank as they arrive at the table, and Ashtyn can't help but admire her makeup. She's applied the sharpest eyeliner Ashtyn thinks she's ever seen in her life.

"Ashtyn," Drew purrs as he pauses next to their table.

She keeps her face neutral, even as adrenaline floods through her entire body. "Sorry, do I know you?"

Drew throws his head back and lets out a laugh that injects itself right into her bloodstream. It brings her back to New Year's Eve... and she has to shake her head to clear her thoughts. Her body thrums, as it always seems to do around Drew, with something like anticipation.

"Nice to see you, too," he says. He sticks his hand out to Spencer. "Andrew Mitchell. Ashtyn's certified best friend."

"Again, I've never met this man in my life," Ashtyn says, taking a sip of wine to try and compose herself.

Spencer just furrows his eyebrows in confusion and takes Drew's hand. "Right. Uh, nice to meet you. Spencer Davis."

"Seriously. He's not my best friend," she reiterates. She stares daggers in Drew's direction, trying to convey her anger at him with just a look. His smile is so wide it makes Ashtyn's skin itch with irritation. She's about to snap at him when the waiter walks up and shows Drew and his date to their table. Which just so happens to be right next to Ashtyn and Spencer's. Unbelievable.

"I will give you one thousand dollars to move them to another table," Ashtyn says to the waiter. He chuckles, thinking she's joking, when she is in fact very serious. He notices her face, the grave expression etched into her features, and scurries away without another look.

Drew's date frowns as she sits down and flips her hair over her shoulder. Spencer looks confused, the poor guy. Drew is still all smiles as he sits down next to them. "It's like a double date!" he says, excitedly.

"You stay on your side of the room, and I'll stay on mine," Ashtyn says through gritted teeth. Drew gives her a mock salute and turns his attention back to his date.

Andrew "Drew" Mitchell is the bane of Ashtyn King's existence, ever since he dropped a moving box on her foot. Last year, Ashtyn and her best friend, Ava, got a new roommate, Shiloh. And with Shiloh, came his best friend, Drew. His charm, good looks, and overall positive attitude made Ashtyn bristle with annoyance every time they were forced to hang out. And then the New Year's Eve kiss happened...

Ashtyn likes to tell herself that it didn't really mean anything. Everyone else had someone to kiss, and it just happened. He'd been staring at her when the clock struck midnight, and she couldn't help herself. She can't remember who moved first, just that they were both suddenly on each other, their lips pressed lightly together. She tells herself it was a moment of loneliness and weakness and tries to forget about it, but it comes back to her in her dreams. Dreams she has no control over, mind you.

She hasn't seen him since, nor have they spoken. It's better this way. It keeps her feelings in check. Not that she has any feelings for Drew... absolutely not. No, he flirts with her, and she ignores him. That's how it will stay. It's safest that way.

"Is there some kind of history there?" Spencer questions, voice low, bringing Ashtyn back to the present.

"No!" she exclaims, too defensive and a touch too loud. She clears her throat and lowers her voice. "There is no history there. He's just my roommate's best friend."

"Oh. Sorry, I thought you lived alone—"

"I have two roommates," Ashtyn interrupts. "I know. Everyone's always surprised I still live with friends." She can feel Drew's presence heavily. Even though he's not looking at her, it's like she can't escape him. She *knows* he's right there, listening to their conversation.

"That's okay. I know how expensive it can be to live on your own," Spencer replies.

Ashtyn sighs. It was exactly this reason that she and Ava had found Shiloh. Their best friend, Brooke, had just moved out, and they couldn't afford the rent on their house without a third person. Enter, Shiloh. He was the perfect roommate: quiet, kept to himself, and overall, a good person. It was no wonder he and Ava fell in love. Ashtyn is so happy they found each other, even if they tried to keep it from her for a while. Shiloh is like a brother to her, and Ava is the Meredith to her Cristina. She can't imagine her life without them. Although now, with their coupling, sometimes Ashtyn feels more alone than ever. It's not that she *wants* a relationship, because she definitely doesn't, but sometimes she feels that familiar pang of loneliness when she watches her friends act completely in love with each other. Whenever that happens, she just shoves it deep, deep down.

"Psst."

Ashtyn ignores the sound coming from the other table.

"Psst!"

She looks over at Drew, annoyed. "What do you want?"

"Who is this guy?" he whispers, pointing at her date as if Spencer isn't literally right in front of them.

"None of your business."

Spencer clears his throat. "Uh, I'm pretty sure I gave you my name—"

"Don't talk to him," Ashtyn snaps at Spencer, interrupting him. "He thrives on the attention. And we can't all fit in the room if his ego gets any bigger."

"Hey, can we switch places for a minute?" Drew asks Spencer. Ashtyn's mouth drops open in utter shock. He can't be serious.

"Uh—"

"It'll just be for a minute. Cara here will keep you company. Won't you, babe?" Cara, Drew's date, looks up from her menu with a frown and rolls her eyes. Drew gets up and ushers Spencer out of his chair. Spencer, stunned, doesn't even put up a fight. Ashtyn watches it all unfold, and her heart starts to race.

Drew plops down in the now unoccupied chair, lazy smile on his face. "Hi."

"What the fuck are you doing?"

"Just saying hi."

"You're insane, you know that right?"

Drew actually takes a sip of Spencer's wine. "So, how's it going?"

"Are you purposely trying to ruin my date? Or are you just naturally this fucking annoying?"

He places a hand on his heart, eyebrows raised. "I'm offended you think I'm ruining your date, when I know for a fact that I'm saving you from it."

"Uh, I'm still right here," Spencer says. Both of them ignore him. Not even Cara looks at him. So much for keeping him company.

"I'm seriously considering drowning you in my soup right about now." This just makes Drew laugh, which infuriates her even more. "Seriously, Drew. Can you just let me enjoy my date?"

"You were enjoying yourself?"

Her blood runs cold, and she rolls her eyes. "Does it matter?"

"Yes, Ashtyn, it does." The way he says it sends shivers through her. They stare at each other, so many unspoken things vibrating between them. His cologne wafts over the table, a familiar scent among the chaos of the restaurant.

"Is this about what happened at New Year's?" She's surprised the question comes out of her mouth. "Do I need to let you down easy?"

"Let me down? That would imply there was something between us." The way he says it, with just a tad bit of seriousness in his voice, makes her face flush with heat.

"*Is* there something between you?" Spencer asks, eyes still locked on the both of them.

Drew and Ashtyn snap their heads up in sync and say, "No." Cara snorts, but doesn't look up from her menu. Spencer sighs, as if wondering how he ever ended up here in the first place.

"Can you just go back to your own date?" Ashtyn questions.

Before Drew can answer, Spencer gets up and takes some cash out of his wallet. He holds it up, setting it on the table. "You know, I think I'm gonna go. This should cover everything."

"Wait, Spencer, please," she pleads. She gets up from the table, but Spencer turns and places a hand out in front of him.

"You know, I've been on some pretty bad dates in my life, but I think this might be the worst." His words stun her into silence. "Have a good rest of your night." She can do nothing but watch him leave.

Once he's outside, she whirls on Drew, venom in her voice. "What is your fucking problem?"

"Ash—"

"What did I say about calling me that?"

"You weren't serious about that guy, were you? He's an asshole."

"Really? Cause from where I'm standing, you're the asshole. You had no right to come in here and interrupt us!"

To his credit, Drew actually looks ashamed, a blush staining his cheeks. He frowns, clearing his throat. "I'm sorry. I-I didn't—"

"Didn't what?" Ashtyn interrupts. "Think I'm capable of going on a date just for the fun of it? Have the desire to go home and fuck someone just for the sake of fucking someone? Did it really fucking matter if I liked him or not? I don't need anyone's permission to go out."

"Ashtyn, that's not—"

She gathers her purse and coat from the back of her chair. "Can you just leave me alone, please? I don't know if you got the wrong idea during New Year's, but I'm not interested. So, just leave me alone." She doesn't care if her words are mean. She doesn't care if she hurts his feelings. She doesn't care. She turns to Cara, who is looking between them with her eyes narrowed. "I'm sorry."

Before anyone can utter another word, Ashtyn stalks out of the restaurant without a backward glance.

* * *

As she enters the house, Ashtyn hears the TV playing softly in the living room. She strips off her heels and tosses them in the corner along with her coat, her height decreasing significantly without the shoes. She pads into the living room and sees her roommates on the couch, Ava's head in Shiloh's lap as his fingers twirl lazily in her hair. Ashtyn plops next to them, resting Ava's feet gently in her lap, careful not to disturb her.

"She's missing her favorite part," Shiloh whispers. *The Proposal* plays on the screen, Ryan Reynolds about to confess his love to Sandra Bullock.

"I'm not asleep," Ava mumbles and then promptly lets out a soft snore, followed by an incredibly loud one.

"I don't know how you handle her snoring," Ashtyn says, smiling at her friend, remembering the days when they shared a dorm room. She'd had to wear earplugs to bed.

"It helps that she's cute." Shiloh looks down at his girlfriend in adoration. "So, how was your date?"

"Terrible," Ashtyn replies, sighing heavily. "Your stupid best friend interrupted us."

Shiloh frowns. "Drew was there?"

"Yes, and he literally made my date get up and leave."

"You're kidding."

"Unfortunately, I am not."

"I'm sorry. I can talk to him if you want me to."

"Oh, I think he got the message that I was mad at him." She sighs again. "It's whatever. It was a shit date before that, anyway. How was y'all's night?" The remnants of Chinese takeout litters the coffee table.

"Are you going to punch me if I say perfect?"

"Yes."

Shiloh stares down at Ava with more love in his eyes than Ashtyn thinks she has in her whole body. "It was perfect."

Well, at least someone had a good night. Ashtyn smiles at her friends. "I'm glad you guys had a good night."

"And I'm sorry you didn't."

Ashtyn waves him off. "It's fine. I'm used to it." Their cat, Jess, jumps up on the couch and snuggles into Ashtyn's lap, purring loudly. She's nearing one year old already, and she's grown immensely since they rescued her outside of a bar alleyway as a kitten.

Shiloh raises his eyebrows at Ashtyn. "You know what she would say to that, don't you?" He looks down at Ava, pointedly.

"Yes, which is why I'm glad she's sound asleep." Ava lets out another snore, and Ash stifles a giggle. "Let her enjoy the last few hours of her Valentine's Day. She doesn't need to get upset because of me."

The credits roll, and Shiloh sighs. "I don't think there's any point waking her up, anyway. I should probably bring her up to bed."

Jess perks her ears up as if she understands what he's saying. "Oh, no you don't," Ashtyn says, holding the cat close to her chest. "I need you tonight more than he does."

Shiloh scoops Ava into his arms effortlessly and carries her up the stairs toward whichever room they're sharing for the night. Jess struggles out of Ashtyn's arms until she plops to the floor and scurries after them. Ashtyn sighs.

It looks like she's going to bed alone tonight.

Chapter 2

It's incredibly rare for Drew Mitchell to have an empty bed. Especially on Valentine's Day, of all days. And yet, here he is, bed empty and heart racing.

What the fuck had he been thinking ruining Ashtyn's date like that? He wasn't thinking, that's the problem. He'd seen her, in that gorgeous fucking dress, and lost all sense of time and space. He'd forgotten Cara was right there. He'd forgotten everything that wasn't Ashtyn King and made an utter fool of himself.

He thinks back to the day he first saw her, copper hair tied up in a bun, black leggings hugging her ass, and an oversized sweater hanging off her shoulder. He'd been so stunned at her presence that he dropped the box he was holding right on her foot, infuriating her senseless. He'd felt all the bravado he usually employed in these types of situations seep out of his pores, and he was left utterly helpless. She was the most beautiful woman he had ever seen. And he'd spent the last year trying to get her to know that. He'd put on as much charm as possible, bought her drinks, done *anything*, just to get her to look at him. But she'd refuted him every step of the way. And then New Year's happened...

He'd already promised himself he would not kiss her. He was afraid that he wouldn't survive it, and he had been right. The clock struck twelve, all of their friends around them, coupled up and kissing, and he'd just looked at her. And she looked back. He's not sure which of them moved first, but it didn't really matter. All that mattered was that their lips met, and Drew knew he was fucked. She tasted like champagne and cherry lip gloss, and the way her lips felt against his own... words could never describe it. And then they'd separated, and the look in her eyes almost broke him then and there. Without a word, she turned away from him and hid in the kitchen for the rest of the night. They hadn't spoken since. Until tonight...

Until he ruined everything.

Drew slams his fist down on his mattress and gets up, unable to sleep. He can't stop thinking about her, about everything he said to her. He steps out onto the balcony of his new apartment, a perk of the new promotion he got at work, and the crisp February air is like a shock wave to his system. He takes a deep breath, his exhale coming out in a plume of frosty air.

He thinks about texting Cara and apologizing, *again*, but she probably doesn't want to talk to him right now. Even though they aren't anywhere near serious, just the occasional hookup here and there, she was pissed at the way he behaved at dinner. He can't blame her. He's such a fucking idiot.

He stares out at the city, lights bright and twinkling. He loves the location of his new apartment: top floor, downtown view, right next to work. He's still settling in, having moved in a few weeks ago. He's getting used to the new layout. It doesn't quite feel like home just yet. Something's missing...

He taps his phone anxiously when it starts to buzz with an incoming call. He looks down at the name and sighs. He probably should have seen this coming. "Let me guess. She told you?" he answers.

"What the fuck is wrong with you?" his best friend, Shiloh, asks as way of greeting.

"Yeah, I've been asking myself the same thing all night."

"Seriously, man, we've talked about this." Oh, they had talked about this, alright. Shiloh had made it very clear that his roommates were off-limits to Drew when he moved in with them. But now, Shiloh has Ava. And Drew still doesn't have anyone.

Drew sighs. "You don't need to remind me how much of an idiot I am. I know I fucked up."

"Tell me what happened." So, Drew does. When he's finished, Shiloh lets out a low whistle. "Man, I feel like I should punch you for that poor guy. And for Ash. Mostly for Ash."

"Trust me, that guy didn't give a fuck about her."

"And how do you know that?"

"I just do."

Shiloh lets out a breath. "You're just lucky Ava was asleep when Ash came home and told me what happened. Otherwise, you know she'd be on the phone with you right now instead of me."

Drew laughs. "I'm sure I'll get an earful tomorrow. Er, I guess today." He looks at his watch. It's nearing 1AM. He hears a soft snore from the other side of the line. "You really sleep with that jackhammer every night?"

"Careful, or I really will punch you," Shiloh warns, but Drew can hear a hint of a smile in his voice.

Drew laughs, again. "You know I love her."

"Yeah, she loves you too. Which is why she's going to call you tomorrow and yell at you."

"I'll put her in my calendar."

This time it's Shiloh that laughs. "I'll try to tell her to go easy on you."

"Nah, I deserve her wrath if she so chooses to unleash it upon me." Drew doesn't think he could ever be mad at Ava, even if she yelled at him every day. She's just a good person, and perfect for his best friend. "Alright, man. I gotta get some sleep. I'll talk to you later."

"Night, buddy."

Drew hangs up the phone and feels his chest deflate. There's no way he's sleeping peacefully tonight, not when his thoughts are full of a certain redhead...

* * *

Even though he barely slept a wink, Drew's up bright and early, five miles logged on his peloton and coffee brewing in the pot. He's showered, dressed, and on his way to work before most of the world is even awake. He feels most at peace in the early morning, when the sun is rising, and the world is slowly awakening. His mind feels quieter somehow.

He's always been a morning person, even as a child. When his sister was running wild during the night, he was waking up early and helping his father in the garage or assisting his mother with breakfast. It helps him feel grounded.

With his new apartment, he's able to walk to work instead of driving. He likes the chill of the morning on his face, the warmth of his coffee cup in his hand, the sound of traffic in his ears. It all makes him feel alive, happy to be walking on this earth.

He's the first to arrive at the office, and he flips on the lights, illuminating the dark space. He makes his way to his new office, *another* perk of the promotion, and settles into his desk. It feels good to have his own space after so many years at the same company. He'd been stuck at the same cubicle next to Robbie, who was a great guy, but also had to tell Drew about fifty different stories a day. Now, Drew can shut the door and actually get work done. He boots up his computer and gets started.

A knock on his door startles him. He looks up, seeing that it's already past noon. He's been lost in work the last few hours. His coworker and friend, Jordan, pokes his head in.

"Hey, got a minute?" Drew waves him in. "Geez, have you even looked up from your computer since you got here?"

Drew rubs his tired eyes. "Sorry, I didn't get much sleep last night. Guess I got lost in work."

Jordan wiggles his eyebrows. "Oh, some late-night Valentine's Day activities?"

Drew huffs a laugh. "Yeah, definitely didn't happen. Cara left early."

"Seriously? You went home alone? That's very un-Drew like."

"Believe me, I know." He pauses, debating telling the truth. It slips out anyway. "I ran into Ashtyn last night."

Jordan frowns. "Ashtyn King?"

"Yes, Ashtyn King. You know, your wife's best friend? She was in your wedding?"

"That's not what I meant, you fucker. I meant, what was Ashtyn doing out on Valentine's Day? Doesn't seem like her."

"Yeah, hence why I lost my mind." Drew tells Jordan the story, ignoring the way Jordan's eyebrows keep raising the longer Drew talks.

When he's finished, Jordan lets out a low whistle, reminiscent of Shiloh's from the night before. "You're lucky you didn't leave with a black eye. Or bruised balls."

Drew gives him the finger, but he knows his friend is right. What he did was unacceptable to everyone involved. He thinks that if he ever sees Spencer again, he might have to run in the other direction like a coward. "Trust me, I've already gotten an ass reaming from both Shiloh and Ava."

Ava called him bright and early this morning, just as he arrived to work, and talked to him for an entire hour during her free period. He didn't mind the call, actually. He likes talking to Ava. It was just the scolding he didn't particularly care for, even if he deserved it. She went relatively easy on him, though, and they ended with plans to meet for lunch next week.

Jordan interrupts his thoughts. "I'm guessing you haven't spoken to her."

"No, I doubt she ever wants to speak to me again. I mean, I made her date leave—"

"Drew? I was talking about Cara."

Shit. He scrubs a hand down his face. "Yeah, of course, I knew what you meant. Uh, no, I haven't spoken to her. But we've never been serious, anyway."

"Well, I would hope not if you ditched her in the middle of your date for another woman."

Drew hates the way the words embarrass him, his cheeks heating. "T-that's not..." But he doesn't have any more excuses, because that is exactly what happened, and he can't change that fact.

"You gotta figure out what you want, man," Jordan says, twisting the wedding ring on his finger. "You're nearing thirty."

"Since when is thirty the cut off for having your shit figured out?"

Jordan shrugs. "I just want you to be happy."

"I am happy," Drew retorts. He's always been happy. He has a stable job, a great apartment, friends, family, people that occupy his bed... he doesn't need anything else, does he? He's never really considered settling down with someone before. It's not that he's against it, he's just never thought about it. Maybe it's time to start. "Anyway, don't you have work to do?"

Jordan laughs and salutes him. "Yes, boss."

As the door to his office shuts behind his friend, Drew lets out a breath. He doesn't have time to think about this shit. He has work to get done. He puts in his Airpods and shuts out the world until the end of the day.

Chapter 3

"Clarence! We do not eat pine cones!" Ashtyn exclaims, hands on her hips. "Put it down!"

The small child looks at her with determination on his face and takes a ginormous bite out of the pine cone. The moment it touches his lips, his face scrunches with disgust, and he lets out a wail that echoes across the playground.

"What did I say?" Clarence cries louder, and Ashtyn sighs, taking the pine cone from his tightly gripped hand. She chucks it over the fence and kneels in front of the boy. "Hey, look at me." Clarence looks at her, tears streaming down his face. "What did we learn?"

"Yucky!"

"Yeah, yucky. Now we know not to eat pine cones."

"I just wanted to be a squirrel."

"Okay, well, we can pretend to be squirrels in other ways," Ashtyn says, gently. She ruffles the boy's hair. "You have five more minutes until recess is over." Clarence's eyes widen, and he bolts across the playground, rejoining his friends, pine cone debacle forgotten.

"Gosh, he's a handful, isn't he?" Daisy, her friend and coworker, asks, coming up to her.

"Yeah, but he's a sweet kid," Ashtyn replies. She loves her students, even though they tend to drive her crazy. She turns to look at her friend, and she's blinded by the rock sitting on Daisy's third finger. "Oh my god!"

Daisy bites her lip and showcases her new jewelry. "Derek asked last night."

"Oh my god, Daisy! Congratulations!"

She blushes. "Thanks, Ash. I know it's kind of soon. We only just celebrated our one-year anniversary, but I just can't picture my life without him." She wraps her arms around herself with a happy smile on her face.

"No, I don't think it's too soon," Ashtyn replies. "I think you guys are perfect for each other. I'm so happy for you." And she means it. She remembers the night of Ava's birthday last year, when Derek and Daisy were paired together for the game of Blockbuster, and they'd clicked immediately. The same night she was paired with Drew. Ashtyn shakes her head, clearing her mind from thoughts of him. She's still pissed about last night. "How did he ask?"

Daisy goes into excruciating detail about the proposal, and Ashtyn has to be mindful of the expression on her face. She's happy for her friend, she really is, but sometimes too much talk of love and marriage and happily ever after makes her feel sick. She'd barely been able to make it through Brooke's wedding last year, and even that had ended in a panic attack. She smiles at Daisy, making sure to give her the enthusiasm she deserves.

Ashtyn and Daisy have been coworkers for the last five years. Daisy teaches right next door, and they hit it off the day they met. Daisy is sweet and joyful, very much like Ava, where Ashtyn is more of the pessimistic, realistic friend. They balance each other out nicely.

"I know it literally just happened last night, but I'm already thinking we might want to just do a courthouse wedding. And a party afterwards."

Ashtyn doesn't miss the way relief floods through her system. No wedding means no reliving the Brandon situation, *again*. "I think that's a great idea."

"Really? I know my mom will be pissed, but I don't really care. This day is meant for Derek and I."

Ashtyn puts a hand on her friend's arm. "Do what is going to make you and him happy. That's all that matters."

Daisy smiles, genuine joy and love reflected in her expression. "Thanks, Ash." She doesn't hug her, knowing Ashtyn hugs very few people in her life. They're just too personal. Too comfortable. She reserves them for very special occasions only. Or her mom.

Another teacher blows the recess whistle, signaling the kids to line up. Ashtyn's class rushes toward her, some kids barreling into her legs. "Back to it," Daisy says, waving to her friend as she lines up her own kids.

Once they're in a semi-formed line, Ashtyn raises her hand and yells, "Okay, one, two, three, eyes on me!"

The kids snap to attention, their gazes laser focused on Ashtyn. She counts out each kid until she reaches twenty-three, and she knows they're all there. "Okay, what do we do when we get to the hallway?" she asks.

"Catch a bubble!" the kids yell.

Ashtyn smiles. "Okay, Clarence, lead us in."

* * *

Ashtyn is the first to arrive home after the school day. Jess greets her with a meow and headbutt to the shins.

"Hi, stinker," she says, stooping down to pat the cat on the head. Jess purrs happily, rubbing her head against Ashtyn's hand. "What did you get into today?" There's an assortment of hair ties strewn about the room. As if on cue, Jess bats one playfully. Ashtyn smiles and plops to the floor, tossing the hair tie across the room as Jess chases it and brings it back. They do this for a few minutes until there's a knock on the door.

Ashtyn frowns and checks the time on her phone. Shiloh and Ava should be home soon. Who would be at the door? They aren't expecting company. She gets up with a groan and answers the door.

Michael, their landlord, stands there sheepishly, a large coat hugging his skinny frame. "Uh, hey there Ms. Marshall."

"King," Ashtyn corrects. "Ava is Ms. Marshall."

"My apologies, Ms. King. Um, is it alright if I come in?"

Ashtyn looks at him skeptically. "Uh, sure. Is everything okay? We paid next month's rent already."

"No, yeah, I got it. It's not that..."

Ashtyn holds the door open wider for him, and he enters. He avoids her gaze as he wipes his muddy boots on the welcome mat. "Sorry to be barging in like this. Are you the only one home?" Jess scurries into the foyer, excited at the prospect of a guest. She slides across the floor and right into Michael's legs. She meows as she looks up at him.

"Yes, it's just me right now. The other two should be here soon, though. If there's a problem..." Ashtyn lets her words dangle.

"Not a problem, per se..." Michael reaches a wrinkly hand down to scratch Jess under the chin.

"Just spit it out." She's tired of the runaround. Subtlety is not her forte.

"I'm selling the place."

His words make Ashtyn's heart skip a beat and her blood run cold. Anxiety starts to spiral in her gut. "Excuse me?"

"Well, you know, I'm getting older. And, I just don't have it in me anymore to keep this up. So, I'm selling all my property and retiring to Florida. I'll need y'all out by the first of June."

Ashtyn doesn't believe the words coming out of Michael's mouth. This house, the one they've been in since college, is being sold. And they're being thrown out. She can't believe it. No, she actually *can't* believe it.

"Could I have a cup of coffee?" Michael asks, eyeing the fancy new coffee machine Ava bought last year after her disastrous date with Brad the barista, as if he didn't just tell her life altering news.

Ashtyn sighs heavily, biting her tongue in the process. "Yeah, sure."

Michael sits at the island while Ashtyn fires up the machine. Her hands begin to shake at the thought of leaving this house, and she has to steady herself before pouring the coffee grounds. She barely knows how to work this damn thing. Ava is normally the one making coffee for everyone.

"I know you guys have been here awhile..." Again, Michael doesn't finish his sentence.

"This year marks eight years," she says, staring at the coffee machine. Ashtyn, Ava, and Brooke had found this place at the end of their sophomore year of college. Tired of living in the dingy dorms, and wanting to live together the three of them, they scoured the internet for a cheap apartment. But, there really weren't any three-bedroom apartments that could be considered cheap. So, they found the house. Ashtyn still remembers Michael showing them the property. They were all working as much as they could in order to save up for their own place, and this had been the one. It was perfect. Affordable, and just big enough for all of them. They'd been here ever since. They didn't even leave when Brooke eventually moved out to live with Jordan. Instead, they found Shiloh. Ashtyn can't imagine leaving after all this time. This is their home. They've been through so much together here.

As she finishes making the coffee and pouring it into a mug, Ava and Shiloh arrive home. They stop short when they see Michael in the kitchen.

"Hi, Michael. Sorry, we didn't know you were coming, or we would have been home sooner," Ava says. She drops her bag in the foyer and hangs her coat in the closet.

"That's okay, Ms. Marshall. I already talked to Ms. King for a bit."

Ava looks at Ashtyn with a concerned expression. Ashtyn gives her a tight-lipped smile, eyebrows raised to let Ava know it wasn't a pleasant conversation. Shiloh places a comforting hand on Ava's shoulder, sensing Ashtyn's foul mood.

"Michael has decided to sell the house," Ashtyn says, dropping the bomb before he can delay it any longer. Ava lets out a gasp, hand coming up to cover her mouth. Shiloh doesn't say anything, his mouth set in a firm line, hand still on Ava's shoulder. Michael looks uncomfortable as he sips his coffee. "We're to be out by June first."

Nobody says anything as the news settles, thick and heavy in the room.

"Well, I mean, could we rent it from the new owner?" Ava asks, already two, three steps ahead of everyone else. "Or maybe, if it's feasible, we could buy it from you?"

Michael sighs into his coffee. "Um, I'm actually selling it to my niece and her new husband. They still need to come and look at it, but they seem pretty set on it from the pictures I showed them. They'd be living here, not renting it out."

Ashtyn's anger starts to bubble to the surface, and she has to bite her tongue to keep from saying something that would definitely get them kicked out early. Ava looks like she's censoring herself, too. Shiloh, to his credit, is cool, calm and collected.

"Well, thank you for the heads up," Shiloh says. Jess paws at his legs, and he picks her up. She immediately nuzzles into his face. "We appreciate knowing now instead of later."

Michael finishes the last of his coffee. "Uh, thank you for the hospitality. And, sorry about the bad news. If you need anything before then, just let me know. I'll, uh, get out of y'all's hair now." Nobody says anything as he leaves.

Once the front door shuts, Ashtyn slams her hands on the counter. "I fucking hate landlords!" Her palms sting from the contact, but she embraces the pain. It helps fuel her anger.

Ava has tears in her eyes as she asks, "What are we going to do?"

"We're going to sue the fucker!" Ashtyn exclaims. Shiloh looks over at her, pointedly. She sighs, holding up her hands. "Okay, sorry, not helping."

"It'll be fine!" Ava says, dabbing at her eyes with a napkin. "We'll figure it out. It'll be fine." Shiloh wraps an arm around her, comfortingly, and Jess licks her face.

Ashtyn's thoughts spiral, most of them negative. She keeps picturing the worst-case scenario. He didn't even ask them if *they* wanted to buy the house. Before she can spiral any further, she decides to change the subject, trying to ease the tension that's threatening to ruin the day. "Daisy's engaged."

Ava smiles and sighs. "Yeah, Derek told us today."

"Looks like everything's coming up roses for everyone else." She doesn't mean for it to come out as bitter as it does.

"I already called Drew and yelled at him," Ava says. "I'm sorry your date got ruined."

"That's not what I meant," Ashtyn replies, rubbing her temples. She can feel a headache starting to form. She needs a hot bath and a strong drink, stat.

"Maybe this is a good thing, Michael selling the house," Shiloh starts. "I mean, we're all in very different places than we were a year ago."

Ashtyn holds up a hand, silencing him. "I'm going to stop you right there."

Ava bites her lip and looks away, guiltily. As if they've already discussed something like this before Michael even walked in the door. "I mean, he does have a point," she says. She won't look Ashtyn in the eye.

The pieces start falling into place for Ashtyn, the truth punching a hole right through her. "How long have you been planning on leaving?"

"What?"

"How long have you been thinking about moving out?"

"That's not at all what's happening here," Ava says, defensively. "We talked about getting our own place *once*, and I shut it down."

Ashtyn's anger finally reaches its breaking point. "Well, I would hope so. You've only been together, what, four months officially?" Her words are harsh, and they hit their mark. Ava winces, her face crumpling. Ashtyn immediately feels guilty, upset that her anger won, but she doesn't apologize. She's spiraling. She's never lived on her own. She's never been away from her best friend. She doesn't even know if she can afford anything on her own.

"Ash," Shiloh says, softly. Ashtyn knows she's putting him in a terrible spot. He loves both of them, but he's only *in* love with one of them. Ashtyn *knows* who he will pick. Hell, she'd pick Ava too. "We have time to figure things out."

She shrugs, flippantly, as if she doesn't care. Even though she does, her emotions battling a war inside her. She cares a hell of a lot more than she's letting on. "It's whatever. I'm going to take a bath. Nobody bother me until I'm out." She heads out of the room without another word.

* * *

Ashtyn takes her time in the bath, letting the hot water soak her tense muscles. Her lavender candle burns steady, filling the room with the sweet scent. She tries to relax and *not* think about the last few days and the bombshell that landed at her feet an hour ago. But, her mind keeps wandering to Drew and their New Year's kiss of all things. And how he'd shown up at the same restaurant, wearing an incredibly flattering blazer with his stupid, blonde hair and wide grin that sent her pulse racing. Okay, yes, Drew Mitchell is attractive. That's undeniable. It's just everything else that infuriates her beyond belief. And now, she's faced with the possibility of not living with her best friend. It's all just too much for her to deal with right now.

It's not like she's never imagined it. She knew they would eventually move on and get their own places. She just didn't think it would be this soon. She thought, like, a few more years at least. Even if it was unreasonable, she's always hated the idea of moving out of the house.

Ashtyn knows Ava and Shiloh probably want their own place. That's what couples do. They live together. Alone. Without roommates. But, what about Jess? Jess was *theirs*. Who would she go with? Shiloh is her favorite, and Ashtyn can't imagine separating them. That would leave Ashtyn...alone.

Alone. Alone. Alone. All alone. The words echo in her head, a vicious reminder.

She lets herself sink under the water and scream. Bubbles whoosh out of her mouth and hit the surface. The sound drowns in the water, and she continues until she has no more air left, her chest left feeling deflated. She breaks the surface, splashing water over the lip of the tub. She doesn't care about the mess. She just feels empty. Empty, and so very alone.

She's cold when she gets out of the bath, her body shaking as goosebumps cover her arms and legs. She wraps a fluffy robe around her, trying to bring herself a tiny bit of comfort. She drains the water and watches it swirl to the bottom. Once it's finished, she wraps her hair in a towel and makes her way down the hall toward Ava's room. Her and Shiloh's voices are muffled behind the closed door, and Ashtyn knocks lightly. They fall silent for a moment before Ava says, "Come in."

Ashtyn opens the door and sees them lounging on the bed. "Can I come in?"

"Of course," Ava says, opening her arms and inviting Ashtyn onto the bed. She flops onto it, in-between the couple. Sometimes she feels like the ultimate cockblock, the friend still living with the happy couple. She lies face down, face hidden in the pillows. It still smells like Ava, but now there's a new smell intermingled with her friend. Shiloh. They're intrinsically linked now, and the change sends a pang through Ashtyn.

"Should I pack my stuff for the streets now or later?" Her voice is muffled by the pillows, but she knows Ava hears her because she sighs heavily.

"Ashtyn." Ash turns her head to peek out at her best friend. Ava's looking down at her with a soft smile on her face. "I love you, you know that, right? We both do."

Ashtyn groans, shoving her face back in the pillows. "Don't use your love against me."

"We're not using it against you," Shiloh says, nudging her with his foot. "We just want to talk through our thought process with you."

Ashtyn says into the pillows, "Let me wallow in my self-pity."

"No," Ava says, fiercely. "We're not doing that."

"No, we're just splitting up." Ashtyn sits up, leaning back against the headboard. Ava hooks her arm through Ash's. "I guess I probably should have seen this coming."

"No, none of us saw this coming," Ava says. "I'm serious, Ash. We weren't planning on getting our own place anytime soon. You know I love living with you."

"I love living with you, too. But I also know the dynamic has changed slightly."

Ava and Shiloh share a knowing look. "Ashtyn, we can get someplace big enough for all of us," Shiloh says.

She knows he would do that for them. But he shouldn't necessarily have to. They need their own place. Ashtyn needs her own place. She's nearing thirty. She should have learned to live on her own by now. Although, maybe she could find a new roommate. Even though all of her friends are happily paired off now. She doesn't know who she would ask. She takes a deep breath and says, "No, you guys need your own place. And I need to find my own, too. I think it's time."

"Ash," Ava starts, but Ash holds up a hand to stop her.

"Careful, or I'll change my mind." Jess hops up on the bed, and Ashtyn has to hold back tears. No one asks who will take her, because they all already know.

They sit in silence, enjoying the company they know will soon be gone. Jess, as if sensing the seriousness of the situation, curls up on Ashtyn's lap and falls asleep, purring loudly.

"If we really can't find anything on our own, then we can reevaluate and find something big enough for all of us," Shiloh whispers. He bumps his shoulder against Ashtyn's, careful not to jostle Jess too much.

Ashtyn looks up at him. "Promise?"

"Promise."

"Besides," Ava starts, "you can't get rid of me that easily." Ashtyn giggles and lays her head on her best friend's shoulder.

"Me either," Shiloh agrees. He wraps his arm around the girls, and they sit like that for a while, trying not to think about the day they will have to part.

MARCH

Chapter 4

The boat cuts through the water effortlessly. The lake is crowded, spring breakers out partying on the water, but Shiloh avoids them all skillfully. He's gotten awfully good at piloting the boat since acquiring it last year. Drew sits back, letting the sun bake his skin as he sips a beer. Ashtyn hasn't spoken a word to him since they boarded the boat, although he doesn't blame her for that. She sits, arms crossed, under the helm in the shade. A large, floppy sun hat sits on her head, her copper hair pulled back in a low ponytail. Drew has to keep himself from staring at her, mostly so he doesn't piss her off.

Ava sits on Shiloh's lap at the wheel, her arm slung across his bare shoulders, wind whipping her hair back from her face. Brooke and Jordan sit next to Drew, beers in hand.

"God, I missed the sun," Brooke says, stretching out her legs.

"We're so close to summer I can almost taste it," Ava says, wistfully.

"Great, my hibernation season is coming up," Ashtyn quips. She doesn't let even a fraction of the sun's rays touch her. It's hot for March, but the breeze helps cool them. So does the beer.

"Where's Mattie?" Drew asks, looking up at his friend from his sunglasses.

Shiloh smiles. "Making up the Mexico trip he missed last year."

"You'd think he'd want to enjoy his own boat."

"Please," Ava says, "this is more our boat than his." She's teasing, but Drew knows how much work Shiloh and Ava put into the thing to get it running. Hell, it was named *Ava* for a reason. Mattie may have bought it, but Shiloh and Ava made it work. It's as much theirs as it is his. "He'll get all the time he wants with it after he graduates."

Drew whistles. "Still can't believe the little bastard is gonna be a college graduate."

"Neither can I," Shiloh replies. "God, life moves fast."

"Hey, speaking of life moving fast, have you guys started looking for a new place, yet?" Brooke asks as she rubs sunscreen into her skin. Drew's ears prick up at her words. New place?

Ashtyn's frown deepens. "We just started looking, Brooke." There's a bite to her words, something hidden in the undercurrent of her tone.

Drew looks around at the group. No one seems willing to give up any more information. Surely Shiloh would have told him if they were moving? He takes it upon himself to investigate. "You're needing a new place?" He feels like he's traipsing through a minefield.

Ashtyn doesn't say anything as Shiloh and Ava share a look. "Our landlord is selling the house," Ava answers. "We're, uh, trying to figure out where to go from there."

Oh.

Drew can see what she's not saying. They want their own place... without Ashtyn. He thinks of the countless apartments he toured before settling on the one he has now. His heart begins to race as he says, without thinking, "I just got a new apartment."

Ashtyn turns to look at him before anyone can say anything. "Okay? Good for you."

Drew clears his throat. "Uh, it's a two-bedroom downtown. Big, you know?"

Everyone is silent as Ashtyn raises her eyebrows at him. "You can't seriously be offering what I think you're offering."

Drew shrugs, trying to act casual. "Just a suggestion." Such a loaded statement. He can't believe he's actually saying these words to her of all people, and in front of their friends no less.

"No offense, but I'd rather sleep on the street."

His heart continues to race, but he teases to lighten the mood. "Offense taken."

"You're right, I did mean that offensively."

"Ah, come on Ashtyn," Drew says, trying to break the tension, even though he can feel his hands start to shake. "You can't hate me that much. Besides, I'd charge you less than any other apartment in the country. Just ask Shiloh, I'm a great host." Shiloh, thankfully, doesn't respond.

"I'm not taking your pity offer," she retorts.

"It's not a pity offer. Call it a friend discount."

"We're not friends."

"Okay, now you're just being mean."

Ashtyn huffs and turns away from him. He still hasn't technically apologized for the Valentine's Day fiasco. He clears his throat awkwardly, heat rising to his cheeks as he continues to ignore everyone else on the boat. "Um, I'm sorry about the whole, you know—"

Ashtyn holds up her hand, silencing him. "Consider it forgotten."

Her words stun him. He really thought he'd have to grovel more. In fact, he planned on it. "Okay, then. The offer does still stand, though." It's a terrible idea, what he's offering, but he just can't help himself. The thought of her even considering it secretly thrills him.

"Like I said, I'd rather sleep on the street."

"Suit yourself." Drew just shrugs and finishes off his beer. "Where are you two looking?" He directs the question at Ava and Shiloh.

Ava looks over at her friend, guiltily. "Um, just some places closer to the school. But we haven't found anything yet." Shiloh kisses her bare shoulder comfortingly.

Drew feels the tension radiating off of Ashtyn's body. She's avoiding everyone's gaze as she stares out across the water, arms crossed. Drew can't even imagine how she must be feeling. Like everyone is abandoning her...

Shiloh stops the boat, the water lapping up the sides. The sun is relentless as it beats down on all of them and their uncomfortable silence.

"Last one in is a rotten egg!" Ava exclaims, breaking the tension, and jumps straight into the water, Shiloh close on her heels. Brooke and Jordan are not far behind, their drinks forgotten. Whether everyone wanted to escape the awkward conversation or just cool off, Drew's not sure. Either way, the others were smart to jump ship. Now, it's only Ashtyn and Drew on the boat, the silence between them unbearable.

"Ashtyn," he says, and she cuts her gaze to him, eyes piercing. "I really am sorry."

Her expression doesn't soften. Drew can count on one hand the number of times her gaze *has* softened in his presence. One, when he'd guessed her clue correctly in Blockbuster at Ava's birthday party. Two, when they'd run into each other at the bathrooms of the camping site where they celebrated Shiloh's birthday, and she'd thanked him for taking care of the Garrett situation. Three, when they'd drunkenly danced together at Brooke and Jordan's bachelor party. Four, New Year's Eve. God, New Year's Eve. He wants to go back there. If he could go back, he's not sure if he'd tell himself *not* to kiss her or to hold on tighter. He would definitely punch himself for offering to let her *move in* with him. What *had* he been thinking?

Ava's shriek of laughter as Shiloh splashes her makes Ashtyn's eyes flick to her friends. They flick back to Drew a split second later. She sighs, as if deciding something right in that moment. "Don't worry about it. It was a shit date, anyway."

Instead of a quip, he says, "Doesn't mean I should have ruined it."

She huffs in agreement. "Did your date leave too?"

"Not until after dinner."

"You deserved that."

"I did."

Ashtyn lets out a small laugh, some of the tightness leaving her shoulders. "I think I might swear off dating for the rest of my life."

"So, then, what's the problem with moving in with me?" He is venturing into dangerous territory, but he can't stop himself.

The look she gives him sends shivers down his back despite the heat. "We'd tear each other's throats out."

Drew scoffs. "Ashtyn, I'm married to my work. I go to work by seven and come home, if I'm lucky, by ten during busy season. Five during the normal season. I'd barely even be at the apartment."

"Yeah, that's what Shiloh said about being a bartender and look how that turned out," she replies, jutting her chin out at her friends who are wrapped around each other, smiles wide.

"Accounting is very different from bartending."

Ashtyn rolls her eyes. "He also hated bartending."

"And I love accounting."

She wrinkles her nose. "How can anyone love accounting?"

"I love math. But, I love the pay most of all."

"Math? Gross."

"Math is never wrong. Besides, don't you have to teach your kindergartners math?"

"They're five, Drew. I teach them to count to one hundred and call it a day."

This makes him laugh as he opens another beer. "I'm serious. You should consider it. No strings attached."

Ashtyn stares at him, and he has to look away. "Thanks, but no thanks. I'll find something on my own."

"Okay, but don't come crawling back to me when you see the state of the market."

She smiles sweetly at him, her eyes hard. "Don't worry, Drew. I'll never come crawling to you."

* * *

The sun won't stop following Ashtyn. No matter how much shade she's under, there's still a ray of sunshine trying to bite at her skin. She can already feel a sunburn starting to form on the tops of her shoulders. With her pale skin and red hair, it's impossible not to burn. Even with a gallon of sunscreen on her body. It also doesn't help that Drew keeps staring at her, and her skin sizzles underneath his gaze. She can't help it. It's just hormones, she tells herself.

She actually cannot believe he offered her a room in his apartment. It's preposterous. It's ridiculous. It's stupid. She shakes her head, cementing her beliefs in her brain. She will never consider something like that. Over her dead body.

"Ashtyn!" Ava yells from the water. "Come on in!"

Ash huffs. "It'll be a cold day in hell when I jump into that water."

"Ah, you're such a party pooper!" Brooke yells, splashing water up into the boat. It lands right at Ashtyn's feet.

"Come on, Ashtyn," Drew says, standing and offering his hand to her.

She looks at it with disdain on her face. "I meant what I said."

"Not even to dip your feet in?"

Ashtyn sighs and relents, trying to not let her bad mood ruin the day. It's spring break, she should be enjoying her time off, not stewing in her misery. "Fine, I'll sit at the end and dip my feet in. But if anyone splashes me, I'll kill them."

Drew lets out a laugh as he makes his way toward the end of the boat, his hands outstretched to catch Ashtyn if she falls.

She rolls her eyes. "I'm fine, Drew. I don't need a baby—" But she's interrupted as a jet ski flies by and sends a wave crashing toward them. It hits the boat violently, and the movement jerks the boat so heavily that Ashtyn loses her footing and slams right into Drew's muscular body. They careen into the water with a huge splash.

The water swallows Ashtyn whole, but before she can panic, she feels Drew's strong hands gripped tightly to her arms. They haul her up to the surface where she takes a deep lungful of air. She flails as she tries to remember how to tread water. Drew's arms go around her middle, and she clings to him, instinctually.

"You're okay. You're okay. I got you," Drew says, as he holds them both above the water. Her thick, wet hair is in her eyes, and she pushes it back so she can see.

Ava swims over, concern on her face. "Ash, are you okay?"

"I'm fine," she gasps. She knows how to swim, she just hasn't done it in a while. Her legs kick out, getting used to the feeling of being suspended in a body of water. Drew doesn't let go of her, and she's grateful for the anchor.

"Fuckers shouldn't have driven so close to us," Shiloh grumbles, hauling himself onto the boat. "Zero awareness of other people." He bends down and holds out a hand to Ashtyn to help her back onto the boat. She wants to get out of the water, but she doesn't want to let go of Drew. He feels safe at the moment. Like letting go of him would mean she'd drown.

"Just give me a minute," she breathes, trying not to show that she's shaking. She's sure Drew can feel it, and he tightens his arms around her even more. She hates how good it feels. How *secure* it feels.

"I can help you get onto the boat," Drew whispers, so only she can hear. "I'll have Shiloh grab your hand, and I'll push your..." He stops, and Ashtyn understands why.

"This is the only time I am going to allow you to touch my ass," she says, but it lacks her normal bite as her teeth begin to chatter.

A slight flush creeps into Drew's cheeks. "I will be a perfect gentleman."

"You better be," she grumbles and then reaches for Shiloh's hand. Drew really is a gentleman, because she barely feels his hands touch her behind as she's hauled up onto the boat. Ava's ready with a towel to wrap around Ashtyn's shoulders, and she takes it gratefully.

"Thanks," she says to her best friend. Ava wraps her arm around Ashtyn's shoulders and rubs, trying to warm her up. Her teeth won't stop chattering. The water wasn't even that cold, it's just all the adrenaline running through her system.

Drew doesn't even look at her as he wraps a towel around himself, but Ashtyn can see that he's shaking a little too. She catches his eye and mouths, "Thank you."

He just nods as he collapses onto one of the seats. Brooke and Jordan also climb into the boat, the mood dissolved by the reckless jet ski driver.

"I don't know about y'all, but I'm starving," Ava says, trying to ease the tension. The group agrees, and Shiloh starts up the boat, piloting it back toward the dock.

Ashtyn tries desperately to forget the feeling of Drew's hands on her. She fails miserably.

Chapter 5

Ashtyn is truly and utterly fucked. There's really just no other way to put it. She's looked at numerous apartments the last couple of weeks and nothing has worked out. They're either too expensive, too far from school, or just plain horrible. Shiloh and Ava, on the other hand, found their perfect apartment, and it was only the third unit they looked at. Situated near the school, perfectly big enough for two people and a cat, and labeled a "quiet" complex. It's perfect for them. Ashtyn had to excuse herself to cry in the bathroom when they showed it to her. She knows that if she really needed to, they would offer her the second bedroom. But, Ashtyn won't do it. She knows Ava wants an office. Knows they both need one. She won't ruin this for them. She can figure it out. She *will* figure it out. It's only March. She still has time.

Her brain won't stop going back to Drew's offer. Ashtyn knows he just got a major upgrade because of his promotion. Downtown apartment, big, nice view...and he would never charge her too much... *no*. She has to stop her brain from venturing into forbidden territory. She won't do it. She was serious when she said she'd rather sleep on the street than in the same building as him. They'd kill each other. There's no universe in which Ashtyn King and Drew Mitchell inhabit the same space without serious repercussions.

She goes back to perusing apartment listings, ignoring the way her heart hurts. She's on the verge of tears when there's a knock at her door. She slams her laptop shut and composes herself before saying, "Come in."

Ava pops her head in, a smile illuminating her face. "Hey, you coming tonight?"

Ashtyn racks her brain for whatever plans she agreed to when she was in a better mood and comes up short. "Um, remind me what's happening."

"Playoffs start tonight for the girls."

Ashtyn sighs. It's Shiloh's first year as Lakeview High School's soccer coach, and he's already led the girls to playoffs. He's an amazing coach, and Ashtyn now remembers she agreed to attend the first playoff game to support him. "Uh, yeah, I'm coming. Just let me get ready."

Ashtyn turns to her vanity as Ava flops onto the bed. "Hey, did you get a Facebook invite today?"

"Invite to what?"

Ava pauses, biting her lip. "Our ten-year reunion."

Ashtyn drops the lipstick she was about to apply. It bounces off the vanity and onto the floor. Jess, who was sleeping peacefully a second ago, hears the noise and jumps up with a meow. She bats the tube underneath the bed where she chases after it. "You've got to be kidding me."

"Can you believe it? Ten years." The way she says it, almost wistfully, makes Ashtyn believe that they are on two very separate pages when it comes to this reunion.

"We're not going," she says, picking up a different lipstick from her collection.

"What!?" Ava exclaims, sitting up. "Of course we're going."

Ashtyn doesn't look at her friend as she swipes on her *second* favorite nude shade. "Ave, there's no way I'm going to be trapped in a room with people I have long since forgotten about. Not to mention, he who shall not be named might be there." Ashtyn shudders at the thought. Even though Ava knows everything about the Brandon situation—as does Shiloh, thanks to a post-wedding ceremony panic attack last October—Ashtyn still doesn't like talking about him, let alone thinking about him. There's no way she'll ever be in the same room as him again. Not if she can help it.

"There's a RSVP list! I can check and make sure he doesn't check 'yes.' Would you come then?"

Ashtyn pretends to think about it for a moment. "No."

Ava bats her eyes at Ashtyn. "Even if I ask really, really, really nicely?"

"Why do you even want to go?"

"I don't know! Maybe because I want to show everyone how hot I am! And also my super-hot boyfriend."

Ashtyn glares at her friend. "Gross."

Ava sticks her tongue out at Ashtyn. "You have no idea just how hot he is."

"And I'd like to keep it that way, please," Ash says, holding up her hand. "That's basically my brother."

Ava just laughs as she falls back onto the bed. Jess, lipstick forgotten, jumps up and starts making biscuits on the blanket. Ashtyn pulls her hair back into a tight ponytail and fastens it with a scrunchie. "You know you have nothing to prove to those people, right Ave?"

Ava bites her lip and pets Jess absentmindedly. "I know." Her voice is small, a telltale sign that she's not being honest with her best friend.

Ashtyn joins her on the bed, grabbing her friend's hand. "Look at me." Ava's brown eyes slide to meet Ashtyn's green ones. "You are the best person I know, and if those stupid fuckers in high school didn't realize that then, they don't get to realize it now. Their loss."

Ava sighs deeply. "I know I don't need to prove anything to them. I guess I'm just curious to see how much has changed, you know? Ten years is a long time. Just think about it for me, will you?"

"Fine," Ashtyn lies. "I'll think about it."

"Thank you!" Ava throws her arms around Ash, squeezing her tightly. Ashtyn won't ruin it just yet. That will come later.

"Okay, I'm ready. Let's go watch some soccer."

* * *

"That's a foul!" Ava screams, and Ashtyn has to put her hands over her ears. The referee, apparently not seeing what Ava does, lets the play continue, and Ava sighs heavily. "Ridiculous."

Shiloh seems to feel the same way. Ashtyn can see him across the field on the sidelines, throwing up his hands in disbelief and shouting something unintelligible. The referee gives him a warning, and Shiloh sits on the bench, a frown on his face.

Ashtyn, for all her hatred of sports, actually does enjoy watching soccer sometimes, if only because her friends love it so much. The stands are filled with supporters to watch the girls in their first playoff game. Derek and Daisy sit next to Ava, and behind them are Parker and Damien, Ava's coworkers and the girls' mutual friends. Even Brooke and Jordan have come out. The only person from their group that isn't here is Drew, and Ashtyn silently thanks whoever lives above for his absence. She still wakes up feeling his hands on her skin, an intense desire filling her belly. It's been torture. Awful, horrible torture.

Ashtyn tries to focus on the game. Shiloh's girls are winning by two points, but the opposing team is on the offensive and aren't letting up. Ava's hands are grasped tightly into fists on her lap as she watches the game intently. Ashtyn is about to get up and head to the restroom when a body plops down next to her, and she knows who it is just by the scent of cologne that instantly hits her nose. It goes straight to her bloodstream, and goosebumps emerge on her forearms. Think about him and he shall appear, apparently.

"Hey," Drew says to everyone.

Ava barely tears her eyes away from the field to say hello back. Ashtyn mutters a greeting and pointedly doesn't look at him. She feels Drew bump his shoulder against hers, and it's like a jolt to her system. She whirls on him, as if she just can't help herself.

"How's the housing search going?" he asks simply.

"Wha—what?" she stutters, her composure slipping.

"How's the search for a new place going? Have you found anything yet?"

Ashtyn takes a deep breath and snaps her mask back into place. "It's fine," she says. "I haven't found anything yet, but I'm still not accepting your offer."

"Good, cause it's rescinded."

Ashtyn whirls on him again, eyes wide. "What?" She's not sure why it bothers her, but it does.

"I'm rescinding my offer for you to live with me."

"You can't just rescind an offer like that."

"Why not? It's not like you were going to say yes." He stares at her with a hint of a smirk on his face. He's playing with her. Teasing her. Seeing just how far he can push her buttons to get a reaction out of her.

Ashtyn huffs and turns away from him. "You're right, I would never say yes to you."

His reply is cut off by the crowd's cheers as Lakeview's defense successfully blocks a shot on goal. Drew's breath is hot on her ear as he leans down and whispers, "You're missing out on a great view, though. Top floor, right downtown."

Ashtyn turns to him, and they're face to face, lips just inches apart. She smiles sweetly and bats her eyelashes at him. "Maybe I *should* move in just so I can push you off the balcony."

Drew's lips stretch into a wide smile that almost touches Ashtyn's. "I'd think about you the whole way down."

A blush splays across Ashtyn's cheeks, and she pulls away as the crowd cheers again, another shot on goal blocked. She clears her throat and focuses on the field. She ignores Drew for the rest of the match, even if the heat on her cheeks is a constant reminder of him.

The girls end up winning, and as soon as the referee whistles the end of the game, Ava is up and out of her seat, running across the field toward Shiloh. He holds his arms out for her, and she jumps right into them. If they weren't her best friends, Ashtyn would think them lovesick fools.

"Hey, Drew, are you coming to dinner with us?" Jordan asks. Ashtyn throws a wide-eyed death glare in Jordan's direction, but he doesn't seem to catch it.

Drew shrugs. "Uh, sure. Where are we going?"

"To hell," Ashtyn mutters.

* * *

Ashtyn was right, they really are in hell. And by hell, she meant a family style buffet. Drew can't remember the last time he was at a buffet. High school, maybe? Either way, it's loud and crowded.

Shiloh's entire team, as well as their families, are here, along with the friend group. Apparently, the school provided a meal ticket to this specific buffet if they won their first playoff game. So, here they all are. He probably shouldn't complain about free food, but the place is so jam-packed with people, Drew can barely hear what Shiloh is saying above all the noise. "What!?"

"I said, thanks for coming!" Shiloh yells back.

"Of course, man." What Drew doesn't tell his best friend is that he really came so he could see Ashtyn. Ever since their tumble into the water, he can't stop thinking about her skin underneath his fingers. How it felt to have his arms wrapped around her. Like he never wanted to let go. He shakes his head, trying to rid himself of thoughts of her. He hasn't been able to for over a year, but it's gotten increasingly bad as of late.

She's sitting next to Daisy, frown on her face, eyes blank. Drew wishes he could read her, get into her mind and figure out what she's thinking. Her phone buzzes on the table, and she picks it up, frown deepening. She excuses herself and takes the phone call outside. Drew looks over his shoulder at her as she leaves. He feels the instinct to go after her and make sure she's okay. But he stays planted in his seat, legs jiggling.

He catches Ava's eye from across the table, and she gives him a knowing smile. He subtly gives her the finger, making her throw her head back in laughter. She shoots him a shooing motion with her fingers, almost like she's giving him permission to go check on Ashtyn. No, he won't. She'll be fine.

Ten minutes later, Drew's getting up, despite everything in him telling him to leave her alone. He just can't help it. Something keeps pulling him toward her.

He spots her immediately, sitting on the curb a few feet away from the front door. Her hands cup the back of her head, and she leans forward, body between her knees.

"Ashtyn?" he asks, as quietly as he can, but she still startles.

"Jesus Christ," she mutters, wiping away a stray tear that he definitely wasn't supposed to see. "What do you want?"

"Just wanted to make sure you were okay," he says, sitting next to her on the curb. He notices that she doesn't move away from him.

"I'm fine," she replies, voice gruff.

"Okay," he says simply. He won't push her. He won't expect anything from her. He will just let her know that he's here for her.

No jokes, no quips, no flirting. No strings attached.

They're silent for a moment before she lets out a breath. "My mom keeps offering for me to move back in with her. You know, if I can't find anything."

"*Have* you found anything?"

Ashtyn just shakes her head. She bites her lip, eyes watering, and she buries her face into her hands. Drew knows she's trying desperately not to cry in front of him. She's always hiding herself away from him, keeping him at a distance. He reaches out a tentative hand and lays it on her back. Electricity spikes through his bloodstream, and his heart begins to race. God, how can one woman have this much of an effect on him?

Surprisingly, she leans into his touch, so he wraps his arm around her shoulders. She sinks into his side, a small sob emitting from her hard exterior. Drew doesn't say anything, he just lets her cry into his side as long as she needs to. Which turns out to be quite a while.

When she's finished, she leans out of his embrace and wipes her tears on the back of her hand. "Sorry," she mutters.

"It's okay," Drew says. "That's what I'm here for."

"You tell anyone I cried, and I'll kill you," she warns, but her tone lacks her usual bite.

Drew puts a hand over his heart. "Your secret is safe with me." He clears his throat. "Um, I was just kidding earlier. If you...really do need a place to stay—"

"I'll be fine," she interrupts him. "It's just taking longer than I thought to find the perfect place."

Drew doesn't say the thought that rises to his mind. *There is no such thing as a perfect place.* If she's looking for perfection, she'll be looking for a while. Instead, he says, "Well, I've lived in quite a few places, so if you need any help, I'm sure I can offer some sage advice."

Ashtyn snorts, a small smile forming on her lips. "I don't think I could afford your lifestyle."

"Hey, my first apartment out of college was a one-bedroom shithole that never had hot water."

She sighs. "And that's what I'm worried about."

Drew frowns, afraid he's upset her. "I mean, they're not all bad. There are good ones out there that are affordable. I'm sure I could look around for you. You know, put out some feelers..." He knows he's rambling, but his mouth just won't stop moving. Ashtyn looks at him, a small smile on her face, and it gets him to shut up for a second. They stare at each other, a palpable tension vibrating between them.

In an instant, she's on her feet, hands on her hips. "Do you want to get out of here?"

Chapter 6

Ashtyn rolls down the window of Drew's truck and lets the wind whip her hair around her face. It dries the tears that rolled down her cheeks not ten minutes ago. It wasn't hard for the two of them to sneak away. Shiloh and Ava were too preoccupied with the team, so when Ashtyn waved goodbye to her friends from the front door of the restaurant, they barely even registered it. They all have each other's locations on their phones anyway; it would be fine.

She leans her arm out the window, letting her hand kiss the wind as it whips past them. She told Drew to just drive, it didn't matter where. She just needs to get away for a bit. She can't believe she let him see her cry. She can't believe she leaned into his embrace and let it happen. But she'd needed someone, and he had been there. He always seemed to be there when she needed him.

She doesn't *hate* Drew, despite what people may think. Sure, he annoys her at times, not to mention the first time she met him he dropped a moving box on her foot that left a bruise for a week. But no, she doesn't hate him. In all reality, she's scared of him. Scared that he's a good guy, with a good heart and good intentions. And that's just too much good for Ashtyn. Too much good for *her* to ruin. So, she keeps him at a distance with her snarky remarks and death glares, because if he were to ever get too close... well, they'd both end up heartbroken. And Ashtyn will not let that happen.

They drive in silence for a while, buildings passing in a blur. It isn't until Drew drives into a residential neighborhood that Ashtyn realizes they've left the city. "Where are we?" she asks, not recognizing her surroundings.

"My old neighborhood," Drew replies, turning up a steep hill. "My parent's house is just down the road." They climb, higher and higher, until they crest the hill and arrive at a small, empty cul-de-sac. Ashtyn can see the lights of the city flickering in the distance. It's breathtaking. No trees obstruct their view, nor houses. It's all just earth and sky and stars.

"Wow," she says, taking in the view. "It's beautiful."

"I used to come up here when I was a kid," Drew says, turning the truck off. "Watched a lot of sunsets back in the day."

"Let me guess, you brought all your girlfriends up here to woo them." She's teasing, but there's a tinge of curiosity laced in her voice.

Drew blushes. "I've actually never brought anyone up here before."

His response stuns her into silence, and adrenaline shoots through her body. After a moment she manages to ask, "I'm the first?"

"You said you needed to get away from it all. This is where I come to do that."

Ashtyn sucks in a breath and looks out at the wide expanse of sky. She opens the door to the truck and slides out. The March air is warm, not too hot just yet. She much prefers the colder weather compared to the warmer months. She thrives in the cold.

Drew gets out of the truck as well and stands next to her as she leans against the hood. She looks up at the stars, mesmerized. Without all the light pollution from the city, it's bright and clear. "Know anything about space?" she asks.

Drew shrugs. "A bit."

"Okay, show off then."

He smiles and looks up. "Okay, so you can spot the big dipper, right?"

Ashtyn shakes her head. "Nope."

Drew points toward the sky. "You see that little group of stars? They make sort of like a square. And there's a tiny little handle that connects them. Some people say it looks like a kitchen ladle. That's the big dipper."

"I see it!" she exclaims, pointing at the stars. "Okay, so where's the little dipper?"

"You're gonna follow an invisible line from the two, top stars of the big dipper. They're called Dubhe and Merak. Do you see them?" Ashtyn nods, and Drew draws an invisible line from the stars downward. "The handle of the little dipper starts with Polaris, the North star."

"There it is!" Ashtyn exclaims, her shoulder brushing against Drew's as he points out the stars. "Wow, it's beautiful."

"I, um—" he coughs. "We could see them better with my telescope. I have it in the backseat."

"You have a telescope?" she asks, turning to face him.

"Of course I have a telescope. How could I be a part of the local astronomy club if I didn't own a telescope?"

Ashtyn, despite herself, laughs. She claps a hand over her mouth the second it comes out. "Sorry, I wasn't laughing at the astronomy club. I just..."

"Didn't think someone as hot as me could be a nerd?"

There's the Drew she's used to. She rolls her eyes. "The idea that nerds aren't hot is an outdated stereotype that I will not be a part of."

"Yeah, I know, I'm living proof."

Ashtyn laughs and shakes her head. "Shut up."

"There's much you don't know about me, Ashtyn King." He bumps his shoulder into hers, and she has to stop herself from shivering.

"Yeah, I've gathered that." After a beat of silence, she says, "Okay, show me the stars up close."

Drew smiles and heads to the backseat to unearth his telescope. It surprises her how big it is. She thought it'd be skinny, like those old telescopes she's used to in movies. No, this one is big. Drew sets up the base, which looks like a tripod, then sets the telescope part on top. It's bulky, again, much bigger than she was expecting.

"You keep this thing handy for impromptu star viewing parties?" Ashtyn asks, teasing.

Drew laughs. "There was a planet alignment not too long ago. Everyone from the club got together to view it. I just forgot to lug this thing back up to my apartment."

Ashtyn nods, biting her lip. Once he's finished setting up the telescope, Drew invites her to look through the viewfinder. "I've positioned it on Polaris. Take a look."

She does and gasps. It's big and beautiful and bright and indescribable. "Oh my god," she breathes. "It's incredible."

"To be honest," Drew starts. "Polaris isn't even that impressive compared to the rest of the sky."

"Hey! You be nice to Polaris. I love him."

This makes Drew throw his head back in laughter. "Okay, okay! Sorry, Polaris."

Ashtyn has to bite back a smile. "Isn't he the brightest star in the sky?"

"No, that's Sirius. It's brighter than the sun."

Ashtyn looks away from the telescope, leaning back against the truck again. "Space scares the shit out of me."

"Why?" Drew asks, looking at her. She keeps her gaze focused on the stars, but she can feel the heat of his stare.

"Because it's just so... infinite, and we aren't. I'm just this tiny human, living on this huge rock, that could die at any second. It's scary."

"And how lucky I am to be living my tiny human life at the same time as you," Drew replies softly.

Ashtyn turns to him, and the look he's giving her scares the ever-loving shit out of her, because it's a look that says more than words ever could. It's similar to the look they shared at New Year's. A look they should never share again.

Ashtyn turns away from him and scoffs. "Maybe a meteor will crash down on Earth and kill us all. Then I bet you wouldn't call yourself lucky."

"Ashtyn the optimist, ladies and gentlemen!"

"Gotta humble the romantics."

Drew frowns as he stars up at the stars. "Is that why you were so against Shiloh and Ava getting together in the beginning? Because it was romantic?"

His question actually kind of stuns her. "I wasn't... against them getting together," she mumbles. "I just didn't think it was a good idea, but I was wrong. Obviously."

"Obviously," he parrots.

She narrows her eyes at him. "Ava's never had her heart broken, that's why she's such a romantic."

"Shiloh won't break her heart."

"I know that," Ashtyn replies. "I'm just saying, she's never felt that... feeling before. So, she's always optimistic about love."

"And you're not?"

"No, I am not."

Drew doesn't press for more information, and Ashtyn sighs with relief. She hates talking about Brandon. Drew doesn't need to hear that stupid story. It'll just make him feel sorry for her, and she doesn't need that from him.

"They're gonna make it. Shiloh and Ava. I have no doubts," Drew says, stuffing his hands in his pockets and looking back up at the sky. She wants him to keep telling her about the stars. Showing her things she's never seen before.

"I don't either," Ashtyn says, truly meaning it. "They're perfect for each other."

"Soulmates?"

"I don't believe in soulmates. But if I did, then I would say yes, they're soulmates."

"I don't think I believe in soulmates either," Drew says. "But I guess they're as close as one could get."

Before Ashtyn can stop herself, she asks, "Then what do you believe in?"

"I don't know. I just know I haven't found it yet."

They look at each other, something charged between them. Ashtyn sucks in a breath. "Out of all the women you've shared a bed with, you haven't found one worth keeping?"

A look that Ashtyn can't decipher passes across Drew's face. It's replaced with a lazy smile a second later, and he gives her a shrug. "Ah, you know what they say, some people just never learn to settle down."

For some reason, she doesn't believe him. Maybe it's the look he displayed for only a second, or the way his body seems tense despite his carefree attitude, but Ashtyn knows he's lying. She's not sure what caused the shift in his attitude, but it doesn't really matter. They were steering too close to personal territory anyway.

She crosses her arms and gives him a tight-lipped smile. "Alright, show me something better than Polaris."

* * *

Drew stands under the freezing water, letting it shock his system out of whatever it was he was feeling earlier. Despite having hot water now, sometimes he misses the old shower that never stayed warm. It was his constant for so long. So, sometimes, he blasts freezing water just to remember what it feels like. And to get him to forget about Ashtyn.

He had come dangerously close to telling her things tonight. Like which stars are his favorite. Like how he wants to settle down. How much he craves a love like his friends'. How he enjoys the company of not just women...

Drew has known he's bisexual since freshman year of high school when he developed a crush on his lab partner, Liam. Drew had taken one look at that boy, dark windswept hair, lazy smile, and he'd been smitten. They ended up sharing a kiss after school one day, and Drew knew. He knew he liked boys *and* girls. It was scary and exhilarating all at the same time.

It's been a part of his identity for so long now that sometimes he forgets not everyone knows. Like Ashtyn, for instance. She'd made the quip about women in his bed, and he'd *almost* corrected her. But for some reason, it didn't feel like the right time. He knows he doesn't owe anyone an explanation about his sexuality, but it also doesn't bother him to tell people. He likes people knowing. He remembers coming out to Shiloh their junior year of high school. It was late on a Friday night, after a football game, and they'd been driving around aimlessly when Drew blurted it out.

Shiloh looked at him, smiled, and said, "Thanks for telling me, brother."

And that had been it. He's supported Drew in any and all relation-ships he's had since then. Although, he wouldn't really call any of them relationships. What he told Ashtyn was the truth. He hasn't found what he's looking for yet.

The water gets so cold that he starts to shiver, and he turns off the shower. Tonight was the most he's talked with Ashtyn since New Year's. Her presence excites something in him that he hasn't felt in years. Something he's worried he's actually never felt before. He would have shown her every star in the sky if she'd asked him to.

He steps out of the shower and wraps a towel around his waist. He brushes his teeth and dries off fully before falling into bed, exhausted. He's about to drift off when his phone buzzes on the nightstand. It continues buzzing, and Drew picks it up. He almost drops it when he sees who is calling.

"Hello?" he answers, voice low, as if he's not sure it's really her.

"Hey," Ashtyn replies, voice equally low. "Um, sorry, I know it's late."

"No, it's okay. Everything good?"

She's silent for a moment, like she's considering her words. "Were you serious?"

Anxiety shoots through him. "About what?"

"About helping me find an apartment."

The anxiety dissipates, and he lets out a breath. "Of course, Ashtyn. Isn't that what friends are for?" As if they're friends.

She's silent for a moment. "I just... I don't want to bother Shiloh and Ava with this, because they've already found the perfect apartment. And I'm still struggling and..." Her words die off, and Drew can picture her biting her lip on the other side of the phone. "I need help."

Those words... he never though he'd hear them coming from her. He feels his heart start to race. "I'll send you a list of places I recommend in the morning. Don't worry, we'll find something. It'll all work out."

He can hear Ashtyn sigh. "Thanks, Drew."

"You're welcome, Ashtyn."

Neither of them hangs up, their breathing the only thing keeping them company. "I'm sorry," she says, after a moment.

"For what?" His hands fist in his bed sheets. He wishes they were having this conversation face to face.

"For the kiss on New Year's. I shouldn't...I..."

She can't seem to find the words she's looking for, so Drew says, "It's okay. Don't worry about it." They're silent again, letting so many unspoken things hang between them.

"Goodnight, Drew," she says, softly.

"Goodnight, Ashtyn."

And then she's gone, and Drew is alone, the echo of her voice still ringing in his ears.

MAY

Chapter 7

"Are we there yet?" Ashtyn groans as the car flies down the interstate.

"Ash, we literally just left," Ava says from the front seat.

"Why did Mattie have to attend school so far away?" Ashtyn grumbles, crossing her arms as she stares out the window.

"It's literally two hours, you'll be fine," Shiloh snaps, and Ava puts a hand on his shoulder to get him to relax. Ashtyn knows he's not angry with her. He's just anxious about seeing his parents for the first time since last September.

Mattie, Shiloh's younger brother, is graduating college tomorrow, and they're all going to his ceremony to support him. But, that also means the Brooks family is going to be there, and Shiloh did not leave on good terms with his parents the last time they spoke. Ashtyn knows how anxious Shiloh is about this unorthodox family reunion.

Mr. Brooks did not leave a good impression on either Ashtyn or Ava. He was rude, snobby, and an overall prick. When he finally pushed Shiloh to his breaking point, neither of the girls were upset when Shiloh cut him off for good. Even though it upsets Shiloh, having lost his relationship with his parents, Ashtyn knows it's for the best.

"I'll play 'I Spy' with you to pass the time," Drew offers from his spot in the seat next to her, redirecting her attention. Why he had to carpool with them, Ashtyn will never know. Probably just to annoy her.

She tries to forget the fact that she called him in the middle of the night and asked for his help in finding an apartment. After their night on the hill, something shifted within her in regards to Drew. He was genuinely being nice to her, and she needed all the nice she could get right about now. He actually ended up helping her find an incredible apartment near the school that was perfect. She was just waiting on their call to finalize everything. It could be any day now.

"I spy something annoying," Ashtyn says, looking out the window.

"Hey, it's not nice to talk about Shiloh that way," Drew retorts. The line gets a small smirk out of everyone, even Shiloh.

"Sorry," Shiloh says. "I'm just nervous."

"It's gonna be okay, babe," Ava says, rubbing her hand on his shoulder. "Besides, I'll be there to protect you. I'll throw hands if I need to!"

"I have no qualms with punching an old man in the face," Ashtyn adds.

"Well, if everyone else is doing it, I guess I will too," Drew quips.

Shiloh laughs softly. "Thanks, guys." He takes Ava's hand in his and kisses her palm. Ashtyn feels that familiar pang of loneliness and stares out the window until it goes away. Sometimes, and she will never admit this, she misses when they were all single. When Shiloh and Ava were just friends, and they all had that easy flow between them. But, Ashtyn also knows she would never trade Ava's happiness for anything in the world. So, she shoves that pang deep down where it won't upset her, or anyone else for that matter.

They arrive at the hotel a couple of hours later, and Ashtyn flops onto the bed, Ava on the one next to her. Shiloh and Drew got their own room, and Ashtyn is excited for the opportunity to be alone with her friend for the first time in a long while. Ashtyn loves Shiloh, and she loves Ava and Shiloh together, but sometimes she misses when it was just her and Ava. She misses the late-night movie marathons in their dorm room, eating so much candy their stomachs hurt, giggling about boys. Now, they're older, wiser, all that shit. It's different. Even if they still have movie night every Sunday. She doesn't want to think about how that will work when they live in different places.

"Have you heard from the apartment people yet?" Ava asks, kicking off her sandals.

Ashtyn sighs. "No, and I don't want to talk about that this weekend. I just want to enjoy the getaway."

Ava throws a bag of Red Vines on the bed. "Good thing I came prepared."

"This is why I love you," Ashtyn replies, ripping into the bag. She tears into one greedily. "God, this brings me back."

Ava brings out a bag of powdered donuts for herself. "*These* bring me back."

"Oh my god, I haven't had those in forever!"

"And you're not going to! This bag is for me."

"You're gonna eat an entire bag by yourself?"

"Yes, do you have a problem with that?"

"Of course not. More Red Vines for me," Ashtyn replies, hugging the bag to her chest. Ava laughs and flops next to Ashtyn. They snuggle into the bed together and turn on the TV, flipping through the cable channels to find something ridiculous to watch.

They're twenty minutes into a movie neither of them has seen before when Ashtyn whispers, "Hey."

"Hey," Ava whispers back.

"I'm scared."

"Ash, it's just some venomous snakes on a plane. It's nothing to be scared of."

Ashtyn narrows her eyes at her friend playfully. "I'm not talking about the movie."

Ava leans her head on Ashtyn's shoulder comfortingly. "What are you scared of?"

"Of being alone." She's not sure if it's the dark room, the only light coming from the TV, or the nostalgia of old times, but Ashtyn feels okay sharing this with her best friend.

"Ash," Ava says, softly. "You're going to find someone..."

"No," Ashtyn interrupts. "I meant... living alone. Without you and Shi. I'm scared that everything is going to be different, and we're going to drift apart..."

"Hey," Ava says, sitting up to face Ashtyn. "That's not going to happen. Look at me."

Ashtyn looks at her friend in the glow of the television. Ava has powdered sugar on her chin, and Ashtyn laughs as she wipes it away for her.

Ava holds up three fingers in a girl scout salute. "I, Ava Danielle Marshall, do promise you, Ashtyn Marie King, that we will never, ever grow apart. We're almost thirty, for God's sake. I don't have time to make any new friends. Besides, I meant it when I said you're stuck with me for life."

Ashtyn laughs, loudly, and grabs Ava's hand, holding it close. "We've never lived apart since college."

"I know," Ava replies, sadly. "I'm a little scared too."

"You are?"

"Yeah, I mean, I'm going to miss you so much. And, I'm worried it's gonna change my relationship with Shi..."

"Ave," Ashtyn starts. "That's ridiculous. Nothing is going to change for you two."

"But, it could. I mean, you were right. We are only a few months into an actual relationship. What if living alone changes the dynamic? What if I end up reminding him too much of Scarlett?"

The mention of Shiloh's ex-wife startles Ashtyn. "Ave, stop. You are *not* Scarlett. And Shiloh is not the same person he was when he was eighteen. I shouldn't have said what I said about your relationship. It doesn't matter how long you've been together, I know what you two mean to each other. You're meant to be."

Ava sniffles, trying to hide the tears forming in her eyes. "I'm gonna miss you."

Ashtyn presses her forehead against her friend's. She will always be brave for Ava. She will always be the strong person if her friend needs her to be. So, that's what she will do right now. She will put aside all her own fears for the sake of Ava. "It's not like we're moving out of the city. We'll both still be there. We can have sleepovers, and obviously I gotta come over to get my fix of Jess."

Ava laughs and squeezes Ashtyn's hand tighter. "No matter what. It's me and you, right?"

"You and me. Always."

Ava's eyes flick to the movie playing on the TV screen. "Even if there are snakes on a motherfucking plane?"

Ashtyn cackles and does a karate chop with her hands. "Don't worry, I'll protect you from anything! Even motherfucking snakes on a motherfucking plane."

* * *

Drew finishes his beer and signals the bartender for another. Shiloh, next to him, does the same.

"You okay, man?" Drew asks his best friend. Shiloh's been unusually quiet tonight.

"Yeah, just nervous about tomorrow." The hotel bartender sets two beers in front of them, and they cheer before taking a sip.

"I wouldn't be nervous. You have two girls that would probably rather go to jail than see you upset."

Shiloh huffs out a laugh as he sips his beer. "Yeah, I know. I just... this is Mattie's day. I don't want to take that away from him."

"I know what you mean. Where is he tonight?"

"Oh, you know Mattie. Probably partying somewhere."

Shiloh's glumness is starting to bring down the mood, so Drew slaps him on the back. "Okay, let's talk about something else. Are you excited about the move?"

Shiloh sighs and bites back a smile. "God, I'm so excited. Not that I haven't loved living with Ashtyn... I'm just excited to have a bit more privacy with my girlfriend."

Drew laughs. "Understood. But, you're not nervous at all? It's a big step."

"We've already lived together for over a year, and I can't imagine my life without her. It just feels like the natural next step. I don't have any doubts."

"And you're not... rushing into anything, right?" Drew hates himself for asking, but he was the one that was there after Shiloh's divorce. It was *his* couch Shiloh crashed on. He never wants to see his friend like that again.

"No, I don't feel rushed with her. Like, if Michael hadn't sold the house, we probably would have stayed there with Ashtyn for a while, and that would have been great. But since he is selling, it feels right to get our own place. Natural. I just feel so fucking peaceful with her, you know?"

Drew doesn't know, but he wants to, so he says, "Yeah." He finishes off the last of his beer in one long gulp.

"Sorry, I'll stop getting all sentimental and shit," Shiloh says, laughing.

"Shiloh Brooks, sentimental? No, never," Drew jokes, and Shiloh shoves him playfully.

"Fuck off."

Drew smiles as his phone buzzes on the bar. He turns it over, sees who it is, and ignores it. He feels a tiny pull of guilt in his stomach, but he pushes it down.

"Let me guess... Haley?" Shiloh questions.

At the mention of his sister, Drew feels a headache start to form. "New subject, please."

"Okay, where did you and Ashtyn run off to the night of playoffs?"

Drew frowns. "That was like, two months ago. You're asking me now?"

"Yeah, well, you've been busy."

That was an understatement. Tax season just started to slow down, and Drew has been working nonstop the last couple of months. Busy season is always intense with so many accounts to manage. He'd barely been able to attend that playoff game, but he made the time. In all honesty, he shouldn't have stayed up so late talking with Ashtyn, but he couldn't help himself. He can never help himself when it comes to her.

He sighs. "She just needed to get away from it all for a bit. We went driving."

Shiloh narrows his eyes at his friend. "Right. And you had no hand in helping her get her new apartment?"

"She asked me for some recommendations. I offered my help."

"That seems very un-Ashtyn like."

"Trust me, I know," Drew replies. "She didn't want to bother you or Ava. I think it's hitting her a bit more than she's letting on." He feels guilty, talking about her without her knowledge. But, it's Shiloh. They tell each other everything.

Shiloh lets out a breath. "Yeah, I was worried about that." He rubs his temple and finishes off his beer. "That's why I wanted them to have the night to themselves."

"Wow, you didn't want to hang out with your oldest and best friend?"

"Oh, yeah, that too."

Drew flips him off but smiles. His phone buzzes again, and this time he doesn't even look at it before turning it off. His sister can wait until after the weekend. Whatever it is, he'll deal with it later. The bartender slips them the bill, and they pay. Yawning, Drew can feel exhaustion start to tug on his bones.

"God, we can't hang like we used to," Shiloh says, also yawning.

"We're old now."

"Don't remind me," Shiloh teases.

As they make their way up to their room, they hear the muffled sound of giggling coming from the room next to theirs. The giggling soon turns to cackling, and the boys can't help but smile at the sound.

"Nothing could ever get between those two," Shiloh says, a fond smile on his face.

Drew laughs. "And if anyone tried, they wouldn't survive."

Chapter 8

The Event Center is sweltering. Ashtyn does not remember her graduation having *this* many people all crammed in the same room. They're already an hour into the ceremony, and Mattie hasn't even been called yet. Many people wave handheld fans in front of their faces, trying to chase away the Texas heat.

They're seated fairly high up, per Shiloh's request, so they don't run into the Brooks family. Shiloh said his father would never be caught anywhere above the fifth row. They haven't spotted them yet, although the center is filled with hundreds, if not thousands of people. It would be impossible to spot anyone in this crowd. That doesn't stop Shiloh's leg from bouncing continuously. Ava has her hand on his knee to steady him, but it doesn't seem to be working.

Meanwhile, Ashtyn keeps checking her phone for an update on the apartment. They should have called her already to confirm everything, but they haven't. Her anxiety is spiraling out of control, worried that something might have happened to hinder her chances at nabbing the unit.

"They'll call you," Drew whispers next to her, sensing her discomfort. "It'll be okay."

She takes a deep breath, trying to relax. She feels the urge to reach out and grab Drew's hand, but she doesn't. She sits on her hands instead, so no one can see them shake. This is Mattie's day. She should be focused on the ceremony, not worrying about herself.

"His degree is up next!" Ava exclaims, getting her phone ready for pictures, even though it's impossible to see anything this high up. Luckily, they have projectors that blow up everyone's faces.

"There he is!" Shiloh points into the crowd. Ashtyn can't tell anyone apart, but she trusts Shiloh to know which one is his brother.

"Matthew Thomas Brooks," the announcer proclaims, and the entire group jumps up and screams.

"Let's go, Mattie!" Ava screams, hands cupped around her mouth as she jumps up and down ecstatically. Ashtyn had to convince her *not* to bring an air horn, for the sake of everyone's ears. Mattie crosses the stage and takes his diploma from the dean, an ever-present smile on his face.

"That's my baby brother!" Shiloh yells, clapping excitedly. Mattie turns toward the crowd, beaming, and takes a bow. Classic Mattie.

Ashtyn's pride for Mattie begins to overshadow her anxiety. Her hands burn from repeatedly clapping, but she can't stop, even after he's left the stage and someone else has been called. Shiloh and Ava can't stop smiling and waving toward Mattie's direction either. Thank God the air horn was left behind.

Ashtyn knows how proud Shiloh is of his little brother, especially since he never went to college himself. Even with all the family drama, Shiloh's love for Mattie has never once wavered.

Once the ceremony is over, the group shuffles their way outside among the throng of people. They planned to meet Mattie at the flagpole after everything was over. Although, it seems as if everyone had the same idea. There are so many people, Ashtyn keeps bumping into strangers on accident. As they try to find an open space to wait, her blood runs cold as she spots the two people they were trying to avoid: Mr. and Mrs. Brooks. Even though she's never met Mrs. Brooks before, she has a striking resemblance to her sons. Better that than their dipshit father.

Shiloh stops short, and Ashtyn runs into his rigid back. His hands are clenched at his sides. "We've got this," Ava whispers, so only they can hear, and tugs on his hand. Ashtyn tries to give him a comforting pat on the back, but it seems to fall flat as his body doesn't relax.

As they make their way over, Mr. Brooks notices them, and the corners of his mouth tip ever so slightly downward. Not enough for a stranger to notice. No, just for them. Ashtyn knows this isn't the time or the place to air out their grievances with each other, but she can't help the rage that settles in her bones. Every interaction she's ever had with Mr. Brooks has been an unpleasant one. Plus, she's heard the horror stories from Shiloh about his childhood. She feels the need to punch the old man right in the face.

Everyone is stiff as a board as they stop in front of the Brooks parents. "Father," Shiloh says, reaching out his hand. Mr. Brooks regards it for a moment before taking it firmly, frown still permanently on his face.

"Shiloh," he replies, stern and gruff. His voice has always set Ashtyn on edge, although most men's voices tend to do that.

"Mom," Shiloh starts, but Mrs. Brooks barely even looks at her son, or the girlfriend she's never met. However, when she spots Drew, her eyes light up. "Andrew! Honey, how are you?" She kisses both of his cheeks as he leans down to hug her stiffly.

"Hi, Gloria. I'm good. How are you?" Ashtyn can tell Drew is uncomfortable, but he's hiding it well. She's not sure if he and Shiloh had a conversation the night before about how they would handle this.

"Oh, I'm wonderful, sweetie. Are you still working at the accounting firm Tom set you up with?"

Ashtyn feels the words vibrate among the group. She didn't realize Mr. Brooks helped Drew get his job. "Uh, yes ma'am, I'm still there. Just got promoted actually."

"Incredible news, son!" Mr. Brooks exclaims. "I bet your father is so proud."

The look that crosses Shiloh's face almost brings tears to Ashtyn's eyes. Ava is grasping his hand so tightly, Ashtyn can see her knuckles turning white. Her face is a mixture of rage and dejection. Drew shifts uncomfortably on his feet, hands stuffed in his pockets. "Ah, you know my dad. He's happy as long as I'm happy."

Mr. Brooks flicks an invisible piece of lint off his charcoal gray suit. "Well, congratulations."

"Thank you," Drew mumbles. He stares at the ground, as if looking too closely at Mr. Brooks will suck him into his orbit.

Ashtyn has to bite back every retort that comes bubbling up to her lips. The things she would say to that awful man if she were alone with him. Luckily, Mattie saves her at that exact moment.

"There he is!" Mr. Brooks exclaims, clasping his youngest son into a tight hug. Ashtyn didn't think Mr. Brooks was capable of giving hugs.

"Thanks for coming, everyone," Mattie says, a small smile on his lips. Ashtyn can only imagine how jarring it must be for him to see everyone together again. He gives his mom a hug and a kiss. Then, he sees his brother.

The smile Mattie gives Shiloh is worth it all. It even warms Ashtyn's heart. The brothers embrace tightly, like they never want to let go, like their love for each other is stronger than their parents' rejection. The Brooks parents busy themselves with checking their phones.

Ashtyn notices Drew's absent stare, hands in his pockets. "You okay?" she whispers to him.

He just shrugs, his expression never changing. "I'm fine. It's Shiloh I'm worried about."

"I think he's gonna be okay," she says, watching him hug his brother. Drew's face softens ever so slightly, a small smile playing at his lips. When the brothers let go of each other, Mattie launches himself at Drew.

Ashtyn feels her phone buzz in her pocket as she watches the exchange. She snatches it up immediately and recognizes the number she's been waiting for all week. "Excuse me," she says, taking the phone call away from the crowd. She doesn't want to leave her friends, but she can't miss this call. When she's a safe distance away, she answers. "Hello?"

"Hi, is this Ashtyn King?"

"Yes, this is she."

"Hi, this is Sarah from Pinecrest Apartments."

"Oh my gosh." Ashtyn breathes out a sigh of relief. "I've been waiting on your call. I was getting worried there for a minute."

"Um, yes ma'am, about that..." Sarah stammers. "Um, after reviewing your application, unfortunately we have decided to go with a different tenant and can no longer offer you the apartment. We apologize for the inconvenience. If you have any other questions, please feel free to contact our office at..."

But Ashtyn has stopped listening. The phone falls to the ground, protective screen shattering as it hits the concrete, case popping off. No. No, no, no. This cannot be happening. This was her only option. She doesn't have any other backup plans. It was this or nothing. She put all her eggs into one basket like a fucking idiot. Her mom's voice comes roaring into her ears: *You could always move back home.*

The beginning of a panic attack starts to take shape as she tries to catch her breath. Her chest constricts, sweat suddenly pouring from every part of her body. She tries to take gulps of air, but her throat feels like it's constricting in on itself. She knows she could go home, but it's so far from everything she's established. Her job is here. Her friends. Everything. A sense of vertigo hits her, and she sways slightly.

"Ashtyn?" At the sound of Drew's voice, her knees give out. Luckily, he's close enough to catch her before she hits the ground. "Oh my god, Ash. Are you okay? Do you need me to get Ava?"

"No!" she manages to exclaim. She doesn't even register that he called her "Ash". Tears start to form in her eyes, but she blinks them away rapidly. Drew's arms steady her, and he's able to pull her back up into a standing position. She grabs his shirt in both hands and turns them so the group can't see that she's about to have a panic attack. "Please. Don't tell them."

Drew's arms snake around her, and she doesn't care what her normal policy is; she sinks into his embrace, burying her face into his chest. The scent of Drew wraps around her like a blanket, soothing her panicked brain. His arms cocoon her in an embrace that is steady, yet soft. She takes deep breaths, letting his comfort calm her into a normal breathing pattern. She hates how secure he feels.

"What can I do to help?" His voice is low and soothing, his hand at the small of her back, rubbing small, comforting circles.

Ashtyn sniffles, then looks up into his blue eyes, composing herself to the best of her ability. Her brain is short circuiting. There's no other explanation for what is about to happen. She's going to regret this. She's so going to regret this, but she has no other option. "Does your offer still stand?"

Drew blinks down at her in surprise. "What offer?"

"To live with you."

His eyebrows shoot up in surprise, then he schools his face into a normal expression. "Uh, ye—yeah. It does. Of course."

"Good. Cause I don't have anywhere else to go."

"Ashtyn, what happened? Did the apartment people call you? I don't understand what's going on."

She doesn't feel like reliving the past five minutes, so she just sighs, hands shaking. She takes a small step out of his embrace. "I need a place to live, and you offered. I'm accepting your offer."

"I don't want you to settle for something you're not comfortable with—"

"Stop," she interrupts him. "I'm not settling. You have never made me feel uncomfortable. And you said you'd charge me less than anyone else in the city. Is that still true?"

"Of course. Honestly, you really wouldn't need to pay rent—"

She holds up a hand to stop him, fingertips inches from his chest. "Don't play the pity card. You're going to charge me rent, and I am going to pay it, because I will be living in your apartment. We are going to set up ground rules, so we don't rip each other's throats out, and we are not going to tell Ava and Shiloh until after this weekend. Does that work for you?"

Drew swallows and says thickly, "Yes, that works for me."

"Okay, then," Ashtyn says, fixing her makeup in her compact mirror and steadying her hands. "It's settled. Let's get back to the shitshow."

* * *

Drew's mind won't stop racing. When he originally offered for Ashtyn to live with him, he never thought in a million years she would say yes. He never thought he would actually hear those words come out of her perfect mouth. But they did. She said yes. She's going to move in with him. They are going to occupy the same, close space. And soon. Oh, so very soon.

Excitement, fear, anxiety, lust, and every emotion in-between courses through him. They're in the car heading home from Mattie's graduation weekend, glad to be done socializing with the Brooks family. Ashtyn is sleeping in the seat next to Drew. Shiloh stares stone-faced at the road in front of him, and Ava has her nose in a book. Drew wanted to tell Shiloh about Ashtyn last night, but he had to respect the fact that she didn't want her friends to know yet. She didn't give him any details, but he can surmise that the apartment complex called and informed her she didn't get the unit. He can't imagine why, but it doesn't really matter. She's out of options, and she went to the only person left. *Him.*

He rubs a hand over his jaw as he stares out at the passing landscape, thoughts running a million miles an hour through his head. Instead of thinking about all the things that could go right, he thinks about all the things that could go wrong. She could end up hating him. They could ruin their tentative friendship irrevocably. They could damage their relationship with Shiloh and Ava. Every horrible thing he can think of floods his system, and he almost wants to turn to Ashtyn and tell her he can't do it. But he won't. She's desperate, and he would never let her suffer. He takes a deep breath to steady himself. This is going to be okay. It's all going to work out.

A small poke to his arm startles him out of his reverie. He turns to see Ashtyn now awake, staring at him. Her hair is mussed from sleep, and Drew thinks this might be how she looks in the mornings. A thrill runs through him at the thought of getting to see her right when she wakes up. Stupid, stupid boy.

"You okay?" she mouths. Drew just nods, lips pressed tightly together, keeping him from saying everything he wants to. He takes this precious moment to study her as she turns her head back to the window. Her thick, red hair is tangled, but she doesn't seem to mind. Her face, normally done to perfection with makeup, is bare. She closes her eyes again, and her soft lashes lay against her pale skin. Her lips, normally plump with gloss, are clear and slightly cracked. She didn't even bother getting dressed, since they were just driving home today. She's in sweatpants and a soft cotton shirt that says, "I Hate Mornings." Drew thinks she is the most beautiful person he has ever seen.

As he looks up with a small smile on his face, he catches Shiloh's eye in the rear view mirror. The two boys share a look that says more than words ever could.

God, what has he gotten himself into?

Chapter 9

As Drew enters the house, he's surprised to find how empty it is despite the raucous laughter that echoes throughout. Most of the big furniture that once dominated the space has been moved or sold already. Music thumps through the echoing house, everyone else having already arrived. Drew is the last. He'd spent the last ten minutes sitting in his truck, trying to hype himself up. He's barely spoken a word face to face with Ashtyn since she agreed to move into his apartment. They've only texted here and there, getting things finalized. Now, tonight is the "goodbye house" party. Next week, Ashtyn will officially move in with him. His skin tingles at the thought.

"Hey! There you are!" Ava exclaims, embracing him in the foyer.

"Hi, sorry I'm a bit late. I brought wine, though."

"Ooh, my favorite," she says, taking the bottle from him. Their cat, Jess, winds her way through Drew's feet, and he bends down to pet her. She purrs against his fingers. He's never considered himself a cat guy, but Jess is the exception. She's the perfect little fluffball. She licks his hand as if she can read his mind. She knows everyone loves her.

"Drew, get your ass in here!" Mattie yells over the music, his voice slightly slurred.

He doesn't see Ashtyn with the group. Mattie, Shiloh, and Jordan are playing Nintendo Switch Sports on the TV that's still mounted to the wall, while Daisy, Derek, Brooke, Parker, and Damien chat amongst themselves. Ava's pouring herself another glass of wine in the kitchen. Ashtyn is nowhere to be seen.

"There he is!" Jordan exclaims once Drew finally finds his way into the living room. The *empty* living room. The large sectional that took up the majority of the space is gone. Instead, lawn chairs are spread out across the room. It feels like a college frat house he used to frequent.

"Come on, I need someone on my team for tennis," Jordan says, handing him a controller. Drew takes it, but his mind is stuck on a continuous loop of *"Where's Ashtyn?"*

While the vibe seems to be good, Drew can't help but feel a little sad at the thought of the house being sold. So many memories flood through his mind: the day Shiloh moved in and he met the girls for the first time. Being so stunned at the sight of Ashtyn that he dropped a box right on top of her foot. Ava's birthday party. Countless game nights and movie nights. The driveway where they worked on that damn boat, when Ava fell and cut her head open. Shiloh's divorce party, where Ava whispered something in Drew's ear that he still thinks about...

His mind wanders to that night, when he circled his arm around Ava's waist and whispered in her ear, slightly drunk and staring straight at Ashtyn, "I think I'm going to fall in love with her one day."

Ava leaned up into his ear and whispered back, breath hot and full of alcohol, "I think she'll fall in love with you too. Just give her time."

Just thinking about it again sends shivers down his spine. He tends to keep that memory tightly locked up in the back of his brain, so he can't go back to it and hope. No, hope is a dangerous thing. A scary, dangerous thing.

"Earth to Drew," Jordan says, waving a hand in front of his face. "Geez, where are you tonight?"

"Sorry," Drew says, shaking his head. "Just out of it, I guess."

"Well, get into it!" Ava exclaims, entering the living room. "We're celebrating!"

"Ave, take my place for a few rounds," Drew says. "I gotta use the bathroom."

She looks at him curiously, but takes the controller anyway. He squeezes her shoulder in a silent thanks. He heads into the hallway, checks to make sure no one is watching, and then takes the stairs two at a time. He reaches Ashtyn's door and knocks quietly.

"Come in," she says softly. Drew opens the door and realizes this is the first time he's ever been inside her bedroom. Moving boxes are strewn everywhere, clothes and shoes peeking out from overstuffed bins. Ashtyn is sitting on her unmade bed, staring at a picture frame.

"Hey," he says. He clears his throat awkwardly. "You okay?"

Ashtyn sighs and puts down the frame. It's a picture of her and Ava, arms around each other, smiles wide. They look young, like they were still in high school when the picture was taken. "No."

Drew perches on the edge of the bed, careful to give her space. "What can I do?"

"There's nothing anyone can do," she says. "I just have to get over it."

He frowns. "You're allowed to be upset."

"No, I'm not. Do you see everyone down there? They're happy. They're excited about the future. No one is sad like I am."

"So, you don't want to go down and celebrate?"

"No, I want to go down and act like it's a funeral, because that's what it is."

"Okay, then let's do that." He thinks he'll do anything she wants right now.

It's Ashtyn's turn to frown. "I'll ruin everyone's good mood. I already bring the vibe down enough as it is." It's a small admission, one that Drew doesn't agree with.

"Don't be ridiculous," he retorts. "You've always been the life of the party. Who did the most tequila shots with me at Brooke and Jordan's bachelor party?" She sticks her tongue out at him, but there's a hint of a smile on her face. When she doesn't say anything, Drew clears his throat. "Do you want to tell them tonight?"

Ashtyn groans and falls back against the pillows. "I guess we should. But they're going to freak."

"It'll be fine."

"I fear you underestimate your friends."

Drew huffs a laugh. "And I think you overestimate them."

"We *do* need to go over some boundaries," she says, biting her lip and sitting up.

"I'm all ears," Drew responds. "Whatever you want."

She takes a deep breath, then looks up at him. "No flirty comments. I am your roommate, nothing more."

"Understood."

"I'm not a morning person, so don't even try to talk to me before ten AM."

"I already knew that."

Ashtyn narrows her eyes at him but continues. "If you have... guests come over, let me know before, so I can... be scarce."

"Okay. The same goes for you."

She snorts. "You think I'm gonna have a cohort of men coming in and out of my bedroom?"

"I don't know. But it doesn't matter to me. The apartment is half yours, so you're free to do whatever you'd like with whomever you'd like. Same goes for me."

A charged tension thrums between them, but they both ignore it. "Fine," she says. "I—I think that's it. We'll just stay out of each other's way."

He hates the way she says it, but he replies, "Sounds good to me. So, you ready to go down there?"

"No," she replies, but gets up anyway.

Drew, deciding to take a chance, holds his hand out to her. She looks at it with a frown, but then takes it, albeit tentatively. Her hand is warm in his, soft and small. He squeezes it ever so slightly and tries to convey to her that he is safe. She can trust him. "We've got this," he says. "Together."

"Am I going to regret this?" She's teasing, but there's a tinge of seriousness in her voice that Drew detects. He's worried about the same thing. So many things could go wrong.

To make her feel better, and to ease his own nerves, he smiles lazily and says, "What could possibly go wrong?"

* * *

As they make their way down the stairs, still hand in hand, Ashtyn has to steady her breathing. She doesn't know why she's so nervous to tell her friends she's moving in with Drew. The sound of cheering hits her ears like a foghorn. It's so loud in here, sounds echoing throughout the bare room. She can barely stand to see it so empty.

"There you are!" Ava exclaims once she sees her best friend enter the living room. "I was worried you weren't ever going to come down."

"I just wanted to finish packing some stuff," Ashtyn replies, voice soft. She lets go of Drew's hand discreetly and instantly longs for it back. God, why did it feel so good in her own?

"Here, Shi made you a drink."

Ashtyn takes the drink gratefully and sips. She almost moans with how good it is. "God, why did he ever stop being a bartender?"

Ava giggles and sips her own drink. "He's a man of many trades." She looks over at him dreamily, and Ashtyn wants to vomit from the cuteness of it all.

"Hey, uh, I need to talk to y'all later," Ashtyn says, trying to gather as much liquid courage as she can.

"Is everything okay?"

"Yeah, I'm fine. I just... have an announcement to make."

Those are the exact wrong words to use, because Ava's eyes widen, and then she's banging on her glass, exclaiming to the entire room, "Ashtyn has an announcement!!!"

Ashtyn tries not to rub her temples in annoyance. It's not necessarily Ava's fault. She's already a few drinks deep, which means she's even more exuberant than normal. Ashtyn sighs and catches Drew's eye from across the room, where he's found a seat on a lawn chair. He gives her an encouraging nod. For some reason, it eases her nerves. She wishes he was standing next to her, holding her hand while she tells their friends the news.

Everyone's eyes are on her as they quiet down. They wait patiently for her to speak. Ashtyn takes a huge gulp of her drink, then says, "I'm moving in with Drew." The entire room freezes. Nobody says a word, the only sound coming from the TV. Nobody even blinks as they process the information. You'd think they just heard the world was ending.

Ashtyn rolls her eyes. "The apartment I wanted flaked on me, so Drew was my last option. That's it. If anyone makes this a big deal, I'm kicking you out early."

"Ash," Ava starts, her mouth agape from shock. It then turns into a bright, beaming smile. "That's great news!" She wraps her friend into a hug, and Ashtyn lets it happen.

"Are we taking bets on how soon one of them kills the other?" Jordan asks, loudly.

Ashtyn glares at him over Ava's shoulder. Brooke also gives him a death glare and pinches the underside of his arm. "Kidding, kidding!" he says, hands raised in surrender. He stares down into his drink, brown cheeks tinged pink. "Geez."

"I have vowed to be a perfect gentleman," Drew says, his ever-present charm fully locked in. Ashtyn thinks it's rare to see him without it, and yet, every time they're alone, it's not there. She tries not to think about it. She knows he's doing this for her benefit, acting like it's not a big deal.

Shiloh hasn't said a word, and Ashtyn looks over at him nervously. He gives her a small smile and raises his drink. "To your new adventure."

The group cheers, and Ashtyn chugs the rest of her drink. She heads to the kitchen to get herself another one and avoid the eyes of her friends. Shiloh joins her a moment later. She could have bet money on this happening. She's surprised Ava isn't with him.

"Hey," he says.

"Are you here to lecture me?"

"No," Shiloh scoffs and crosses his arms, looking nervous.

"You're a terrible liar."

"I'm not here to lecture you. I just... want you to be careful."

"Consider me careful."

"Ash." The tone of his voice makes her look up at him. "Are you sure this is what you want?"

"I don't think it really matters what I want, Shiloh," Ashtyn says carefully. "Every apartment I looked at was either too expensive or rejected me. I literally have no other options."

"We could have found someplace together—"

"No, it's too late for that. Plus, you and Ave found the perfect place. You deserve that. I'll be fine."

"Ash," Shiloh starts, reaching out to her. She accepts his embrace, albeit reluctantly, and leans into him. She's come to love hugs from Shiloh, even if she doesn't want to admit it. She never wants to admit that she's dependent on someone else.

"I promise. I'm going to be okay."

"I know," Shiloh says into her hair. "Drew will take care of you, even though I know you don't need anyone to take care of you. But, he will. He's a good guy, otherwise he wouldn't be my best friend."

"I know."

"I love you, you know that right?"

"Yeah, I love you too. Besides, you know you can't get rid of me that easily, right? I'm still coming over every Sunday for movie night. Plus, Jess is still half mine. I should at least get visitation rights."

"I wouldn't want it any other way," he says, squeezing her tight. "You're family. Forever."

Ashtyn feels another set of arms encircle her, and she knows it's Ava. "Ugh, my favorite people in the world," she murmurs. She's tipsy, which makes her even more lovey than normal.

"Stop it, you two. You're going to make me cry," Ashtyn teases.

Ava pulls back. "Ashtyn King, crying? I don't think I've ever heard of such a thing!"

"I think I've cried more the last few weeks than I have in ten years. It's disgusting."

"Crying is good for the soul," Ava says. "You gotta release all those negative emotions!" She shakes out her arms dramatically, sloshing some of her wine over the lip of her glass.

"Okay, I think that's enough wine for you," Ashtyn giggles, taking the glass away from her friend.

"Hey!" Ava whines, sticking out her bottom lip in a pout. "I wasn't done with that."

"Mine now," Ashtyn says, taking a sip.

"Here," Shiloh says, handing Ava a glass of water. "So you don't have the world's worst hangover tomorrow."

Ava groans but relents, taking the water. She gulps it down in record time, then yells, "Okay, everyone into the living room!" She grabs both Ashtyn and Shiloh's hands and drags them behind her.

"What's all this about?" Ashtyn asks.

Shiloh just shrugs. "Beats me."

Ava turns off the TV in the middle of Mattie and Jordan's game, and they turn around, eyes wide. "Ave, I was just about to win!" Mattie exclaims.

"Shh, it's time for the goodbyes."

Mattie and Jordan look at each other, confused, but they shrug and collapse into the lawn chairs. Ava stands at the front of the living room, facing everyone with a bottle of wine. How she got the bottle from their time in the kitchen to now, Ashtyn has no idea. She's a sneaky one, that Ava Marshall. But God, she loves her best friend.

"Okay, I want everyone to come up here and tell us your favorite memory of the house! And no one is exempt! Everyone has to do it." She narrows her eyes and points at everyone in the room. "Okay, I'll go first." She clears her throat and holds up the bottle in a toasting gesture. "I honestly have too many memories of this house that I will cherish forever. From the day that Ash, Brooke, and I moved in, to the day I met the love of my life, this house has been there for us. And I couldn't be happier to have made all these memories with you all." She takes a long pull from the bottle, then holds it up above her head. "To this house!"

Everyone cheers, and then Shiloh is pulling Ava into a kiss, taking the bottle from her. She stays next to him as he takes his turn. "My favorite memory is obviously the day that I moved in. But, also, the first time that I kissed you in that hallway." Ava radiates under his gaze as they press their foreheads together. "I wish I had done it sooner."

"Gross!" Ashtyn yells, but there's a smile on her face as she watches her friends kiss.

"To the house that gave me my family," Shiloh says, breaking away from Ava and taking a pull from the bottle.

"Do we really all have to take a drink?" Brooke asks, taking the bottle from Shiloh. "I feel like that's kind of gross."

"Don't be a spoil sport!" Ava says, wrapping herself around her boyfriend.

Brooke rolls her eyes but smiles. "Fine. My favorite memory, besides when we moved in, is when Jordan proposed to me in the backyard." She looks at her husband lovingly.

"Hey, that was gonna be my memory!" Jordan exclaims, getting up and wrapping his wife in an embrace.

"We can share," Brooke says, kissing him. They both take a sip from the bottle.

"Ugh, there are too many couples here," Ashtyn grumbles. Mattie raises his glass in agreement.

"Well, we won't be any better, because I think our memory is the same," Daisy says, taking the bottle from Brooke. "My favorite memory is when Ava paired Derek and I together in Blockbuster."

Derek snakes an arm around her. "I couldn't agree more. Although, I will never forget when Ava made us all watch *Mamma Mia* on her birthday a few years ago, and it ended up being a karaoke singalong night."

"Oh my god, that was so fun!" Ava says.

Derek and Daisy take a sip, then pass the bottle to Parker and Damien. "The first time we ever came to game night," Parker starts, adjusting his glasses, "I was so nervous. I had just moved to town, and my new coworker invited me over to her place, and the second I walked in the door, I felt so welcomed. We played Catan until, if I recall, almost two in the morning, and it was some of the most fun I've ever had."

"Parker," Ava says, tears forming in her eyes.

"Don't cry or you're going to make *me* cry!" Parker says, taking a sip from the bottle. He passes it to his husband.

"And my favorite memory," Damien says, "is also the *Mamma Mia* karaoke night, because Ashtyn and I had the best duet in the history of duets."

Ashtyn smiles and raises her glass to Damien. "No one has ever sung 'Dancing Queen' better, I think."

"Never," he replies, taking his drink. He hands the bottle to Mattie, who gets up and smiles.

"Well, I know I haven't been here as long as most of you, but I've had some good times in this house. My personal favorite is when we played Monopoly, and Ashtyn got so mad she flipped the entire board over."

The friend group bursts into laughter as Ashtyn's jaw drops. "I did not flip it! It was an accident! It was already precariously perched on the edge of the table!"

Mattie laughs and takes a long gulp from the bottle. "Pretty sure I saw your hand slip, then."

Ashtyn grunts and takes the bottle from him. "I hate you all. My favorite memory is when we got Jess." As if on cue, Jess bolts into the room, chasing a hair tie.

"Oh come on, Ash!" Ava protests. "Be a little more sentimental."

She rolls her eyes. "Fine. I love this house, and I love you all. I'm glad we moved in. There." Ashtyn takes her gulp and turns to Drew. He's the only one left. He's looking at her with a softness in his eyes that makes her shudder. She hands him the bottle.

"My favorite memory," he says, his fingers skimming against hers, "is the night of Shiloh's divorce party."

Shiloh furrows his eyebrows. "Your favorite memory of the house is my divorce party?"

Drew smiles, eyes crinkling at the corners. "Yeah, I got some pretty good advice that night." His gaze slides to Ava, and she beams, as if she knows exactly what he means. Ashtyn looks at the two of them, unable to figure out what is passing between them.

"To friends," Drew says, finishing off the bottle. "To moving out. And to our continued celebrations, wherever they may be."

Everyone cheers, the room brimming with love and celebration. And yet, Ashtyn can't help but feel the enormous loss that's coming. This house, her friends, all this love... it's going to change. No matter how much they tell themselves it won't, it will. Something is shifting. Ashtyn just has to hold it together until everyone leaves.

They drink and talk long into the night, sharing stories and memories from the past few years. Ashtyn doesn't cry once. Instead, she tries to focus on the here and now, reveling in this feeling, because it won't be here tomorrow. Tomorrow, everything changes.

Chapter 10

Ashtyn tapes up her last remaining box and sets it in Drew's hands with a scowl. "If even one eyeshadow palette is damaged, I'm making you buy me a new one," she says, sternly.

"Don't worry, I'm not in the habit of dropping boxes anymore," Drew retorts with a wink.

"You better not be."

The house is empty. Completely barren. The only things left are the sleeping bags laid out on the living room floor. Ashtyn, Shiloh, and Ava decided they wanted to spend their last night in the house together, as a family, like old times.

"Alright, is that the last of the boxes?" Drew asks. The back of his truck is filled with Ashtyn's belongings. They moved her furniture earlier in the day, and she'd gotten her first look at her new apartment. She hates to admit it, but it is ridiculously nice. Way nicer than anything she could afford on her own, with huge windows overlooking the city. The view is spectacular. Even if a particular blonde nuisance is sharing it with her.

"Yeah, I think that's everything," Ashtyn says, crossing her arms over her chest. She catches a glimpse of the old movie wall and feels a pang in her chest. She and Ava had spent most of yesterday divvying up the DVDs, trying to figure out who owned what. She feels like separating the DVDs defeats the purpose of the collection, but she didn't tell Ava that. She just enjoyed the time she spent with her friend. Now, as she stares at the blank wall, the loneliness starts to set in.

"You sure you don't want to stay, Drew?" Ava asks, setting the pizza boxes on the floor next to their sleeping bags.

"Nah, y'all enjoy your last night together. Besides, I gotta unload all these boxes to the top floor."

"I told you I'd come and help," Ashtyn argues.

"Don't worry about it," Drew says. "I'll take care of it."

"Andrew."

"Ashtyn. I'm serious. I got it. Go, enjoy your time together."

Ashtyn relents and lets him go. The thought of lugging all those boxes up to the apartment sends her stomach roiling. Drew leans out the window of his truck and waves as he drives away, all of her belongings with him. Ash turns back toward the house, the porch creaking as it has always done. No more front porch evenings, sipping wine after work and watching the sunset. No more watching Ava and Shiloh pass a soccer ball back and forth in the front yard. Ashtyn sighs, leaving the porch behind as she enters back into the house and plops down on her sleeping bag. Jess curls into her lap, purring loudly.

"You better not forget me," she whispers to the cat. "Because I'm still gonna see you at least once a week, if not more."

Shiloh sits across from her, and Jess immediately gets up and goes to him. "Sorry," he says.

"It's fine, I know where her loyalties lie."

"Don't worry, we'll put your picture right next to her cat tree," Ava says, passing her friend a plate of pizza.

Ashtyn sticks her tongue out at her but smiles. "There better be pictures of me everywhere!"

"Everywhere," Ava agrees. "Besides, it's almost summer, which means we won't be working, and you can come visit every day."

Ava and Shiloh's new apartment is only about ten minutes away from Drew's without traffic. But ten minutes feels like a lifetime when you're used to five seconds. Ashtyn *hates* change. Hates the impermanence of life.

She blows out a breath. "Yeah, I'm sure I'll need a break from Drew sooner rather than later."

"You're sure this is what you want?" Shiloh asks for what seems like the hundredth time, concern on his face. He strokes Jess absent-mindedly, her small cat body limp and relaxed in his lap.

"Yes, Shiloh," Ashtyn sighs. "This is what I want. Drew is... a good friend."

Ava's eyebrows shoot up at Ashtyn's proclamation. "I'm pretty sure you threatened to drown him in soup a few months ago."

"And I'd do it again!" Ashtyn retorts, then sighs. "But things change." She shrugs. "I didn't think I would be on the verge of homelessness a few months ago."

"Ashtyn, you know you will never go without a roof over your head. You have us, your mom, Brooke and Jordan, all our friends. You are never alone," Ava says, putting a hand on Ash's shoulder. "No matter what."

Ashtyn bites into her pizza to stop herself from getting emotional. "Enough with the sentimental shit."

Ava laughs and digs into her own piece. "Well, what should we do on our last night together?"

They laugh. They laugh so hard their sides hurt and tears leak out of the corners of their eyes. They laugh so long, Ashtyn doesn't think she could ever be happier, even if she tried. They laugh loud and unabashed, their voices echoing throughout the house.

They reminisce about the good times. Like when Ashtyn and Ava watched the entire *Friday the 13th* franchise in one weekend, only stopping for pee breaks and food, jumping at every little sound they heard out in the hallway. They tell Shiloh about the college parties they left early, the late-night study sessions, the copious amounts of money they spent on powdered donuts and Red Vines and used DVDs.

Ashtyn french braids Ava's hair, like she used to in their dorm room before parties, while Shiloh tells them about Drew's twenty-third birthday party, a story they've heard a million times but always makes them laugh. They try and see who Jess will come to if they're all on separate sides of the room. Shiloh always wins, even when Ashtyn offers her treats. They play hide and seek even though there's nowhere to hide, the house open and empty. Still, Ashtyn wins when she squeezes herself into a kitchen cabinet for twenty minutes.

They debate about the mysterious brown stain on the ceiling that no one will take credit for. At this point, they don't even know when it happened, but Michael will probably take it out of their security deposit. They don't care. They giggle uncontrollably as they theorize who it could have been, and *what* exactly it is. They walk into each bedroom, sharing their favorite memories, Ashtyn remembering so many long nights studying at her desk for her teacher's certificate exam. They make sure each room gets its moment to shine.

They list their four favorite movies per their Letterboxd accounts, which they made Shiloh get a few weeks after he moved in. But they can't stop at just four, so they keep going, listing every movie they love, every movie that means something to them, and why they need to have a marathon of them all soon. They try to list every DVD they own, from memory, and Ashtyn tries not to let her gaze linger on the empty wall where the shelf used to be. They revel in the world of film, one Ashtyn feels more comfortable in than real life sometimes.

They sit in silence, letting the house settle in their bones, so they never forget it. So it becomes a part of them. So they never forget the feeling this night gives them. They hold hands, trying to remember what they feel like to each other, every curve and imperfection and callus. And eventually, they fall asleep in the early hours of the morning, their bodies not far from each other.

That's how they spend their last night together, and it's all they could have ever asked for.

JUNE

Chapter 11

It feels weird having another person living in the apartment with him. Drew has never had a roommate, besides college and the stint where Shiloh slept on his couch. But other than that, he's always had a place to himself. He's kind of excited to have Ashtyn living with him, even if she's been in a foul mood ever since she stepped foot across the threshold.

She's only been here about a week, but she's still hesitant around him. They've barely seen each other as she cleaned out her classroom for the summer break and moved into the apartment. Drew's been making himself scarce, to let her adjust.

Since she's not working over the summer, Drew knows he'll be seeing more of her. His own work is starting to slow down as well, and he's nervous at the prospect of both of them being home on the weekends, nothing to do except talk to each other. Or ignore each other. Drew has bets on the latter.

It feels like all the progress they've made in their relationship, if you can even call it that, has vanished. It's like they're strangers again, Drew trying ridiculously hard to impress her, Ashtyn pointedly ignoring him. He knows, logically, she's just grieving the loss of her home. She's sad and upset and adjusting to a new place. But, still. It hurts to see her frown more often than smile.

It's Friday afternoon, and Drew is finishing up his work at the office.

He's nervous to go home and to see Ashtyn. Nervous that he made the biggest mistake of his life when he asked her to move in with him. Drew waves to his boss as he leaves the office, and the Texas heat envelops him as soon as he steps outside. He shrugs off his blazer and lays it across his arm as he makes his way down the sidewalk. His heart beats in rhythm with his footsteps, but soon starts to accelerate as he nears his building. He takes the stairs, rather than the elevator, to buy himself more time.

By the time he reaches the top floor, he's out of breath, and his heart is still racing. He has no idea why he thought the stairs were a good idea. Even with his morning peloton workouts, he's no match for the stairs. No one is. He takes a steadying breath then opens the door. The aroma of spices and herbs hit him all at once. She's cooking. Well, that's an improvement to the sulking she's been doing as of late.

He lays his stuff on the entryway table and heads into the kitchen, where the smell is mouthwatering. Ashtyn has her Airpods in, so she doesn't hear him enter. She's humming to herself, swaying her hips to the beat as she stirs a pot of sauce on the stove top. It's intoxicating, watching her relaxed and at ease. He almost doesn't want to disturb her.

Drew clears his throat, but she still doesn't hear him. He starts toward her with a hand up to tap her gently on the shoulder, but she must see him out of the corner of her eye, because she whirls around with a gasp and flings the spoon straight at his head. It hits him with a *thunk,* and a trail of sauce runs down his forehead.

"What the hell!?" Ashtyn exclaims, her chest rising and falling rapidly as she tears her Airpods out of her ears. "You can't just sneak up on someone like that!"

"To be fair, I tried to get your attention," Drew says, biting back his smile. He grabs a dish towel and wipes his forehead. "It smells great in here."

Ashtyn sighs and retrieves the spoon from the floor. She tosses it in the sink and grabs a new one from the utensil holder. "I, um, figured I should cook since we haven't really had dinner together yet. You know, with work and moving and everything."

"Thanks," Drew says, loosening his tie.

"No problem. It'll be ready in a minute."

"Okay, I'll just get out of these clothes." He makes his way to his room, tugging off his work clothes as he goes. He tries very hard not to bring work home with him at the end of the day. Work is for the office. Home is for… everything else. For Ashtyn. He takes the world's quickest shower, and by the time he's done and dressed in sweatpants and a t-shirt, Ashtyn has the table set for dinner.

When she sees him, her throat bobs, as if she's not used to seeing him like this. Barefoot and relaxed in his own home. He looks at the table and realizes she's set the plates on the complete opposite side of the table from each other. The distance is glaring.

"Are we really going to eat at opposite heads of the table?" Drew asks, chuckling.

"I didn't know where you usually eat."

He takes his plate and scoots it closer to where Ashtyn is sitting. She stiffens, but doesn't protest as he sits down next to her. "I actually can't remember the last time I sat at this table."

"Not a big dining table guy?"

"I normally don't make it home before dinner. So, I usually grab something on my way home and scarf it down on the walk."

"Geez. That's sad."

"I just try to remember how well I'm paid."

At his words, Ashtyn looks around at their shared space. It's large, much larger than a standard apartment. Drew had got a two bedroom because he planned on making the second bedroom an office or a workout space. But now, it's Ashtyn's room, and he doesn't seem to mind not having either of those spaces anymore. He's just glad he has a place for her.

"About that," she starts, staring down at her plate of food.

He knows what she's about to say next. "Ashtyn, I already told you your rent. I'm not changing my mind."

"I'm scamming you."

"No, you're saving for something better, right? So you can get out of my hair as soon as possible?"

They talked about this the day she moved in. He was charging her next to nothing for the room, but he really didn't care. He could afford this place without her rent. He just wanted to help her, and he knew she wouldn't take it for free. When she protested that it was too low, he argued that this way she could start saving for her own place. Like this was just temporary. Which it is... temporary.

"Right," she sighs. "Someplace better."

Drew smiles at her as he takes a big bite of food. He sighs contentedly. "God, I can't remember the last time I ate something homemade."

"You like it?"

"I love it."

"To be fair, the noodles are from a box. I just made the sauce. It's my mom's old recipe."

"Well, thank her for me, because it's delicious. Even with boxed noodles," he teases. Ashtyn sticks her tongue out at him but smiles despite herself. Seeing her relax eases something in Drew's chest.

They make idle small talk for the rest of dinner, trying to find a balance between comfortable silence and pleasant conversation. When they're finished, Drew clears the plates and starts on the dishes.

"I can help," Ashtyn says, quietly. She's so much more reserved than she normally is. It's like her snark and sarcasm have shriveled up inside her. Drew misses them, even if they're normally directed toward him.

"No, I got this. You cooked. I clean," he says.

She bites her lip, looking contemplative, then says, "Okay." She heads toward her room and shuts herself inside without another word.

$$* * *$$

They continue this back and forth for the next week. Drew goes to work, Ashtyn sulks in her room until it's time to start cooking, then they share a meal together at dinnertime. After, Ashtyn shuts herself back in her room until she falls asleep.

Her room is fine. It's smaller than the one she had at the house, and the bathroom is out in the hallway, but it's fine. It's better than nothing, she has to keep reminding herself. She knows she should be grateful. Drew has been nothing but kind to her. But, she still feels... empty. Like she lost her best friend and her home. Like she's starting over.

She's talked to Ava almost every day since they moved away from each other. She's gone over to their apartment a few times, cuddled with Jess, and put on her happy face. They're happy, Ava and Shiloh. They have the whole summer to break in their apartment together, and Ashtyn should be happy for them. She *is* happy for them... she is. She just wishes she could also be happy too.

It's Sunday when Ashtyn comes out of her room and shuffles into the living room. Drew is on the couch, feet on the coffee table, playing a video game on the TV. He's relaxed, at home. She wishes she could feel the same.

"Hey," she says tentatively, sitting next to him, leaving a glaring amount of space between them even though the couch isn't *that* big.

"Hey," Drew says, smiling softly at her. He pauses the game and sets the controller down. "You, uh, want the TV?"

"Um, actually, I was going to ask if you wanted to watch a movie with me. It's movie night. Or, I guess, it was." Normally, Ash would be going over to Ava and Shiloh's so they could watch a movie together, but it's the first one they've had to reschedule. Ava's parents came into town to see the new apartment, and they're all going to dinner. Ashtyn was invited, but she declined to go. Self-sabotage, she thinks to herself. She's not sure *why* she didn't want to go, just that her instinct had been to say no.

"Oh shit, it is Sunday, isn't it?" Drew asks, checking his phone. "Here, you can have the TV." He turns off the game, and Ashtyn looks at the space by the TV mournfully. There should be shelves full of DVDs in here for her to choose from. Instead, just a blank wall stares back at her.

"You okay?" Drew asks, noticing her sour mood.

Ashtyn sighs and decides to tell him the truth. "I miss the movie wall."

"I have pretty much every streaming service—"

"No, it's not about that," Ashtyn interrupts. "It's being able to see them all, you know? All your favorite movies at your fingertips. Lined up alphabetically so you know where they all are. It's just...it's silly, I know, but I love it. Er, loved it, I guess I should say."

"You know, you can put a shelf out here if you want," Drew says softly. "I know you and Ava split up your collection, but if it makes you feel more at home, you can set them up out here."

Ashtyn turns to look at him. "Really?" She hadn't even considered putting anything in the shared spaces of the apartment. She'd shoved everything in her room and closet and called it a day. The apartment doesn't feel like hers yet. No, just her room, hence why she stays holed up in there most days.

"Of course. I told you to make yourself at home. If a movie wall makes you feel that way, then please, be my guest. Besides, I think I may have a DVD or two around here somewhere..."

Ashtyn feels a smile tug at her lips. Right now, all her movies are shoved in the closet, unable to be seen by anyone. This offer... Drew's offer to set up her own movie wall makes her feel just a little bit more settled.

"Thanks," she says. "I'd really like that."

"Okay, then let's go get a shelf!"

"What, now? It's late."

"Yeah, and? Target doesn't close until midnight. We've got plenty of time." He gets up and pulls on his shoes, twirling his keys on his index finger. The look he gives her, one of anticipation and excitement, gets her up off the couch and following him out the door.

* * *

"I'm supposed to be watching a movie right now," Ashtyn groans. "Not debating which shelf is going to look better in the living room."

"We can't just pick a random shelf," Drew counters. "It has to match the aesthetic of the apartment."

"And what aesthetic is that? Single man that works too much and keeps things just a little too clean?" Drew frowns at her, and Ashtyn bites back a smile. "Kidding!"

"Maybe I should try out the 'see it in your home' feature," Drew mutters to himself.

"No, that's it. I'm picking the white one. It's my shelf, and I want this one." She goes to grab the ginormous box and almost topples over from the weight of it. Drew steadies her, then takes the box from her, easily. His biceps bulge under the weight, and she has to look away. She does *not* think about how easily those arms could pick her up.

"Show off," she mutters.

Drew just laughs and carries it over his shoulder like it weighs nothing. "If it doesn't match, I'm blaming you."

"It's white. White matches everything."

They continue their banter until they round the corner and come face to face with a beautiful blonde woman that makes Drew stop in his tracks. Ashtyn bumps into him with an "oof," but his grip doesn't falter on the box. Ashtyn doesn't think she recognizes the woman, but then she frowns, and Ashtyn knows exactly who it is. Cara. From the disastrous Valentine's date night. *Shit.*

"Cara. Hey," Drew says, his voice seemingly catching in his throat.

Cara looks between the two of them, her frown deepening. She scoffs "Looks like you finally figured it out."

"Wha—what?" Drew stutters.

Cara looks at Ashtyn with a look she can't decipher. "Have fun with him."

"Cara—" But Drew doesn't get a chance to finish, because Cara just smiles and walks away with a swish of her hips. Drew stands there, mouth slightly agape.

"Well, you really fucked that one up, didn't you?" Ashtyn asks, crossing her arms.

Drew lets out a deep breath. "Yeah, but I'm pretty sure it was doomed from the start."

They resume their walk to the checkout in silence. When they get there, Drew doesn't even pretend like he's going to try paying for the shelf. He's completely checked out, his eyes far away. Ashtyn pulls out her wallet and pays. They load it into the back of the truck and get in, silence settling over them. The awkward tension is palpable.

"You, uh, okay?" Ashtyn asks, shifting in her seat.

Drew seems to snap out of his trance as he turns on the truck. "Uh, yeah, I'm fine. Sorry, guess I zoned out there for a sec."

"You know, you're allowed to be upset. You don't always have to be this happy, go-lucky guy you portray to everyone."

For a second, Drew seems like he's going to be vulnerable with her. But, a moment later, he smiles lazily. "You want to get some ice cream?"

So, they do get ice cream and bring it back to the apartment, where they start to unbox the shelf. Ashtyn insists she can do it herself tomorrow morning, but Drew decides he needs to build it right now. Pieces of it litter the ground, along with their discarded ice cream cups.

"Hand me piece B," he says, holding out his hand. Ashtyn hands it to him, and he attaches it skillfully to the correct place.

"So, uh, are we going to talk about what happened at Target?" Ashtyn asks, hating herself for bringing it up. Why? Why is she bringing this up? She should just let it go. But Cara's words keep nagging at her. *Have fun with him.*

"Not really sure what there is to talk about," Drew replies, not looking up from the shelf. He attaches another piece to the base.

"You seem upset."

"I'm not upset, Ashtyn. I'm mad at myself for being a dickhead to her. She didn't deserve what happened that night and neither did you."

"Were you two, you know, together?"

"Not exactly. It was casual, like most of my relationships." This is the first, tiny glimpse Ashtyn has gotten into Drew's personal life. For all his teasing and flirting, he really has kept himself closed off from her. Or maybe she just hasn't been paying attention. Either way, she feels the need to dig deeper.

"You not big into dating?" she asks.

"Are you?" he replies.

Her defensive walls immediately slam into place, and she rolls her eyes. "Okay, point taken."

"It's not that I don't want to settle down eventually," Drew says. "I just haven't found anyone I've felt like I wanted to with."

"And Cara?"

"She's beautiful and fun, but that's the extent of our relationship. I didn't picture it going on longer than a few months anyway."

"So, there's no one you can picture yourself settling down with?" Ashtyn asks, feeling the weight of her words settle over them.

Drew looks up at her, something unspoken in his eyes. "I didn't say that."

She shivers and laughs to break the tension. "Well, I'm sure you'll find someone eventually."

Drew just smiles sadly and goes back to his work. They assemble the rest of the shelf in relatively comfortable silence. Once it's finished, Drew looks at his work triumphantly. "You were right. White looks good."

The shelf sits next to the TV stand, bare and empty, ready to be filled. Ashtyn smiles at it, then runs to her room and grabs the ginormous tote that's currently housing her DVDs. It's too heavy to carry, so she drags it across the floor and into the living room. How, exactly, Drew got all her stuff up to the top floor, she'll never know. She just knows that when she arrived on her first day, everything was in her room, not a scratch in sight. All eyeshadow palettes were in perfect condition.

"You need help?" Drew calls, settling himself onto the couch.

"I got it," Ashtyn huffs as she pulls the tote up to the shelf. She's out of breath just from pulling a freaking tote full of movies a couple of yards. She breathes heavily, hands on her hips, and stares daggers at Drew, who is laughing behind his fist. "Is something funny?"

"Not at all," he says, biting a knuckle.

"Let me guess. You didn't even break a sweat lugging this shit up to my room?"

"I'll never tell," he teases, crossing his feet at the ankle and bringing his hands up behind his head. He's the picture of relaxation.

Ashtyn scowls and opens up the top of the tote. "Come on. We've got sorting to do."

They alphabetize for what seems like hours, Ashtyn continuously having to fix Drew's mistakes.

"Come on, Drew," she admonishes jokingly. "Even my kinder-garteners know that *Candyman* goes before *Captain America*."

"Listen, I'm good with numbers, not letters," he teases. "Also, if your kids are watching *Candyman,* then I'm worried about your teaching credentials. This looks scary."

Ashtyn laughs, loud and unabashed. "Yes, Drew, I make my kids say 'Candyman' in the mirror five times every time they ask to go to the bathroom."

"Hey, I don't know what they're teaching the kids these days!" he jokes. "That could be true for all I know."

Ashtyn rolls her eyes and bites back a smile. "Here, put this in the 'P' section."

Drew takes the collection of movies and frowns. "You really like this stuff?" He gestures to the stack of *Paranormal Activity* movies he's holding.

"I do," Ashtyn says. "Horror is my favorite genre."

"Really? Is that because your last name is King?"

"Probably. When I saw the name Stephen King in my local library, I knew I had to read whatever it was he was writing. Turns out, I loved it." She had devoured almost everything Stephen King had ever written by the time she graduated college. She still picks up his new release every year.

"Huh." Drew huffs.

"Does that surprise you?"

"Honestly? No, it doesn't. Not a lot surprises me when it comes to you."

That surprises her. She looks at him in bewilderment. "Well, everything about you surprises me."

Drew sighs. "I'm not a closed book, Ashtyn. You can ask me anything you want."

"Noted." She feels her walls starting to rise again as she puts more DVDs on the shelf.

"You don't want to ask me anything right now?"

Ashtyn sighs. "What's your favorite movie? And if you say *Pulp Fiction*, I'm moving out."

Drew grins broadly. "*Shrek.*"

She looks up at him, something between shock and amusement crossing her face. "Your favorite movie is *Shrek*?"

"What's wrong with *Shrek*?"

"Nothing!" she exclaims. "I guess, I just didn't expect that. It's a great movie."

"Well, yeah, of course it is," he says. "It's the best."

Ashtyn smiles, grateful to have gotten this piece of information from him. It feels... special somehow. She decides to let him in as well, just a little. "My favorite movie is *Scream*."

Drew looks sheepish. "I've never seen it."

"What!?"

"I'm not normally a horror movie person."

"Ugh, you and Shiloh both," she grumbles. "We'll have to fix that."

"You'll have to give me a horror movie education," he says, voice suddenly slightly lower.

Ashtyn clears her throat and puts the rest of the movies on the shelf, not looking at him. The idea of the two of them sitting on the couch, watching scary movies in the dark... it's all just a bit much. She puts the last movie on the shelf and admires her work. It's filled to the brim, but they all fit. The movies stare back at her, and she feels a sense of nostalgia wash over her. It's not completely the same, but it's close, and that's a start.

"What do you think?" Drew asks. She slides her eyes to him. He's got a lazy smile on his face. Her throat tightens against the feeling that she doesn't belong here, in his space, with her movies filling his walls. The nostalgia is shattered, imposter syndrome settling in, like she shouldn't be here.

"Fine," she mumbles. "Better than nothing."

"Oh, come on! It looks great."

"I said it's fine," she snaps. Drew's face falls and regret instantly tugs at her heart. But instead of apologizing, she digs herself deeper, farther into this role she's assigned herself. "Maybe it'll make living here tolerable." Shame washes over her, cold and shocking. She hates that she said it, but she can't take it back.

Drew, to his credit, doesn't say anything. He just gives her a tightlipped smile and leaves the room. She can hear the *snick* of his door closing without another word. Ashtyn stands in the living room, alone, only the movies on the shelf staring back at her accusingly. They didn't even watch a movie, she realizes.

She swallows against her shame as she heads into her room. Why does she have to ruin everything? They were having a nice conversation, and she messed it all up. As she closes the bedroom door behind her, she falls against it, hugging her knees to her chest as she sits on the ground. She sits like that for a long while, the apartment's glaring silence the only thing to keep her company.

Chapter 12

The last few days, Ashtyn and Drew have been cordial with each other, at best. Ashtyn has stayed hidden in her room even more than usual. She's stopped cooking dinner for them, and instead, eats in her room where she can't make a fool of herself anymore. She feels like an idiot, like she ruined everything. Normally, her snark isn't that untamed, or frankly, rude. The words burn under her skin, making her itch with discomfort. She should apologize, even if it's been almost an entire week since it happened. God, she's such a bitch.

Bitch. The word feels branded to her forehead; one she's been unable to scrub away for a while now. Bitch. A word used predominantly by men to make women feel bad for reacting in a certain way. To make them seem like they're in the wrong when they get angry. Ashtyn's always hated hearing the word come out of men's mouths, yet she can't stop herself from using it against herself. For living up to this namesake that people bestowed upon her when she stood up at Brandon's wedding. *Gosh, what a bitch move.* She can still hear the words echo in her brain every time she says something remotely mean. Bitch. Bitch. Bitch.

As she lays in bed, agonizing over her past mistakes, she hears keys in the doorway. Well, she guesses, she might as well get her shit together and go apologize. She doesn't even realize that it's not at all the time Drew normally comes home until she's near the door, her socked feet barely making any noise on the floor. She stops abruptly in the hallway as she comes face to face with a young, blonde woman, the tips of her hair a fading box-dyed pink. For a crazy moment, Ashtyn thinks it's Cara, but then she sees the woman's face better. It's a stranger. In Drew's apartment. In *her* apartment. A motherfucking stranger in the motherfucking apartment. The thought almost makes her laugh.

The women stare at each other for a moment, unblinking. Ashtyn debates screaming or running, but she's frozen in place, unable to make a decision, her blood freezing over. Goddamn her fight or flight instincts right now. Her feet betray her by not running, and her brain betrays her by short circuiting. The woman cocks her head, brows furrowed in confusion.

"What are you doing in my apartment?" Ashtyn asks, voice coming out weaker than intended. She clears her throat, trying to make it go deeper. "How did you get in?" Jesus, this is pathetic. She can be scarier than this.

The woman frowns, dropping a duffel bag to the ground as she juts out a hip. "Goddammit, did he move and not tell me? That's real shitty on his part, because I still have the key."

Ashtyn just blinks at the woman. For a moment, she forgets that this isn't even technically her apartment. "Who—who are you talking about?"

"Andrew Mitchell. Tall, blonde, annoying. Does he still live here?"

"Y-yes," Ashtyn stutters, and the woman sighs with relief.

"Oh, thank God." She shuts the door with her hip and slips off her shoes, padding toward Drew's bedroom. "I'm gonna go take a shower."

And with that, the woman shuts the bedroom door behind her. First, Ashtyn is shocked. Then, she's mad. Livid, even. They had agreed they wouldn't have dates over in front of each other. She dials Drew's number furiously, fingers shaking with rage.

"What's up?" he answers, voice nonchalant, like they haven't been ignoring each other for a week.

"What's up is that you have a woman caller breaking into our apartment and showering in your shower. That's what's up," Ashtyn growls, barely taking a second to breathe. "You're supposed to tell me before that happens. We had an agreement."

There's a beat of silence before Drew says, "What are you talking about?"

This just infuriates Ashtyn even more. Her grip on the phone tightens. "A fucking blonde woman came into the apartment, with keys I might add, and is now in your shower! She didn't give me a name, but I can only assume she's one of yours since she knew your name and had a goddamn key."

Drew's only response is, "Fuck." Then, "I'm on my way."

He hangs up before Ashtyn can say another word and anger floods her system. She grabs the baseball bat that sits in the entryway and positions herself so her back isn't toward Drew's room. She doesn't know who this woman is, but Ashtyn isn't letting her sneak up on her again.

Drew is home before the woman is even out of the shower. By the look on his face, Ashtyn wonders if he even knew she was coming. Ashtyn doesn't say anything as he rushes toward his room, and she hears him bang on the bathroom door. She keeps her hands firmly on the baseball bat, just in case.

"Haley!" Drew yells. "Get the fuck out of the shower! Now." Ashtyn can't hear what the woman, Haley, replies, but it must annoy Drew, because he sighs heavily. "You have five minutes." He heads back toward the hallway and stops when he sees Ashtyn with the baseball bat, his eyes going wide. "Jesus Christ, were you going to bludgeon her?"

"Well! I don't know who she is, and you didn't offer any explanation!

I had to protect myself." She loosens her grip on the bat, but doesn't let go.

"I'm sorry," Drew says, rubbing his temples. "I—I forgot to tell her I got a roommate."

"Who is that?"

"My little sister."

Ashtyn drops the bat to the ground, the loud clatter ringing in her ears. She didn't even know Drew had a sister. God, what else does she not know about her new roommate? "Your sister?"

The shower turns off, and Drew turns toward the bedroom with a heavy sigh. "Prepare yourself."

* * *

It takes all of Drew's self-control not to strangle his sister as she comes out of the bathroom with her hair tied up in a towel. It appears she borrowed one of his old high school t-shirts without asking. It hangs loosely off her too skinny frame.

"Hi, big brother," she drawls. "How've you been?"

"Haley, what did I tell you about breaking into my apartment?"

"You said to make yourself at home! Otherwise, you wouldn't have given me a key."

"I also told you to call before you did that."

"And you didn't tell me you got a new girlfriend," Haley counters.

"She's not my girlfriend," Drew says, quickly, eyes glancing to Ashtyn. She observes them from her spot in the kitchen, eyes wide and guarded. She seemed surprised when Drew told her Haley was his sister. Had he never mentioned having a sister? He can't remember. He can't remember anything right now when his baby sister is invading his space, *again.*

"Is she the redhead you kept whining about at Christmas? I mean, she's pretty—"

"Haley," Drew interrupts her. "What are you doing here?" His patience is already wearing thin with her.

Haley sighs dramatically. "Jimmy kicked me out, the bastard."

Drew rubs his temples. His sister headache is starting to form with a vengeance. "What did you do this time?"

"Hey, that's not very nice! I didn't do anything. Why do you always blame me for everything?"

"Haley," Drew warns.

"Okay!" she relents. "I might have thrown all of his clothes out the window and onto the street. But, like, it wasn't a big deal! He overreacted. Plus, he cheated. So, you know, we were supposed to be even!"

Drew doesn't even have words for what he's hearing. It's the same old sob story with Haley, just different details each time. "Let me guess, you figured you'd crash here until you figured something out."

"Ugh, you're the best big brother ever!"

"You're not staying here," Drew says, and Haley's face falls. It tugs at his heartstrings, his brotherly instincts starting to rear their head. He tries to smother them, remembering that he has Ashtyn to worry about now.

"What?"

"I have a roommate now. We don't have room for you."

"Oh, come on! I'll sleep on the couch. You know I've slept on worse. And I can't go back to Mom and Dad, they'll kill me."

"No, Haley—" But before he can finish, Ashtyn clears her throat.

"It's okay," she says, voice small. "I don't mind if she stays."

Both Drew and Haley whip their heads to Ashtyn. "Oh, you're the best, girl! What's your name? Sorry, I probably should have introduced myself before breaking in, but I thought you were just a one-night stand that wouldn't be here tomorrow."

"Ashtyn." Her words are clipped as she crosses her arms against her chest.

"I'm Haley. I promise you won't even know I'm here!" Haley exclaims and goes off to grab her stuff from the entryway.

"Ashtyn," Drew starts, but she puts her hand up to stop him.

"It's okay," she says, not meeting his gaze. "And also, I'm sorry about the other night. I-I shouldn't have said what I did. I didn't mean it."

"Is that what this is about? You feel guilty?" He remembers her words and how badly they hurt him. He didn't want to admit it, but they'd torn a hole right through him.

"Yes. But, also, she's your sister. I don't mind if she stays. I'm just... I'm sorry, Drew. I shouldn't have said that. I didn't mean it, okay?"

"Thank you," Drew replies. He feels some of their previous tension start to melt. "I appreciate it."

"And I-I appreciate you." She swallows, like the words are hard for her to admit. "Maybe it'll be fun to have your sister here?" She forms it like a question.

"Oh, you don't know Haley then," Drew says, sighing heavily. No one knows Haley the way he does. He loves his little sister, he does, but she's also the root cause of most of his stress induced illnesses. She's been trouble since the moment she was born. "I'll make sure she's gone by next week."

"It's okay, Drew. Really." She places a hand on his arm, and a shiver runs through him.

"You have no idea what you just agreed to."

Chapter 13

Drew was right. Ashtyn had *no* idea what she agreed to when she decided to let Haley stay. Holy shit, the girl is a wreck and a half. She talks a million miles a minute, always something crazy coming out of her mouth.

"Listen, all I'm saying is that if they didn't want people to graffiti the courthouse, they shouldn't have made it so ugly."

"That's a federal building, Haley," Drew counters. "You could have been arrested."

"Yeah, but I wasn't. Besides, the world needs more art."

"Legal art."

Haley rolls her eyes and takes another big bite of food. They're all sitting at the dining table, trying to be very normal about this whole situation. Well, at least Ashtyn is. Haley, mouth full of food, says, "Legal art is boring. You gotta take risks to make good art. Everyone knows that."

Drew just sighs and rubs his fingers against his temples. Ashtyn has never seen him like this before. He's so tense and rigid. He's normally relaxed and charming and cracking jokes when he's around the friend group. When he's around Haley, he acts like the most mature adult Ashtyn's ever seen. It's weird. She figures it's the big brother mentality.

"So, Ashtyn," Haley starts, changing the subject. "What do you do?"

Ashtyn stirs the food on her plate absentmindedly. "I'm a kindergarten teacher."

Haley blanches. "And you like doing that?"

"I do," she replies. "Kids make a lot more sense than adults sometimes."

"Well, I don't know about *that*. Every kid I've come across these days has been a brat."

"Were they being a brat, or were you just not being understanding?" She doesn't mean for it to come out harsh, but her tone has an edge to it.

Haley though, to her credit, doesn't seem upset. She just laughs. "God, you're just like my brother. No wonder he likes you so much."

"Haley," Drew warns, cheeks warming. "That's enough."

Haley turns to her brother, a mischievous smile on her lips. "What?" she asks innocently, batting her lashes at him.

But the words ring in Ashtyn's head. *You're just like my brother.* Ashtyn does something she normally wouldn't. She presses, turning toward Drew. "Do you want kids?"

The question must surprise Drew, because he freezes, fork poised between his plate and mouth. He puts it down and clears his throat. "Um, yeah, I think so. Obviously not right now, but yeah, in the future I could see myself as a father." Haley makes a *blech* sound in response.

Ashtyn's not sure why, but the answer shocks her. Maybe it's because she's so used to Ava and Shiloh both saying they never want to have kids. She felt outnumbered when she expressed that she was open to the idea of being a mom. She loves her little rugrats at work, even if they aren't technically her own kids. But, for roughly eight hours a day, she's responsible for them, and she takes that seriously. Even when they drive her absolutely crazy. Even when they try to eat pine cones. Even when they *are* being brats. Regardless, she loves them. She wants that for herself, she thinks. A family. One day.

She doesn't say anything as she looks at Drew, his cheeks reddening under her gaze. Haley looks between them with flickering eyes, a smirk on her face. "Y'all bang yet or what?"

"Haley!" Drew exclaims at the same time that Ashtyn drops her fork with a loud clang. It's her turn for her cheeks to flame, and she looks down at her plate, ignoring the comment. Moment officially ruined. Drew narrows his eyes at his sister. "Can you pretend to have a filter for one second, please?"

"Oh, come on, I'm just kidding!" Haley protests, biting back a smile that argues she was definitely trying to stir the pot.

"Sorry Haley, but I don't see your brother like that," Ashtyn says, trying to ignore the blush erupting over her face.

"We're just friends," Drew reiterates.

"And barely that." Ashtyn ignores the way Drew's mouth tightens at her words and the guilt that floods her system.

Haley looks between them skeptically. "Okay, whatever y'all say." She inhales another bite of food. "This dinner slaps by the way. I haven't eaten this good in a while."

"What have you been eating lately?" Drew asks, his tone casual but shoulders tense.

Haley rolls her eyes. "Oh, you know, the usual. Poptarts and energy drinks."

"Hales—"

Haley holds her hand up. "I did not come here for a lecture. I came here because you're the one person that never makes me feel like shit about my life choices. Just... let me breathe for a bit."

Ashtyn feels guilty being here for this conversation. The look Drew gives his sister is heartbreaking, like he wishes he could wrap her up and keep her safe from every harsh thing life has to offer. But he can't. No one can.

"You know," Ashtyn starts, trying to lighten the mood. "One time in college, I ate like three packs of Red Vines and chugged way too many Redbulls while cramming for a midterm. And I'm still here to tell the story."

Haley's face softens at Ashtyn's words, and she smiles. Her eyes tell Ashtyn thank you. But her mouth says, "See, Drew? I'll live."

An awkward silence settles over them as they finish their dinner. Ashtyn offers to clear away the dishes as Drew sets Haley up on the couch.

"You know, if you were a real gentleman, you'd let me take your bed, and *you'd* sleep on the couch," Ashtyn hears Haley say.

"Yeah, well, if you weren't my annoying little sister, maybe I'd think about it."

Instead of being offended, Haley just laughs. "You're such a little shit."

"Same goes for you."

"Hey, Drew?"

"Yeah?"

"I love you."

"I love you too, Haley."

Once the dishes are done, Ashtyn tiptoes to her room to give them privacy. She shuts the door and collapses onto her bed, ignoring the way her heart pounds. *We're just friends.* She repeats the words to herself for a few minutes, until a knock on the door startles her. "Yeah?"

"It's me," Drew says through the door. "Can I come in?"

She takes a deep breath. "Um, sure."

The door opens a crack, and Drew peeks his head in. He stops just inside, as if debating on whether or not to enter her space. If they've really set that boundary. "It's okay, you can come in," Ashtyn says. Drew steps fully into the room – for the first time, Ashtyn realizes – and closes the door behind him. He looks around at her decorations, pictures of her and her friends framed on the wall. Vanity tucked in the corner, makeup spread all over it. A million pillows on the bed.

"What was this room going to be originally?" she asks as his eyes travel over every surface.

"Ah, I didn't really have any plans for it," he says flippantly, hands in his pockets.

She narrows her eyes at him. "Really?"

Drew shrugs. "I mean, besides maybe a home gym, I really didn't have any need for a two bedroom. I just felt like I should have one. Turns out, I was right."

Ashtyn's cheeks burn as she turns away from his gaze. She clears her throat. "Is there a reason you're here?" It sounds rude, but she doesn't mean it that way. "Sorry, that sounded accusatory. I really gotta work on my delivery."

Drew laughs lightly. "Um, I just wanted to apologize for Haley. You know, for the stuff she said at dinner. She doesn't really have much of a filter."

"It's fine, really."

Drew pauses by the edge of the bed and then slowly lowers himself onto it. It sinks under his weight, and Ashtyn pulls her knees up to her chest. She's very aware of where his body is. Where hers is. The space between them.

"I really didn't expect her to just show up without at least calling me first. She's kind of a mess, but I've always been there for her when she needs me—"

"Drew, it's okay," Ashtyn interrupts. "I understand. I just didn't even know you had a sister."

"There's a lot you don't know about me," he says softly.

"Yeah, I guess the same could be said about me."

They sit in silence for a moment. "I don't normally talk about Haley with other people. I love her, she's my sister, but she also stresses me out. She makes a lot of stupid choices that I feel like I need to help her fix."

"She's an adult, Drew. She can fix her own mistakes."

"Yeah, but in my mind, she's still that annoying little five-year-old that followed me around everywhere. I was her protector. And even though we are adults now, I still feel like I need to look out for her. No matter what."

"I don't have any siblings, but Ava is the closest thing I have to a sister, and I feel the same way with her sometimes. I get it."

Drew looks at her and smiles a little. "I promise she won't stay long. It's only a matter of time before Jimmy calls crying and apologizing, and she takes him back."

"Is that a normal occurrence?"

"Oh, yeah," he says, letting out a breath. "Haley loves to make the same mistake over and over again."

Ashtyn can't help but laugh. "Don't we all?"

Drew smiles. "I guess. I love my sister so much, but goddamn if she doesn't make my life difficult sometimes."

"She really likes to air out your thoughts and feelings, doesn't she?"

Drew blushes. "She doesn't know what she's talking about. I told you, no filter."

Ashtyn feels like toeing the line, so she says coyly, "Oh come on, Drew. I know you have a crush on me."

He actually throws his head back and laughs. It reverberates through Ashtyn's entire body. God, that laugh. "A crush? No, I don't do crushes."

"But you liiiiiike me," she teases.

"Of course I like you, Ashtyn. Who wouldn't?"

His frankness makes her blush, again. "Trust me, lots of people don't like me."

"Well, their loss then." He gets up off the bed and heads toward the door. His hand touches the doorknob when Ashtyn says, "Drew?"

He turns toward her, eyes soft. "Yeah?"

"Thank you."

"For what?"

"For being my roommate. And my friend."

Drew smiles. "I wouldn't want it any other way. Goodnight, Ashtyn."

And then he's gone, and Ashtyn has to tell herself that his words don't crack her wide open and expose her racing heart.

Chapter 14

"Hi, Mom," Drew answers, phone gripped tightly in his hand.

"Hi, sweetheart," Flora Mitchell says, her voice sweet like honey. "How are you?"

"Oh, you know, I'm good." He's on his way to work, the Texas heat already soaking through his shirt. It's almost getting hot enough for him to want to drive rather than walk, something he hates doing. "How are *you*?"

"I'm okay, sweetie. Thank you for asking." She pauses, and Drew can picture her biting her lip, debating on how to bring up the difficult subject.

He decides to save her the effort. "Haley's with me."

His mother sighs heavily. "Andrew, you can't keep rescuing her."

"I'm not rescuing her," he argues. "I'm just providing her a safe space to get back on her feet." His sister's words come flooding back: *You're the one person that never makes me feel like shit about my life choices.* He will be that person for her, always. No matter what.

Drew loves his parents, but they have very different views on Haley. His parents have tried tough love on her for far too long now, and he knows it doesn't work. It just pushes Haley further and further away. He knows that they would let Haley stay with them, but he also knows Haley doesn't want to hear a lecture. So, he lets her crash on his couch. She never stays longer than a few weeks anyway. Sometimes she just needs a break from the real world, and Drew can't blame her for that.

"Honey, I love your sister, but she also needs to learn to grow up. You can't coddle her for the rest of her life."

He has to keep himself from snapping. "I'm not coddling her, Mom."

"And you have a roommate now. How does she feel about your sister disrupting your lives?"

"Ashtyn is fine with it."

"But she shouldn't have to be."

"Mom," Drew says, rubbing his eyes in frustration. "Please. Just let it go. She's staying a few days, and then she'll be back with whatever dipshit boyfriend wants her back." He hates himself for how harsh the words come out, but he doesn't feel like having this conversation right now.

His mother sighs. "If you say so."

A memory snaps to the front of his brain at his mom's words. The first time Haley found herself on Drew's doorstep. She was a senior in high school, and Drew was living in that shitty apartment with no hot water. His first apartment after graduating college. It was pouring, the sky dumping its tears onto the earth, when there was a small knock on his door. When he opened it, there stood Haley, drenched head to toe, yet still smiling.

"Hey, mind if I crash for a bit?" That's all she had said before plopping onto the couch. His parents called a few hours later, worried sick about where their high school daughter had run off to. When Drew told them she was safe and staying with him, his mom had released that same heavy sigh. "If you say so."

Now, back in the present, Drew grips the phone tightly in his hand. "I do say so. I just stepped into the office, Mom. I gotta go."

"Okay, honey. Have a good day. I love you."

"I love you too." As he hangs up the phone and steps into the air-conditioned building, his tense shoulders start to relax. Nothing like crunching numbers to put him at ease.

At lunch time, he gets a text from Haley: *Hey, Ash and I are having a girls' night tonight in the apartment! So can you find something to do that's not here? K thanks love youuuuu!*

Just as he finishes reading the message, Jordan pops his head into Drew's office. "Hey, want to grab a beer tonight?"

"God, yes," Drew says without a second thought.

* * *

"To girls' night!" Haley exclaims, clinking her glass against Ashtyn and Ava's.

"Thanks for inviting me," Ava says, sipping her drink.

"Any friend of Ash's is a friend of mine!" Haley exclaims. Ashtyn doesn't even bother correcting her. What Ashtyn doesn't tell Ava is that she was worried about having a girls' night with *just* Haley. She's worried she'd bring up Drew having a crush on her again, and she doesn't want to get into that tonight. She needs Ava here. Plus, she misses her best friend.

"I've never really had a girls' night before," Haley admits to her drink.

"You never had sleepovers when you were younger?" Ava questions.

Haley shakes her head, still not looking up from her drink. "I didn't have a lot of girlfriends."

"Well, to your first proper girls' night, then," Ashtyn says, clinking her glass against Haley's again. "May we live up to the expectation."

"I guess it's a good thing I brought all these face masks," Ava says, spreading out the array of facial products.

The girls each select one and apply it to their face as Taylor Swift croons in the background. Ashtyn relishes the cooling cucumber against her skin. She sips her frozen margarita and sighs. It's been too long since she's had a night like this.

"You seem happy," Ava says softly from her spot next to Ashtyn. Her charcoal mask has dried on her skin, and it starts to crack at the edges.

"Yeah, I guess I am," Ashtyn replies. "I mean, as happy as I can be."

Ava smiles at her friend. "Jess misses you. She carries around your hair scrunchie everywhere. It's adorable."

Her friend's admission makes Ashtyn's heart crack. God, she misses that cat. Maybe she could convince Drew to let her get a cat…

"Hey, um, have you thought any more about the reunion?"

The question makes Ashtyn freeze, her body going tense. Haley's ears perk up at the mention of a reunion, her sheet mask slipping off her forehead. "Ooh, what reunion?" she asks, already having finished her first margarita.

"Our ten-year high school reunion," Ava says. "I really want to go, but Ash doesn't want to."

"I just don't think reminiscing with people I barely tolerated sounds like a fun time," Ashtyn counters. She peels off her mask and rubs the rest of the moisture into her skin.

"But I'll be there! And Shi too. Plus, we liked some people."

"*Some* is the keyword there."

"I bet Drew would go with you," Haley says nonchalantly. Nobody makes a sound as her words settle over the group.

Ashtyn chugs the rest of her margarita, afraid of the words that might tumble out of her mouth right now. Alcohol will help, she thinks. When she's finished, she sighs. "I don't want to subject him to that. I don't want to subject *anyone* to that."

For once, Haley is quiet and thoughtful. "You know he'd do it for you."

Ash hates the way the words pierce her heart. She *knows*. She knows Drew would do anything she asks, and she hates it. Instead of being vulnerable or honest, she just rolls her eyes. "Nah, even he wouldn't do that for me."

Haley doesn't say anything as she gets up to make another drink, her mask fluttering to the floor. Ava is silent, chewing her bottom lip, her own mask now crumbling at any facial movement. "Well, I'm not going if you're not going."

"Oh come on, Ave."

"I'm serious."

"But you want to go."

"So? I'm not going without you."

"Ava..."

"Ashtyn." The determination on Ava's face makes Ashtyn hesitate. Haley comes back with three more margaritas. How she made them so fast, Ashtyn has no idea, but she takes her drink gratefully. She takes a long sip, the coldness going straight to her brain. She presses her thumb to the roof of her mouth, easing the brain freeze slightly. She sighs. "I don't know..."

"I'll race you for it."

The words have Ashtyn raising her eyebrows. "You'll race me for it?"

"You know exactly what I mean."

"Ava, I say this with all the love in the world, but you have never won a round of Mario Kart in your life. Ever."

"Exactly. So, if I win, you have to come to the reunion with me. If you win, you can skip it."

"Ooh, can we all drink at least three more margaritas to make this race fair?" Haley asks, wiggling her eyebrows.

"Now *that's* a good idea, Haley," Ava says, snapping her fingers.

Ashtyn narrows her eyes at the girls. "You want to drunk Mario Kart race me? All for this stupid reunion?"

"Actually..." Ava says, finger on her chin. "I think I have an even better idea."

Three shots of tequila and two blindfolds later, Ashtyn and Ava race their way through MooMoo Meadows at Haley's direction.

"Ava, keep going straight! Ash, take a harsh left! No! Not that harsh! You fell off!"

"You're cheating!" Ashtyn yells at Haley. "You want her to win, so I have to go to this stupid reunion!"

"No, I swear!" Haley says, and Ashtyn swears she can hear the grin on her face. "Ava, you're doing great sweetie! Keep going!"

Ava laughs maniacally. "Who knew I just needed to get drunk and drive blindfolded to finally beat Ashtyn."

"This is so unfair," Ashtyn whines, feeling the urge to cheat and peek out of the blindfold. She did always say she could drive these courses blindfolded, and now she's eating her words.

"Hit the boost, Ava! You're almost there!"

"What about me?" Ashtyn asks. She whips off her blindfold, consequences be damned, and comes face to face with her car at a standstill, a ginormous cow blocking her path. Ava zooms through to the finish line.

"You won!" Haley yells, enveloping Ava in a hug. Ava whips off her blindfold and smiles triumphantly. That smile alone might be worth this stupid fucking reunion, Ashtyn decides.

Ashtyn glares at her friend. "I guess you won."

"So, this means you'll come?"

Ashtyn sighs. "I'm staying an hour, tops, and you're paying for my ticket."

"Deal!" Ava squeals, tackling her friend in a hug. "Oh, this is going to be so much fun!" Ashtyn doesn't have the heart to tell Ava that it might be the worst possible way she could imagine spending her time. But, fair is fair. She said she would do it, so she will.

"I need another drink," Haley says with a wicked grin.

The girls drink almost three more pitchers of margaritas. It's nearing one in the morning when Drew and Shiloh walk in on the girls drunkenly performing karaoke. *Bad* karaoke. Apparently, Haley had once been in a metal cover band. Ashtyn's sure she sounds better sober, but...

"Oh, I love this song!" Drew exclaims, running over and grabbing the ladle Ashtyn was using for a microphone from her hands.

"Hey!" She hiccups. "My solo is coming up!"

"You gave her the solo!?" Drew looks at Haley like he's been wounded.

"Well, someone had to do it! And you weren't here."

"You literally told me to get lost tonight."

"And yet, here you are, interrupting our performance."

Drew gives Ashtyn back the ladle. "Spoil sport," he says to his sister.

"Baaaaaby," Ava slurs, slinging her arms around Shiloh. He holds her close, like he hasn't seen her for weeks. Ashtyn misses her cue for the solo, because she's watching her friends.

"Hey Drew," Haley says, the karaoke now completely forgotten. The music is a dull ache in Ashtyn's head. "Want to go to Ashtyn's ten-year reunion with her?" Ashtyn whirls toward Haley, eyes wide. She feels her margarita almost come back up.

"You convinced her to come?" Shiloh questions, looking between the girls.

Ava nods furiously. "I beat her in Mario Kart! For the first time ever! And I did it blindfolded!"

"Wow!" Shiloh exclaims, biting back his smile at his incredibly drunk girlfriend.

Ashtyn rolls her eyes. "They totally cheated."

"I did not! I won fair and square! But, Drew should totally come with us," Ava says, eyes lighting up as she hangs from Shiloh's shoulders. "That way you can protect her if Bra—" She stops herself, hand slapping against her mouth as Ashtyn glares at her best friend.

Drew looks between them warily. "Protect her?"

"Oops," Ava says around her hand. "Wasn't supposed to say that."

"Okay, I think it's time we got you home," Shiloh says to Ava, breaking the tension. "Haley, always good to see you again."

Haley salutes him with her whisk microphone. "Hey, tell that little brother of yours he owes me ten bucks."

Shiloh frowns. "What for?"

"Oh, he knows."

Shiloh just shakes his head and smiles. Drew waves to his friends, eyebrows knitted together in confusion. "Get home safely."

"Bye everyone! I love you!" Ava yells behind her as they leave. And then, Ashtyn is left with Drew and his sister. Her stomach roils, the margaritas wanting to come back up. She says as much before rushing to the bathroom and hurling her guts up. She really should not have had those tequila shots earlier.

She's in there for ten minutes before a small knock startles her. "Leave me alone, Drew," she groans.

"It's me," Haley says softly. She doesn't sound like she just chugged three pitchers of margaritas. Ashtyn gets up on shaky legs and lets her in. Haley hands her a glass of water.

"Thanks," Ashtyn mumbles, chugging the water then sliding down the wall to the floor.

Haley joins her with a plop. "Sorry, maybe we shouldn't have had so many margaritas. Or the tequila shots."

"Yeah, I should have paced myself better," Ashtyn replies. She hasn't been this drunk since Brooke and Jordan's bachelor party last year. They sit in silence for a moment, the toilet gurgling from being flushed so many times.

"He's worried about you, you know?"

The words confuse Ashtyn, and she wrinkles her brow. "Who's

worried about me?"

Haley just sighs, setting her hands on her lap. "My brother cares about you. A lot. Whether he wants to admit it or not."

It's Ashtyn's turn to sigh. "We're just friends, Haley."

"I know. Doesn't mean you shouldn't bring him to the reunion. Especially if you need protecting."

Ashtyn feels her stomach churn. "I don't need protecting. Ava's just being dramatic, per usual."

"You sure?"

Ashtyn's not sure if it's the sincerity that laces Haley's voice or her own drunkenness, but she feels tears start to spill out of the corners of her eyes. Her words are almost as sour as her stomach. "How can it be almost ten years, and I'm still not over it?" She grits her teeth, willing the tears away. "I fucking hate him. I hate his guts, yet he still haunts me." Haley doesn't pry. She doesn't ask questions. She just lays her head on Ashtyn's shoulder in comfort, those pink dyed tips tickling her neck.

Ashtyn's hands turn to fists. Maybe it's because Haley doesn't know anything about the situation, or really anything about Ashtyn at all, that she continues, "He left me. He just decided not to love me anymore one day. And *I'm* the bad guy. I'm the girl that stood up at his wedding and made a scene. How the fuck is that fair?" She's never been this honest with anyone other than Ava and Shiloh. "And now I'm terrified to go to some stupid reunion, because he *might* be there. How pathetic is that?"

Haley grasps Ashtyn's chin and turns her face to her own. "Don't let him win," she says fiercely. "Whatever you do, don't let him win. Don't let him scare you into not going to something, because he might be there. Don't let him haunt your dreams. *Don't let him win.* Whoever he is."

The words knock around in Ashtyn's brain. "H-how? How do I do that?"

"By being brave. Go to this reunion and show him that he doesn't mean a thing to you anymore. Prove that he doesn't have a hold on you by letting yourself be happy. Let yourself fall in love again if you want to."

"But what if I get hurt? What if I don't survive it?"

"I can't promise that you won't get hurt again, but I can promise that you'll survive it. Just look at me. So many failed relationships under my belt, and I'm still kicking."

Her words make Ashtyn giggle, and she wipes away her tears. "Thanks, Haley."

Haley smiles. "You're welcome. Besides, what girls' night doesn't have someone ending up in tears, right?"

Ashtyn laughs again, her head clearing slightly. "We really hit all the staples tonight, didn't we?"

Haley chuckles, snuggling closer to Ashtyn. "We really did. Also, you tell me this guy's name and address, and I'll kick his ass for you."

They're silent for a moment before Ashtyn asks, "Do you really think Drew would go to the reunion with me?"

"Babe, he'd move heaven and earth if only you asked."

And it's those words that scare the ever-living shit out of Ashtyn. Because she knows they're true.

"I know I may be biased," Haley starts, "but my brother really is the best."

"I know," Ashtyn admits. What she doesn't say, but thinks is, *that's what scares me the most.*

JULY

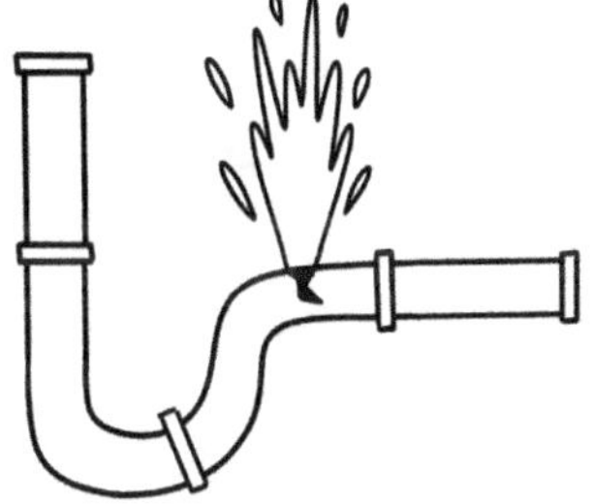

Chapter 15

"Happy Birthday!" The entire room erupts as Shiloh and Ava walk through the door. Shiloh's eyes widen, and his mouth drops open in surprise. Ava grips his arm tightly, a huge smile on her face.

"Surprise!" she exclaims, bouncing on her toes.

When Ava told Drew and Ashtyn that Shiloh wanted a "lowkey" birthday this year, she was adamant about throwing him a surprise party. So, a surprise party they threw. Ava had taken Shiloh out for lunch while Drew, Ashtyn, and Haley snuck into their apartment to decorate. Mattie and the rest of the friend group had arrived a little later to help as well. Drew did not miss the way Mattie and Haley skillfully avoided each other, even within the confines of Ava and Shiloh's tiny apartment. It confused him, as he thought they were friends. At least, they were when they were younger. Whatever, those two have always been weird around each other.

"Guys," Shiloh says, smile permanently etched to his face. "You didn't have to do all this."

"Of course we did," Mattie says, hugging his brother through the tinsel hanging from the door. "Ava wouldn't let us *not* do it."

Ava blushes and swats Mattie. "Not true," she grumbles. "I just wanted to make sure you had a good birthday."

"Thank you," Shiloh says, pressing a kiss to Ava's lips. Drew has to look away from the intimate moment, something deep in his chest aching.

Haley bumps her shoulder against his, startling him. "You okay?" she asks softly.

Drew just nods, giving her a smile. "Never better. You?"

His sister shrugs. "You know me." Her eyes slide to where Mattie is laughing from across the room. Something sits behind those eyes, but Drew knows better than to ask. Instead, he slings an arm around her and lets her silently sink into him.

Shiloh and Ava's apartment is much smaller than Drew's, and especially smaller than the old house, so the friends are spread out, occupying different rooms, coming and going as they please so no room feels overcrowded. Jess sits at the top of her cat tower, surveying the chaos. Ashtyn stands next to her, rubbing the top of her head, right where the brown spot is. She chats idly with Ava and Shiloh. Drew watches them from his perch in the kitchen where he shares a beer with his sister.

"So, are you ever going to make a move?" Haley asks, catching Drew's gaze on Ashtyn.

Drew scoffs. "Trust me, I've made myself pretty clear with her."

Haley rolls her eyes. "Somehow, I doubt that."

"Drop it, Haley. Or I'll bring up the thing *you're* avoiding."

Haley's eyes widen, but it doesn't stop her from glancing at Mattie. "I don't know what you're talking about."

"Uh huh, sure."

She huffs and takes a long pull from her beer. "Things change. We're not the same people we were back in high school."

It's such a loaded statement, but Drew doesn't press her. Haley may be loud and extroverted, but she's always been able to keep the things important to her close to her chest, where no one can find them. Drew guesses she keeps a lot of secrets from him. "Whatever you say, Hales."

She sighs, scuffing her toe against the floor. "I guess I should probably tell you I won't be staying much longer."

This makes Drew pause. "What do you mean?"

"It means," she says, picking at the label on the beer bottle with her nail, "that Jimmy called. Said he missed me."

"Haley—"

"I don't want to hear it."

They both fall silent as Mattie enters the kitchen, grabbing another beer from the fridge. "Hey," he says, his normal exuberance toned down. Drew remembers a time when, if both Mattie and Haley were in a room, both could be distinctly heard from any direction.

"Hey," Haley replies, her own voice dulled.

Drew doesn't say anything as he watches the awkward exchange. Mattie grabs his drink, gaze lingering on Haley, before leaving the kitchen as quickly as he entered.

"I thought you guys were friends?" Drew asks once Mattie is out of earshot.

"Yeah, me too," Haley grumbles, finishing off the rest of her beer. She chucks it in the trash and is about to leave when Drew catches her elbow softly.

"Will you talk to me, please?"

Haley sighs, turning to her brother. "About what?"

"About not going back to Jimmy's."

She sucks in a breath. "I thought you'd want me out of your hair."

"Yeah, well, turns out I'd rather see my sister in a place where she's loved and cared for than going back to some asshole that cheated on her."

Haley rolls her eyes and something tightens in Drew's chest. "You sound like Mom."

Having his baby sister stay with him has felt different this time. He's not sure if it's watching her interact with Ashtyn or the rest of his friends, but he feels the need to keep Haley in a healthy environment and away from this Jimmy person. She's barely told him anything about him, but it doesn't matter. Drew doesn't like him. In fact, he just might hate him.

"Speaking of Mom," he starts, and he feels Haley tense. "They both want to see you."

"Yeah, well, they know where I'm staying."

Drew has to bite his tongue to keep himself from snapping at her. "I told them we'd meet them for dinner tomorrow."

"What the fuck, Drew? What, are you three conspiring against me now?"

"No," he says fiercely. "That is not what's happening."

"Well, it sure feels like it."

"If you don't want to go, then you don't have to. But, I think it would mean a lot to them if you came."

"And they couldn't have told me that themselves?"

The words make Drew's throat tighten. He hates having to be the middleman between his parents and his sister. He loves them all so much, but why does he have to be the go between? Why can't they talk to each other like adults? "Maybe we could have that conversation with them," he probes. "Together."

Haley looks at him, chewing on her bottom lip. "Would you be on my side?"

"I'm always on your side, Hales."

The look she gives him is worth every headache she's ever given him, every late night worrying about where she is or what she's gotten herself into. It's worth the go between with his parents. It's worth it *all*.

She wraps her arms around his middle, laying her head on his chest. "Thanks," she says softly. She takes a deep breath, then says, "Is this a good time to tell you that I think I broke your Peloton?"

"What!?"

"Shhhh, this is a peaceful moment," she says, squeezing him so hard he can barely crane his head down to look at her incredulously.

"Oh, I'm going to kill you," he says, pinching her side. She yelps and spins away from him in an instant.

"Hey, there y'all are," Ashtyn says as she enters the kitchen. Haley pulls Ashtyn to her, using her as a human shield, so Drew can't pinch her again.

"Help! Protect me from my brother's wrath!" Haley yells, and Ashtyn looks between the siblings with a bemused expression.

"She broke my Peloton!" Drew exclaims, trying to get around Ashtyn. Haley's hands are gripped tightly on her shoulders, swaying her back and forth.

"Wait, *you* broke it?" Ashtyn asks, whirling on Haley. "I thought *I* broke it!"

"You BOTH broke it?"

"I didn't mean to!" Ashtyn exclaims, turning back to him. "I saw it in your room, and I was curious since I've never seen one before, and I may have accidentally spilled some coffee on the screen."

"And I may have accidentally broken a pedal by trying to use it," Haley says, still hiding behind Ashtyn.

"Jesus," Drew laughs, rubbing his forehead. "I can't afford to have both of you under the same roof."

"See! Then it's a good thing I'm leaving."

"You're leaving?" Ashtyn asks, a tinge of sadness in her voice as her face falls ever so slightly.

"Uh, yeah, Jimmy called," Haley says casually, shrugging.

"Oh." Ashtyn frowns but doesn't say anything else.

"You're leaving?" Ava asks, appearing out of nowhere, Shiloh at her side. The kitchen is suddenly extremely crowded with all of them occupying the tight space.

"Geez, I didn't mean to announce it to the whole party," Haley mutters, looking at the floor.

Drew catches her eye and gives her a reassuring smile. "You know you can stay as long as you need."

"Yeah, I liked having someone to team up with against him," Ashtyn teases.

Haley laughs. "I'm sure I'll be back eventually. Nothing keeps me away for long."

"Our door is always open," Ashtyn says. Her words send chills down Drew's entire body, a rush of affection heating his cheeks. *Our door.* God, he'll never forget those words for as long as he lives.

"You're the best," Haley says and pulls Ashtyn into her embrace. The entire room freezes except for Ashtyn. She accepts the hug without even a blink, arms holding Haley securely to her. Haley must notice everyone staring, because she whispers into Ashtyn's ear, "What's everyone's problem?"

"I don't do hugs," Ashtyn whispers back, small smile on her face.

"Well, you're doing a pretty bad job of it then," Haley says, tightening her grip on Ashtyn.

"I know," Ashtyn says, and she catches Drew's eye from over his sister's shoulder. She gives him a shy smile that he tucks into his heart. A precious moment he can look back on later, when she closes herself off again. To prove that, slowly, she's opening up to him. And he'll cherish it forever.

Chapter 16

The July heat is thick and heavy in the air, leaving everything sticky in its wake. Ashtyn knows that as soon as she gets up from the leather couch, she's going to leave sweat stains from the back of her thighs. The AC has been on the fritz, so they have portable fans blowing throughout the apartment to try to mitigate the heat. Ashtyn is currently staring blankly into the swirling fan in front of her, sweat trailing down her temples.

"Here," Drew says, handing her a fresh ice pack from the fridge.

"Thanks," she says, taking it gratefully. She raises it to her forehead, relishing in the brief relief. It really does not help that their apartment is on the top floor. It also does not help that Drew is currently shirtless, in only a pair of basketball shorts. She's seen him shirtless countless times, including this past weekend when they all celebrated the Fourth of July on the boat out at the lake. But this time, it feels more intimate, only the two of them in the sweltering apartment. She averts her gaze discreetly.

Haley left a couple of days ago, keeping true to what she said at the surprise party. Ashtyn's not sure how Haley could have given her such sage advice that night in the bathroom, just for her to go running back to her shitty boyfriend. When Ashtyn had asked, Haley just shrugged and said, "Do as I say, not as I do."

Despite her craziness, Ashtyn misses Drew's sister. She was fun to be around and always had something interesting to say. Apparently, the two siblings had met their parents for dinner before Haley left, and by the attitude Drew came home with, it seemed to have gone well. Ashtyn didn't want to pry, so she didn't ask questions. She's just glad they all seem to be on better terms now.

Ever since that night in the bathroom with Haley, Ashtyn's felt herself start to soften around Drew. She's even tried out some friendliness, for the hell of it. She could be brave. She could stop letting the past define her. Right?

Now, as they sit together in front of the fan, each holding a Nintendo Switch controller, Ashtyn feels somewhat peaceful. It's not as awkward or tense with Drew anymore. Instead, it actually feels like they're becoming friends. Very, very slowly.

"Okay, focus up," Ashtyn says, sitting up straighter. "You're cooking meat, and I'm chopping vegetables."

"But I like chopping vegetables!"

"Too bad. I'm doing it."

"Fine," he grumbles. "Who's plating?"

"You. I'll do dirty dishes."

Since the start of this unbearable heatwave, no one has wanted to venture outside for too long. Even for Texas, it is sweltering. Even poor Drew had to drive to work yesterday, because it was too hot to walk. So, to keep themselves busy, they've started playing the game Overcooked together. Drew walked in on her playing it one day, sat down to watch, and the rest was history. Now, they play it every night, trying to beat their scores from the day before.

"Those rat fuckers better watch out," Drew says, taking a sip of beer as he settles into the couch. "They're not stealing anything tonight."

"You say that every night. And every night they steal your food."

"Yeah, but tonight I'm extra focused."

Ashtyn giggles and starts up the game. "Ready?"

"I was born ready." Drew was, in fact, not born ready. "Put down my onion, you stupid rat!" he screams.

"Forget about the onion!" Ashtyn yells. "The meat is burning!"

"Fuck!"

"Drew, the entire kitchen is going to get set on fire! This is what you get for chopping *my* vegetables."

"Where's the fucking fire extinguisher!?" Drew's character is running around wildly on screen, and the look of absolute horror on his face brings immense joy to Ashtyn as she throws her head back in laughter. She can't even be mad that the stove is burning and setting the rest of the kitchen on fire. Normally, she's extremely competitive and hates losing. In this instance, it's hysterical.

"You're laughing!? Our kitchen is burning, and you're laughing." This just makes Ashtyn laugh harder, her abs hurting from the motion. The kitchen is now half on fire, dishes abandoned, and rats stealing all their ingredients. She sets the controller down, wiping her eyes on the sleeve of her shirt.

The timer runs out as the rest of their kitchen is engulfed in flames, and the final score is revealed. They didn't even get one star. It has to be their worst run yet, but Ashtyn can't stop laughing. She clutches her side in amusement.

"Okay, that's it," Drew says, plucking the controller out of her hand with a smile. "This game is getting banned."

"What!?" Ashtyn exclaims, her smile falling. "You can't ban Overcooked just because you're bad at it!"

"I can, and I will!" He gets up to hide the controllers, and Ashtyn bounds toward him, trying to snatch them back. He holds them up over his head, using her height against her.

Ashtyn frowns in amusement. "Really? It's come to this."

"I can't have my gamer reputation soiled by this... ridiculous game." He bites back a smile as Ashtyn tries to jump for the controller. She's never noticed the glaring height difference between them until now.

"Gamer reputation? I don't think your Call of Duty bros will care, frankly." Drew doesn't relent, so she tries a different tactic instead. She places her hand on his bare torso and looks up at him from underneath her lashes. "Please," she says prettily, batting her eyes at him.

"Oh, I am not falling for that," he says, pressing closer into her hand, the distance between them getting less and less. "Because I can play that game just as well as you. If not better."

Ashtyn's throat bobs, feeling the tight muscles of his abdomen underneath her fingertips. She thinks she's about to do something stupid when Drew's phone pings loudly from the coffee table. Ashtyn instantly recognizes the notification sound as Drew's eyes go wide. A mischievous smile forms on her lips.

"Looks like someone just got a match on Tinder," Ashtyn says, biting her lip. Before he can move, she runs toward the table and scoops up his phone. She's planning on teasing him, just a little, so he'll give her the controller back. "Let's see who the lucky lady is."

But as she looks down at the home screen notification, she stops in her tracks. A man named Sean matched with him. A man, not a woman. She looks up at Drew, her cheeks reddening, voice caught in her throat. "S-sorry," she stutters, tossing him the phone. He doesn't even glance at it as he catches it, never taking his eyes off her. "I-I didn't mean to invade your privacy. I was just messing around—"

"I'm bisexual," he says simply before she can continue. She blinks at him, not knowing how to respond. She knows she crossed a line, picking up his phone like that. She just assumed his sexuality without ever actually asking him. Shame floods through her as she remembers every terrible comment she's made about him and women. She just... assumed. Like an asshole. "Does this change anything?" he asks, taking a tentative step toward her.

"No!" Ashtyn exclaims too loudly. She blushes again. "God, no. Sorry, I just… I'm sorry. I shouldn't have assumed." God, Ava would kill her for this. "And I shouldn't have looked at your phone."

"It's okay," Drew says, taking another step closer to her. "It's not like I ever told you. You didn't know."

"You didn't have to," Ashtyn says softly. "Whether you wanted to tell me or not, I shouldn't have assumed. I'm sorry."

"I did… want to tell you. I just didn't know how to bring it up. Most people know, but it's not something that generally comes up in casual conversation. Besides, coming out is different for everyone. I've always been very casual about it, which I acknowledge is a privilege not everyone in this world has."

"I know, but still. I shouldn't have looked at your phone. That was rude and stupid—"

"Ashtyn," he says, interrupting her. He closes the distance between them, hand coming up to caress her arm. "Stop apologizing. You said this doesn't change things, so don't let it."

She lets out a breath and smiles. "Okay. Thank you for telling me." She pauses, then says, "But you're still not banning Overcooked." She snatches the controller out of his hand with a triumphant grin.

"Oh, you're gonna get it now," Drew says, and Ashtyn bolts across the room with a shriek, Drew close on her heels. He catches her around the middle in a matter of seconds, lifting her up effortlessly. She can feel his biceps tighten around her, and it's a glorious feeling.

"Drew!" she exclaims. He swings them toward the couch when his foot catches on the edge of the rug, sending them crashing down onto the cushions. His bare chest hovers just above her as he catches himself on the back of the couch. Their faces are inches apart, noses just barely brushing. She'd barely have to move to kiss him. The look in his eyes sends a jolt of desire through her, right between her legs. Her brain almost short circuits, just from looking at him at this angle.

God, he's beautiful. Those blue eyes boring into hers...

The phone loudly pings again, jolting them apart. Thank God, too, because if they'd crossed that line... Ashtyn's not sure how they'd ever come back from that. She straightens, her back slick with sweat. She'd wanted to cross that line though... she'd wanted to.

Drew lets out a breath as he sits up, running a hand through his hair. "Sorry," he says, a blush tinging his cheeks.

"It's okay," she says breathlessly. She squeezes her legs together, trying to subdue the pulse that's starting to build there. It's been so long since she's been with someone. So, so long, her brain can't help but wander in that direction when she's in the presence of an attractive man. Even if that attractive man is Drew. *Drew.*

She shakes her head, throwing those thoughts out of her head. She's treading some seriously dangerous waters right now. "Um, are you gonna get that?" she asks, gesturing toward the phone.

"Oh," he says, shaking his head. "Uh, maybe later."

"You can answer. I mean, you don't have to ignore it because of me." She's nervous. She's actually nervous around Drew. What is wrong with her?

Drew swipes the phone open for only a moment before locking it again. "It's not important."

"When did you know?" she blurts, brain short circuiting again. Drew looks over at her curiously. "When did you know that you're bisexual? If you don't mind telling me."

Drew smiles, his shoulders relaxing. "I don't mind telling you. I knew my freshman year of high school. There was this guy named Liam..."

And so, he tells her. He tells her of his first kiss, how nervous he was. He tells her about coming out to Shiloh. When he told his parents and sister. He tells her about the local LGBTQ+ youth shelter he volunteers at once a month. About the kids he's met, their stories, and how he doesn't understand how anyone could kick a child out of their home just for being themselves. And she listens, reveling in this new side of Drew that she discovers. He shows her the real Drew, not the cocky, ever so charming Drew he tends to show everyone else. No, he shows her the *real*, honest Drew. And Ashtyn finds that the real Drew... the real Drew is someone she genuinely likes. Someone she likes a lot.

* * *

They talk for hours, long into the night. Drew realizes this might be the longest they've ever talked without a quip or playful banter between them. No, tonight is all real. All truth. As he tells Ashtyn about himself, he can see her holding herself back. Like she's on the precipice of telling him the thing that keeps her from opening up to people. But, she doesn't. Instead, she listens to him and his stories, smiling and laughing at all the best parts. Accepting him for who he is.

She's finally relaxed in the apartment. In *their* apartment. It feels like they're sharing the space equally, no longer tiptoeing around each other. He's not exactly sure what transpired the night Haley talked to Ashtyn in the bathroom, but something shifted, if ever so slightly. He might just have to thank his sister for that.

Drew lets out a yawn and checks the time. It's nearing three in the morning. "Geez, get me talking and I just don't stop."

Ashtyn laughs softly, legs tucked neatly up against her chest. "I like hearing about you. I learned a lot of valuable information."

"To torture me with at a later date?" He's teasing, just like they always do, but Ashtyn's face tightens just a tiny bit. Blink and he might have missed it.

A second later, her smile is back. "Exactly."

"So, is that why you didn't share anything tonight? So I don't use it against you?"

"What could you possibly want to know about me?"

Everything, he thinks. *I want to know everything about you.* Instead of saying that, he says, "I don't know, give me a fun fact. Something nobody else knows."

She raises an eyebrow at him. "Seriously? What is this? An icebreaker on the first day of class?"

Drew chuckles. "Maybe. Sometimes that's what getting to know people is like."

Ashtyn smirks, "Okay, fine. Wanna know something nobody else knows, not even Ava?" Drew raises his eyebrows, waiting for her response. "I have never, and I truly mean never, had a man make me come."

He freezes, his eyes going wide as the words land between them like a bomb. "You've never..."

"I've always had to do it myself. The men I've chosen to spend my time with have been unable to please me."

"Ashtyn," he starts, like he can't believe what she just admitted. Maybe it's because it's three in the morning, an apt time for secrets to spill, or because he just told her more than he's ever told her before, but Drew's astonished at her words.

She rolls her eyes. "Hence why I don't occupy many beds anymore."

Drew steadies his gaze on her, his heart starting to race. "Is that a challenge?"

Ashtyn sucks in a breath. "No, it is not."

"Because I have never come before anyone that occupies my bed." He feels a thrill run through him at the thought of Ashtyn in his bed, at learning what makes her sigh in pleasure.

"You know, pride is a sin," she chides.

"Am I not allowed to be proud of things that are true?"

There it is again. That expression he can't read yet. She twirls a piece of hair around her finger, then sighs. "Whatever, this was stupid. You don't need to hear my sob story."

"I didn't realize it was a sob story."

"Of course it's a sob story. You think I'm normally this cynical and hateful without a sob story?"

The words land right in Drew's chest. "You're not hateful, Ashtyn."

Her face is hard and unreadable, a harsh contrast to only moments ago. "That's not what I've heard."

Anger floods his system. "Who the fuck said that about you?" He'd break anyone's face that said those horrible words to her. She doesn't look at him as she balls her hand into a fist, her jaw set. Their carefree mood from an hour ago shattered. He shouldn't have pushed. He should have just let it go...

"It doesn't matter," she mutters.

"It does matter!" Drew protests. "You are not..." He clears his throat. "You are kind. You are caring and incredible. Fuck anyone that doesn't think that."

"You wouldn't think that if you knew what I did."

"Nothing you say to me would ever make me change my mind about you, Ashtyn. Even if you told me that you murdered someone. But, please tell me you didn't murder someone."

This elicits a small laugh out of her, and Drew's heart soars. Yes, keep her laughing. Keep her happy. "No, I didn't commit any crimes." She sighs heavily. "Your sister gave me some sage advice when she was here. She told me to be brave. So, I'm going to do that." Drew doesn't say anything as Ashtyn closes her eyes. "You were vulnerable with me tonight, so I'll be vulnerable with you. I push people away because a long time ago I chose someone, and they didn't choose me back. So, I promised myself that I would never choose *anyone* ever again. That I would never let anyone make me feel like that again."

Drew reaches his hand out to her, and she takes it, squeezing hard as her eyes stay shut. Like she can't face him when she's saying these words. He thinks he'll hold onto her for as long as she needs him. He'll never let go.

"His name is Brandon. He was my high school sweetheart," she starts. "We'd been friends forever until he finally plucked up the courage to ask me out during our freshman year. I felt like the luckiest girl in the world. Who wouldn't want to date their best friend? I was fourteen years old, and I just knew we'd get married. How fucking stupid is that? God, I was such an idiot..."

Drew still doesn't say anything. He just squeezes her hand comfortingly, letting her know that he's here. He'll always be here. She continues, "He was so intrinsically entwined in my life. Like, we did everything together. He was my first everything. And when we graduated, we had planned on going to the same college, but we didn't get accepted to the same places. So, we decided on long distance like fucking idiots. I really thought we could do it. If anyone could do it, *we* could, because we were strong. I thought everything was fine. I mean, we didn't see each other as often as we wanted, but we talked. It was *fine.*" She emphasizes that word again. "Then, one day out of the blue, he calls me and breaks up with me over the phone. He tells me he met someone else, just so casually, as if it was the most normal thing in the world. He didn't... he didn't even cry or anything. He just hung up the phone, and that was it."

Before he can stop himself, Drew closes the distance between them and puts his arms around her. She doesn't even fight it. She just leans into his chest, neither caring that they're sweaty and the heat is pressing in on them relentlessly. He strokes her hair as she takes a deep breath. "It felt so cruel," she says. "Like our entire lives were a lie. I just sat there in complete shock. Ava found me a few hours later, just sitting on the bed and staring at the wall. It wasn't until she asked me if I was okay that I burst into tears. I don't think I stopped crying for a week straight. Another reason why I hate crying. It reminds me of my weakest moment."

"Ashtyn," Drew starts, but she ignores him.

"Two months later, I check my mailbox, and I find a wedding invitation. From him." She practically spits her words. "He's barely nineteen years old, and he's marrying a girl he's known less time than he's known me. And he fucking invited me to the goddamn wedding. As if we were still supposed to be best friends after he ripped my heart out. As if I would *want* to be there." Drew tenses, his arms holding her tightly. If he ever finds this Brandon...

"I actually couldn't believe it. I thought it was a practical joke, honestly. But, no, it was real. It was all just so fucking real and cruel. So, I went. I don't know why I did. Ava tried to talk me out of it, so did my mom, but I just felt like I had to. Maybe to prove a point? To prove he didn't hurt me, even though I was split open and aching. I still can't rationalize it, even today.

"But I went. And I watched this beautiful girl walk down the aisle to him. To *my* Brandon. The Brandon I had known for half my life. And he was crying as he looked at her. He didn't cry when he tore inside of me and ripped out my beating heart. No, he cried when he saw *her*. It was supposed to be me. It was supposed to be *us*. He was supposed to look at me like that. So, when the minister asked if anyone had any objections... I stood up."

Her hands grip Drew's, so tight, like she's anchoring herself to him. To keep from getting lost in the past. He holds on to her for dear life. Their bodies beginning and ending in all the same spots.

"I stood up, and everyone looked at me. I'm pretty sure someone even gasped. I think it was his mom. I just kept thinking, what about me? Don't you remember me? Don't you remember what we used to be? I was screaming at him with my mouth closed. I wasn't trying to ruin the wedding. I just needed him to know I had come. That I wouldn't be forgotten. And then he looked at me, with a look I'd never seen before. It was almost like he didn't even recognize me at first. And then I realized that *I* didn't recognize him. He wasn't the same person I had fallen in love with in high school. He was a complete stranger.

"I opened my mouth, maybe to say something or to scream, but nothing came out, and as I continued looking at him, he just shook his head. Like he was disappointed in *me*. I couldn't take it anymore, so I just ran. I ran out of that chapel with all those eyes on me, and I didn't look back. I-I haven't seen him since, and I never plan to. But, I know the rumors that spread after something like that. That I ruined the wedding. That I'm the reason a bride cried on her wedding day. That it's all my fault. Of course he wouldn't stay with someone as crazy as me, someone who shows up to another person's wedding..."

"Ashtyn," Drew whispers, and his words must break something in her because she finally lets out the sob she's been holding in. It shatters his heart completely, hearing those sounds come out of her.

"Why?" she asks, her voice thick with emotion, emotion Drew's never seen or heard from her before. "Why wasn't I good enough?"

"You are perfect," Drew says, taking her face in his hands. "You are more than enough for anyone. If he didn't see that, then he's an idiot. In fact, it makes him the stupidest man on the entire fucking planet. Anyone would be lucky to have you."

She looks up at him, tears staining her cheeks. "Anyone?"

"Anyone," he repeats.

A fire burns bright in her green eyes. "And what would you do? If you had me?"

Those words, God those words... He doesn't know how to think, how to breathe, hearing those words come out of her mouth. He shivers. "I'd worship every single inch of you."

Her lips are on his before he even has time to blink. He tastes the saltiness of her tears first, and they dissolve on his tongue. One of his hands curls in her hair, securing him to her while the other wraps around her hip. She propels forward, straddling him, hands coming up to his cheeks, caressing him. He's instantly hard underneath her, desire coursing through him. The number of times he's dreamed of this moment must be in the thousands. Their New Year's kiss was sweet, but this is scorching.

Ashtyn opens her mouth, and Drew's tongue finds hers. She lets out a moan that goes straight to his cock. His hands skim just barely underneath her shirt, and he can feel the goosebumps erupting over her skin, despite the heat in the apartment. Every inch of them is burning, their hands mapping out each other's bodies.

"Ash," he murmurs against her lips, and she hums in pleasure. The sound rips through him like an avalanche, leaving him aching for her.

They break apart, foreheads resting against each other's, breathing hard. They're crossing every single boundary they set up. They're crossing too many lines. They're sharing too much...

She must realize this at the same time as him, because she gets off his lap in one swift motion. He already misses the way she felt on top of him. "I–I'm sorry," she stutters. "I shouldn't have done that."

He's so glad she did, though. And he wants to tell her that. He wants to tell her so many things, but the look on her face stops him. "Ashtyn," he says, and she looks up at him. "It's okay."

She shakes her head. "This doesn't change things."

The words punch a hole right through him. They rip him open and leave him bleeding, aching for her. All he can manage to say is, "Okay."

Her smile doesn't meet her eyes. "Goodnight, Drew."

She's gone before he has a chance to calm his racing heart.

Chapter 17

"Fuck," Ashtyn groans, rubbing her tired eyes with the heels of her hands. She wakes the next morning around noon, full of regret and embarrassment. Why the hell did she tell Drew all that stuff last night? Because Haley told her to be brave. Stupid advice, really. She wasn't born to be brave. She was born to hide her feelings and wallow in self-pity.

And then she kissed him... God, she's such an idiot. They were finally becoming friends, and now they went ahead and ruined it all by crossing that line into forbidden territory. But goddamn if it wasn't one of the hottest kisses of her life.

I'd worship every single inch of you.

Just thinking about those words coming out of his mouth sends a ripple of desire coursing through her. His mouth on hers, his hands touching her skin, her name on his lips. God, he knew exactly what he was doing. It almost makes the Brandon memories sting a little less. Almost.

She groans again and sits up in bed. Her sheets are damp with sweat, either from the heat or the explicit dreams she had last night. Either way, she needs a shower. Drew is definitely at work by now, so she's not worried about running into him. She feels a twinge of guilt for keeping him up so late on a work night. But before the kiss, they'd opened up to each other. It felt... right. Like it was supposed to happen.

In the hallway, the heat is suffocating, and Ashtyn gathers her hair into a bun before stepping into the bathroom. She takes a deep breath and turns the shower to cold. The pipes let out a groan that echoes throughout the bathroom. Water sputters out of the shower head then stops, turning to a tiny trickle. She wiggles the handle again, but the pressure doesn't change.

"You've got to be kidding me," she mutters, wrapping a towel around herself as she tries turning it on and off again. Nothing. The pipes groan again ominously. "You'd think this fancy apartment would have working water."

She secures the towel more tightly around herself and peeks out of the bathroom door. All is quiet, so Drew is definitely at work. She wanders into the kitchen, where a cold pot of coffee and a blue sticky note await her.

Water's out. Maintenance said it should be fixed later today. D

Well, that explains it then. She sighs and makes herself an iced coffee with the leftover pot. She takes a sip and smacks her lips. "Not as good as Ava's, but it'll do."

She changes into shorts and a tank top before collapsing onto the couch, her skin instantly sticking to the leather. She's half an episode into *New Girl* when her eyelids grow heavy, not even the coffee able to keep her awake. When she falls asleep, her dreams are full of Drew's hands on her.

* * *

Plink. Plink. Plink.

Ashtyn wakes from her nap to the steady drip of water on her nose. She blinks a few times, trying to understand *why* exactly her face is wet. Surely it's not hot enough that her entire face is sweating. It's then that she feels another drop of water hit her face, this time right between her eyes, and she sees the leak coming from the ceiling above her. It must have been leaking for a while, because there's a dark water stain blooming across the ceiling.

"What the?" she groans and gets up from her spot on the couch. "You've got to be kidding me." She wipes her face on her shirt, a mixture of sweat and ceiling water dampening the fabric. First, there's no water, and now it's leaking from the ceiling. Just perfect.

She heads to the kitchen to find a bucket to put under the leak, so the floor doesn't get damaged. An ominous groan from the pipes sounds throughout the apartment as she tests the kitchen sink. Still no water. A tinge of anxiety spikes through her. She finds the mop bucket under the sink and trudges back toward the living room.

The stream from the ceiling is steadier now, the couch taking most of the damage. Ashtyn looks out the window, not a rain cloud in sight. It's bone dry out there. She sighs and goes to put the bucket on the couch, under the stream.

"You'd think for how expensive this goddamn place is, shit like this wouldn't—" She's interrupted as a section of the leaking roof collapses in on itself, an avalanche of water and plaster pouring into the living room like a waterfall. Ashtyn screams as the water hits the floor, soaking her instantly from head to toe. Luckily, the water doesn't hit her directly on top of her head. A million reactions rush through her, but the biggest one tells her to run, forgoing all other options.

So, she does. She runs out of the apartment and down the stairs as fast as she can. She's barefoot, having forgotten to put on shoes, so she slips on the bottom stair. Her arms flail for the banister, and she just barely catches it as her tailbone smashes directly onto the tiled floor. Pain lances its way up her spine, the wind knocked from her lungs as she lets out a cry of pain. Her chest constricts, fighting for air. She tries to catch her breath, tears on the precipice of falling. The pain of her now bruised tailbone emanates down to her toes.

No one else seems to have had their ceilings collapse, because no one comes out of their apartment to flee or check on the girl gasping for breath at the bottom of the stairs. Her fingers grasp the banister as tightly as she can muster, and she pushes up on her feet despite the pain. She tries to ignore the injury as she makes her way slowly down to the lobby, one foot in front of the other.

Once there, she dials Drew's number. He answers on the first ring. "Hey, did they finally fix the water?" His voice is light, airy, not at all bothered by what transpired last night.

Ashtyn tries to school her voice into something calm, but she can barely get any words out. "Water... burst... avalanche... apartment."

She can hear Drew rustling on the other side of the line. "Ashtyn, what are you talking about? Are you okay?"

"I'm... fine," she grits through her teeth, trying not to sound like she just fell down the goddamn stairs. "But your apartment is fucked."

There's a beat of silence before he says, "I'll be there as fast as I can."

Turns out, Drew runs the entire way home, and he's drenched in sweat by the time he arrives in the lobby, hair plastered to his forehead. He skids to a stop in front of Ashtyn, hands coming up to her shoulders as he looks her over. "What happened?"

She's been standing stock still in the lobby since their phone call, trying to ignore the pain at the base of her spine and to calm her heartbeat to its normal rhythm. Her hands shake as she says, "Your roof collapsed. Or a pipe burst. I'm really not sure. I didn't stay long enough to check. But there was a lot of water."

"Oh my god, Ashtyn," Drew says, crushing her to him. She lets out a hiss of pain that has Drew immediately stepping away from her, scanning her from head to toe. "Are you hurt?"

For some reason, she doesn't want to admit that she's in pain. So instead, she says, "It-it was right above the couch. I was napping, and then I woke up to water dripping on me. So, I went to get a bucket, and then the roof collapsed and water got everywhere and—"

"Ashtyn," Drew says, looking at her fiercely. "Are you okay? Are you hurt?" His hands run up and down her arms, whether to warm her or check for injuries, she's not sure.

"I'm fine," she replies, breathlessly. "But your couch—"

"I don't care about the couch or the apartment," he says adamantly. "I only care about you."

If she wasn't completely full of adrenaline, she might have gotten butterflies. But she can't feel anything other than her racing heart, and the dull ache that's now at her tailbone. The pain has gotten slightly better since it happened, but it still hurts. "I'm fine," she says. "Just very wet."

Normally, she'd expect Drew to make some funny quip about what she just said, but he doesn't. Instead, he pulls her tighter against him, his clothes dampening at their contact. After a moment, he loosens his arms but doesn't fully let her go as he pulls out his phone and calls the building manager. The manager and the entire maintenance team are there within minutes, and Ashtyn recounts the entire story again, omitting her fall from the stairs. It's too embarrassing to admit anyway.

They go up to investigate while Ashtyn and Drew wait in the lobby. A few curious onlookers have gathered to hear the news. Fred, the manager, arrives back downstairs looking disheveled and worried. "I cannot apologize enough," he says frantically. "This should have never happened."

"No, it shouldn't have," Drew says gruffly, arm never leaving Ashtyn's shoulders.

"I'm fine," Ashtyn replies, trying to diffuse the situation. "It's all good."

"No, it's not," Drew grumbles. "Our apartment is flooded, and she could have gotten seriously injured."

"Drew," she says, placing a hand lightly on his arm. "I'm okay." Again, she doesn't mention her fall. It would just make everything way more complicated than it needs to be.

"We will make it up to you," Fred says. "Let me go and make some arrangements."

He's gone for about thirty minutes. All the while, Drew paces the lobby back and forth, seething, his eyes always flitting back to Ashtyn to make sure she's okay.

"You're gonna burn a hole in the floor," Ashtyn says lightly, perching as gently as she can on the edge of a chair, careful of her injury. It feels like someone punched her right in the tailbone. She's pretty sure she can already feel a bruise forming, large and purple.

"Yeah, well, it would serve them right."

"It's not their fault the pipes burst. Shit like that happens."

Drew sighs, scrubbing a hand over his face. "I know. I just... I'm really glad you're okay."

They hear footsteps on the stairs, and Fred reappears, face grim. "Well, the good news is that most of the damage is contained to the living room. The bad news is that it's going to take a week or so for us to fix the damage. In the meantime, we can set y'all up at one of the nicest hotels in the city, no cost. Plus, compensation on one month's rent. Again, we are so sorry that this happened and promise that it will never happen again."

"Can we at least go up and get some of our stuff?" Ashtyn asks.

"Of course. Just please steer clear of the living room. We're bringing in equipment to get started as soon as possible. Once you're ready, come by the main office, and I'll give you the hotel information."

Drew shakes Fred's hand, and they make their way back up to their now flooded apartment. Ashtyn insists on taking the elevator, not sure she could actually make it up the stairs without limping. The pain has dulled, whether because of her adrenaline or something else, she doesn't care. She's just glad she can walk. Water has already spread from their unit into the hallway, where maintenance men lay towels and wet floor signs along the ground.

The portion of the ceiling that collapsed lays in pieces on the floor and the couch. Water no longer gushes from it; instead, a few plops leak onto the now ruined couch. Water stands a few centimeters from the floor, the bottom shelf of the movie wall already slightly warped. Ashtyn looks at it sadly, afraid the movies on the bottom shelf have been ruined.

"I'll replace them," Drew says quietly, placing a hand on her shoulder. "Whatever's been damaged, we can replace it."

Ashtyn just nods, not letting Drew see how upset she really is. He's right, things can be replaced.

They pack quickly and head back down to the lobby when they're ready. Fred meets them and gives them the hotel's information. "Again, we are so sorry about this."

They nod and thank the man. When they get to the parking garage, Drew sighs. "I need to head back to work. You okay to head over there by yourself? I can take the rest of the day off if I need to."

"No, don't worry about it. I'll get us checked in," Ashtyn replies. "Maybe now I can finally take a freaking shower."

Drew laughs. He pauses, looking at her intently. After all the chaos, Ashtyn now realizes this is the first time they've seen each other since last night's kiss. She doesn't even have time to be embarrassed or regretful. "Just call if you need anything," he says. He touches a hand to her elbow before turning toward his truck. Ashtyn shivers, even though she's changed into fresh clothes, and gets into her own car. As she sits, her tailbone gives a lick of pain up her spine that has her gripping the steering wheel for dear life. Maybe she should have said something...

She turns the key in the ignition, trying to ignore the pain like she does all of her other problems. On her way to the hotel, she drives slowly, trying not to aggravate her tailbone any more than she already has. She calls Ava and informs her of the day's adventure.

"Oh my god, Ash!" she exclaims. "Do you need to come stay here? You know you're more than welcome."

"No, the apartment got us a hotel. A pretty nice one, too."

"Okay, well you're still welcome here whenever you need it."

Ashtyn knows Ava means it. But, she doesn't want to crash their party. They've barely been in the apartment for two months now. It's still too early for Ashtyn to be invading their space. She can't admit defeat this early.

"I'll be fine," Ashtyn reassures her best friend. "Besides, Drew's growing on me."

Ava whistles. "Wow, who would have thought you two could ever get along?"

Ashtyn laughs. "Yeah, well, weirder things have happened."

They talk a little longer until she reaches the hotel and tells Ava she'll call her later. She hikes her bag up over her shoulder and makes her way toward the front reception desk, limping slightly. This is going to be hard to hide from Drew.

"Hello!" a woman whose name tag reads "Sharon" says brightly. "Checking in?"

"Um, yeah," Ashtyn replies. "I'm not sure what name it's under. I'm from the apartment that had the flooding. Our landlord set us up here. I'm Ashtyn King."

"Oh, yes, of course!" Sharon chirps. "We have you and Mr. Mitchell in our king suite."

Ashtyn blanches. "Oh, wow. Um, just out of curiosity, does the king suite come with two beds?"

Sharon smiles. "No, sorry, just one king bed. But there is a pull-out couch."

"And we're only booked in one room? Not two?"

"That's correct. I apologize, we're all full up right now. We might have a spare room free up a few days from now, but Mr. Alvarez only paid for one room."

Ashtyn sighs, ignoring the tightening in her gut. "No, that'll be fine. Thank you so much."

"If you have any questions, please feel free to call." Sharon hands her two keys with a smile. "Have a great stay!"

As Ashtyn takes the elevator up to their room, she shoots a text to Drew: *Just a heads up. They put us in one room with only one bed. No other rooms available.*

He replies a second later: *You okay with that? I can sleep on the couch.*

Ashtyn: *Yeah, that's fine. The couch pulls out. We can take turns.*

Drew: *I'll take the couch.*

Ashtyn just rolls her eyes as she unlocks the door to the room. Of course he would try to be a gentleman.

A nice living area and kitchenette welcome her. To her right is the bedroom with, exactly as described, one king bed. Their kiss plays in her head again. *I'd worship every single inch of you.*

She runs a hand through her hair as she flushes. He can sleep on the couch. That's an entire room away. It's fine. Ashtyn drops her bag and flops onto the sheets, tailbone protesting against the movement. They're crisp and clean and smell like linen. She eyes the bathroom and sees the walk-in shower staring back at her. It's flirting with her, its sparkling glass door wide open and inviting. This is going to be the best shower of her life.

Chapter 18

By the time five-o-clock rolls around, Drew feels like he's lived a million lifetimes. When he woke up this morning, the only thing on his mind was his and Ashtyn's kiss from the night before. Now, his thoughts race through every little thing that's happened today. When he got that phone call from her...

Instinct took over, and he'd run the entire way from his office to the apartment, not stopping once. The way her voice sounded... it had sent him spiraling. And then he'd seen her, soaking wet and shaking, and he felt... scared. Scared that something terrible happened to her. Scared to lose her in some way. Scared that things *have* changed, and he ruined the tentative friendship they created.

He really doesn't care about the apartment, just as long as Ashtyn is okay. He hates that he wasn't there to protect her. And now they're stuck in the same hotel room. Sharing an entire apartment is very different from a small hotel room where they won't have privacy away from each other. And then there's the matter of the kiss...

He's kissed her twice now, and his body begs for him to do it again. He doesn't think he's ever tasted anything as sweet as her. Not even in his wildest dreams could he have dreamed her up, perfect pink lips and soft curves. She's always been perfect. He shakes his head, clearing his thoughts of her as he heads out of the office and toward the parking garage. He drives over to the hotel, trying desperately not to think of kissing Ashtyn King, and when he gets to do it again. If ever. It's the longest drive of his life.

He pulls into the hotel's parking lot, and as he slides out of the truck, he slings his bag over his shoulder. He packed the bare minimum, and now he's certain he's forgotten something in all the chaos. It doesn't really matter, though. Just as long as he has Ash. He checks the room number she texted him earlier and makes his way toward the elevator. It's agonizing, waiting for it to arrive. Once it does, a family stumbles out, kids loud and rambunctious. Luckily, no one else gets on as Drew presses the button for his floor.

He double checks the room number one last time as he steps off the elevator. His feet carry him down the carpeted floor and deposit him in front of room 603. He knocks lightly, heart in this throat. "Hey, it's me."

"Uh, just a sec!" Ashtyn yells from the other side of the door. "I just got out of the shower."

He does *not* imagine her naked, dripping wet from the shower. He does not think about what it would be like if she opened that door naked, waiting for him to come in and kiss her senseless. He does not think...

"Sorry," she says, opening the door and stopping his thoughts in their tracks. Her hair is wrapped in a towel, and she has on a pair of sweatpants and a tank top. "Come on in."

She holds open the door for him, and he takes a tentative step inside. When she texted earlier about the one bed situation, his mind had conjured up a million different fantasies. But then he sees the couch, and reality hits him in the chest. This is for the best, he thinks.

He sets his bag down in the shared living area and collapses onto said couch. "This is nice." The couch is definitely smaller than he was anticipating, but he can make do. At least there's a wall between the living area and the bedroom, in case they need space from each other.

"Just wait until you see the shower," Ashtyn sighs. "It's glorious."

Under any other circumstances, Drew would have quipped something about them sharing it. But, something's shifted. Something suddenly feels a little too real, and it scares the ever-living shit out of him. He clears his throat. "I'm gonna see what the pull-out situation looks like." He immediately blushes as Ashtyn raises her eyebrows, a surprised smile crossing her face. "That's no—Uh, sorry, I did not mean it like that."

She laughs, crossing her arms over her chest. "Never thought I'd see the day that Andrew Mitchell gets flustered."

Drew sighs, a small smile tugging at the corner of his mouth. "It's been a long day." He stands and runs his hands under the cushions, trying to find where the couch pulls out. Once he finds the lever, he pulls, but something creaks and cracks, the lever flying right off the handle. It hits the ground with a soft thump.

"Well, that's not good," he mutters. He tries to finagle his way around the couch, pulling it this way and that, but it doesn't budge. He sighs in defeat, staring at the broken handle on the floor. "Well, I guess it's just the couch for me."

Ashtyn frowns. "Drew, the couch is tiny. I don't even think you'll fit."

"It's fine," he says, waving his hand.

"No," Ashtyn protests. "You take the bed. I'll take the couch. I'm short anyway."

"Ashtyn, I'm not letting you take the couch."

"And why not?"

"Because... it's not... I can't..." He's grasping at straws, words suddenly becoming foreign to him. "You're not sleeping on the couch."

"This is ridiculous. Just let me sleep on the couch."

"No," Drew says, flopping his body across the sofa, trying to claim it as his. She's right, he's too big, and he hangs half off of it. He smiles at her, lazily. "See? Perfect."

"Andrew," she says, arms still crossed across her chest. The use of his full name sends shivers down his spine. "You look ridiculous."

"It's *so* comfortable."

"It is not."

"Are you calling me a liar?"

She narrows her eyes at him. "Is this your way of trying to be a gentleman?"

His gaze slides to hers. "Is it working?"

"Just sleep in the bed with me," she says suddenly.

He actually falls off of the couch at her words. His ass thuds against the carpet. "Wha-what?"

"I'll make a pillow fort in the middle, so we don't accidentally touch each other. It'll be fine." This time, it's her turn to wave her hand in front of her face.

"Since when are you okay with sharing a bed with me? A few months ago, you barely agreed to share an apartment with me."

"Yeah, well," she starts, biting her lip. "We're friends, right? Friends can share beds. If you were Shiloh, I wouldn't think twice."

Drew arches his eyebrow at her. "But I'm not Shiloh."

Something glazes across her eyes. "No, you're not." She takes a small step toward him, and that's when Drew sees it. A wince. A limp. She's limping.

"Ashtyn?" he questions, looking at her curiously.

She stops, standing up straight. "What?"

"Why are you limping?"

"I'm not limping."

"Then come here." She doesn't listen to him. She doesn't take another step. His voice deepens into something even Drew doesn't recognize. "Ashtyn."

"I'm fine!" she protests. "I just smacked my tailbone on the stairs."

Something fierce and urgent roils through him. "You fell?"

"I really wouldn't use the word fell," she says, rolling her eyes. "I just slipped. A little. Barely."

"Ashtyn," he says again, gruffly. He takes a step toward her, reaching out to... to what? Hold her? Make her feel better? He's not sure. He just knows he needs to get to her.

"I'm fine, honestly," she says. She tries to take a small step back, but there's that wince again. Her face scrunches against the pain, her hand instinctually going to the small of her back. Like she can hold the pain back.

Something cracks in Drew's chest as he closes the distance between them. "Please, let me help," he says, voice soft. He leans down to pick her up, but waits for permission. With her face still scrunched, she just nods slightly. He's careful, so very careful, as he scoops her up in his arms, careful of her spine. Her hands curl into his shirt, breath hot at his neck. "Thank you," she says, so softly he almost misses it. There's a slight wobble to her voice that has him holding her closer.

"I've got you," he says, making his way into the bedroom. The single king bed takes up most of the space, and he places her gently onto the mattress. It sinks under her weight, and she sighs contentedly.

He sits on the edge, careful not to jostle her too much. "Why didn't you tell me?"

Ashtyn blows out a breath. "I didn't want to worry anyone. Besides, it barely hurts."

"That's not what your face said." She rolls her eyes. She adjusts in the bed, wincing again. Drew gives her a pointed look. "There is no way you're sleeping on the couch."

"You're so stubborn," she grumbles, pulling the blankets up around her.

"*I'm* the stubborn one!?" Drew asks incredulously. "Ashtyn King, you are the most stubborn woman I have ever met."

She huffs out a bitter laugh. "Yeah, I've been told it's one of my biggest flaws."

Drew frowns. "When did I ever say that was a flaw?" She blinks up at him, surprised. "In fact, I'd say it's one of the things I like most about you."

She scoffs. "One of the things? I thought you just liked me because I'm hot."

"Of course I think you're hot, Ashtyn. But that's not why I like you." She stares at him as if he just said something crazy. "I like you because you're smart and stubborn and determined. I like you, because you make me laugh on days where my fucking roof collapses in on itself."

She bites her lip as a small smile adorns her face. "Yeah, I guess I like you too." It's an admission that means a hell of a lot more to Drew than he'd ever admit to her. "But only a little."

"Because I'm hot?" he quips.

"Don't push it," she says, but her smile remains. She snakes her arm out from under the blanket and places a hand on his knee. "Thank you."

"Can I get you anything?" he asks, heart in his throat. She bites her lip, as if she's too proud to ask. "Please?"

"Some ibuprofen would probably help," she says quietly. "And some ice cream?"

"Your wish is my command," Drew says, getting up off the bed. He turns and salutes her. "I'll see what I can do about the sofa bed, too."

His heart pounds as he rides the elevator down to the lobby. At the front desk, he meets a lovely woman named Sharon, who informs him that there's nothing they can do about the sofa bed right now, but they can get a replacement for them tomorrow. Looks like it's the couch for him tonight. He thanks her and buys the ibuprofen and ice cream. It costs him an arm and a leg, but he doesn't mind. He'd pay anything to make Ashtyn happy.

When he gets back to the room, she has the TV playing an episode of *New Girl* he recognizes, and she's tucked up in the middle of the bed. She takes the goods gratefully, popping the medicine immediately.

"There's nothing they can do about the sofa tonight," he says. "I'll just deal with it for now until they can fix it tomorrow."

Either she forgets her offer for them to share the bed, or she's gone back on it, but she just says, "Okay."

Drew takes the hint and heads back to the sofa. He takes the world's quickest shower, gets ready for bed, and lays down on the stiff couch. He hangs half off of it, his long legs bent at the knee over the arm. He's barely closed his eyes when he hears Ashtyn calling from the other room. His eyes spring open, and he's in the bedroom before he can even think.

"What's wrong? Are you okay? Do you need more meds?" It's dark, and he's unable to see much more than a few feet in front of him. His knee hits the edge of the bed, and he almost topples onto it.

He hears Ashtyn sigh. "Will you please just sleep in the bed with me?"

He swallows thickly. "Ashtyn, I-I don't want to make you uncomfortable."

"You won't," she says. "Besides, I made a pillow fort." She smacks what Drew can only assume is the border between the two sides of the bed. "Nothing's getting past this."

Drew chuckles. He reaches out into the dark to find the border, a huge stack of pillows keeping them appropriately separated. "You sure?"

"Yes, just get in here."

He doesn't question it anymore, sinking into the mattress, the sheets welcoming after trying to lie on that hard couch. He groans into his pillow, his back already relaxing. Ashtyn giggles from her side of the bed. She feels so close, yet so far away. He thinks about their kiss again.

Neither of them has brought it up...

They both agreed it didn't change things between them. It wouldn't change things. Drew sighs, wiping it out of his mind for the night. "Goodnight, Ashtyn," he says, sleep already tugging on his bones.

"Goodnight, Drew."

Chapter 19

It is the world's slowest Friday to ever exist. Drew stares at the clock above his desk, fingers twitching as he watches it count down to the end of the day, ever so slowly. He awoke this morning, face full of pillows, with the knowledge that Ashtyn was just on the other side of the bed. He could see just the top of her red hair from his side. The urge to reach out and touch her, to feel her warm skin underneath him, was unbearable. So, he got up, took a cold shower, and hurriedly got ready for work. She was still asleep by the time he slipped out the door.

Now, he stares at the clock, willing it to go faster. If he worked for a boss that was with the times, he'd be able to work remotely half the time. But, Franklin is old school. Like, really old school. He thinks coming into the office provides the company with a sense of comradery. When in reality, it just makes everyone a little grumpier on Fridays.

"Hey man," Jordan says, popping his head into Drew's office. "Heard about your roof collapsing."

"How?" Drew asks. When he'd run home yesterday, he hadn't told anyone what was going on. Just that he had an emergency, and he'd be back. No one asked any questions, not even gossip prone Robbie.

"Ava called Brooke. Brooke told me."

"Geez," Drew says, rubbing a hand down his face. "Word travels fast around here."

"You guys okay?"

"Yeah, we're fine. Manager put us up in a fancy hotel for the week."

"So, you and Ashtyn, stuck in a hotel together all weekend…" Jordan wags his eyebrows, and Drew sends him a death glare.

"Just because I was a groomsman in your wedding doesn't mean I won't punch you in the face."

Jordan rolls his eyes, but raises his hands in surrender. "Sorry, I forgot you're sensitive about her."

Drew grounds his teeth. "I'm not sensitive about her. I'm respect-ful."

"Riiiiight," Jordan trills. "Respectful. And is that why you haven't made a move yet?"

Drew throws a pencil at Jordan that he dodges expertly. "Get out."

"Okay, okay! I'm just messing. Besides, you know mine and Brooke's apartment is always open if you need it. I'm sure you and Ash could fit on the couch—"

Drew throws an entire box of paperclips at Jordan as his laughter echoes throughout his office. "I hate you!" Drew calls to his retreating back.

"Right back at you, asshole," Jordan teases.

Drew rolls his eyes, but smiles. Then he sighs, looking at the mess he made on the floor. Well, this would at least waste some time until he can finally get back to the hotel and to Ashtyn…

* * *

It's 5:01PM when he's pushing the button in the hotel elevator for their floor. He'd barely been able to keep himself still that last half hour in the office, and he slipped out early before anyone could notice. Consequences be damned.

His key touches the automatic lock, and he's opening the door right as Ashtyn steps out of the steamy bathroom, hair wet, white robe secured tightly around her. She blinks at him in surprise. "You're back early," she says from her spot in the doorway.

"Uh, yeah, slow day," he says, swallowing the desire he feels at seeing her in a robe. He just couldn't wait to get back to her. Couldn't wait to see her again. Now that he's here, he doesn't know where to look, to stand, to breathe.

"Gotcha," she replies. She crosses her arms across her chest and clears her throat. "You, uh, didn't happen to bring dinner, did you? I'm starving."

Idiot, he thinks. He didn't even think about dinner. All his thoughts were focused on her. He scrubs a hand down his face. "Sorry, I completely forgot."

"It's okay," she says. "I'm sure we could order room service. Oh, they came and fixed the sofa bed by the way. It should be good to go."

"Oh," is all he's able to say. Disappointment floods his system. Disappointment and shame for wanting her so bad, when she clearly couldn't be more uninterested. "How's your tailbone?" he asks as a way of distracting himself.

"Fine," she says. Her limp looks better today, but it's still noticeably there. "Hot shower helped."

"Good," he says.

She frowns at him, leaning her hip against the wall. "What's wrong?"

"Nothing," he says, making his way over to the sofa bed. He pulls the newly restored lever, and the bed springs forth immediately, thin and creaky. He sits on the edge precariously, the springs letting out an ominous groan as he puts his full weight on it. He lays back, and he can feel every spring dig into his spine. "Wow, this might be the most comfortable bed I've ever laid on," he jokes.

"Great, then I'll take it," she says, joining him in the room.

"Uh, no."

"Uh, yes."

"Ashtyn, you're not taking the sofa bed."

"Why? You just said it's the best bed you've ever laid on," she counters, cocking an eyebrow at him.

"Exactly. So that means I should take it."

"Since when are you so selfish? Where's the gentleman act you employed yesterday?"

"I'm not a gentleman," he says, gruffly, sitting back up. "I've always been a selfish asshole. I want the bed all to myself."

"Selfish," she hums, coming to stand right in front of him. He can see the white cotton of her robe, the knot holding it together. Her bare skin just underneath. His breath catches in his throat as he looks up at her. She stares down at him, a thoughtful look on her face. She takes another small step toward him, and he sits up straighter. The mattress creaks again. "Doesn't sound very safe," she muses.

"T-totally safe," Drew stutters, swallowing his growing desire as he watches her get closer and closer in that fucking robe.

"What about that perfectly good pillow fort I made?" she questions. "You didn't have any objections to that last night."

Drew tries to compose himself. "A temporary solution to a temporary problem." He pats the sofa bed. "Problem fixed."

"You know," she sighs. "I saw them fix the sofa bed. I just don't think they did a very good job. It could snap in the middle of the night, folding you right up into the couch. Think of how sad our friends would be if you were permanently molded into a couch."

"And you? How would you feel?" He's stepping into dangerous territory, but she started it, goddamn it. She's playing with him, seeing if he'll play back. And he will. Oh, he'll play if she wants him to.

"I'd be mildly disappointed," she says, rueful smile on her face.

It's that look that makes Drew teeter over the edge. "Okay."

"Okay?"

"Okay, I'll sleep in the bed with you again." She smiles, but doesn't step away. She's daring him. Daring him to ask. He swallows, thickly. "What if we dismantled the fort?" Oh god, this is such dangerous territory, one he's wanted to cross into for so, so long. "Just for one night."

Her lips purse into a perfect "o", and her eyebrows shoot up. She crosses her arms defiantly. "And what makes you think I'd agree to that?"

His brain and his heart are at war. He wants to continue, but he's also worried about ruining everything they've built so far. *Fuck it*, he thinks. "Because of the way you kissed me the other night."

She sucks in a deep breath, obviously not expecting him to mention it, even though she's the one challenging him. "I thought I said it didn't change anything."

"It doesn't."

"Then why are you bringing it up?"

"Because I want to do it again." He looks up at her from underneath his lashes. She doesn't move away from his gaze. She stands her ground, looking down at him through her own lashes. She seems to be debating something, the corner of her bottom lip tucked neatly underneath her teeth. Her eyes slide to his, and she must make a decision, because she steps into the space between his legs, her knees against his. He sucks in a breath as she fingers the knot holding her robe closed. Slowly, ever so slowly, she undoes it, her robe tumbling open, revealing her naked body underneath. He's not sure what comes out of his mouth, but it sounds like a mix between a moan and a whimper as he takes her in. The peak of her breasts, down to her navel, to the tops of her thighs. She's so fucking beautiful, Drew's afraid he'll drop to his knees in worship and never be able to get back up. He stays where he is, letting her come to him, letting her set the pace. And she does, his eyes devouring every inch of her. He feels his heart travel to his throat, his dick already hard in his pants.

"No fort?" she breathes, her fingers going to his hair. He closes his eyes as he noses the spot of skin between her breasts, her skin smelling of lavender. His hands skim the backs of her thighs, just barely below her ass.

"No fort," he agrees, looking up at her. His fingers find their way to her hips, and her eyes flutter at the contact, goosebumps erupting on her skin. He can see her nipples harden at the contact.

"This doesn't change anything," she says so softly, he almost doesn't hear her. He doesn't care. He doesn't care if this changes everything, he just needs to taste her, touch her. He nods against her stomach.

"Nothing changes," he agrees. He waits. He waits for her permission, her initiative.

She sinks into his lap, her face finally coming down to the same level as his. "Then please kiss me."

* * *

Drew's mouth lowers onto Ashtyn's, and she has to keep in the groan that's been building within her ever since he walked in the door. Her hands grasp the front of his shirt, desperately trying to rip it off of him. He obliges her, and it's gone in one swift motion, their chests now crushed together. Her nipples pinch in pleasure at the contact. She's not sure what came over her, deciding to remove her robe and expose herself fully to him, but she's not complaining. They'd been making their way toward this moment for far longer than either of them would like to admit.

Drew's hands find their way to her backside, and she can feel how hard he is beneath her. Everything about them is hungry. They don't take their time or slow down. They are a mess of hands, skin, and teeth.

Every single nerve ending in Ashtyn's body is on fire, screaming at her to get closer, closer, closer. Drew's hands on her are strong and secure, sending her spiraling with desire. The moan he lets out sends a pulse through her body that needs release.

"Bed. Now," she breathes, barely even taking her lips away from his. The way he gets up off the sofa bed without even jostling her might be the hottest thing she's ever experienced. With her legs secured around his waist, he walks them through the living room and toward the bedroom, his arms tight around her. God, why had she wasted all that time being annoyed by him, when they could have been doing this?

He lays her gently on the bed, his body over hers, his mouth finding the hollow of her throat. She throws the pillow fort to the floor, so they have the entirety of the bed to themselves. She reaches down for the button on his pants, unfastening it. She palms him through his underwear, and he lets out a groan that zaps right through her.

Drew's off her in an instant, kicking off his pants at the end of the bed. He stands, and she can see the outline of him through his underwear. Jesus fucking Christ. She stares at him with lustful eyes, biting her bottom lip in anticipation.

He crawls over to her tantalizingly before grabbing her thighs and pulling her to the edge of the bed, gently and ever so slowly. "Are you in pain?" he asks, fingers caressing her hips. Ashtyn completely forgot about her bruised tailbone. She can't feel anything other than the pulsating desire coursing through her. She shakes her head and spreads her legs in front of him, aching and wet. He kneels, his mouth trailing kisses down her navel toward where she wants him most.

"Good," he says, gently biting the inside of her thigh. "Now, do you have any idea how long I've wanted to know what you taste like?"

She whimpers as he places a kiss where he just bit her. She feels like she might just combust from his mouth alone, from hearing him whisper those words to her and her alone. Oh, how long she's waited... "Please," she gasps, her fingers fisting in the sheets.

"I'm going to be the first man that makes you come," he says, voice gruff. "Me." His mouth lowers between her thighs, and she moans as his tongue swirls where she's most sensitive. Her toes curl as her pleasure builds, Drew's hands gripped onto her hips as his mouth explores her, devours her, takes his time with her. How had no one before him been able to do this?

"Fuck, Drew," she says, her back arching as he flicks her clit with his tongue. It's the most intense feeling she's ever felt, her pleasure building so quickly, she almost can't believe it. Her pleasure builds and builds until her orgasm explodes out of her, blinding and brilliant. She moans so loud, she's worried the entire state of Texas can hear her.

She's breathing heavily as Drew makes his way up her body, his mouth caressing the shell of her ear. "I think that was the best sound I've ever heard," he whispers.

A laugh escapes from Ashtyn as he nuzzles into her neck. She's not sure if it's the post-orgasm high, or the fact that it's Drew, but she thinks this might be the happiest she's ever been in bed with another person. "How did you do that so fast?" she breathes.

"I told you I never come first," he replies huskily. His voice, so intimate, has her wet again. She spins him so he's underneath her, her hips bracketing him.

He stares up at her with glazed eyes. "You are so beautiful." His hands graze the tops of her thighs, and she shivers. Her fingers skim the edge of his underwear, his eyes rolling back in ecstasy. She works them down his legs, letting his cock spring forward, thick and ready. She takes his length in her hand, and he moans. It's the most glorious sound she's ever heard.

"Condom?" she asks, pumping him once.

"Wa-wallet," he stutters, fists grasping the sheets.

"Really?" she teases. "The wallet condom?"

"Are you complaining?" he asks, cocking an eyebrow at her, smile on his face.

"No, I'm not," she says, retrieving the condom swiftly. She tears it open with her teeth, and she swears she hears Drew whimper. She puts it on him in one fluid motion and settles over him.

"Is this okay?" she asks breathily.

"God, yes," he says, sitting up to kiss her again. She can still taste the remnants of her pleasure on his tongue, and it thrills her, knowing his mouth had been full of her. He's so hard and solid underneath her. And then she's sinking onto him, his length filling her utterly and completely as their arms wrap around each other. He's buried fully inside her, and she gasps, her eyes rolling to the back of her head in pleasure. He groans as she rides him.

"Goddamn, Ashtyn," he says.

They move steadily, pleasure and ecstasy building between them. Her nipples rub against his chest, the friction cascading her closer and closer to the edge, *again*. Ashtyn reaches down to touch herself as they continue. "I'm close," she breathes. How he's able to give her multiple orgasms, when no one else has before, is baffling. But goddamn, if it doesn't feel like heaven.

Drew kisses her again, his tongue wrapping around hers as he spins them so he's on top, her legs spread wide before him. He fucks her expertly, slowly, deeply. She moans into his mouth as her orgasm crests, her body about to collapse from the sheer euphoria of it all.

"Drew!" she cries.

"I'm here, sweetheart," he says, his own breathing labored. "I'm right here with you."

And then they fall together, their orgasms washing over them as they collapse into each other, their bodies intertwining until they're a mess of limbs and sheets and kisses.

Chapter 20

Drew wakes to the warm figure of Ashtyn next to him, her auburn hair strewn across his chest. Normally, he wouldn't complain, but a loud beeping has startled him out of his slumber. He's bleary eyed, the room still draped in darkness. He waits, not wanting to wake her up, but there it is again, a long, loud beep. Muffled, but still obvious.

"Ashtyn," he mumbles, rubbing his tired eyes.

She stirs and—he wouldn't believe it if he hadn't heard it himself—growls. "It better be past ten AM."

He checks his phone on the nightstand. "Try three AM."

"Then why are you waking me up?" The loud beeping starts up again, and Ashtyn groans. "What the fuck is that?"

"Stay here. I'll check it out." He leans down and kisses her head as she snuggles deeper into the sheets. He doesn't mean to do it, it just happens. It feels natural.

He gets up and finds a pair of sweatpants that he puts on as quietly as he can. The beeping continues, getting louder as he heads toward the hallway. He unlocks the door and peeks his head out. The noise is much louder out here, and he has to cover his ears. There are other patrons peeking their heads out of their doors, eyes blinking rapidly as they adjust to the light, hair disheveled.

"What's going on?" a man asks gruffly. Drew shrugs in response.

The elevator dings down the hallway, and a man rushes out. "Please, no one panic," he explains, voice raised so they can hear him above the beeping. "But I'm going to need everyone to evacuate the building. Our sensors have detected a gas leak." Despite the man's warning, panic floods through Drew's system. "If I could please have everyone evacuate using the stairs. Please leave your belongings." The man begins ushering people toward the exit, the crowd murmuring amongst themselves.

Drew rushes back into the room, flipping on the lights as he goes. Ashtyn groans loudly, burying herself deeper into the pillows.

"I'm sorry, Ash, but we gotta go." He starts scouring through their bags and discarded clothes to find something she can put on quickly.

"What?" Her voice is muffled by the sheets.

"They're evacuating the building. There's a gas leak."

At his words, Ashtyn sits up straight, hair obscuring half her face. "A gas leak? Oh my god, we're gonna die."

"We're not going to die. Come on, get up and get dressed. Quickly." He tosses her a shirt, and she pulls it over her head. He tries not to think about how she was still naked under the sheets. How badly he wanted to wake up next to her and continue what they started last night. Instead, he pulls on his shoes and gathers his wallet and keys, trying to clear his mind. They leave their bags per the staff's request and head into the hallway, hands finding each other and holding on tight. Whether they meant to do it or not doesn't really matter right now. The man from earlier ushers them into the stairwell, and they make their way down with the hoard of other guests, alarm still blaring. There are hundreds of sleepy patrons littering the parking lot as people try to make sense of what's going on.

"Geez, disaster just keeps following us," Ashtyn mutters, hugging her free arm around herself. She doesn't let go of Drew's hand, her palm sweaty in his. If Drew believed in fate, he'd think they were cursed. He's about to say as much when a firefighter stands in front of the crowd and asks for everyone to back up at least fifty feet. The crowd scuffles along, Drew and Ashtyn among them.

"How long do you think this'll take?" she asks, stifling a yawn.

"No idea," he replies, wanting to sling an arm around her, to comfort her, but he doesn't. Instead, he just keeps holding her hand. This is safe. Innocent. Nothing like what happened last night...

It's an hour before anyone comes to talk to them. Ashtyn is dozing on his shoulder as they sit in the bed of his truck when the hotel manager announces, "We are so sorry for the inconvenience. Unfortunately, we won't be able to get back into the building tonight. We are working on relocating everyone to other hotels."

The crowd groans, and many rush up to the manager, demanding more answers than he can give. "Please, everyone! Form a line."

"Well, this could take a while," Drew says, sighing. Ashtyn lets out a whine, burying her head into his shoulder. She can barely keep her eyes open. "You know, we could always call Ava and Shiloh—"

"No!" Ashtyn shouts, suddenly wide awake, hands gripping his arm tightly. "No, we don't need to bother them."

"Why? You know they'd let us crash."

"No," she says firmly, offering no other explanation.

Not wanting to push her, Drew says, "Okay, well we can wait. It might take a few hours, though. Hopefully they put us somewhere nice."

Ashtyn sighs, rubbing her forehead. "I... might have somewhere we can go."

* * *

Two hours later, they pull up a dirt driveway to an old farmhouse. The porchlight is on as the sun begins its ascent over the hill. Thank God it's Saturday, and Drew doesn't have to call in to work. Ashtyn's mom sits on the porch, coffee mug in hand. She waves as she sees the truck pull up the driveway. He's never met Ashtyn's mom, but he's heard stories from Ava. She and Ashtyn are extremely close.

Ashtyn's been dozing the entire drive, not a peep out of her. As he turns off the truck, she awakens with a yawn, and her eyes light up as she sees her mom. They exit the truck, and Mrs. King meets them halfway up the drive. Ashtyn envelops her mom in a big hug.

"Hi, Momma," she says. "Sorry to barge in on you this early."

"Oh, honey, you can always barge in," Mrs. King says. She turns to Drew with a sparkle in her eye. "You must be the roommate."

"Andrew," Drew says, sticking out his hand, always using his full name when meeting parents. Mrs. King forgoes the hand and wraps her arms around him in a hug.

"Sorry, I'm a hugger," she says, patting his back.

"And you say she's your daughter?" Drew teases, eliciting a laugh out of Mrs. King.

"Watch it," Ashtyn warns, but there's a hint of a smile on her face.

"Thank you for letting us stay, Mrs. King. I hope this isn't too much."

"Oh, please honey, call me Carol. Any friend of my daughter is a friend of mine. Besides, I've got plenty of room."

The house is big for just one woman. With a wraparound porch, two stories, and three bedrooms, Drew's not sure how Carol keeps it so clean. The hardwood floors are spotless as they enter, leaving their shoes in the doorway. The hallway is filled with framed pictures of a tiny redhead, smiling brightly in each photo. Drew could have stopped and stared at them all day.

"I've set you up in the guest room, Andrew," Carol says, snapping his attention away from the photos. "Ash can have her old room. Or sleep with me like we used to."

A blush tinges Ashtyn's cheeks, but there's a warm, familiar smile on her face that says she doesn't mind much. "You don't have to call him Andrew, Mom. He'll get a big head."

Carol laughs as Drew catches Ashtyn's gaze. "Does this mean you'll finally let me call you Ash then?"

Her eyes narrow, but that smile doesn't leave her face. "I'll think about it."

Drew's heart skips a beat at her words. Carol looks between him and her daughter with a sparkle in her eyes. "Oh, this is going to be a fun weekend," she says.

Drew sleeps until noon. He probably could have slept longer, but his body is hard wired to be up by now. He pads down the stairs with socked feet, careful not to wake Ashtyn. The aroma of coffee leads him to the kitchen, where Carol sits at the breakfast bar, working on a crossword. At his entrance, she looks up at him and smiles. "I thought the coffee might rouse one of you."

"Well, it's definitely not going to be Ashtyn," Drew teases, and Carol laughs, eyes crinkling at the corners.

"No, my daughter is not much of a morning person."

"So I've learned." He pours himself a mug of steaming, black coffee and sips it gratefully. "Thank you again for letting us stay. I'm sure the hotel would have put us up somewhere fine, but Ashtyn was really tired, and we both agreed she'd be more comfortable here."

"I'm surprised she didn't call Ava first."

Drew frowns. "She... didn't want to bother her. You know, the new apartment and all that."

Carol nods. "Oh, I know all about it. Sometimes Ash can be too stubborn for her own good." Drew just laughs and takes another sip of coffee. Carol clears her throat. "I, um, am very grateful to you, Andrew. She had nowhere else to go, and you were there for her."

This makes Drew pause. He sets the coffee down, wrapping his hands around the warm mug. "Ah, I was just the last resort," he teases. "Besides, she's just waiting for something better to come along."

Carol shakes her head, short graying hair swishing against her shoulders. "No, she's not." Something about her words makes Drew bite back a smile. "I know you couldn't bring any of your belongings, so I set out some extra clothes for you. Sorry if they're a little musty. I haven't exactly brought them out in a while."

He doesn't want to pry, so he just smiles. "Thank you. I appreciate it." He'd noticed the clothes sitting on the bed when he'd entered the room early this morning. A warm, faded flannel. Old, worn jeans that seemed a little too big for him. He wonders who they used to belong to. They sit in silence for a moment, before curiosity gets the better of him. "So, what exactly do you know about me?"

This makes Carol smile. "It's not what Ashtyn says, but what she doesn't say that you should always pay attention to." When he doesn't respond, Carol continues, "I know what she's said about you. How you dropped that box on her foot the first time you met and stared slack-jawed at her like an absolute, oh what was the word she used..."

"Blonde fucker?" Drew supplies.

"That's the one!" Drew chuckles into his coffee, the memory sending a shiver through him despite the warm drink in his hands. Ashtyn's mom sighs, a small smile on her face. "But I also know what else she's said about you. She told me about the time you threatened to break Garrett Smith's jaw for speaking rudely about Ava. You should have seen the way she talked about you, then."

A memory surfaces in Drew's mind from last July. They were here, in this town, camping for Shiloh's birthday weekend. One of Ava's old boyfriends was there, slightly drunk, and said some things that pissed the entire group off. Drew took him off to the side and let him know he wasn't welcome near their group again. Later that night, after he'd issued said threat, Ashtyn had cornered him near the campsite bathrooms, a determined look on her face. He'd tried to tease her, play with her, but she wasn't having any of it. She was... thanking him. Her hand gripped his arm, and her eyes softened. The air was hot and thick, and all Drew could think about was that he'd die to see her expression soften in his presence again. How he knew he'd do anything for her, no questions asked, even if she hated him, even if she couldn't stand the sight of him. He would do anything just to see her happy.

"Yeah," Drew says, coming out of the memory. "She's pretty great."

"I've heard more about you than you might realize," Carol says, twirling her pen through her fingers. "I've been dying to meet you."

"Well, I hope I don't disappoint."

Her eyes crinkle as she smiles. "You could never disappoint, honey."

He warms at her words. He takes in the kitchen as Carol fills in another answer on her crossword. The house feels rustic, like something you might find straight out of *Pioneer Woman*, a show his own mother frequently watches. His eyes settle on a framed picture hanging above the sink, a man with fierce red hair holding a small toddler with that same scarlet mane.

Carol must notice Drew looking at the picture, because she says, quietly, "My husband, Phil. Ashtyn's father. We lost him when she was four."

Drew's never heard Ashtyn speak about her father. "I'm sorry," he says sincerely. "I didn't know." He must have been the owner of those old clothes.

"I don't think she likes talking about him," Carol admits. "She never really got the chance to know him."

"I can't imagine what that must have been like."

"Some days, I see it as a blessing that he passed before she could fully know him. Other days, I think it might be the greatest tragedy of her life." The words are so honest, so open. Her eyes water with decades of tears held in. "It just seems so unfair that I got to love him for so long, and she didn't." Drew reaches out to gently pat Carol's hand. She grabs on like it's a lifeline.

"Well, I'm glad she has a mom as great as you to take care of her," he says.

She sniffles, and the tears disappear. A smile takes their place. Drew wonders if Ashtyn got that trick from her mother. "Thank you, Andrew," Carol says, patting his hand. "Okay, no more tears. Now, let's get that girl awake."

Chapter 21

Ashtyn wakes to the smell of her mom's famous French toast and the sound of Billie Holiday crooning softly from downstairs. She checks her phone on the nightstand. It's almost 2PM, and she groans loudly.

She sits up, her back cracking from the stiff mattress. God, how did she sleep on this thing all through high school? Her feet hit the floor, an eerie sense of déjà vu washing over her. She follows the mouthwatering smell down the stairs, yawning all the way. She probably could have slept the entire day away, her body tired from last night's trysts. Before entering the kitchen, she hears her mother's laugh followed by Drew's. It halts her in her tracks. It's something she never, in her wildest dreams, thought she'd ever hear.

She peeks around the corner and into the kitchen discreetly. The radio plays softly on the counter, a stack of French toast sitting tantalizingly on the breakfast bar. But, the craziest sight of all is Drew, in her childhood home, washing dishes at the sink while her mother dries. They're shoulder to shoulder, laughing with each other, like they've known each other for years instead of hours. He's wearing a flannel that causes a lump to form in her throat.

The last forty-eight hours rush through her brain like a tidal wave. The flooded apartment, the gas leak at the hotel, *other* things that happened in that hotel... She feels a full body shiver run through her at the thought. *This doesn't change things*, she reminds herself. Even as she stares at the man she swore was her enemy looking right at home in *her* home. Making her mother laugh. Doing the dishes. Swaying slightly to the music of Billie Holiday. She wouldn't have believed it if she wasn't seeing it with her own two eyes.

She was wrong to bring him here. This is a mistake. First, she sleeps with him, then she brings him home to meet her mother? What on earth is she thinking? The gas leak must have gone straight to her head. Who knows how long she'd been inhaling toxic fumes. Before she can spiral further, a bright voice bellows, "Good morning, sunshine!"

She snaps her attention to Drew, a wide smile on his face as he turns off the sink. "It's about time you got up," her mother says. "I figured if anything could get you out of bed it was my famous French toast."

"Well, it worked," Ashtyn says, leaving her hiding place now that she's been discovered. She seats herself at the breakfast bar and looks at the food ravenously. She's starving. The only thing she consumed last night was Drew. He places a steaming cup of coffee in front of her, and she nearly snatches it out of his hands. She drinks deeply, letting the caffeine wake her bones and her brain.

"Thank you," she says, quietly. She can't look him in the eye, not when he's wearing her father's clothes and charming her mother. She's not sure what the feeling is that's coursing through her, but she knows she doesn't want to face it right now. It's all a bit too much.

Her mother slides a plate of toast in front of her. "The King special." She kisses Ashtyn's forehead, and for a moment, she feels fifteen again. But, instead of Brandon at the table with them, it's Drew. Annoying, agitating, makes her want to tear her hair out, Drew. He sits across from her, lazy smile on his face, blue eyes bright. Drew, who would do anything for her. Drew, who has never actually done anything to warrant her sour attitude toward him.

Drew, Drew, Drew. Her mind won't stop saying his name. Repeating it until it's branded into her skin, intertwined with her bones. She must be staring, because he looks at her funny.

"Everything okay?" he asks.

"Perfect," she makes her mouth say. "Perfect."

And that's what scares her the most, because nothing is supposed to be perfect. She thought her relationship with Brandon was perfect and look how that turned out. If she found perfect again, she'd always be waiting for the other shoe to drop. For her heart to be ripped out of her chest and tossed in a drawer, forgotten by everyone but her. No, she can't put herself through that again. *Won't* put herself through that again.

She takes a bite of food, forcing it down her throat. "Thanks, Mom," she says. "It's delicious."

* * *

Ashtyn finds her mom outside in the garden a few hours later. Drew's on the phone with the hotel, trying to figure out when they can be let back in. He said he'd take care of everything, and Ashtyn is grateful for that.

"Hey," her mom says, dirt staining the knees of her jeans. "Coming to help?"

Ashtyn huffs out a laugh. "That's hilarious."

"How did I get a daughter allergic to the outdoors?"

Ashtyn plops onto the rocking chair on the porch. She can see the top of her mom's head over the railing. "I was born with red hair and pale skin. The sun hates me."

Her mother chuckles. "You can thank your father for that."

Ashtyn's heart constricts at the mention of her father. Seeing his flannel this morning on Drew... it tore a hole right through her. The man that helped create her feels like a stranger, and she hates it. She hates how cruel the world is for taking him away from them. She decides to change the subject. "So, what did you and Drew chat about while I was passed out?"

"Oh, you know, this and that."

Ashtyn peers over the railing at her mother with raised eyebrows. "Just this and that?"

"Yes, Ashtyn. He told me a little about his work. I told him about my garden. I also told him how much of a petulant teenager you were."

"Mom!"

Her mom laughs and gets up, joining Ashtyn in the neighboring chair on the porch. She pats Ashtyn's knee comfortingly. "I'm kidding. But I did thank him for letting you move in with him."

"Mom," Ashtyn groans, rolling her eyes. "It's not a big deal."

"I disagree."

Ashtyn sticks her tongue out at her mother, channeling that teenage petulance she mentioned. Her mom just laughs, grabbing Ashtyn's hand. Her palm is warm and worn. "You kept fighting me about coming back home. I'm just glad you were able to find a solution that didn't take you away from your life in the city. But, I am glad you came to see me," she says.

The words spear right into Ashtyn's heart. "I'm sorry it's been a while."

"It's okay. I know how much this move stressed you out. Are you at least happy with him?"

Ashtyn stills. "The apartment is fine. Besides the flooding part."

"That's not what I asked."

"We're... just friends, Mom. And barely that. We tolerate each other at best," Ashtyn stutters, trying to convince not only her mother, but also herself.

"Oh, I think he does a lot more than tolerate you," her mom replies, squeezing Ashtyn's hand.

"That's ridiculous." Her mind wanders to last night, and she has to squash those memories before a blush is splayed upon her cheeks. She presses the heels of her hands to her eyes.

"Is it?"

"Can we change the subject please?" Ashtyn asks, pressing her hands harder, so she starts seeing spots.

"Okay, are you going to the reunion?"

Ashtyn inwardly screams. "Goddammit, Ava."

"Hey, don't blame Ava! At least she calls me."

"I call you!" she protests.

"Yeah, every other month."

Ashtyn chuckles, then sighs heavily. "I told her I would go."

"But?"

"You know what."

"Ah," Carol says, patting her daughter's hand. "Him." Her mom doesn't utter his name, just like Ashtyn doesn't.

"I don't know what to do."

"Well, do you want to know what your father would have said?" Ashtyn feels that pain in her heart again, old and deep and aching. She doesn't say anything as she squeezes her eyes shut against the pain. Her mother tucks her finger under Ashtyn's chin and lifts her face. She opens her eyes to see her mom's expression. "He would have said fuck him."

Ashtyn gasps. "Mom!"

Carol throws her head back in laughter. "It's true. He would have said 'fuck him'. Fuck him and everything he did to you. That man didn't, and still doesn't, deserve a single one of your tears. He never did." Her mom's eyes sparkle as she continues, "And you know what else? Your father would have gone to that wedding with you. He would have stood up and booed if you wanted him to. That's how much he loved you. He would have done anything for you."

A sob escapes Ashtyn's tough exterior. Her mother wraps both arms around her, holding her tightly. "I wish I could remember him better," Ashtyn admits quietly.

"Oh, honey, you can always ask me about him. His memory lives on through us and the stories we tell."

"It doesn't upset you? It doesn't make you miss him?"

"Of course it makes me miss him. But, that's how I know we lived the best life we could while we had him. Because of how much it hurts to miss him."

Ashtyn's tears begin to flow, and her mom wipes them away with the pad of her thumb. "How did you survive it?" Ashtyn asks breathlessly. "How did you survive losing someone you loved so much?"

"Well, for one, I had you. And every time I look at you, I see him too. I see all the things he gave you, including this wildfire hair." Her mother strokes Ashtyn's hair. "I see him in your stubbornness. In your tenacity. In your humor. But, I also had a community of people to surround me when he died. I leaned on others to help me through."

Ashtyn squeezes her mom tightly. "Weren't you scared you might lose them too?"

"Of course, sweetheart. But that's what being human is. Loving someone so much you're afraid to lose them. But, you can't let fear hold you back. You have to walk hand in hand with it."

"How?"

"You love. Love is always stronger than fear. You love as much as you possibly can. I promise you, it's worth it."

Ashtyn feels the words wrap around her heart. "I love you so much, Mom."

"I love you most, my sweet girl."

The porch door slides open, and Drew freezes when he sees the two women embraced. "Is this a bad time?"

"No, come on out," Carol says. "We're just reminiscing."

Ashtyn discreetly wipes her tears as Drew leans on the railing. "Well, the good news is that we'll be able to go back to the hotel tomorrow."

"And the bad news?"

"We'll be there about a week until the apartment is fixed."

"Well, you know you're more than welcome to stay here," Carol says. "Lord knows I've got the room."

"As much as I'd love to stay, I unfortunately have to work," Drew says. "Boss doesn't believe in remote work. No matter the circumstances." He pauses, scrunching his brow in concentration. "But, Ashtyn can stay if she wants. I don't mind picking you up when the apartment's ready."

With the way her mom's face lights up, Ashtyn knows there's no way she can say no. Honestly, this might be the best outcome, since she's not ready to have the "we slept together" conversation with Drew just yet.

"Are you sure?" she asks, looking up at him. "I'd feel bad leaving you all alone."

"I'll be fine," Drew replies, shrugging. "I've lived alone this long, what's another week?"

"Right," Ashtyn says, biting her lip. She won't admit to herself that she'll miss him. That her body begs her to share a bed with him again. No, she'll bury those feelings like she always does. She looks to her mom, who is beaming at her. "Can we have macaroni and hotdogs like we used to?" she asks with raised eyebrows.

"We can have whatever you want."

"Deal!"

Her mom wraps her in a tight embrace, and Ashtyn catches Drew's gaze over her shoulder. He has a soft smile on his face as he leans against the railing of the porch, as if he's always belonged here. As if he was meant to always end up here. Ashtyn closes her eyes, but the image is forever branded in her memory.

Chapter 22

Carol puts Drew to work for the rest of the day. When she asked him to fix a leaky faucet in the bathroom, he didn't have the heart to tell her he had no idea what he was doing. Thankfully, Shiloh answered on the second ring and talked him through the whole thing. Now, she has him repairing loose floorboards on the porch. At least this was relatively intuitive, and he's able to do it without calling Shiloh for help.

As he's hammering the last board into the porch, the sun descends behind the hill, coating the porch in dim light. The sliding glass door opens, and Ashtyn stands above him, bathed in the light from the kitchen.

"Dinner's ready," she says softly. He looks up at her, noticing how relaxed she is, and smiles.

"Perfect timing," he replies. "I just finished."

"You didn't have to do that."

Drew frowns. "Of course I did. Your mom asked me to." He stands, wiping his sweaty forehead on his shirt. He doesn't miss the way Ashtyn's eyes glaze as she stares at the sliver of bare torso. "Besides, it's the least I could do to thank her for letting me stay here. And for letting me borrow your dad's old clothes." He hikes up the jeans that are definitely too big for him.

Ashtyn swallows and doesn't say anything. She's staring just above his shoulder, avoiding his gaze. "Ash," he starts.

She slides her eyes to him. "Andrew."

This exchange, him using her nickname, her using his full name, sends his heart racing. It's a test. A line in the sand. Are they willing to go further?

"Dinner's getting cold!" Carol yells from the kitchen, shattering the tension between them.

"Coming!" Ashtyn yells back. She holds Drew's gaze for a moment longer before turning and heading back into the house. Drew follows her, heart in his throat.

As they sit at the table, Drew feels a sense of peace settle over him, like he could get used to this, even though he knows he shouldn't. He knows deep in his bones that he shouldn't want this. That he *can't* want this. But goddamn if he doesn't yearn for it.

Carol sighs as she sits down. "Shall we pray?"

Ashtyn actually chokes on her drink, spraying water all over the tablecloth. She coughs as Carol pats her on the back. "Mother, when have we ever prayed at this table?"

Carol shoots her daughter a look as she hands her a napkin. "Ashtyn Marie, we have a guest. And we shall be respectful of whatever beliefs our guests have."

Drew bites back a smile. "It's okay, Carol. I don't have any religious beliefs that need to be practiced. Just very grateful for this dinner you made."

Carol lets out a breath as she wipes her forehead in relief. "Oh good, cause I didn't actually have a plan for what I was going to say." Drew laughs, the sound loud and bright in the room.

"You are ridiculous," Ashtyn says to her mom, shaking her head with laughter as she passes the bread basket around the table.

"You know, my parents actually used to pray at the dinner table when I was younger," Drew supplies. He remembers it clear as day, opening one eye during his father's prayer, seeing that Haley had opened her eye as well. He'd stick his tongue out at her, trying to make her laugh, kicking her under the table when it wouldn't work. And when he would eventually elicit a giggle out of her, their mother would shush them, a small smile on her face. The memory is one that brings him joy, despite the fact that their family isn't religious anymore.

"But you don't anymore?" Ashtyn asks, taking a sip of water.

"No, none of us do," Drew replies. He clears his throat when Carol and Ashtyn look at him like he should continue. "Back in the day, my parents used to be pretty active in the church. We'd go every Sunday, my sister and I dragging our feet, because we thought there was much more fun to be had on a Sunday morning than spending it in church. We went on and off the entirety of my life, until high school. When I, uh, came out as bisexual to my parents, they were extremely supportive. But, when the church found out, which is still a mystery to me *how* exactly they found out, they called us in for a meeting. They sat me and my parents down and told us that I wasn't allowed to be who I am. That there was something wrong with me." Drew hasn't told this story in a long, long time, and the words stick in his throat as the memory resurfaces, his fingers clenched around his silverware. "They told us, and I quote, 'You can go back to normal or leave the church.'"

Ashtyn's face is hard across the table, her hands balled into fists of anger. Carol looks shocked, a hand to her mouth. Drew lets out a shaky exhale. "I'll never forget the look on my dad's face when the pastor said that. He stood up, looked that pastor up and down, and said, 'A church that doesn't accept people for who they are is no church of mine.' And that was that. We never went back, and we stopped praying at the dinner table."

"Oh, Andrew," Carol says, sliding a hand across the table toward him. He takes it gratefully, smiling at her. "Your dad is right. Anyone that doesn't accept people for who they are is no friend of ours."

Drew feels a tear leak out the corner of his eye, and he wipes it away quickly. "Thank you, Carol." His gaze slides to Ashtyn, her mouth a thin, firm line.

"You tell me where this so-called pastor lives," she says, eyes dark. "I'll make sure he never speaks again."

Drew barks out a laugh. "He's dead, actually."

"Good. I hope he's rotting in Hell."

"Ashtyn Marie!" Carol exclaims. Her eyes are wide, but there's still a hint of a smile on her face.

"That is not the worst thing that has ever been said at this table, and you know it," Ashtyn counters.

Carol blushes. "You hush." She flicks a pea at her daughter, and it hits her directly on the forehead.

"Careful, Momma. Last time you started a food fight, Aunt Debra had a heart attack."

This time, it's Drew's turn to choke on his drink, eliciting a cackle out of Ashtyn. He wipes his mouth on his napkin and places his elbows on the table, his heart feeling lighter. "Okay, this I gotta hear."

* * *

Ashtyn tosses and turns in bed, unable to sleep, sheets sticking to her sweaty skin. She peels back the blanket and sits up, scrubbing her face with her hands. Her feet hit the bare floor, and she makes her way down the stairs toward the kitchen, not really sure what she's searching for. She stops when she sees the porch light on, a figure sitting in one of the rocking chairs. Drew's back is to her as he looks up at the night sky. Her heart clenches, remembering what he shared at dinner. The rage she felt for him was blinding. How did he keep that anger from taking hold in his heart? She would have punched that pastor right in the face if he was still alive.

She slides open the door as quietly as she can and slips onto the porch, settling into the chair next to him.

"Hey," he says, eyes to the sky. "Can't sleep either?"

"No," she admits. She pulls her knees up to her chest, wrapping her arms around them. The world is quiet except for the symphony of cricket chirps and the occasional owl hoot.

He turns to her slightly. "You okay?"

"Fine. You?"

"Fine."

They're silent for a moment. "Are we going to talk about it?" Drew asks quietly.

Ashtyn closes her eyes, sighing deeply. "No." She's such a coward. Nothing in this world scares her more than her feelings.

"So, that's it then?"

"What do you want from me, Drew?" she asks bitterly. She turns toward him. "It was fun. We got it out of our systems. Isn't that enough?"

He doesn't look at her, eyes permanently fixed on the sky. "So, what, we go back to normal?"

"This isn't normal?"

"No, Ashtyn," he says gruffly. "It's not."

The way he says it has her shivering despite the oppressive heat. "I can't give you what you want." She whispers it like a secret.

He finally turns fully to her. "When have I ever asked you for anything?"

She blinks, surprised by his question. Sure, he's flirted with her, teased her, flattered her... but he's never asked her for more. He's never pushed her into something she doesn't want. He's always been there when she's needed him.

"Friends," she whispers. "We're friends."

"Friends," he repeats, eyes going back to the sky. She wants to reach out and touch him, let him know she means it, but she doesn't. No, she lets that word hang in the air: *friends.* Like if she repeats it enough times, she'll actually believe it to be true. She'll finally believe that's all they'll ever be.

Friends.

Friends.

Friends.

She feels like the stupidest girl in the world.

Chapter 23

Drew is gone by the time Ashtyn wakes the next morning. The guest room door is slightly ajar, bed made and empty. She enters the kitchen, her mother sitting at the bar, doing her usual crossword.

"When did Drew leave?"

"Just a little while ago," her mother says. "He didn't want to wake you up. Said for us to have fun and not get into too much trouble."

Ashtyn smiles, but it doesn't reach her eyes. "Ah."

Her mom furrows her eyebrows together, pen twirling between her fingers. "Is there something you're not telling me?"

"Of course not," Ashtyn replies, pouring herself a cup of coffee.

"Okay, well then can I tell you that I think Drew is very cute?"

"Mom!"

"What? It's true. He's handy, too. And respectful. I like him."

"Great, you date him."

"Who said anything about dating? I'm talking about marriage."

"Jesus Christ, Mom," Ashtyn mutters into her coffee. "Just sell me off to the highest bidder."

Carol laughs, setting down her pen. "I'm just saying, I think he's a good guy."

"He's a great guy," Ashtyn says. "Doesn't mean I want to marry him."

"I don't think you want to marry anyone, really."

Something about her mother's words set her on edge. "So? Why does marriage have to be the ultimate goal?" Ashtyn snaps, sounding harsher than she means to. "Marriage ends in divorce. It ends in death. Maybe I don't want that."

Something like pain flickers across her mom's face. "It's okay to not want something. It's okay to never get married. But, don't fool yourself into thinking marriage is the enemy, when it's really a person you're mad at."

She's right. Ashtyn hates the idea of marriage because of Brandon. Because of her father. Because of Shiloh. Because of the pain she associates with it. Shiloh's pain at his divorce from Scarlett. Her mother's pain at the death of her spouse. Her own pain, for not being picked by Brandon. All this pain, not caused by marriage itself, but by the person in the marriage, sometimes through no fault of their own. Her father didn't choose to leave her mom. And Shiloh, Shiloh found Ava after his divorce. As for Brandon... Ashtyn's not sure where he is now, but she knows how she feels. How his marriage made her feel.

Ashtyn sighs, rubbing her temples. "Can you stop being the smartest woman on the planet?" she asks, laying her head on her mom's shoulder.

Carol chuckles, arm wrapping around her daughter. "Maybe when you stop being the world's most stubborn daughter."

Ashtyn grins. "You might be waiting a long time for that."

Her mom presses her forehead against her own. "So, what should we get up to this week?"

* * *

Ashtyn and her mom have the best week of their lives. They stay up late watching movies, eating junk food, and laughing more than they have in years. They talk about Ashtyn's dad, and she revels in the stories she's never heard before. She feels closer to him, just by talking about him, by reliving memories she thought she forgot.

Halfway through the week, Ava joins them, bringing Ash some clean clothes and a lecture. She was pissed when she heard Ashtyn hadn't come to her when they'd been relocated out of the hotel. But, she'd gotten over it pretty quickly when Ash invited her to spend the last few days with them.

The temptation to tell her best friend about what happened with Drew eats her alive. She doesn't keep secrets from Ava. But, she refrains, knowing how big of a deal Ava will make it out to be. Besides, it's never going to happen again. Even if it had been spectacular. It doesn't matter. It's *not* happening again.

Friends. Friends. Friends.

"Earth to Ashtyn," Ava says, waving her hand in front of Ash's face.

"Sorry," she replies, shaking her head. "Drifted off for a minute."

"Is it because we're talking about the reunion?"

Ashtyn rolls her eyes. "Yes."

"I still think you should ask Drew to go with you."

"And why would I do that?"

"I don't know. Maybe you could pretend he's your boyfriend. You know, in case the devil shows up."

"Gross," Ashtyn says, even though her heart skips a beat at the thought. Stupid, treacherous heart. "Besides, you told me he hasn't RSVP'd."

"Yeah, but it's not until late September. He could RSVP late."

"Oh goody."

Ava winces. "Sorry."

Carol must notice her daughter's annoyance, because she changes the subject. "So, Ava, how's the new place?"

Ava blushes. "It's good. It definitely took some getting used to. It's weird not being able to see Ash every day." She reaches her hand out and takes Ashtyn's.

"I'm glad you're here," Ashtyn says, squeezing her friend's hand.

Ava gives her a small smile. "I am too. I miss you."

"I miss you more."

"Geez, you'd think you two lived on different continents," Carol teases. Ashtyn tosses a pillow gently at her mother's head, making her laugh. "Don't make me ground you."

"Go ahead. I'm leaving tomorrow anyway."

Carol sighs. "Don't remind me."

Ashtyn gets up off her spot on the floor and sits next to her mom. She wraps her in a warm embrace. "I promise I'll come visit more often."

"You better."

"Don't worry, Carol," Ava says, joining in on the hug. "I'll drag her here if I need to."

Ashtyn pinches Ava's side, and she squeals. "Hey, no tickling!"

"Then quit teasing me!"

"I wasn't teasing! Teasing is when I make fun of you for getting so drunk that you passed out in—" But Ava doesn't have a chance to finish, because Ashtyn tackles her off the couch. She shrieks, and the girls tumble to the floor, laughter echoing throughout the house.

* * *

Drew hears the knob of the front door turn as he pushes the new couch into position. He's finished just as Ashtyn steps into the living room.

"Wow, nice upgrade," she says, dropping her bags to the floor. The previous couch was ruined by the flooding, so Drew had gone out and gotten a new one before she arrived home. How was she supposed to watch movies if she didn't have a couch?

"You like it?" he asks.

"It's bigger than the old one," she says, inspecting the new sectional.

She runs a hand over the material before flopping onto it. "I like it."

He swallows at the sight of her sprawled on the couch. *Friends*, he has to remind himself. He would take anything she gives him, even if it's just friendship. But now she's here. She's back home. *This doesn't change things.* He repeats it over and over again in his head like a mantra.

"So," he starts. He clears his throat when he realizes he doesn't know what to say.

"So," she repeats, sitting up.

"Did you, uh, have a good time with your mom?"

"I did. Did you... have a good time by yourself?"

"Eh, it was alright," he says with a shrug. They stare at each other for a moment, silence settling thick in the room.

"Well," she says, "I'm glad to be home."

"Yeah, me too," he agrees. He doesn't point it out, but his heart soars at the use of "home." *Home.* This is home to her. He doesn't have time to think too hard about it, because she clears her throat.

"Um, I've been meaning to ask you something," she says. He tenses, not knowing where this conversation is headed. "Remember last month when your sister was here, and she mentioned my ten-year reunion?"

"Vaguely," Drew replies.

"Well—" She stops, frowning. She stares at the wall next to the TV, where a new movie shelf sits. "Is that..."

"Oh, yeah!" Drew exclaims, coming around the couch to stand in front of the shelf. "The shelf had a lot of water damage. It was sagging really bad, so I went out and got a new one. It's the same one we picked out at Target."

"Drew," she starts, hand coming up to her throat.

"Some of the DVDs on the bottom shelf got ruined, so I went out and replaced them. I tried to get the exact copies you had, but some were really old, so I had to get an updated cover. I had to go to like three different Walmarts to find all the *X-Men* movies, but I did it!"

Ashtyn looks up at him in amazement. "There were like, twenty DVDs on that shelf," she says.

"Thirty-two," he corrects. He looks at the floor like he's embarrassed that he put all this effort into something. "It's not a big deal. Most of them were easy to fin—" He's cut off as Ashtyn crushes him into a hug.

"Thank you," she whispers into his chest. His arms go around her, heart hammering wildly.

"Of course," he says. He lays his cheek against the top of her head, reveling in the feeling.

After a moment, she sniffles and steps out of his embrace. He hates letting her go. "You were going to ask me something?" he probes, stuffing his hands in his pockets.

"Oh, right," she says. "Um, my ten-year reunion. It's coming up in September, and I was wondering if you, uh, wanted to go with me?"

"Go with you?"

"Yeah, you heard me." She crosses her arms against her chest, like she's closing herself off from him again. He desperately wants to hug her.

Drew bites back a smile, opting for a teasing tone. "You mean, like a date?"

Ashtyn narrows her eyes at him. "Don't push it."

He raises his hands in innocence. "Okay, okay. Sure, I'll go with you. Any particular reason you're asking me?

She takes a deep breath. "Because we're friends. And I might need support if... if *he's* there."

She doesn't have to say his name for Drew to know she's talking about Brandon. He clenches his fists in his pockets. "And you're asking me? As friends?"

"Yes, I'm asking you," she says, almost exasperated. "Don't make it a big deal. This is what friends do."

"Okay."

"Okay?"

"Okay. I'll go with you." He can see some of the tension from her shoulders drop. "As friends."

She lets out a breath. "Perfect, thank you. Now, I've got some laundry to do." She gathers her bags and heads toward her room. "Oh, before I forget, we're hosting Daisy's engagement party here in a few weeks."

Drew bites back a smile as he watches her enter her bedroom. She doesn't close the door behind her.

AUGUST

Chapter 24

"Oh my gosh, Ashtyn, thank you so much for hosting," Daisy gushes. Her stunning engagement ring glistens under the lamp light. "It's amazing."

"Of course. But, honestly, thank Drew. He helped decorate a lot."

A knowing smile lights up Daisy's face. "Who knew you two would ever learn to live together?"

Ashtyn huffs out a laugh. "So everyone keeps saying."

Their friends gather in Ashtyn and Drew's apartment to celebrate Derek and Daisy's engagement. Ashtyn and Drew have been mostly normal for the past few weeks. They watch movies together. They eat dinner together. They even started playing Overcooked again. But they *never* touch. It's become an unspoken rule between them ever since that night in the hotel. They do not touch each other, because Ashtyn knows that if she touches him, she won't be able to stop. And friends do not touch each other like how she wants to touch him.

She sees him across the room, talking with Shiloh and Derek, head thrown back in laughter. She thinks about his throat, licking up the length of it, to where she can claim his mouth with hers...

"Ashtyn?" Daisy's voice startles her out of her fantasy.

She turns her attention back to her friend. "Yeah?"

"I asked how you guys are doing after the busted pipe."

"Oh, right! Yeah, we're great. You can hardly even tell the roof caved in," she says, pointing to the spot where the leak was. The maintenance men had done an excellent job fixing up the damage. She doesn't tell her friends about Drew buying every one of her DVDs that got ruined. No, that was just for her to know. To cherish.

"Hey," Ava says, joining the girls, drink in hand. "Great party, Ash."

"Okay, fine, I'll take all the credit," Ashtyn teases. In all honesty, Drew had done most of the decorating. Even though he's not as close to Derek or Daisy as Ashtyn is, he'd taken charge of the party planning, turning their apartment into streamer heaven. Large, inflatable engagement ring balloons litter the floor. It had been a hassle to blow them all up, but seeing Daisy's smile as she entered the room was worth it.

"Honestly," Daisy says. "Thank you for doing this. We feel very lucky to have such amazing friends."

"Is Ashtyn taking credit for all my hard work again?" Drew asks, joining the group. He slings an arm around Ashtyn nonchalantly, and her skin is instantly ablaze. *We're not supposed to touch*, she thinks to herself. Touching is dangerous. It's off limits. Did he miss the memo? Or is he just pretending everything is normal in front of their friends? Trying to act like they're not tiptoeing around each other?

If anyone notices her stiffen underneath his touch, they don't let on. Her body feels like a bomb, like she might explode if Drew shifts even an inch. But he doesn't. His arm is relaxed but firm around her shoulders. Like they're just two best friends...

Jordan and Brooke join their little circle, and Jordan whistles under his breath at the sight of them. "Wow, that is something I never thought I'd see." Brooke smacks her husband lightly, but her eyes give away that she feels the same.

"That's how I feel about you turning in any of your projects on time," Drew quips back at his friend. He's casual about it, but he removes his arm from Ashtyn's shoulders. It leaves her feeling like something's missing. *See*, this is why they're not supposed to touch.

Jordan flips him off, laughing. "Hey, I'm just glad you two could put your swords down and inhabit the same space without killing each other."

"Who says we haven't tried?" Ashtyn asks, smiling sweetly. Drew snorts into his drink, knowing damn well they've done way more than attempted murder.

Before Jordan can retort, Derek sidles up to his fiancée and wraps an arm around her. "So, before it gets too late, Daisy and I have a small request." The group's ears perk up, except for Ava, who smiles like a madwoman, bouncing on her toes. Derek clears his throat. "Since it was the game Blockbuster that ultimately brought Daisy and I together, we'd like to play a round tonight. If that's okay with everyone. Same teams as that night."

Ava squeals as she unveils the game from her bag. Ashtyn feels her blood run cold. The same teams as that night... that was when she and Drew were paired together. They'd won their first round, but Derek and Daisy ultimately won the game. But that first round with him, she'd crushed him into a hug for getting the answers right. It was completely out of her comfort zone, but she'd been so excited about winning that she threw all her rules out the window. It was ultimately the start of the Ashtyn and Drew saga.

"This is totally unfair," Parker says, overhearing Derek's request from his spot on the couch. "Ava and Shiloh always win now."

Ava sticks her tongue out at her friend. "We'll go easy on you."

They do not, in fact, go easy on them. It is absolutely neck and neck, all teams having a similar number of points for the first time in what seems like forever. Everyone has upped their game lately. Even Ashtyn and Drew get into a rhythm. It helps that Drew's been watching way more movies with her lately, joining Sunday movie nights.

As Ashtyn looks at her cards, she feels her confidence start to shrink.

She looks at Drew, narrowing her eyes at him. "Okay, I'm going to need you to lock the fuck in. One of these is really hard."

"Hey! No hints!" Shiloh yells. Ashtyn whips him a look that tells him to be quiet. He's smart and does exactly that.

"Okay," she breathes. "Start the timer." They've always played loosey goosey with the rules of this game, making the quotes for the movie incredibly obscure, so only their partner will know what they're talking about. Nobody ever complains, though. It's what makes the game fun for them. "Okay, one word: bowling."

Drew frowns, thinking for a moment, then snaps his fingers. "*The Big Lebowski.*"

"Yes! Okay, quote it: This movie stars the most fuckable version of Jeff Goldblum we've ever seen."

"*Independence Day!*" he screams, jumping up and down with excitement.

Ashtyn has to bite her lip to keep herself from laughing. They'd both been drooling over Jeff Goldblum's character in that movie not two weeks ago. He was, arguably, hotter in that movie than *Jurassic Park.* She shakes her head and focuses. "Okay, charades." The timer is ticking down. This was the hard one. She'd made him watch the movie, but he fell asleep halfway through. This one was risky to choose for charades, but she's ready. It's one of her favorites, after all.

She starts her Oscar-worthy performance, pretending to hold up a handheld camera to her face. She begins to fake cry, staring into the make-believe camera, sniffling heavily. She wails, trying to sell the performance to the best of her ability. She even whips up a few fake tears.

Drew is looking at her like she's crazy. "What the fuck is that supposed to be?"

Ashtyn wails louder, but Drew isn't understanding, shaking his head back and forth with furrowed brows. She groans and looks around, trying to figure out a new plan. It clicks a second later, and she runs toward the opposite wall, where she stops and stands, stock still, face against the wall. She stares and stares at that wall, back ramrod straight and hands at her side. She can practically feel Ava jumping up and down, knowing the answer.

"Oh my God," Drew says, something clicking at her posture. "It's that stupid fucking movie I fell asleep while watching. And when I woke up, that guy was just staring at the wall like a weirdo... what the fuck was that?"

Ashtyn peeks behind her and sees Ava actually holding her hand over her mouth, almost bursting with the information. She can steal the answer if Drew doesn't get it, cementing her and Shiloh's win. Drew rubs his forehead furiously, time ticking down. "Oh, what was it called? Something project... stupid idiot project? Dumb kids in the woods? Project, project," he repeats, trying to figure it out. The timer almost runs out when he snaps his head up and yells, "*The Blair Witch Project!*"

"Yes!" Ashtyn screams, turning and launching herself at him. He catches her instantly, picking her up and spinning her around. She doesn't even care about the no touching rule. "We got the last horror card! We win!"

Everyone's mouths drop open, either in shock that Ashtyn and Drew just won, or that they're still wrapped around each other willingly. He sets her back on her feet, but she doesn't step away from him.

"When did y'all get so good at this game?" Ava asks, a sparkle in her eyes.

"You told me to watch more movies, Ave. So, I did," Drew replies, not letting Ashtyn go. The longer he holds onto her, the longer she wants to jump his bones. She untangles herself from him gently and takes a small step away, a blush tingeing her cheeks.

"We're cheating," Ashtyn says flippantly. "We got earpieces to feed each other information." She's kidding, trying to diffuse the situation, but no one seems to take the bait.

"Looks like we're about to have new champions," Derek says, smiling. "Although, it is mine and Daisy's party. Shouldn't that automatically make us win?"

The group groans playfully as Derek kisses his fiancée. "I'm gonna kick y'all out early if you keep it up," Ashtyn teases, knowing she would never do such a thing.

"I demand a rematch!" Ava declares.

They rematch three more times, Ashtyn and Drew winning every single round. It's as if the universe gives them only the best cards, just to prove to their friends how good of a team they make. As if the universe is urging them together. It's ridiculous, honestly.

"We're going to have to start switching up teams again if y'all keep this up," Parker teases, setting his glass on the counter as they begin to clean up. It's late, time having slipped away while they played round after round of Blockbuster.

"Yeah, good luck separating those two," Ashtyn chides, gesturing to where Ava and Shiloh are canoodling in the corner, lost in each other.

Parker laughs and wraps an arm around his husband. "Remember when we were in that phase?"

"You mean we aren't still?" Damien asks, pressing a kiss to Parker's cheek. Parker blushes, and Ashtyn smiles at her friends. Her heart aches, ever so slightly, as she looks away from all the kissing couples.

It's nearing two AM when everyone finally gathers up their belongings and heads out the door, thanking them for a great party. When everyone's gone, Ashtyn sighs and hops up onto the kitchen counter, leaning against the cabinets.

Drew throws away the last of the beer bottles, unbuttoning the top button of his shirt when he's finished. He stands across from her on the opposite counter, lazy smile on his face. "We make a good team," he says.

Ashtyn crosses her arms as she looks at him. "We got easy cards."

"You really think *Lawrence of Arabia* was an easy card?"

She snorts, knowing it wasn't. No one, in the history of their time playing this game, has ever been able to successfully guess *Lawrence of Arabia*. Never. Until tonight. "Lucky guess," she breathes. Drew frowns and takes a step toward her. She gives him a warning glare. "Stay where you are."

"Why?"

"Because if you get too close, I'm going to want to touch you." She's not sure if it's the wine she's consumed or the high of winning every round of Blockbuster that has her revealing this to him, but it doesn't matter. "And we're... we're not supposed to touch each other. Friends don't touch."

Drew's frown deepens, and he takes another step closer to her. "We've been touching each other all night."

"I know," Ashtyn says, eyes never leaving his. "And we shouldn't have. It makes it harder to..." But she trails off as he closes the distance between them, stepping in between her legs. His hands sit on the top of the counter, bracketing her hips. She inhales sharply, very aware of how close they are. Her eyes fall closed at the feeling of his breath on her neck. "Harder to..."

"Harder to what?"

To resist you, she thinks. She swallows and looks into his blue eyes. "No touching."

"No touching?"

"Correct. It's supposed to be an unspoken rule. I thought you knew about it."

"I don't know about any unspoken rules." His lips graze her earlobe, and she arches her back, her breasts just barely grazing his chest. Her nipples pinch under her dress, aching for him.

He pulls back, mouth inches from her. "So, no more touching?"

She's barely able to shake her head, trying to stand firm in her decision. "No more touching."

He chuckles, low and deep, the sound going straight to her bloodstream. "You really think I need to touch you to drive you crazy?"

Her nostrils flare, and her eyes widen at his words. He's taunting her. Tormenting her. Two can play this game. They're good at games, apparently. "Is this how you want to play?" she asks, running a hand down her neck, dipping low into the neckline of her dress. She pulls it down so her bra is exposed, and she runs a hand down her breast, just barely grazing her nipple through the fabric. Drew's eyes widen, and his breathing becomes ragged as he realizes what she's doing. Her hand travels lower and lower until she hitches up her dress and fingers the edge of her panties.

"Ashtyn," he warns, voice low.

She dips her finger inside her underwear, stretching the fabric aside. "Who said anything about touching myself?" Oh, she's playing a *very* dangerous game right now. But her desire has been building all night, and she needs release. Friends don't touch each other, but they can easily touch themselves while the other watches.

Drew lets out a breath, hands staying planted on the counter. His eyes burn into hers as she touches herself, feeling how wet she already is. She gasps slightly, and Drew's pupils dilate. His hands turn to fists, and she can see his cock straining against his pants.

"You can touch yourself too," she says, eyes fluttering as she begins to circle her clit with her finger. God, she wishes his mouth was on her, but she won't give in.

He groans, but he doesn't move to touch himself. He just keeps looking at her, breath hot at her neck, lips so close to her skin. He's restraining himself, not giving in to temptation.

"Enjoying the view?" She's trying to tease, but her pleasure is building as she works herself, and she throws her head back, smacking it on the cabinet lightly. It doesn't faze either of them.

"You have no fucking idea," he replies, voice gruff in her ear. "You are so goddamn beautiful."

The temptation to grab him and kiss him is intoxicating, but she resists. Her finger circles her clit faster and faster, her breathing becoming ragged as her pleasure builds. She's already so close, it's almost embarrassing. But with the way Drew is looking at her, nothing feels embarrassing right now. No, right now, she only feels desired.

"Look at me," he says. Her eyes slide to his, their mouths only millimeters apart. "Look at me when you finish."

His words tip her over the edge, and she orgasms, their eyes locked tight as she does. He groans as he watches her come undone, but his hands never move off the counter. Her orgasm is long and drawn out, washing over her entire body. When it's over, her limbs slacken, and she feels like she could melt right off the counter. She's warm and satiated, tucked safely in the presence of Drew.

"Still think we don't make a good team?" he asks lightly, breathing hard.

She smiles and laughs softly. "Goodnight, Drew," she says, sliding off the counter and stepping around him. She doesn't look back at him as she makes her way to her room. She can feel his eyes on her the entire way.

* * *

He's barely touching himself before he's finishing, the spray from the shower washing over him. Holy fuck. Ashtyn fucking King. Drew's orgasm spills out of him as he thinks of her touching herself. The way she looked when she climaxed, her pupils dilated and her mouth moaning. God, he'd wanted to touch her so badly. Now, as he holds himself, he can't get her out of his head. He hasn't been able to get her out of his head since the day they met, but this is different. This is so, so different. This feels dangerous. It feels... real. It feels like more than friends.

He wants her. Not just physically, but in every single way he can have her. He wants to wake up with her next to him. He wants to kiss her every single night before bed. He wants to cheer on her accomplishments. He wants to be the person she comes to when she's feeling sad. He wants to show her every star in the sky. He wants to care for her, love her. He wants every single second the universe will give him with her. He wants it all. The good, the bad, the ugly. All of it.

And he knows... he knows it's just a pipe dream. He knows it'll never happen. Knows she'll never choose him. She's said as much. *No touching... just friends.*

So, when he gets out of the shower, heart aching and pounding, he gets into bed and opens his phone. The guy he matched with on Tinder still sits in his inbox, message unread. He opens it and replies.

Chapter 25

"You have a date?" Shiloh looks at Drew from across the restaurant table like he's crazy, eyebrows raised and mouth slightly agape.

"Uh, yes, that's what I just said," Drew replies.

"You're acting like it's a crime," Mattie teases his brother, signaling the waitress for another round of beers.

Shiloh crosses his arms. "I'm just trying to make sense of how this all happened."

Drew sighs. "Tinder. Tinder is how it happened."

Shiloh leans back in his chair, bemused expression still on his face. "I guess I'm just surprised you said yes."

"Why, exactly?"

"Well, because of Ash—"

"I'm gonna stop you right there," Drew says, holding up his hand to his friend. Mattie watches the exchange with curiosity, his eyes flicking back and forth between them. "Ashtyn and I are just friends." He hates that fucking word. If he has to hear it again, he might just explode.

"Since when?" Mattie asks. Drew sends him a death glare, but it doesn't faze Mattie. He just grins. "What? It's a serious question. You've been at each other's throats since the day you met."

"Since... since whenever! We're friends. Just friends. Hence why I'm going on a date with someone else." He doesn't know why he's getting flustered. *Nothing* is supposed to fluster him. Except Ashtyn King.

Shiloh and Mattie share a knowing look. "Right," Shiloh says. "Just friends. Just like Ava and I were 'just friends.'" He puts air quotes around the phrase.

Drew narrows his eyes at his best friend. "You were obsessed with Ava the second you saw her."

"Brother, what's been the past year with you and Ashtyn then?"

"That was before. She's made her intentions clear, and I backed off. She's not interested."

Shiloh scoffs. "You two are ridiculous."

"Just because you're madly in love again doesn't mean you can start dishing out dating advice."

"Can I?" Mattie quips.

"No," Shiloh and Drew both say at the same time. "Unless you're going to man up and admit that you've had a crush on my sister for the last ten years, I don't want to hear it," Drew replies.

Mattie's eyes go wide. "Woah, woah, woah! Who said anything about crushing on someone's sister? That's insane." His face turns beet red as he chugs the rest of his beer.

Drew smirks. "Yeah, that's what I thought."

"By the way," Shiloh starts. "Haley told me to tell you that you owe her ten bucks."

Mattie sinks further into his chair, arms crossed over his chest. "No, she owes *me* ten bucks," he mutters.

Drew laughs and sips his beer. "Look, things between Ashtyn and I... they're complicated." At least that's the truth. "Obviously we're both attracted to each other, but she doesn't want anything more and—"

"Wait," Mattie says, holding up his hand, eyes going wide. "Something more? So, you're saying something *has* happened."

"No, that's not—"

"Holy shit, it has!" Shiloh interrupts, smacking the table. "Look at your fucking face."

Drew grips the table so hard, he's afraid it might snap in half. He can feel the blush splayed across his cheeks as he tries to avoid his friends' eyes. If anyone can read him like a book, it's Shiloh and Mattie. "Okay, one time—"

"Let me guess, it was in the hotel, wasn't it? I told Ava she should have pressed harder to have Ashtyn stay with us. I mean—"

"Shiloh!" Drew exclaims, interrupting him. Shiloh's eyes widen, his mouth shutting. "Can you let me explain?" Shiloh places his elbows on the table and makes a "go forth" motion with his hands. Drew knows how much Ashtyn means to both Shiloh and Ava. How protective they are of her and vice versa. He lets out a breath, the noise of the restaurant a dull chatter around them. "We slept together *once*. It wasn't... it wasn't just some random hook up. It meant something. But, she doesn't want more. She's still fucked up from her past, and as much as I want to help her move on, I can't if she's not ready. So, we're friends. Okay? End of story."

"Friends who've slept together."

"I don't need your fucking permission to sleep with someone," Drew counters, an edge to his voice.

Shiloh sighs. "I didn't mean it like that." He pauses, hand rubbing his chin. "Has she told you about him?"

"Yes," Drew says, his anger toward Brandon roiling in his stomach.

"Then you know." When Drew only raises his eyebrows, Shiloh continues. "You know why she's held you at a distance since the moment you two met."

"Yes," Drew replies softly. "I understand why."

"And this is why you're going on a date with someone else?" Mattie asks, inserting himself into the conversation again.

"Yes," Drew grits out, angrily sipping his beer. "What do they say?

Plenty of fucking fish in the sea."

Shiloh's contemplative as he looks at his friend. "Give her time. She might still be healing."

Drew knows that Shiloh understands this better than anyone. He just nods, his head full of Ashtyn and what they *could* be. No, he won't lead himself down that path. It will only end in heartache. And he's not sure he could handle it if it was *her* breaking his heart.

"You know what I think this conversation needs?" Mattie asks, a mischievous smile on his face as he changes the subject. "Shots!"

* * *

"You have a date," Ava blanches, like Ashtyn just said the most insane thing of her life.

"Yes?" Ashtyn forms it like a question, as if she's just as confused as Ava.

"With whom?" Brooke asks.

"Uh, Spencer," Ashtyn admits, feeling her cheeks heat. She pets Jess absentmindedly, trying to find comfort with the cat. They're all spread out on Ava's living room floor, yarn spilling every which way. They are trying to learn to crochet, much to Ashtyn's chagrin.

"The guy who literally ditched you halfway through Valentine's Day!?" Ava exclaims, dropping her crochet hook in shock. "You've got to be kidding me."

"That was one hundred percent Drew's fault. Besides, I ran into Spencer at the store the other day," Ashtyn says. "I apologized, and we just kind of agreed to... try again." What Ashtyn doesn't say is that when Drew told her he had a date next week, she'd lost her goddamn mind. She knows, realistically, that of course he should date other people. But in that moment, she'd been so overcome with jealousy that she stormed out of the apartment, grumbling about needing ingredients for dinner. And when she just so happened to run into Spencer during her tirade, she just couldn't help herself. Not her best moment, if she's truthful with herself...

"Try again," Ava says, parroting Ashtyn's words.

"Correct." Ashtyn dangles the yarn in the air for Jess to bat at playfully.

"You'll have to make sure Drew is far away from that date," Brooke teases.

"He will be. He has his own date that night."

Both girls snap their heads to Ashtyn in sync. "What?"

"You both have a date on the same night," Ava says.

"Jesus Christ, are y'all hard of hearing tonight? Yes, that's what I said. I don't see what the big deal is." Ava bites her lip, obviously censoring herself. Ashtyn narrows her eyes at her friend. "Spit it out."

"Spit what out?"

"Whatever it is you're dying to say."

Ava sighs heavily. "I'm just glad you and Drew are friends, that's all."

Ashtyn rolls her eyes. "You guys act like we used to be mortal enemies."

"Well, it kind of felt like that," Brooke says, avoiding her friend's eyes as her fingers fly in a blur of yarn.

"Y'all are so dramatic."

The girls are silent for a moment until Ava speaks up. "What changed?"

Ashtyn's head whips up at her friend's words. "Wha-what do you mean?"

"What changed?"

"Nothing changed," Ashtyn says, swallowing. "We just got comfortable as roommates. As friends"

Ava looks right through her, eyes piercing, and Ashtyn shrinks under her glare. She pushes down the cold hard truth. They slept together, that's what changed. She got to know him, the real Drew, and she likes him. She *likes* him, that's what changed. But she can never admit that to herself, let alone her best friend. No, she can't admit that to a single soul. She ripped herself open in front of him, and he didn't back away. He saw her childhood home, her mom, and he looked like he belonged there. It scared the ever-loving shit out of her.

Ashtyn decides she hates crocheting and discards her project to the side. She lets Jess have her way with the yarn when Ava asks, "Did you sleep together?"

Ashtyn freezes, head held down, so she can't look at Ava. "N-no," she stutters.

"You did, didn't you?" The way Ava asks, like she already knows the truth, has Ashtyn looking up.

She swallows the urge to lie. "Once." She can't believe she's admitting it.

Ava sucks in a breath. "Ashtyn."

"I don't want a lecture," Ashtyn mutters. "We did it once, got it out of our systems, and now we're just friends. Okay?"

"That's why you two were so comfortable around each other at Daisy's engagement party," Brooke says softly, eyes still on her yarn.

"That's ridiculous," Ashtyn admonishes. "We're just used to each other. We're roommates, okay? That's it."

"Roommates that sleep together," Ava mumbles.

"We're not like you and Shiloh, Ave," Ashtyn says. "We're not meant to be."

Ava looks at her, sadness on her face. "But what if you are?"

Ashtyn scoffs and rolls her eyes. "Can we change the subject please? I'm tired of talking about Drew." Neither Ava nor Brooke say anything, their hands busy with their crocheting. The vibe of the room has shifted, and Ashtyn sighs.

Ava must sense Ashtyn's discomfort, because she says, "The only other thing I have to complain about is that we have to go back to work soon."

"You know, some of us still have to work over the summer," Brooke says, nudging her.

"What a sad life you must live."

Brooke cackles and throws a ball of yarn at Ava's head, which Jess chases greedily. Ashtyn smiles at her friends, grateful they're willing to pick a new topic of discussion. Talking about sleeping with Drew was not something she wanted to discuss with her friends. Instead, she's happy for this time they've created for themselves, to just be. She remembers when she got to see her friends every single day. Now, she's lucky if she sees them once a week.

"I love you guys!" she blurts. Ava and Brooke turn toward her, their own projects now discarded.

"And we love you," Brooke replies, a soft smile on her face. She scooches closer to Ashtyn, so she can wrap an arm around her. "No matter what, okay?" Ashtyn nods, letting her friend hug her.

Brooke sighs. "I actually have something I want to tell you guys."

"You're pregnant!?" Ava blurts, eyes wide.

Brooke chuckles. "No, not yet. But, we are planning on trying soon."

"Brooke," Ashtyn marvels, a smile erupting over her face. "Oh my god."

Ava squeals, launching herself across the room toward the girls. "Does this mean we can be honorary aunties?"

"Hopefully, yes," Brooke replies. "It was actually at Derek and Daisy's engagement party that I decided I was ready. Jordan's been ready, but I was still a little hesitant. But then, seeing all of our friends happy that night, I just realized I was ready. That I wanted to start a family."

Ava has tears in her eyes at Brooke's words. "Oh my god, Brooke!

This is so exciting! Now, I *have* to learn to crochet. I have to make baby Torres a blanket! Or a hat. Ooh, or little baby socks!"

Brooke laughs. "Well, you'll have plenty of time."

Ava snatches the yarn away from Jess, who's been chasing it across the room. "We have to save it, Jessica. We need this for baby clothes!" Jess lets out a pitiful meow and slinks over to Ashtyn, who gives her a new ball of yarn to play with.

"Look at that, Ashtyn's already got the role of Fun Aunt," Brooke says with a smile.

Ashtyn throws her head back in laughter. "What does that leave you with, Ave?"

Ava sticks her tongue out at her friend. "I can be the Fun Aunt, too."

"In all actuality, I'll probably be the perpetually single Aunt."

"Hey, you never know, maybe this Spencer guy is the one," Ava counters.

The thought actually makes Ashtyn sick. Sure, Spencer is a nice guy, but he's not… forever material. At least, not for her. She's not sure if she'll ever find someone that's meant to be hers forever. Instead of saying any of that, she fakes a smile and says, "Yeah, maybe."

"Speaking of 'the one,'" Brooke starts. "Ave, how are you and Shiloh doing?"

Ava blushes deeply. "We're good," she says, a fondness in her voice that warms Ashtyn's heart. "God, I love him so much."

"And the future?" Brooke probes.

"You know, before we got together, he used to tell me that he never saw himself getting married again. At first, I thought I couldn't live with that. Like, I *had* to get married. But, ever since falling in love with him, I'd be okay never getting married. Loving him and being with him is enough. It will always be enough."

Hearing her friend, who loves so hard and deeply, say that… it moves something within Ashtyn. "You're not scared?" she asks quietly.

Ava looks up, smile on her face. "Not anymore. Not with him. Never with him."

Her words ring in Ashtyn's ears. *Not anymore.*

Brooke and Ava continue talking, but Ashtyn isn't listening anymore. She just keeps replaying the last few months with Drew in her head, over and over again. Every little thing he's ever done to keep her safe and cared for. And then she thinks of her upcoming date with Spencer and the dread it fills her with.

We're not meant to be.

But what if you are?

Chapter 26

Drew can smell Ashtyn's perfume before she even leaves her bedroom. The sweet, floral scent drifts through their shared space, intoxicating him. God, he would drown in her if he could. He would do a lot of things if he could.

As he swipes up his keys from the coffee table, she walks into the hallway. They both freeze, staring at each other. She's wearing a pale blue sundress and heels that make her at least five inches taller than her normal short stature. Her pale, creamy skin is on full display, her red hair pulled up to expose her face. She blinks at him, makeup done to perfection, lips pink and glossy. Drew doesn't say anything as he swallows all his desire and shoves it deep, deep down.

"You look nice," she says, breaking the tension. Drew snorts and shoves his hands into his Chinos.

"Not nearly as nice as you," he replies.

There's a hint of a smile on her face. "You think?" She twirls, and as the dress fans around her thighs, Drew has to suck in a breath.

He's barely able to manage a strangled, "Yes."

"Well, I'll probably be out late tonight. Don't wait up."

As she clacks away from him, Drew can't help but think what it would be like if it was *him* that she was meeting. He can picture it so clearly, standing in a restaurant, seeing her fire-red hair first. Then, her perfect face, smiling shyly as she spots him. Her eyes brightening, footsteps hurrying toward him, as if she can't wait to be with him. And he'd meet her halfway, taking her in his arms, kissing those cherry lips, and he'd melt. He'd melt right into her, not caring who saw. She'd pull back, a blush tingeing her cheeks, and look up at him, eyes sparkling. "Hi, you," she'd whisper. He'd take her in, look her up and down for hours and say...

"You look beautiful." He says to the closed front door. All that remains is the lingering smell of her perfume. She's gone, off to meet someone who is *not* him. Someone who will never be him...

The buzzing of his phone stops his spiral, and he looks down at the message. Shit, he's late.

* * *

"Thanks again for giving me another chance," Ashtyn says, absolutely hating the way it sounds coming out of her mouth. Desperate, pleading, weak. She doesn't look at Spencer as she scans the menu, fingers gripped tightly around it.

"Ah, one bad date doesn't have to define us," Spencer says flippantly. The word "*us*" sets her on edge. The menu bends as her grip tightens even more.

Ashtyn bites her lip, trying to forget the fact that Drew is on a date with someone else across town. When she'd seen him, dress shirt slightly unbuttoned, shorts hugging every inch of his ass, and muscled legs on display, she'd almost stumbled in her heels. Her breath had caught in her throat, her heart pounding so fast she was afraid it would burst right out of her chest, bleeding and aching in front of him. And then he'd know. He'd know how much she wants him. How much she... cares for him.

She shakes her head, clearing her thoughts of Drew. No, she's here with Spencer. She's happy, she tries to reiterate to herself. She's so happy to have been given this second chance.

Spencer clears his throat awkwardly. "So, what have you been up to?"

Ashtyn swallows, trying to muster the courage not to run away from the table. "Um, well, I moved."

"Oh, that's fun," Spencer replies, smiling.

No, actually, it's not fun, she thinks. Not when you're living with the person you're supposed to hate, but instead desperately want to kiss. Instead of saying that, she just gives him a tightlipped smile and no other information.

"Um," he starts. "How's work?"

"I've been on summer break," she says. "I go back next week."

"Oh, right, duh!" Spencer says, snapping his fingers. "Teacher, right?"

"Yeah."

At her lackluster response, he goes back to perusing the menu. The silence that settles over the table is awkward. Shit, what is she doing? This was a terrible idea. She needs to be more enthusiastic. More endearing. "Uh, what about you?" she asks, trying to fill her voice with interest. "What have you been up to?"

"Oh," Spencer starts, as if he wasn't expecting her to ask him about himself. "I've been good. Working a lot."

Shit, what is it that he does again? She cannot, for the life of her, remember what it is he does for a living. Instead of asking, she just nods, biting her lip.

This is going to be a long, long night.

* * *

"Hey, sorry I'm late," Drew breathes as he slips into the chair across from his date. "Traffic was a nightmare."

"It's okay," Sean replies, smiling softly. Never, in the history of his life, has Drew been late for a date. He blames it on Ashtyn, seeing her in that blue dress, nailing him to the floor in a state of perpetual shock and angst.

"It's not okay," Drew says. "It'll never happen again." As if there will be another date after this. *Probably not*, he thinks to himself. Sean's probably already written him off.

Sean smiles again, as if nothing ever bothers him. "Trust me, I've had way worse on a first date." He's cute, with a sleeve of tattoos covering his bicep, something that would normally make Drew flush with desire. Instead, he's so flustered that he barely notices until now.

"Still, I apologize," Drew says, taking a sip of the water that's already on the table. He lifts it toward Sean. "To starting over?"

Sean clinks his class against Drew's. "Sure. I'm Sean."

"Drew. Nice to meet you." They share a smile, and Drew tries desperately to forget all about Ashtyn and the date she's currently on across town.

They're at a crowded sports bar, Sean's choice, and Drew can already feel the noise start to grate on his nerves. Normally, he thrives in these kinds of conditions, but he's on edge, courtesy of Ashtyn. His normal charm and swagger have been dulled at the edges, just waiting until they can get home and banter with Ashtyn again.

Ashtyn. Ashtyn. Ashtyn. She won't get out of his mind. All his synapses are firing in her direction, crying out for her.

"You okay?" Sean asks, frowning at him from across the table.

Drew tries to employ a carefree smile that doesn't give away the storm raging inside him. "I'm great."

* * *

Ashtyn still hasn't worked up the courage to ask Spencer what exactly it is that he does for work. Instead, she lets him prattle on and on about computers and security information and... Her mind wanders again, wading into thoughts of blonde waves and piercing blue eyes...

"Ashtyn?" Spencer's voice pops her back into the present. She has to stop a scowl from forming on her face. Instead, she smiles politely.

"Sorry, did you say something?"

"Uh, I was just asking about your move." Spencer takes a sip of his wine. Ashtyn has to force the bite of food she just took down her throat.

"Oh, yeah. I moved out near the end of May. The stupid landlord sold our house, so I moved into an apartment with a friend."

"Still didn't want to live alone?"

The question makes Ashtyn bristle. "Couldn't find anything affordable in the city."

"Really? That's surprising."

She has to refrain from rolling her eyes. "Yeah, well, teachers are severely underpaid in this country, so." She forces herself to take another bite of food, if only to keep herself from going on a rant.

"I mean, it can't be that hard, can it?"

The question makes her pause, eyes flicking up to him. His expression is serious, as if he really believes wrangling twenty five-year-olds all day is *easy*. As if she doesn't try to teach them numbers, letters, and how to be a good person all in a day's work. "Excuse me?"

Spencer actually shrinks under her glare. "Sorry, didn't mean to bring up a sore subject."

"No, please, continue. I'd love to hear how you think my job is easy."

"I wasn't trying to offend you."

She gives him a saccharine smile. "No, of course not."

He clears his throat, the tension between them palpable and awkward. "I'm, uh, glad you were able to find someone to live with. Since it's so expensive on your own. As a teacher."

Ashtyn scoffs. "Trust me, it wasn't my first choice to live with

Drew—" She stops herself, catching the mistake a second too late. Her throat dries, sweat starting to pool in her armpits.

Spencer frowns, his body language suddenly tense and rigid. "Who did you say is your new roommate?"

"Uh, I didn't," Ashtyn evades, busying herself by chugging her entire glass of wine.

"Did you say Drew?

"Did I? I can't remember."

"Drew, as in the guy that interrupted our first date on Valentine's Day?"

"Uh, yeah, about that—"

"You've got to be kidding me," Spencer mutters, looking up to the ceiling like a higher power should come down and save him from this disastrous date.

"Look, Spencer, it's really not that big of a deal. We're just friends. There's nothing between us."

Spencer scoffs, his gaze sliding back to hers. "Really? Cause from where I was sitting that night, it looked like you both were obsessed with each other."

It's Ashtyn's turn to scoff. "Don't be ridiculous."

"I'm the one being ridiculous? It was my date that was ruined by that guy."

"*Our* date," Ashtyn corrects, voice hard. "We were both on that date."

"Yeah, and it seemed like you'd rather have been on one with him."

"Are you kidding me? I literally begged you to stay."

"Not hard enough."

Ashtyn sucks in a breath at his words. "Why did you agree to this second date, then?"

Spencer looks at her, hands on the table like he's ready to bolt. "Because I really didn't think he could possibly ruin more than one date."

The words punch through her, one syllable at a time, reverberating through her entire body. "You're letting him ruin it, and he's not even here."

"Isn't he, though? You've been checked out this entire night. It's obvious you don't want to be here."

"But I am here," Ashtyn says, hands turning to fists under the table. She's here, and she's trying. Isn't that enough?

"Not really, you aren't." The waiter brings the check at that exact moment, and a silence falls over them, thick and heavy. Ashtyn has to swallow all the things she wants to say. Spencer takes out cash and hands it to the waiter, asking for no change. "I think this should be the last date we go on, Ashtyn."

She doesn't say anything as Spencer gets up and leaves the table. *Again.* She's being left again, and it's all Drew's fault. It's *his* fault that she's alone again. Ashtyn sits there for a long while, seething as she stares at the empty chair in front of her.

* * *

"You don't like movies?" Drew asks over the chatter of the crowded restaurant.

Sean shrugs. "Not really. Find most of them boring."

Drew finds this date boring, if he's honest with himself. Instead of saying that, he forces himself to smile. "Maybe you just haven't seen the right ones."

"Maybe," Sean says blandly. Geez, getting information out of this guy is like pulling teeth. They sip their beers in silence, the room around them livelier than their conversation. When Sean doesn't say anything, Drew tries a different approach. "What do you like to do for fun?"

Sean looks at him like he just asked the dumbest question to ever exist. "Uh, you know, stuff. I go to the gym a lot."

"Oh, I love working out! You ever use a Peloton? I love mine."

"No." The word lands flat on the table, neither of them trying to pick up the pieces of the failing conversation. Drew's about to make an excuse to run to the restroom when Sean tenses, seeing someone over Drew's shoulder.

"Sean?" a woman's voice asks. As she comes into view, Drew can see the confusion on her face. "Hey, what are you doing here?"

Sean straightens in his chair, clearing his throat as he says, his voice a touch deeper than before, "Just grabbing a beer with a coworker."

The words aren't exactly shocking to hear. Drew's been on plenty of "dates" with men who either aren't out or aren't comfortable in a public setting, but he still feels a twinge of disappointment at being shoved back in the metaphorical closet.

The woman turns to Drew with a smile. "Oh my gosh, you must be Ricky!" she exclaims. "Sean's told me so much about you. I'm Erica."

Drew catches Sean's eye from across the table and interprets the look he gives him easily. Drew smiles at the woman and sticks out his hand. "That's me. Nice to meet you, Erica."

Erica chats with them for a few minutes before excusing herself back to her own table. "I'll see you around, Ricky! It was so nice to meet you."

Sean visibly relaxes as soon as she's gone, and he takes a long gulp of his beer. "Sorry," he says once he's finished. "That was..."

"Complicated?" Drew supplies.

"Very," Sean replies. He doesn't look Drew in the eye as he wrings his hands together.

"Who is Ricky?"

Sean looks up at him, a blush on his cheeks. "He's a... friend."

Drew can tell there's more Sean's not telling him. "Yeah, I got one of those too."

"I'm not... out to anyone. Except Ricky. And, I thought if I went out with someone else he'd..."

"Get jealous and figure out what he's missing?" There's a hint of a smile on Drew's face as he says it.

"I'm sorry," Sean says guiltily.

"Honestly, you picked the perfect guy to ask out," Drew says. "Because I'm pretty sure I was doing the exact same thing tonight."

Sean actually laughs, the first sign of emotion on his face all night. "Damn, what are the odds?"

Drew smiles, finishing the rest of his beer. "Depends on how many people you swiped left on before me."

"Honestly," Sean says sheepishly, "you were the only one I swiped on."

"Oh, you can't tell me that. I'll get a superiority complex." The tension has eased, probably because they can both tell there's nothing between them. Both of them obviously want other people.

"Sorry if I wasted your time tonight."

"No such thing as wasted time," Drew says, signaling the waitress for another beer. "Now, tell me about Ricky."

Chapter 27

Ashtyn slams the front door, not caring how late it is. She kicks off her heels and rips out her ponytail in one fluid motion, hair cascading down her back. Tears prick her eyes, either from the pain of her baby hairs being ripped out or the disastrous date. She heaves a sigh, dropping her purse on the entryway table.

"That bad?" Drew asks from the dark of the living room. Ashtyn jumps, not having seen him when she came in.

"What the hell are you doing in the dark?" she asks, flicking on a lamp. Drew sits on the couch in the same clothes he had on earlier, eyes staring blankly at the wall.

"Making sure you got home safe," he mutters.

Ashtyn rolls her eyes. "I don't need you watching out for me."

"God forbid someone cares about you, right?"

There's an edge to his tone, and Ashtyn whirls on him, the events from the night wearing her thin. "What the hell is your problem? Date go badly?"

Drew lets out a bitter laugh. "Yeah, you could say that."

"Well, don't take it out on me. It's not my fault."

"Actually," Drew says, getting up from the couch. "It is your fault."

She looks at him, eyes wide. "Excuse me?"

"You heard me. It's your fault."

"Fuck off, Drew. I didn't do anything."

"What about you, huh?" he presses. "You didn't exactly come in here acting like a ray of sunshine. How'd your date go? You find yourself a nice boyfriend?"

"No, actually, I didn't. And it's *your* fault."

"So, we both ruined each other's dates? Is that what I'm hearing?"

"Apparently." She crosses her arms in front of her chest. "Spencer found out I'm living with you and didn't exactly love that."

"Oh, boohoo. Maybe he should grow a spine."

Ashtyn's blood begins to boil, anger simmering in her veins. "You're such an asshole."

"Right, I'm the asshole. *I'm* the reason the relationship didn't work out. You can blame me for the first time, but not this time. I wasn't even there."

Instead of saying something mean, she just rolls her eyes and says, "You know I don't do relationships, anyway. They're stupid."

"That is such bullshit!" Drew yells, causing her to jump. His tone doesn't scare her, it angers her. When she doesn't reply, he continues. "You have a relationship with everyone you meet."

Ashtyn huffs bitterly. "You know what I meant."

"No, I don't," Drew says. "Every relationship takes work, even if they're not romantic. Your friendships, your colleagues, your family. They're all a type of relationship. So don't tell me you don't do relationships, because that's bullshit."

Ashtyn curls her hands into fists. "You know exactly what I fucking meant. Don't twist my words."

Drew sighs, relenting slightly as he runs a hand through his hair. "I wasn't trying to twist your words. I just—all relationships take work. They all require trust that the other person isn't going to run away when things get tough. I just want you to know that the people that love you aren't going to leave you. That I'm—" He catches himself, sighing heavily and closing his eyes. "All relationships are hard. But they're worth fighting for."

"So then, where's *your* date?" Ashtyn asks, bitterness in her voice. "Was he not worth fighting for? I don't know about you, but I think I have all the relationships I want."

It's quick, but she sees Drew's face fall. He ignores her question and asks quietly, "Then why did you go on a date tonight?" It's a challenge. She can't tell him the truth. She can't tell him that it was just to make him jealous. To get him out of her system. To forget the feelings that are starting to burrow under her skin. She's worried that if they burrow too deep, she won't ever be rid of them.

"Because I wanted to," she replies, voice wobbling slightly.

"Again, I'm calling bullshit."

She groans angrily. "You're really starting to piss me off."

"Good!" Drew exclaims, throwing his arms up. "Get pissed at me. Yell at me. Do anything other than fucking hide from me. At least when we're arguing, you're being real with me."

"Oh, you wanna fight? Okay, let's fight. You only went on a date tonight to make me jealous."

"Yeah, I did! And you know what? I'd do it again."

She scoffs. "You're such a child."

He raises his eyebrows at her. "And what about your date?"

"What about my date?"

"Did you not agree to it just because I had one? If I recall correctly, I told you I had a date, and not a few hours later, you had one on the same day. What a coincidence."

"That's ridiculous."

He narrows his eyes at her. "Don't fucking lie to me, Ashtyn."

"Fine! Yes, I did!" she yells, taking a step toward him. "I dragged poor Spencer into another horrible date that I knew wouldn't go anywhere, just because I wanted to make you jealous. Just so I could stop thinking about you for one goddamn minute of my fucking day.

But, guess what? It didn't work. All I could think about was you on your own stupid fucking date. And when Spencer called me out on it, I didn't have a defense, because it was true. All I wanted was for it to be you there with me."

They're both breathing heavily, staring at each other. "Yeah, well, I couldn't stop thinking about you either," Drew replies.

"Great, I'm glad we got that out of the way."

"Great!"

"So now we can go back to normal."

There's something charged between them, their fight uncovering layers they never even knew were there. "Why?" Drew asks, his voice pleading. "Why won't you let me in?"

"Because I'm an unlovable piece of shit!" Ashtyn yells, the truth exploding out of her like a cannon. Drew stills, stunned at her words. She charges on. "Because I ruin everything I love. Because I don't deserve someone as perfect as you! Because one day, you'll wake up and fucking hate me. Because I don't even know how to love myself, so how am I supposed to love you?"

"Ashtyn," Drew starts, his voice pained.

"That's why I push you away," she says, voice trembling. "That's why I push everyone away. Because I'm unlovable."

Drew takes a step toward her, and when she doesn't run, he closes the distance between them, gathering her into his arms. She's stiff, not sure how to accept his embrace. "No, sweetheart," he says, gently. "You're not unlovable."

"Yes, I am," she mumbles into his chest. "Everyone always leaves. They change their minds. And I–I wouldn't survive if it was *you* that changed your mind. Yo—you're too good."

"Ash," Drew whispers, pressing his forehead against hers gently. "I'm just a guy. No one is too good for anyone." He pauses, taking a deep breath. "I have wanted you from the moment I met you, Ashtyn.

I have desired every inch of you since I first kissed you. I have yearned for you my entire life, before I even knew you. All I have wanted, for the last year and a half, is to hold you in my arms and show you how much I care about you."

She blinks up at him, words caught in her throat. His thumbs catch her tears, his hands cradling her face. "I don't know how..." To what? To love someone again? To let someone in?

"Together," he says, nose skimming hers. "We can learn together. I'm not going anywhere, I promise."

"Together," she repeats, the words foreign on her tongue, but sounding just right. "Me and you."

"Us." It's that word that has her stepping onto her tiptoes and kissing him. His lips slip over hers effortlessly, like they've always belonged there. Like they were made just for her.

"I want you," she admits quietly against his lips. "I've wanted you for so long, but I was too scared to admit it to myself. That's why I pushed you away, because I was scared."

"You don't have to be scared with me." He doesn't take his hands away from her face, keeping her anchored to him.

"But it's what I'm used to," she says. "I'll wake up every day scared that you'll change your mind."

"Then let me prove it to you," he whispers. "Let me prove to you that I'm not going anywhere."

So, she does. She wraps her arms around his neck, his hands traveling down to her waist where he hauls her up, so she's wrapped tightly around his hips. Their kisses, normally hungry and untamed, are slower this time. Gentle and curious, tasting what the other is offering.

"Your room or mine?" she asks between kisses, the words intimate and lovely.

"Wherever you want, sweetheart."

"Yours," she breathes.

* * *

Drew carries them to his room where he sets Ashtyn gently on the bed. His lips don't leave hers as they settle on the mattress, his fingertips dragging up the top of her thighs, goosebumps erupting over her entire body. She hums into his mouth, sending a lick of desire down his spine and straight to his cock. He will prove to her how much he cares for her. How much he loves her, even if she isn't ready to hear it. How much space she takes up in his mind. Together. They will do it together.

He takes his time exploring her body with his mouth. He traces a line of kisses down her jaw to the hollow of her throat, where he can feel her heart race against his lips. He sighs into her ear, chasing her earlobe with a nip of his teeth that sends her heartbeat racing even faster. His fingers slide the straps of her dress down, as slow as he can manage, touching as much of her skin as he can. Ashtyn whines in protest, trying to shimmy out of the dress as fast as she can.

"Slow," he breathes into her mouth. "I have so much to prove to you."

She catches his mouth in a searing kiss, biting his bottom lip gently. It drives him crazy, but he keeps his gentle pace, slowly pulling the neckline of her dress lower and lower until her breasts are exposed. He groans into her neck as he rubs his thumb over one of her nipples, and she gasps in pleasure, back arching.

Even though they've had sex before, this feels like the first time he's seeing her. The first time he's getting to know every inch of her, exposed and unafraid. He kisses down her front, catching her nipple in his mouth, biting down gently. She moans so loud, he can feel it reverberate throughout his entire body. He's already so hard, he's worried he might finish just from watching her, just from hearing her.

His hands travel up her dress until he fingers the fabric of her panties. He remembers the night she touched herself in front of him, and he shudders.

"Touch me," she whispers, hips arching forward, so he can do exactly as she says. He slips a finger into her underwear where she's wet and aching for him. His touch is featherlight, teasing her just the right amount. She grinds her hips into his hand, impatient, and he chuckles into her neck.

"Drew," she pleads, her voice sending shivers down his back. She reaches down to touch him through his pants, and he hisses, the feeling almost unbearable. He tears his shirt off in one fluid motion, so they're chest to chest, his hands going into her full, thick hair. He presses another searing kiss to her lips, that glorious taste of cherry lip gloss coating his throat.

She unbuttons his pants and touches him through his underwear. He thrusts into her hand, moaning unabashedly. He's so lost in the moment, he's powerless to her as she flips them, straddling his waist. He looks up at her, eyes glazed.

"Ashtyn," he starts, but she just looks at him with a small smile on her face.

"I have things to prove, too," she says, sliding down his lap until she's on her knees in front of him, working his boxers down his legs. His cock springs forward, and it's instantly in her hand. She smirks up at him, then licks up his length, his hands fisting in the sheets at the feeling. Holy fuck. His eyes flutter as she works him with her mouth, her teeth barely making an appearance, but sending him into a tailspin when they scrape gently against his shaft.

"You like that?" she asks, kissing his hip.

Drew doesn't think he remembers how to speak. "Ye-yes," he stutters. She kisses her way up his body, slow and tantalizing. She licks the base of his throat, then shimmies fully out of her dress, so she's naked and on top of him. "I need to kiss you," he says, hands on her hips. She lowers her mouth to his, and he shakes his head. "Not there."

Her eyes widen, and her pupils dilate as she understands his meaning. His hands urge her ass forward, until she's hovering over him, hips bracketing his face and hands on the headboard. "Lower, baby," he urges, hands at her hips. Her legs shake slightly as she lowers herself onto his mouth, his tongue instantly finding her clit. She exhales a moan as he begins to devour her, bit by bit. She's glorious in her pleasure, her hands finding his hair and pulling gently when he hits the right spot. She's panting, her release building and building until she's trembling above him. He stops, and she actually growls, looking down at him with blazing eyes. So, he finishes her, letting her orgasm long and deep into his mouth. When she's finished, she collapses next to him, eyes glazed from her pleasure. She touches him and slings a leg over his hip.

He reaches over her and pulls a condom from the bedside table. He slips it on and then rolls on top of her, kissing the hollow of her throat. Her legs spread before him, and he can feel how wet she is from her orgasm, ready for him. She guides him to her entrance, and then he's thrusting into her, both of them gasping at the feeling.

They find their rhythm easily, as if they've done this a hundred times, and Drew revels in the feeling of her wrapped tightly around him. He fucks her deeply, sensually, intimately until he's seeing stars, his orgasm coming quick and hot. She sucks at the hollow of his throat, her nails scraping gently down his back as he groans. He rests his forehead against hers when they're finished, noses skimming and lips nipping at each other.

"You and me," he says, holding her close.

"You and me," she repeats, tightening her grip like she's afraid he might let go.

"Us." He tucks her in against his chest, their bodies hot and sweaty and clinging to each other like they were always meant to end up here. Together.

Chapter 28

Sunlight trickles through the blinds, bathing the room in a warm glow. Ashtyn opens one eye cautiously, coming face to face with Drew's bare bicep. He breathes heavily in his sleep, his chest rising and falling in a steady rhythm. She feels a flutter in her stomach at the sight of him. Butterflies. She has butterflies in her stomach.

For once, the thought doesn't make her want to hurl. Instead, she reaches out and brushes her fingertips across his skin. He sighs and snuggles deeper into the sheets, a hint of a smile on his sleepy face. Ashtyn has to bite back her own smile as she watches him.

She turns, careful not to disturb him, and checks the time on her phone. She almost drops it when she sees a big seven staring back at her. She woke up at 7AM. On her own. She's never woken up before seven during the summer. She waits for the urge to go back to sleep to tug at her, but it doesn't happen. Instead, she's swinging her feet out of the bed, throwing on one of Drew's shirts, and tiptoeing toward the kitchen where she turns on the coffee pot. She wraps her arms around herself, remembering the feeling of Drew last night. She let him in, let him see every inch of her. Instead of embarrassment, she feels unabashed, relaxed. Like she wants to show him *more*. More, more, more. She's selfish when it comes to Drew. Craves the attention he gives her. She thinks she might want it all with him.

Last year, when she snipped and snarked at him, she secretly reveled in the attention he gave her. She couldn't believe anyone would want *her* for her. So, she kept him at a distance, afraid he'd just end up hurting her. Or worse, she'd hurt him. But something's shifted. Something has changed. Maybe her heart. Maybe her head. She's not sure which, just that she wants to get back in bed with that man and never leave.

She makes two cups of steaming coffee and brings them back into the bedroom. At her entrance, Drew rouses. She places the mugs on the nightstand and stands before him, a soft smile on her face. He smiles back at her, fingering the bottom of her shirt, or more accurately, his shirt.

"Hi," he says, tugging her gently onto the bed with him. She falls forward, face inches from his.

"Hi," she replies.

"You're up early."

"Trust me, I'm just as surprised as you," she says, nipping at his bottom lip. Her hands go to his hair, mussed from sleep, fingers savoring the soft curls.

"Does that mean you slept well?" he asks, closing his eyes against her touch.

"You could say that." She kisses him, not caring about morning breath, or her tangled hair, or anything else. No, she doesn't much care about anything right now.

Drew hums, his hands gripping her waist where the fabric of her shirt bunches. Heat blazes through her as Drew flips them, her head softly hitting the pillow, and his lips chasing her throat.

"The coffee's gonna get cold," she murmurs.

"You like it iced anyway," he says into her neck, groaning softly. Her heart warms at the fact that he knows that. He *knows* her.

She hooks her ankles into his thighs, bringing him, already hard, closer to her. "What if I wanted it hot this morning?"

"I'll put it in the microwave for you," he mumbles against her cheek, kissing his way across her face. She giggles at the sensation, arms snaking around his neck and pulling him close.

"I need to shower," she whispers.

He hums. "Funny, so do I."

She laughs into his mouth, a husky sound that has him grinding into her again. "Then what are we waiting for?"

His shower is so large, it's actually ridiculous. "I cannot believe you've been letting me shower in that tiny bathroom when you've had this the whole time." The standing shower takes up the entirety of the far wall, a built-in bench thick and sturdy across from the showerhead. Not to mention the rain showerhead in the middle. Ashtyn's jaw drops the second she sees it.

"You didn't know about the open invitation?" Drew questions as he turns on the water, a sly smile on his face.

She blushes. "You know what I mean."

"Oh, I think you know what *I* mean."

She sucks in a breath as he steps under the spray, full body on display through the glass door. A body she is now intimately acquainted with. She watches as the water falls over every crevice of him, an utter masterpiece.

"You coming, or are you just going to ogle me until I'm done?" he teases.

"Don't act like you don't like it," Ashtyn retorts, pulling off the shirt and stepping into the warm spray of the water.

"I like this much better," he says, pulling her close to him.

Here, in the shower, things feel safe. There's no one else here, just them. Outside, things get complicated. She frowns, leaning her forehead against his chest. His fingertips dance over her ribs, sending shivers down her body.

"What are we doing?" she asks, too much of a coward to look at him.

He sighs, kissing the top of her head. "What do you want to do?" He's letting her choose, even though she knows what he wants. He's never been shy about it. She looks up at him. She doesn't know what she wants. She just wants... him.

The word boyfriend seems juvenile for a feeling like this. A far distant memory sparks in her brain. The day she and Ava met Shiloh, Ashtyn had asked Shiloh if he had a girlfriend.

Partner, Ava had corrected. Partner.

The word rattles around her head as she stares at Drew. He lets her take her time. He lets her think. She tries to make sense of the feelings shoving their way up her throat.

"I think," she starts, swallowing hard. "That I want to try. With you. As my... partner."

His eyebrows raise, the corners of his mouth twitching. "Partner." He doesn't phrase it like a question. No, it's never a question between the two of them.

"Yes," she says. "Is that okay?"

"I like the sound of that. Partner."

Hearing him say that, about her, has butterflies erupting in her stomach again like a goddamn teenager. She kisses his chest, hand traveling down to grasp him where he's hard and ready for her. He moans into her shoulder, biting down softly. She presses her bare breasts into his chest, the trickling water adding to the sensation.

"I-I don't have a condom in here," he rasps, hands gripping her waist.

"It's okay," she says. "I'm on birth control."

He nods against her. "I get tested regularly. I'm on PrEP."

"Andrew," she says, silencing him with a kiss, long and deep. "I trust you. Now, fuck me already."

September

Chapter 29

Rain patters against the window, the room ensconced in darkness as Drew's phone buzzes on the nightstand next to him. He groans, Ashtyn shifting slightly next to him in bed. She's been sleeping with him, in his bed, for the last couple of weeks as they learn each other. As they learn how to be together. As partners.

She's gone back to work, so they both get home around the same time now, their clothes instantly vanishing as soon as they see each other. They've devolved into a mess of skin and heat, unable to keep their hands off one another. When they do manage it, they cook together. They eat dinner, watch movies, play Overcooked with Ashtyn's feet in his lap, his hand more likely to draw absentminded circles on her skin rather than actually play the game. They laugh together, loud and unabashed, as they learn new things about the other every day. Like where Drew is most ticklish, right in the crook of his neck. Like when he calls her sweetheart, and she melts into a puddle of desire at his feet. Like which episodes of *New Girl* are her favorite. Every day, they learn something new about each other, and it feels like a privilege.

They haven't exactly told their friends yet, neither wanting to pop their bubble of secrecy and intimacy. Not that they're a secret... just that *this* doesn't feel like it needs to be announced to the whole world. Drew likes it just being the two of them for now.

His phone buzzes again, rousing him from his thoughts. He's

instantly awake when he sees five missed calls from Haley and the current time: 1AM. He shoots up, swiping open his phone and calling her back immediately.

She answers on the third ring, her voice low, sending panic rushing through Drew. "Hello?"

"Hales? Are you okay? What's wrong?" Ashtyn is awake now, sitting next to him, eyes wide.

"Drew," Haley whispers. "I need your help."

"Where are you?" He's up and pulling on sweatpants quickly, the phone pressed against his ear and shoulder.

"I'm at my place. Er, I guess what used to be my place. Jimmy broke up with me, and he's kicking me out for real this time, but he won't let me get some of my stuff. He locked the bedroom." Her voice is wobbly, like she's been crying. Haley, normally so stoic and strong, sounds like she's moments away from breaking down completely.

"I'll be there as fast as I can," he says before hanging up the phone, not needing any other information.

Ashtyn pulls on a shirt as she asks, "What happened?"

"Haley needs me," he says. "And you're staying here."

"The hell I am."

"Ashtyn," he says, voice hard. "Please."

"It's Haley," Ashtyn replies. "I'm coming."

The way she says it has Drew's chest cracking open. He pulls her into him for a brief moment before nodding. "Okay. Let's go."

The rain makes it hard for him to speed, the roads slick and dangerous. It's dumping, Drew's windshield wipers working overtime to clear away the water. His hands are clenched on the steering wheel, only Ashtyn's comforting hand on his leg keeping him from spiraling. If even one hair on Haley's head has been touched, Drew doesn't know what he'll do, but he knows he'll do it to Jimmy. The thought sours in his stomach, anxiety clawing its way through his chest.

"It's okay," Ashtyn whispers. She tightens her hand on his leg, and he grabs it, holding onto her so he doesn't stray too far into "what ifs."

"It's never okay with Haley," he replies, eyes never leaving the road. He's rescued her from bad situations before, but never at one in the morning and crying. He speeds up slightly, the anxiety getting worse the closer they get. He's never felt this afraid before.

They've barely pulled up to the curb before he throws the truck in park and hops out, not caring about the rain that instantly soaks through his shirt. Ashtyn is close on his heels as he buzzes Haley's apartment. The front door unlocks a moment later with a loud screech. He swings it open roughly, taking the stairs two at a time.

"Slow down," Ashtyn hisses, breathing heavily as she tries to keep up with him. But Drew doesn't slow down. He climbs and climbs until he gets to Haley's door, which is slightly ajar. He bursts inside, his heartbeat racing, eyes scanning the entire room.

Haley sits on the couch, knees tucked up to her chest, tears staining her cheeks. There's an array of trash bags filled with clothes and other various belongings strewn across the floor. Drew is instantly before her, pulling her into a fierce hug as she sobs into his shoulder.

"He–he won't let me into the bedroom. I just need one thing. It's important." She hiccups against his shoulder, tears soaking into the fabric of his shirt that's already wet from the rain. "I can't leave without it."

"It's okay," Drew says, holding her close. "I'll get it." Ashtyn finally arrives, huffing and puffing in the entryway. She kneels in front of Haley, gathering her hands in hers, shushing her and telling her it's going to be okay.

"Stay here," Drew tells them, and makes his way to the bedroom near the back of the apartment. The TV blares on the other side of the door. Drew bangs his fist against it, trying to keep himself as calm as he can. "Jimmy! Open up, man."

"Fuck off," a gruff voice replies, muffled by the door.

Drew grits his teeth and bangs again, louder. "Open this fucking door. She just needs to get one last thing."

"Fuck you both!"

Drew's composure finally slips, and he feels his anger take the reins. "Haley?" he calls. "Do I have your permission to break down this door?"

"Yes!" she yells, voice wobbly. "Yes, whatever it takes. I can't... I can't leave it."

Drew takes a deep breath and kicks the door, the impact reverberating up his knee. The door splinters, but doesn't fully open. "What the fuck are you doing?" Jimmy yells from the other side. Drew kicks it again, this time the door cracking and falling off the hinges. Jimmy's face is a mix of rage and shock as he jumps up off the bed. Haley is lightning fast as she sprints in the room the second it's open, tumbling down in front of the nightstand. She rips the drawer open and grabs what looks to be a notebook. Drew, not sure of Jimmy's intent, steps in front of him as he takes a step toward Haley. He places a warning hand on Jimmy's chest, which Jimmy does not take kindly to.

"Take your fucking hands off me," he spits.

Drew doesn't, staring him down with narrowed eyes. "Take another step and we're going to have a problem."

Jimmy seems to want to test the limits, because he takes a small step forward. Drew, true to his word, slams him up against the wall in one swift motion. Suddenly, he's sixteen again, pushing bullies up against the wall for using slurs. Nobody ever messed with Drew, because he was always so much bigger, unafraid to put bigots in their place. Jimmy is no different. Drew will fuck him up if he has to.

"Do you have what you need?" Drew asks his sister, never taking his eyes off Jimmy.

"Yes," she breathes. "I've got it."

"Get the fuck out of my house you dirty bit—" But Jimmy doesn't get the chance to say the word, because he's flinching as Drew punches the wall next to his face, stunning him into silence. Pain lances up Drew's arm, but he doesn't care. He holds his fist inches away from Jimmy's face.

"Say it again. I fucking dare you."

Jimmy's mouth hangs open, eyes wide and flicking back and forth between Drew and the door. Drew tightens his grip, fist still poised to strike.

"Drew." Her voice is soft, a true contrast to the storm raging inside him. When he doesn't look at her, Ashtyn places a hand on his shoulder. He's not sure when she entered the room, just that she's here now. "Baby, look at me," Ashtyn says. He turns to her, his fist lowering slightly. "He's not worth it."

She's right. He's not worth his anger, his fists, his anything. Drew turns back toward Jimmy, fist now lowered to his hip. "If I ever see you again, I will break your face." He releases him roughly. Jimmy clambers backward toward the bed and as far away from Drew as he can get.

"Ye-yeah, same to you," Jimmy stutters, brushing himself off. He doesn't look at any of them as they head back into the living room. A clap of thunder booms throughout the apartment.

Drew gathers Haley's belongings in his arms. "Is this everything?"

She's clutching the notebook to her chest in a vice grip, not seeming to care about anything else. "Yes. That's everything."

"Let's go," Ashtyn says, placing an arm around Haley and guiding her out of the apartment. Drew's behind them, trash bags in hand, as he slams the door on his way out. The rain hasn't let up, and he's drenched by the time he gets Haley's things in the bed of the truck, the protective covering firmly in place.

As he slides into the driver's seat, both girls huddled together in the back seat, he lets out a sigh, his heartbeat still a jackhammer in his chest. "Are you okay?" He catches Haley's gaze in the rearview mirror.

"Yes," she says, as she looks up at him, clutching Ashtyn's hand. "Thank you for coming to get me."

"Always," Drew says, holding her gaze. He starts the truck, knuckles protesting in pain. He flexes them, seeing the broken skin for the first time, and shame washes over him. Shame and humiliation at letting his anger get the best of him. At letting both Ashtyn and Haley see that side of him. He shouldn't have done that.

It's nearing 2:30AM when they get back to the apartment and set Haley up in Ashtyn's room. Haley doesn't even question it, falling asleep as soon as her head hits the pillow. Drew leans against the kitchen counter, his body still wired from all the adrenaline. He'll never get back to sleep now. Ashtyn joins him, placing an icepack next to his hand.

He takes it gratefully, letting the ice cool his throbbing knuckles. He doesn't catch her eye as he says, "Thank you. I'm sorry that you had to see that."

"No," she says, grabbing his chin so he has to look at her. "Don't you dare apologize."

"I shouldn't have lost my temper like that."

"Drew, I wanted to watch you punch that guy's teeth in," Ashtyn admits. "But I knew you'd regret it the minute you did it. That's why I stopped you."

He exhales heavily, rubbing his eyes with the heels of his hands. "Thank you," he whispers to the darkness. He feels Ashtyn's arms go around his middle, and he holds onto her gratefully, burying his face into her hair. "Thank you."

"She can stay as long as she needs," she says into his chest. And it's those words, mixed with Ashtyn's arms wrapped around him, that has him choking out a sob. Not from the pain or the adrenaline, but because of how much Ashtyn cares for his sister, for him. How much her presence is keeping him afloat. How he never wants to let her go.

She holds him through it, letting him cry into her neck, her hands soothing his back in a steady rhythm. "I'm here," she whispers. "I'm here."

The rain continues its steady downpour outside, thunder echoing all around them.

Chapter 30

On his lunch break, Drew heads back to the apartment to check on Haley. He figures she'll still be asleep, but he's surprised to see her sitting on the couch, bag at her feet, when he walks in. Dread pools in his stomach as he looks at her, hands contemplative on her chin, elbows on her knees.

"Haley, no," he starts, but the look she gives him stops him in his tracks.

"Don't worry, I'm not going back," she says, picking at her nails anxiously. "I'm never going back to that bastard."

Relief floods through him. "Good, because I don't think I'd let you even if you wanted to."

She lets out a small laugh, toeing the corner of the rug with her foot. "I appreciate it. I don't know what I ever saw in a guy like that."

"It's okay, Hales," Drew says, sitting next to her.

She leans into him, sighing. "I think I want to go home."

"Home," Drew says the word like he doesn't know what it means.

"Yeah, home. To Mom and Dad."

The words land like bombs at his feet. Haley has never wanted to go home before. She's avoided their parents like the plague, unless it's an obligated holiday. "Hales, are you sure?"

She sighs heavily, scrubbing her hands through her hair. "No, but something is telling me I need to.

"For what it's worth, I think it's a good idea."

Haley scoffs. "You just want me out of here, so you can have privacy with Ashtyn."

"Haley," Drew warns, cheeks warming.

She knocks her shoulder against his. "Don't think I didn't notice whose bed I went to sleep in."

"We're..." Drew pauses, letting out a sigh. "We're trying something new. Together."

Haley gives him a wry smile. "Okay." She doesn't pry, she doesn't tease, she doesn't say anything else, and it settles something in Drew.

"Okay, have you told Mom and Dad about your plan? About coming home?"

"Um, not exactly," Haley says, biting her lip. "I was hoping maybe you could help me with that."

* * *

"Miss King, are you tired?"

The child's voice causes Ashtyn to jerk her head up, eyes heavy from lack of sleep. "Yes, Addie, I'm tired. I don't get to have nap time like you."

"Well, I'm *not* tired," Addie says, sitting up from her spot on the floor. She crosses her arms defiantly.

"Then sit there and be quiet," Ashtyn sighs, rubbing her eyes. Her phone buzzes on her desk, Drew's name flashing. She snatches it up, not caring that she's not supposed to be on her phone during the work day. "Hey," she answers softly.

"Hey," Drew replies, his voice equally soft. "Is this a bad time?"

"Miss King!" Addie whines. "Henry keeps poking me!"

"If we can't keep our hands to ourselves, nobody is getting a story after nap time," Ashtyn threatens. The kids seem to get the hint and quiet down. "Sorry, no, now is fine."

Drew chuckles. "You're so bossy."

"Yeah, well, if I wasn't they would run all over me."

Drew laughs again, then clears his throat. "Um, so I talked to Haley. She wants to stay with our parents. We called them earlier, and I'm gonna drive her up there after work."

"Wow," Ashtyn breathes. "Okay. Is she sure?" She's not sure what makes her ask this.

"Yeah, I think it'll be good for her," Drew replies. "Do you, uh, want to come with?" Ashtyn's breath stills, her heart starting to constrict in her chest. "If it's too soon, I understand. I just figured I'd ask in case you wanted to, you know—"

"Andrew," she says, stopping his rambling. "I'd love to come with you."

She can hear the smile in his voice as he says, "Great. I'll see you after work."

* * *

Walking into Drew's childhood home feels like crossing a line Ashtyn never thought she would cross again. She's nervous, her hands shaking despite the warmth of the house. The floorboards creak under her shoes, worn from years of family and friends crossing over the threshold. Now, it's her turn. It welcomes her, even if she's hesitant to accept it. Drew places a hand on her lower back, steadying her. It feels good.

Haley's a step ahead of them, almost hesitant to fully give herself over to her childhood home. However, as soon as her parents see her, they envelop her in a hug that tries to mend all her broken parts. Their mother has tears in her eyes as she embraces her daughter, whispering something into her ear that's meant for just the two of them.

Haley sniffles, tightening her grip. "Thanks, Mom."

When they're done, the Mitchells take one look at Ashtyn and start beaming. "Oh my gosh, you must be Ashtyn!" Mrs. Mitchell says, charging forward and taking Ashtyn into her arms.

"Mom, Ashtyn isn't really—" But Ashtyn silences him with a look. She will hug his parents. That, she can do.

"Oh, we have heard so much about you," Mrs. Mitchell says, taking a step back to look at Ashtyn. Her hands grip Ashtyn's arms tightly.

"Oh, have you?" she asks, sending a knowing glance in Drew's direction. He blushes and looks away. Guilty. The idea of Drew telling his parents about her, before they were even friendly toward each other, sends a flight of butterflies soaring through her stomach.

The hallway is lined with childhood photos, baby Drew and Haley posing together in various pictures, smiles wide. There's one of Drew, missing his two front teeth, that makes Ashtyn's heart squeeze.

"Drew's never brought someone home for us to meet," Mr. Mitchell says, voice deep and weathered. His eyes crinkle at the corners as he smiles at Ashtyn.

Ashtyn whips her head to Drew, mouth parted slightly. He doesn't catch her gaze, but his cheeks grow even redder. "Never?" she asks, not looking away from Drew.

"Never," Mr. Mitchell repeats. Ashtyn turns toward Drew's father, her heart a lump in her throat, and smiles.

"Well, then, it's an honor to meet you."

For the first time since they started doing whatever they've been doing, doubt starts to creep into Ashtyn's mind. Even though she agreed to come meet his parents, it all suddenly seems to be moving at lightning speed. What happened to their private nights, just the two of them, learning each other's bodies? Now, parents are involved. Families. Life is being shared. And it scares the ever-living shit out of Ashtyn.

Even here, with Flora Mitchell welcoming her with a warm embrace at the dining table, and Sam Mitchell stirring a pot of sauce on the stovetop, laughing with his daughter. And Drew, nudging Ashtyn's foot under the table with a small smile on his face... even with all of this happening, Ashtyn feels the fear start to creep in.

"You have no idea how long we've been wanting to meet you," Flora gushes, smile wide.

"Mom," Drew mutters.

"I mean, honestly, we never thought we'd see the day!"

"Ma!" Drew exclaims. "Relax, you're gonna scare her."

Ashtyn giggles as Flora sticks her tongue out at her son. "Let me get to know my future daughter-in-law."

"Jesus Christ," Drew says, getting up from the table. "And this is why I've never brought anyone home."

Flora pats Ashtyn's hand. "Ignore him. So, tell me about yourself."

Despite her anxiety, Ashtyn gives Drew's mom a rundown of her life. She revels in Flora's stories about Drew and Haley, the love she has for her children evident. Ashtyn wonders what made Haley so hesitant to come home for help.

"Oh, you work with kids? That's amazing. You know, I've always wanted to be a grandmother..."

"Mom!" Drew exclaims from the kitchen. "I swear to Christ, if you don't stop with this shit—"

"Andrew James, swear jar! Now!"

Drew groans, pulling out a dollar from his wallet. Haley laughs. "We're still doing this shit?"

"Haley Margaret, swear jar!"

"So much for a savings account," Haley mutters, putting a dollar in the jar that sits on the kitchen counter. It's overflowing with ones and fives.

"Who's contributed the most?" Ashtyn asks, eyeing the jar.

"That would be me," Sam replies, entering the dining room. He carries a steaming pot and sets it in the middle of the table. He sighs and seats himself at the head of the table. "Swear like a sailor."

"And you wonder where we got it from," Haley teases her mom, taking a seat next her father.

"That swear jar has paid for many a date night," Sam says, staring fondly at his wife. "So, I'd say it's worth it."

Haley and Drew look at each other with similar disgusted looks, then burst into laughter as Flora tries to swat both of them from across the table. "We have a guest!" she admonishes. "Behave yourselves."

They absolutely do not behave themselves. Haley and Drew both crack inappropriate jokes that make their mother blush and their father roll his eyes. Ashtyn's pretty sure Drew contributed almost one hundred dollars to the swear jar, just tonight. She has a sneaking suspicion he did it on purpose, if not to pay for one more date night for his parents.

"Now, Ashtyn," Flora says, handing her three Tupperware containers full of leftovers after dinner. "You must join our book club. We've been dying to get some younger faces in the group."

Ashtyn laughs. "That sounds like something my best friend would love."

"Oh, please, bring whomever you want! Just not him," Flora says, pointing at her son. She lowers her voice. "It's ladies only."

"Count me in," Ashtyn replies, and Flora beams, clapping her hands together excitedly.

"Oh, wonderful! Can I have your number? I'll text you what book we're reading, and I'll add you to the group chat."

As Ashtyn gives her number to Flora, she spots Drew shaking his head and laughing in the corner. *Sorry*, he mouths, sending her a sympathetic look. Ashtyn shoots him a smile, trying to convey with her face that she doesn't mind at all.

His parents wave to them as they pull out of the driveway, Haley all settled in her old room. When they're farther away, the road stretched out before them, Drew turns to look at Ashtyn, her hand in his. "Was it too much?"

He asks it gently, like he's afraid to scare her. "A little," she admits, tightening her grip on him. She wants to be vulnerable with him, not hide away her feelings like she's used to.

"I'm sorry. My mom can be a lot."

"No, it's okay. I'm just... I'm scared."

"Scared of what?"

"Of what this all means."

Drew sighs. "Me too. Sometimes I'm afraid this is too good to be real."

His words sit heavy in her chest. "I'm not too good—"

"But you are, Ashtyn," he interrupts. "To me, you are. I don't care what you think or what you've been taught. To me, you are too good to be true. I–I never thought I'd find someone like you."

She has to stop herself from trying to dispute him. She has to trust him. Trust that what he's saying is *his* truth, whether she believes it or not. She looks over at him. "Did you swear just so you'd have an excuse to give your parents money?"

Drew bites his lip. "Yes."

His admission sends butterflies soaring through her. "And you think *I'm too good...*"

Drew squeezes her hand. "What if we're just right for each other?"

There he goes, scaring the shit out of her again. Because she doesn't think she could ever be "just right" for anyone. She sighs, reveling in the feeling of his thumb tracing circles on her skin. "Just right," she mumbles.

Drew brings her hand up to his lips, kissing it. "Just right."

Maybe, just maybe, he's right.

Chapter 31

"We have something to tell you," Ashtyn says, causing Ava to freeze with a chip halfway to her mouth. She returns it to the bowl, turning her full attention to Ashtyn and Drew.

They're at Ava and Shiloh's apartment for movie night, an array of snacks laid out on the kitchen bar. Ashtyn and Drew sit next to each other on stools, across from where Ava and Shiloh stand in the kitchen. They both look at them expectantly.

Drew squeezes Ashtyn's knee under the bar comfortingly. They discussed telling Ava and Shiloh about their relationship earlier in the week. Drew was gung-ho, ready to tell the entire world now that his parents know, while Ashtyn felt more reserved, wanting to keep them close to her heart for just a little while longer. But, with the reunion only a week away, Ashtyn knew they needed to tell Ava and Shiloh sooner rather than later. Plus, she remembers how it felt to have Ava and Shiloh keep their relationship a secret from her. She doesn't want to repeat the mistakes of the past.

"Drew and I are..." She pauses, narrowing her eyes at Ava, who is bouncing on her toes, a smile on her face. Shiloh wraps his arms around her middle, whispering something in her ear that has her settling, eyes still bright. "Together," Ashtyn finishes.

Ava's mouth opens, and Ashtyn holds up a finger to stop her. Ava slaps a hand up to her mouth, Shiloh biting back a smile as he nuzzles into her neck. "Hold your thoughts to yourself for five minutes," Ashtyn says. Drew laughs into his hand as he leans his elbows onto the bar.

"We will behave," Shiloh says, making a zipping motion on his lips. Ava nods furiously, hand still over her own mouth.

Ashtyn takes a steadying breath and clears her throat. "I don't want anyone making a big deal out of this, okay? We promised no more secrets, Ave, and I'm holding myself to that. Drew is my partner, and we're still learning what that means for each other. We are asking for you not to freak out and make it a big deal. Just act normal."

Drew grabs her hand and squeezes encouragingly, the smile on his face meant just for her. She squeezes back, looking up at her friends. Ava has tears in her eyes, and Shiloh smiles at them. "Okay," Ashtyn says, letting out a breath. "That's it."

Ava squeals and runs around the bar, launching herself at Ashtyn. The hug from her best friend feels like the acceptance she was looking for. "Oh, Ash," Ava whispers. "I'm so happy for you."

"I said not to make a big deal out of it," Ashtyn mumbles, watching as Drew and Shiloh hug over her shoulder. Shiloh whispers something to his friend that has Drew smiling and nodding.

"I won't, I promise," Ava replies into Ashtyn's hair. "Just let me revel in this for a minute."

Ashtyn laughs, holding tighter to Ava as Jess jumps down from her cat tower to see what all the commotion is about. She hops up onto the bar, batting her head against Ashtyn's arm before checking out the array of food.

"Jessica, what did I tell you about getting on the counters?" Shiloh admonishes, as she tries to dip her paw into a bowl of dip.

Both Ashtyn and Ava look at him with twin expressions of amusement. "Says the guy who used to give her bowls of cream on the counter," Ashtyn says, pulling out of Ava's embrace.

Shiloh blushes as he scoops up Jess. "That was one time," he mutters, rolling his eyes. "Now that she's older, I'm trying to teach her some manners."

Everyone's attention is now on Jess as she scrambles onto Shiloh's shoulder, licking his ear. Drew turns to Ashtyn, hand on her thigh, and mouths, *You okay?*

She nods, hopping down from her bar stool and placing a swift kiss on his cheek. "I'm starving. Let's eat."

* * *

Drew can't focus on the movie at all. No, all he can focus on is Ashtyn's feet in his lap, the feel of her skin under his fingertips, the ability to touch her freely in front of their friends. It feels like a gift. One he never wants to return.

A jump scare on screen startles him, and Ashtyn giggles, nudging him with her foot. "Scared?" she teases.

"No," he mutters, sinking deeper into the couch, arms crossed over his chest.

"Don't worry, Drew," Ava says. "You can pick the movie next time. Preferably one a little less gory."

"Hey! You're not allowed to complain about my pick until after I leave," Ashtyn grumbles.

"I'm not complaining!" Ava protests. She winces as a man gets chopped in half on screen. "It's just a little much."

"Weenie," Ashtyn teases her friend. Ava sticks her tongue out in response, and Ashtyn throws her head back in laughter.

When the movie ends, none of them rate it very high, except Ashtyn, who grumbles about no one understanding horror the way she does. They stay to help clean up, Ava talking nonstop about the reunion. Drew can see Ashtyn tense at the mention of it.

"We gotta have a game plan," Ava says, placing dishes in the dishwasher. "It's next weekend."

Ashtyn groans. "Ave, it's really not that serious."

"Says the one that wouldn't go until I kicked her ass in Mario Kart."

"You cheated, and you know it."

"And yet, you're still coming."

Ashtyn smacks her with a dish towel, making a loud *thwak* that echoes in the kitchen. "Ow!" Ava whines. She picks up her own towel and raises it above her head in warning.

"Oh, no. We are not doing this again," Shiloh says, standing between the two girls. "Last time we did this, you flooded the kitchen, Ash."

"I did not!" Ashtyn protests. "I barely even squirted her with the faucet. Ava is the one that went full psycho and threw dirty dishwater on me!"

"It wasn't dirty! It was clean, I swear!"

Drew smiles as he watches the exchange, grateful that he gets to be a part of this dynamic. "Drew, can you please be a buffer?" Shiloh asks, trying to keep the girls wielding dish towels at bay.

"Oh no, I'm new to this. I'm just an innocent bystander."

Ashtyn whirls on him. "You can't be a bystander! You're supposed to be on my team!"

At her words, he stands and salutes. "Yes ma'am. What are my orders?"

Ashtyn smiles mischievously, finger perching on her chin in thought. "Well, the apartment is too small for a jousting tournament."

"NO jousting!" Shiloh exclaims. "I almost ended up with a broken arm last time."

"That's because you didn't take my advice on proper posture," Ashtyn counters.

Ava nods and pats Shiloh's shoulder. "She's right, you didn't."

Drew raises his eyebrows at his friends. "Jesus, what have I been missing?"

"Chaos," Shiloh replies. "Ash, you already agreed to come to the reunion. No more competitions."

She sighs, but relents. "Fine. But I will have my revenge one day."

"Suuuuure," Ava teases, provoking Ashtyn just like a little sister would. Ashtyn's eyes widen, and then she's chasing Ava down the hallway with a dish towel raised over her head, their shrieks echoing throughout the apartment.

"It's best if you just let them work it out for themselves," Shiloh says to Drew as he leans against the counter. "It's just a *them* thing."

"Sometimes they act more like sisters than friends," Drew replies, fondly.

"Hey, speaking of sisters. How's Haley?"

Drew sighs, the echoes of the girls' laughter floating down the hallway toward them. "She's better. I think going home was the best decision she could have made. I just hope she sticks with it and doesn't run off with some other idiot that treats her like shit."

"Yeah, me too," Shiloh agrees. "Hey, did Mattie tell you he got an apartment here in town?"

"Oh yeah? Good for him."

"Yeah, I'm just worried he's going to be roped into working for Dad."

"Fuck, you think he would do that?"

Shiloh sighs. "I think it might be inevitable."

Drew frowns and claps a hand on his friend's shoulder. "Well, at least Mattie will be in town now. Easier for you to keep an eye on him."

Another shriek of laughter comes from the bedroom, followed by a crash and a loud thump. There's a beat of silence before Ava yells, "It wasn't me!"

Shiloh lets out a laugh, scrubbing a hand down his face. "Come on, let's go see what they broke. You're part of the club now."

Drew smiles, his heart warming at his friend's words. He thinks he's going to like this club.

Chapter 32

This time, when Ashtyn enters her childhood house with Drew at her side, she doesn't feel worried. No, she feels like he belongs here with her. She gave her mom the same spiel she gave Shiloh and Ava: don't make it a big deal. Now, as her mother ushers them inside, smile wide, Ashtyn doesn't feel as weird as she thought she would.

"Oh, Andrew honey, could you help me with my computer? I think I got a virus," Carol says as soon as they're over the threshold.

"Mom, we just got here. Let the poor man rest."

"It's okay," Drew replies, setting his bag down. "I can take a look." He presses a kiss to Ashtyn's head before heading into the kitchen to help her mother with the laptop. Ashtyn has to remind herself that she's allowed to *want* Drew's affection. That he can freely give it to her in front of other people. She doesn't have to hide her desire for him. How much she cares. She's still getting used to it, especially in front of her loved ones.

She lets out a breath and heads upstairs to her old bedroom. Her popstar posters have been taken down, the walls still full of holes from where she tacked them all up. She collapses onto the worn mattress, the room relatively barren of her past teenage self. She moved most of the furniture out when she went to college. Now, it feels more like an old storage unit for stuff she's mostly forgotten about. Memories tucked deep away in old boxes.

She fingers the old quilt, worn at the edges, and tries to calm the storm raging inside her. She shouldn't be worried about this reunion, especially with Drew at her side, but the anxiety won't ease up. It feels too much like wading into the past, when she should be focused on the future. Her mom has laid out her old yearbooks, and she picks one up absentmindedly.

She flips to the first page and immediately slams it closed. Why hasn't she burned this thing? Even just seeing his handwriting has nausea threatening to spill out of her. She tosses it across the room with a loud *smack*.

"Wow, what did that book do to you?" Drew asks, entering the room. He sets his duffel on the ground, joining her on the edge of the bed.

"Bad memories," she mutters, leaning into his embrace. "Did you help my mom with her virus?"

Drew chuckles. "Yes, I fixed it. You'd be surprised how often my boss gets the same type of virus." Ashtyn laughs, and Drew tucks her in close. She swings her legs onto his lap. "You know," Drew starts. "We don't have to go to this thing tomorrow."

Ashtyn sighs. "I promised Ava."

"And you know she'd understand if you cancelled."

She groans into his shoulder. "We already bought the tickets."

"Ash," Drew whispers. "Why are you fighting me on this?"

"Because we're good at fighting."

Drew chuckles into her hair, his lips caressing the shell of her ear. "We're good at not fighting now, too."

She buries her face into his neck. "I need to go. If only to prove to myself that I can do it. Haley told me that I can't let him win. Not going feels like letting him win."

"You're going to take the advice of my sister, of all people?"

Ashtyn giggles. "Hey, she has good advice when it's directed toward other people."

Drew nips at her ear, then kisses her cheek. "If you say so." His hands tighten on her waist. "You know, I never thought I'd see the inside of your childhood bedroom."

His words make her shiver. "It's tainted with bad memories," she whispers, afraid to admit what those memories are. Who they're about.

"Then let's make new ones." He kisses the hollow of her throat, his fingers cascading up her thigh. Her own fingers make their way into his hair, tugging gently as he sucks on her collarbone. His hands skim the edge of her shirt, getting higher and higher...

"Ash! Honey! Can you come down here, please?" Carol yells, causing them to jump apart like they just got caught doing something they shouldn't.

Ashtyn groans as Drew chuckles. "Ten years later, and it's still the same shit as it was in high school," she mutters as her mother yells from downstairs again. "Coming, Mom!"

* * *

"Tell me again why we're doing this," Ashtyn grumbles as Ava swings open the door to the bar. The music from inside wafts out the open door, the smell of beer and sweat nauseating. And Drew's been in his fair share of shitty bars.

"Because this is the only bar this town has," Ava says simply. "I figured we should at least check it out. You know, scope out anyone that might be going to the reunion tomorrow."

"I really don't think there's anything more embarrassing than going to a bar in your hometown," Ashtyn replies, nose scrunched in disgust.

"Ah, come on," Drew reassures her, placing a hand on her back. "It'll be fun."

It is, in fact, not very fun. The bar is dingy, even for small town standards, the floor sticky and suspicious. Drew's chair wobbles to the left every time he shifts his weight, and Ashtyn looks miserable, something he desperately wants to fix.

"Okay, so maybe this was a bad idea," Ava admits, sipping her martini then frowning. She sticks her tongue out in disgust. "I didn't think it was possible to mess up a martini."

"You're just spoiled from the ones I make you at home," Shiloh says.

"True," Ava sighs. The music cuts off abruptly as someone approaches what can only be considered a stage. The microphone screeches loudly, everyone covering their ears from the sound.

"Okay, karaoke time!" a drunk man slurs, his voice booming through the small bar.

"And that's my cue to leave," Ashtyn says, standing up.

Ava bangs her fist on the table, making everyone jump. "That's it. We're doing it old school." She jumps up from the table, barely keeping her glass from falling over.

"Old school?" Ashtyn questions, and a smile erupts over Ava's face.

"We're going to the pool."

The air is warm for a September night. The pool is still, the water glimmering under the moonlight. The chain-link fence around it sags from years of neglect, just begging someone to jump over it.

"You're telling me you two broke into the public pool, regularly?" Drew asks, as Ava steps onto Shiloh's interlocked hands. He boosts her over the edge, and she lands on the other side with an *oomph*. The bag of bottles around her shoulders clinks loudly.

"There wasn't anything better to do," Ashtyn replies, a small smile on her face. "Plus, there's no cameras. We've never been caught before." She grabs onto Drew's shoulder as he helps her over the fence. She lands next to Ava with a grunt.

"And how are *we* supposed to get over?" Shiloh asks, hands on his hips.

"The way our high school boyfriends did," Ava teases, biting her lip.

"Crawl." She points to a corner of the fence that's loose. She pulls it back, the material scratching against the concrete ominously.

"You're kidding," Shiloh says.

Drew pats him on the back. "Here, I'll boost you up. We're no high school schmucks."

"And how will you get over?" Ashtyn asks, eyebrows raised.

"Oh, you'll see." Shiloh steps onto Drew's hands and hauls himself over the fence. Drew wipes his hands on his pants, then takes a few steps backward. "You're gonna wanna clear the area."

Everyone stands back as Drew runs, launching himself at the fence, then grabbing the top and vaulting over it in one fluid motion, landing on both feet. Everyone stares at him with wide eyes.

"That might be the hottest thing I've ever seen in my life," Ashtyn says, and Drew gives her a smirk.

"Bet your high school boyfriend couldn't do that."

Ashtyn shakes her head as she bites her lip at him. "No, he could not."

"I could have done that," Shiloh grumbles, and Ava pats his arm comfortingly.

"Yes, you could have, babe."

"Should I jump back over and prove it to you?" he asks, jerking a thumb over his shoulder.

Ava giggles. "I believe you." She kisses him, then distributes the bottles of alcohol she smuggled in. It's all so juvenile, yet fitting for the occasion.

"Drinking underage, too?" Drew teases.

"She was a bad influence," Ava replies, pointing at Ashtyn.

"I was not!"

"You know, somehow I don't believe you," Drew says.

"Oh, please, like you and Shi weren't doing crazy shit in high school," Ashtyn replies.

"Hey, I was an angel," Shiloh replies as Drew scoffs.

"Right, like when you stole your dad's expensive bottle of scotch, and we got plastered before the homecoming game."

Shiloh grimaces. "Oh yeah. Forgot about that one."

Drew claps him on the back. "I know. I had to carry you home, you were so drunk."

"Okay, enough reminiscing," Ashtyn says, peeling off her shirt. "Let's swim." Her shoes and jeans follow suit until she's just in her bra and underwear, diving straight into the pool.

When she surfaces, Drew looks at her curiously. "Since when do you like swimming?" He remembers every trip they've ever taken on the boat, Ashtyn never once jumping in and swimming with them.

"Since it's dark out, and there's no one else around," she replies. She treads water carefully, looking up at him with a small smile on her face.

Drew laughs, shrugging out of his shirt. Ava is already undressed, and she cannonballs into the pool with a yelp. Shiloh smiles as he tugs off his own clothes, his eyes never leaving her. He's next into the pool, splashing both girls on his way in.

"What are you waiting for?" Ashtyn asks in Drew's direction. Drops of water cling to her lashes that he desperately wants to kiss away. He pulls his jeans down and steps toward the edge of the pool, Ashtyn looking at him with hunger in her eyes. He gets in slowly, the water rising to meet him. He's careful not to splash her as he sinks into the water gently, kicking slowly toward her. He pulls her to him, finally able to wipe those drops of water off her face with the pad of his thumb. He thinks about what it would have been like if he met her in high school, both of them wild and crazy, sneaking into pools with their hearts on their sleeves.

"What are you thinking about?" she whispers, nose bumping against his. Her body is soft against his.

"I'm thinking about what it would have been like to know you back then."

"I was a mess," she says, eyes fluttering closed as his thumb traces down her jaw and into the hollow of her throat.

"You still are," Drew teases. She peeks one eye open and splashes him gently, a playful frown on her face. "But now you're my mess." He kisses her deeply, sucking lightly on her bottom lip, and she groans into his mouth.

"Uh, hey, PG-13 please," Ava teases from the other side of the pool.

Drew can feel Ashtyn flip her off behind his back. "We should have left them back at the bar."

"Hey!" Ava exclaims, sending a splash of water in their direction. "That's not very nice."

"Oh, I'll show you not nice, Ava Marshall," Ashtyn says, leaving Drew's embrace and heading in Ava's direction. Ava squeals and flails in the opposite direction, sending a torrent of water at Ashtyn. The two girls shriek as they splash each other incessantly.

Drew leans on the edge of the pool, taking a sip from his drink. "How does it feel?" Shiloh asks, joining him. "To finally get the girl."

"Fuck off," Drew replies, smile on his face, eyes never leaving Ashtyn as she laughs with her best friend.

Shiloh chuckles. "I am happy for you. Honestly."

Drew turns to his friend. "Thanks, man. I'm happy for you, too."

"A lot's changed in ten years."

"You wanna go to our reunion?"

"Fuck, no."

Drew laughs, finishing his drink, as a loud siren whoops from the parking lot. Everyone turns to look with widened eyes.

"Shit," Ashtyn says, pulling herself out of the pool in one swift motion. Drew thinks it's the fastest he's ever seen her move. "We gotta go." Everyone scrambles out of the pool hurriedly, making way too much noise to be inconspicuous.

"Hey!" a voice exclaims, flashlight searching through the dark for the trespassers. "Stop right there!"

Ashtyn dashes across the pool, trying to gather her clothes while Ava stands ramrod straight, hands in the air. "Don't shoot!" she screams.

The police officer lumbers through the front gate, his flashlight landing on Ava as she stands frozen in place. Ashtyn smacks her forehead with her hand, the two girls obviously having very different ideas on what to do when the cops crash the party. "We're innocent!" Ava exclaims. Drew and Shiloh stand, clothes halfway over their wet bodies, poised to diffuse the situation if need be.

"Ava Marshall?" the officer asks, stepping closer to Ava, his flashlight illuminating her in the darkness.

Her raised arms falter just a bit, a shocked expression crossing her face. "Garrett?"

Garrett Smith's face comes into view, and Drew swallows, remembering the last time he saw Ava's old high school boyfriend. It ended with a threat, and not a subtle one.

Garrett drops the flashlight, no longer shining it directly into Ava's eyes. "Holy shit! What are the odds?"

Ava laughs nervously, hands coming down to her sides. "We're in town for the reunion, so I guess the odds were pretty high."

"Oh, y'all are going to that? Me too! Hey, Ashy," he says, waving to Ashtyn, who is trying very hard to hide her face. He notices the boys next, and his eyes narrow.

Drew waves, casually. "Hey, man. Long time no see."

Garrett frowns and rests his hand on his gun. *Jesus Christ.* "Yeah," he says. "Long time."

"Look, Garrett, I'm sorry we snuck in," Ava says. Garrett's eyes travel down Ava's body, still only in her bra and underwear, and Shiloh takes a protective step forward. Drew puts a hand to his chest, not wanting to aggravate Garrett any more than they have to. Who knew the fucker was a goddamn cop.

"She's got this," Drew whispers to Shiloh. Shiloh tenses, but backs down, letting Ava do what she needs to.

"We just wanted to reminisce on the good times," Ava says, sweetly. "Remember when we used to do this?"

Garrett sighs, scrubbing a hand across his chin. "Well, since the reunion is tomorrow, and I wouldn't want you to miss it…"

"Oh, thank you!" Ava exclaims. "You're the best!"

Garrett blushes under Ava's praise, then narrows his eyes at the boys. "I don't want to see you here again."

Drew salutes him. "You got it, boss."

Ashtyn snickers into her hand, and Drew nudges her, trying to bite back the smile on his face. "Hush, you're gonna get me arrested." This just makes Ashtyn snort, her shoulders shaking with silent laughter.

Garrett eyes them wearily, but his gaze slides back to Ava. "Uh, see you tomorrow?"

"Yeah, definitely," Ava replies, nodding her head furiously. Only her friends can see her cross her fingers behind her back.

"Alright, get out of here. Get home safe, Ava." And with that, Garrett lumbers back to his police car and drives away, not even waiting for them to leave.

Ava sags against Shiloh with a deep sigh. "Whew, that was close."

"He even looks at you tomorrow—" Shiloh starts, and Ava laughs loudly.

"Okay, calm down, caveman."

"Caveman must protect!" Shiloh exclaims, picking Ava up over his shoulder. She squeals, the sound echoing across the pool.

"God, they're so corny," Ashtyn says fondly from her spot next to Drew.

"We could never," he replies, arm snaking around her waist. He squeezes her butt, and she yelps, smacking him lightly on the chest, cheeks heating with a blush. "Ready to head back to your mom's?"

"Only if you promise to ravish me as quietly as you can when we get there," she says, a coy smile on her face.

"Challenge accepted."

Chapter 33

Walking into her old high school gym, Ashtyn feels a sense of dread mixed with nausea roil through her stomach. Luckily, Drew's hand in hers helps steady her, just a bit. She clings to him as nostalgia sits heavily in the air. She takes a deep breath, reading the huge welcome banner that hangs at the entrance to the gym: *Welcome Home 2014 Graduates!*

A projector screen has been set up, streaming old pictures from games, events, and other activities that Ashtyn doesn't think she was ever a part of. There are tables spread out, a buffet table against one wall that's serving an assortment of food. She stares at it ravenously, stomach grumbling.

She recognizes a few people from a distance, but many feel like strangers to her. It's crowded, much more than she expected. Much more than the RSVP list had indicated, and that dread inside her intensifies, hand starting to sweat in Drew's.

"Hey," Drew whispers, breath tickling the shell of her ear. "Have I told you how beautiful you look tonight?" He fingers the bottom of her black dress, goosebumps erupting onto her thighs.

"Yes," she whispers back, her heart warming, anxiety dissipating slightly. "Many times."

"Good. Add another one, then."

She laughs softly. "You look pretty nice, too."

"What, this old thing?" He spins, showing off the slacks that fit him just right, his dress shirt slightly unbuttoned and revealing just a sliver of skin. His name tag sits across his right pectoral, "Drew" scrawled in his messy handwriting. She thinks about tearing off that shirt later tonight, making him wear only the name tag. Chasing his skin with her tongue.

Ava interrupts her thoughts by squeezing her arm. "Garrett sighting," she whispers. "Run."

"Shit," Ashtyn says, steering them toward the refreshment table, Drew and Shiloh scrambling behind them. "You think we can successfully avoid him all night?"

"One can only hope," Ava replies. "I forgot how small this gym is." She surveys the table, then pops a cheese cube into her mouth. "Mmm, I love cheese cubes."

"Oh my gosh, same," a girl with brown hair that matches Ava's says from next to them as she grabs a handful of cheese. Ashtyn feels like she vaguely recognizes her, but she can't place her face.

"Hey, Marlee girl! Get your ass over here!" a tall man with dark hair yells. He's waving her over, a blonde man holding his hand tightly. The girl, Marlee, shoves five cheese cubes into her mouth at once, then yells a muffled, "Coming!" before heading toward her friends.

"Man, I feel like I don't know anyone here," Ashtyn mutters, picking up a glass of champagne from the table.

"Besides fucking Garrett," Ava retorts, causing Ashtyn to snort into her drink.

"Did y'all not meet Brooke in high school?" Drew asks.

"No, we met her our first day of college," Ava answers, fond smile on her face. "She was our next-door neighbor in the dorms."

As Ava delves into the story of when they met Brooke, Ashtyn surveys the gym again. It's like it hasn't changed at all. The same scuffed floors, same weird smell that never leaves, even after the cleaners are done.

She remembers the numerous pep rallies she was forced to attend, to cheer on a football team she didn't care about. For how much she hates change, there's something in her that wishes *this* had changed just a little bit.

"Is it an acceptable time to leave yet?" Ashtyn asks when Ava is finished with her story.

Ava smacks her lightly. "You told me you'd stay at least an hour. It's been barely twenty minutes."

Ashtyn groans, taking another flute of champagne from the table and chugging it. "At least it's an open bar."

They mingle to the best of their ability, seeing old friends and acquaintances from ten years ago, many Ashtyn doesn't recognize, but they seem to recognize her. They make small talk, the monotony of it making Ashtyn grow weary. Drew's hand never leaves her waist, subtly tucked behind her back, so as not to be overbearing. She hates how good it feels, how good having him here with her feels.

When it's been an hour, she turns to him. "Hey, I'm gonna go hide in the bathroom for a bit."

"Want me to come with?" he asks, wagging his eyebrows suggestively.

She giggles, the idea of hooking up in the bathroom sending a thrill through her. "No, I just need a minute to myself. Think I drank too many flutes of champagne."

"Okay," he says, pressing a kiss to her temple. "I'll be here when you're done."

She crosses the gym quickly, trying to avoid any more mingling than she has to. Once in the bathroom, she slumps against the sink, grateful for the reprieve from all the noise and chaos. She's slightly buzzed, using the alcohol to get through all the small talk and pleasantries. So many people she'll forget about it in the morning. So many memories she's trying to avoid.

The toilet flushes, and the cheese cube girl from before, Marlee, exits the stall and begins washing her hands. She catches Ashtyn's gaze in the mirror and smiles. "It's a lot, isn't it?"

Ashtyn lets out a breath. "Yeah. Especially when you're trying to avoid bad memories." She's not sure why she admits it. Maybe it's the safety of the women's bathroom, where secrets always tend to come out.

Marlee laughs, drying her hands on a paper towel. She hugs a black cardigan to her chest. "I feel the same way. Got a lot of history here I wasn't sure if I was ready to revisit."

"You're telling me," Ashtyn scoffs, lowering her gaze to the floor. "But my friends convinced me it would be fun."

"Same," Ashtyn says. "You, uh, graduated in 2014?"

"So they keep telling me."

"Sorry, I don't remember who you are."

"If it makes you feel better, I don't remember you either. But, I was kind of checked out for the entirety of high school. Didn't leave much of a lasting impression."

Ashtyn laughs. "That's fair. I'm Ashtyn. Ashtyn King."

Marlee sticks her hand out. "Marlee Adams, pleased to make your acquaintance."

Ashtyn shakes her hand, a small smile forming on her face. She likes this girl for some reason. "Do you, uh, still live around here?"

"No, actually, I'm in New York City with my fiancée these days. But, my dad's still here, so I come visit every once in a while."

"No shit? What brought you to New York?"

"Film school," Marlee says, smiling. "I'm actually directing my debut indie film this upcoming summer."

"Oh my god, that's amazing!" Ashtyn exclaims. "I'm a huge film buff. What's your movie about?"

"It's a romantic drama. But I should warn you, it doesn't have a happy ending."

"Those are my favorite," Ashtyn replies with a smile.

The two girls talk, exchanging information and social media handles, so Ashtyn can follow Marlee's film journey. "You let me know when it comes out, and I'll be the first to watch," Ashtyn says.

"I'll hold you to that," Marlee replies. "Hey, I gotta go. Perry will be wondering where I am. It was nice to meet you, though."

"You too," Ashtyn says, a small smile on her face. Marlee waves as she leaves the bathroom. Ashtyn's anxiety has eased, this conversation in the bathroom a nice escape from the real world outside. She takes a deep breath, splashes some water on her face, and leaves the bathroom.

As soon as her foot leaves the threshold, the door to the men's restroom, right across from the women's, opens at the exact same time. Ashtyn looks up and freezes in her tracks, her blood running cold. No, it can't be. He didn't RSVP...

Time slows, the air suddenly sucked out of the room. Ashtyn feels like she's suffocating. She's nineteen again, heart bleeding out on the floor in front of her, eyes blank as her brain tries to process what just happened.

"Ashtyn?" Brandon's voice brings her back to the present and makes her knees wobble. Despite herself, her eyes instantly dart toward his left hand, where his ring finger lays bare. *Bare.* When she doesn't say anything, Brandon takes a step forward. "Hey, Ash."

The world feels like it tips over, like she's upside down and doesn't know how to get back right-side up. She's dizzy, her body like jelly. "Don't call me that," she croaks out. Her voice seems to have shriveled up and died. She's alone, her friends nowhere to be seen. Drew, nowhere to be seen. No one is here but her and him. Two people who should not be in the same room as each other.

Brandon laughs lightly, the sound grating on her nerves. "What, is that not your name anymore?" He doesn't seem fazed by her presence.

No, he seems like he was prepared for her.

"Only my friends call me that." Her hands shake uncontrollably, and she tucks them into her armpits, so Brandon doesn't see.

"Oh, come on, Ash," Brandon scoffs. "We used to be friends. It's good to see you." *Used to be friends. Were they not more than that?*

She huffs, trying to find her strength. She stands up straighter. "Can't say the same."

Even though he's aged ten years, she can still see him how he used to be, how she last saw him. Dark hair still cropped short, tan skin glowing under the lights. She's still slightly taller than him when she wears heels, something he always gave her hell for. She tries to remember the last time they were together and happy, but she can't. She only remembers the wedding, the way he shook his head at her. That was the last time she saw him. The last memory she has of him.

"Really?" he says, crossing his arms. "This is how we're going to act?"

She has to bite back every retort she's ever crafted in her brain. She's thought about what she would say to him if she ever saw him again, but now that he's here, she can't think of anything. She just keeps staring at that empty ring finger, her mind empty. "Why are you here?" she eventually manages to ask, when she can't take the silence anymore.

Brandon shrugs, hands now shoved into his pockets. "Don't know. Saw your name on the RSVP list and thought it might be good to see you."

Goddamn that fucking RSVP list. Damn it to hell. "Good to see me?" She has to force the words past the lump in her throat.

"Look, I didn't come here for a fight, okay? I just wanted to say hi."

"Hi?" Her voice is high pitched, cracking on the word. She can't seem to stop repeating him. She clears her throat. "You really thought I'd want to see you?"

Brandon sighs, rolling his eyes. "Come on, Ash. Hasn't it been long enough?" He takes his hands out of his pockets and rubs his ring finger self-consciously, her gaze laser focused on the tan line where a ring should be. Something inside her cracks.

"Was it worth it?" she asks. The words come out harsh, a bite to them. When Brandon doesn't reply, a stupid, confused look on his face, Ashtyn continues, gesturing toward his bare finger. "Losing me for something that didn't even work out?" She thinks back to Haley's words a few months ago. *Be brave. Don't let him win.*

Brandon doesn't smile as he says, "I never thought of it as losing you." The words feel like bullets in her skin, tears instantly springing to her eyes despite her will to keep them hidden. Her mouth hangs open, words no longer forming on her lips. Brandon takes a step toward her. She doesn't have the strength to step away, her body frozen in place. Brandon frowns. "Did you really think we were happy? We were kids. We had no idea what we were doing." His words feel like a cruel joke, meant to harm her and only her.

"Why?" she asks, voice hoarse. "Why did you invite me?" She doesn't need to be specific. He knows what she's talking about. The horrible, unspeakable event has long hung between them, neither one daring to bring it up.

"Because I wanted you to see what it was like!" Brandon explodes, like he's been holding this back for ten years. "Because I wanted you to see me happy, something I never was with you." The pain is so real, it feels like her heart is going to tear through her skin and land on the floor, just like it did all those years ago. "I mean, how could you not see it? All the excuses I made to not come see you? The ignored texts? I thought you'd get the hint, but you never did. You just kept coming back, and I couldn't take it anymore."

Don't let him win. Don't let him win. Don't let him win. But right now, it feels like she's losing, like she's on the precipice of a deep chasm, moments from falling over the edge. "You were never happy?" The way she asks it, weak and pathetic, has her hating herself. Hating that she needs to know the answer.

"I mean, at first I was, sure. But we were teenagers. We fell into a safety net, and we were both scared to go off and find something better. Until I met Callie. When I met her, it felt like waking up."

"So then where is she, huh? If she's so perfect, and you're so happy, where is she?"

Brandon shrugs. "We grew apart. I think I was so desperate for something else that I rushed into a marriage I wasn't ready for. It just slowly fell apart after that."

Desperate. Never happy. How could you not see it? The words echo in Ashtyn's head, over and over again. A mantra of her failures. "What do you want from me? Did you come here just to rub this in my face?"

"Of course not," Brandon says, frowning. "Like I said, I just wanted to say hi. Maybe put to rest some bad blood. But, obviously, you're not ready for that."

His words stun her. "*I'm* the one that's not ready for it? Brandon, I'm the one who had their heart broken. I'm the one that made a fool out of herself at someone else's goddamn wedding—"

He holds up a hand to stop her, like he can just silence her at the drop of a hat. "I'm gonna stop you right there, because that was your own fucking fault, and you know it. Nobody told you to fucking stand up and ruin a wedding. *My* wedding."

She can't take it anymore. "I fucking hate you!" she yells, tears spilling over onto her cheeks. "I-I hate you."

"Ash?" Drew's voice breaks her spiral, her head whipping toward him.

No, she wants to scream. *Don't come any closer. Don't let Brandon win. Don't let him ruin anything else that she cares for.* She holds up a hand to get Drew to stay where he is, but he doesn't. Instead, he grabs it, pulling her close. Her body is rigid, eyes trained to the floor where she doesn't have to face her problems. Drew turns toward Brandon, arms still around Ashtyn. "What's going on?"

Brandon and Drew stare at each other, sizing the other up. Brandon ignores him, turning his gaze back to Ashtyn. "You don't hate me, Ashtyn. You hate yourself."

"What the fuck did you just say?" Drew questions, body tensing.

"I wasn't talking to you."

"Let me guess, you're Brandon?" Ashtyn has never heard Drew so angry before, his voice hard and bitter.

"I see my reputation precedes me. What, you tell all your boyfriends about me?" Brandon asks, and it's this that makes Drew snap. He charges forward, letting go of Ashtyn and pushing Brandon against the wall in less than a second.

"Drew!" she yells, shocked at the sudden outburst.

"What the fuck did you say to her?" Drew growls, arm against Brandon's chest. He has quite a few inches on Brandon, so it's easy for him to look down on the guy.

"The truth," Brandon basically spits, pushing back against Drew. "And she couldn't handle it, per usual."

Ava and Shiloh turn the corner just as Drew raises his fist toward Brandon's face. Ava gasps, and Shiloh is immediately upon Drew, holding him back from smashing Brandon's face into the wall.

"Stop," Ashtyn cries, her voice swallowed by all the noise. "Just stop."

Drew releases Brandon, Shiloh holding his arm tightly. Brandon ruffles his jacket, eyes sliding to Ashtyn. "Control your fucking boyfriend," he snaps.

"He's not..." Ashtyn starts, the words stuttering in her throat. "He's not my..." She can't bring herself to say the word, her throat filling with bile. The look Drew gives her cracks her chest wide open, spilling her pain onto the floor. Everything she was worried about happening has happened. This is her worst nightmare.

Brandon laughs, bitterly. "Even after all this time, you can't move on? How fucking pathetic."

"You utter another fucking word, and I will kill you," Ava says, words like venom, never once raising her voice. She stares daggers at him, her hands curled into fists.

"Wow, Ava, you finally grew a backbone," Brandon says, and Shiloh steps forward, rage on his face.

"Careful, or you'll be dealing with both of us." He lets go of Drew, who shakes out his arm and takes a step toward Ashtyn.

"Ash," he starts, but she takes a step away from him, his face falling. She can't seem to remember how to breathe, how to think, how to do anything.

She sees Brandon's retreating back, her friends' concerned gazes sliding to her as she gasps for breath. "I can't..." she starts, hand going to her chest to try and contain all the feelings bubbling up to the surface. "I can't." She's not sure if she means she can't breathe, or if she can't handle seeing Drew right now, or what, but she just shakes her head furiously.

"Come on," Ava says, taking her elbow gently. "Let's get some air. She turns to the boys. "Stay here. Both of you." Her voice is firm.

Ashtyn doesn't look at them, letting Ava lead her out of the gymnasium as quickly as they can manage. The warm September breeze hits them, and Ashtyn takes deep breaths of air, trying to calm her racing heart and her mind simultaneously.

"It's okay," Ava says, soothing her back comfortingly. "Just breathe. You're okay."

"He-he—" Ashtyn's breath trembles. She can't form the words.

"I know," Ava says, leaning her head on Ashtyn's shoulder. "I know, my love."

Ashtyn sobs, letting Ava hold her in her arms like she did ten years ago. She lets her best friend pick up her shattered pieces, knowing they're safe in her grasp. Ava will be here with her through this. She always will be. She's done this once before, and she'll do it again, no questions asked.

The door to gymnasium bursts open, and Ashtyn turns to see Drew rushing toward them, Shiloh calling after him. No. He can't see her like this. "Ashtyn," he says, breathing heavily. "I'm here."

She shakes her head against Ava's shoulder. She feels Brandon's words echo in her head like drum beats. He was never happy. How could she not see that? All she does is make people miserable. "Go away," she croaks.

He shakes his head furiously. "No. I told you I wouldn't leave, and I meant that."

She squeezes her eyes shut against the pain. "All I do is hurt people."

"That's not true, sweetheart."

"Yes, it is!" she explodes, stepping out of Ava's embrace. She wipes her tears on the back of her hand, her emotions out of control. "One day, you'll wake up and realize all I ever am is mean to you. That you've been unhappy for years and wish you left earlier. That I'm an unlovable piece of shit, just like I always have been. Just like I said from the start."

Ava gasps, hand going to her mouth as she watches the exchange. Drew shakes his head again, eyes watering with tears. "Are you telling me you're going to let some asshole tell you how to feel? How *I* feel about you? Because that's bullshit."

"Is it? What if he's right?"

"I don't care!" Drew yells, throwing his hands up in the air. "I don't fucking care what anyone else thinks, Ashtyn. I love you. I am in love with you."

"No, you aren't," she says, hating the way her body resists the words. She has to say it, to keep him safe from her. He can't love her. She'll just end up disappointing him.

"You're not allowed to tell me how I feel," he says, voice breaking on the last word.

"You'll find someone better," she says. "Everyone always does."

"And if I don't want someone better? If I only want you?"

She closes her eyes, so she doesn't have to look at him as she says, "You can't have me."

Drew sucks in a breath, a small sob emitting from him. "Ashtyn—"

"You can't fucking have me!" she screams, finally looking at him when she says it. They stare at each other, Drew's tears finally leaking down his cheeks. His face, one of complete devastation, will forever haunt her. He looks at her, begging her to change her mind, but she won't. She can't.

"Okay," he manages to get out, before he turns and heads toward the parking lot, not looking back. Shiloh runs after his friend, calling out to him, but he doesn't listen. He just keeps walking. Ashtyn's heart screams and pleads and begs her to stop him. To tell him she loves him too. But she doesn't. He deserves something better than what she can give him. In reality, she doesn't deserve him at all. She never will. And she won't be selfish this time. No, she has to let him go.

As she watches his retreating back, she lets out another sob, sinking to the floor. Ava rushes to her, wrapping her arms around her again. Ashtyn cries harder than she has in a long time, the emotions of so many years finally getting their release. After a while, when all her tears are dried up, she turns to Ava, shoulders sagging and heart in her throat. She asks, hoarsely, "Can I crash on your couch?"

OCTOBER

Chapter 34

The last few weeks have been miserable at best. Every time Ashtyn closes her eyes, she sees Drew's crumpled face as she yells, *you can't fucking have me.* She regretted the words the second they came out of her mouth, but she can't take them back. No, she can't take any of it back, now. No matter how badly she wants to. No matter how much she's haunted by it.

Ashtyn misses Drew something fierce, despite her brain telling her to let him go. How could he ever forgive her? How could he ever love her? She tries not to think about these things, keeping her brain occupied by copious amounts of movies or lesson planning for work. She's taken up residence on Shiloh and Ava's couch, which has been less than ideal. She's pretty sure she's left an Ashtyn-sized divot in the framework by now. Sleeping on it hurts her back, and she wakes with a dull pain in her spine. She's not sure how Shiloh did it for so long before moving in with them.

She takes it a day at a time, only letting herself cry once a day when she takes a shower, so no one can see her. Shiloh and Ava tiptoe around her, careful not to bring up Drew in any capacity. Sometimes, when it's late and they think she's asleep, she can hear them whispering to each other. She can never make out what they're saying, but she has a feeling it's about her. Or Drew. Or both of them. Either way, she doesn't want to know. She puts her hands over her ears and wills herself to fall asleep, praying she doesn't dream of Drew.

It hardly ever works. She dreams of him often, his face occupying so much of her brain she sometimes wants to scoop it out with a spoon, plopping it onto the floor where it can rot. It's never felt like this before. Even with Brandon, it was never *this* bad. This feels insurmountable.

"Miss King?" the little voice startles her out of her self-pity. Ashtyn looks up from her spot on the bench on the playground. Clarence looks up at her with his big, brown eyes.

"Hey buddy," she says, smiling at him. "How's first grade?" Even though he's no longer her student, she still sees him around the school.

"It's okay," he says, sitting next to her.

"Recess is almost over," she says, gently. "Don't you want to go play with your friends?"

Clarence ignores her and asks, "What's wrong?"

The question startles her. Is her face etched in a permanent frown, so even the kids can tell something is wrong? "Nothing's wrong, Clarence."

He sighs, like she's frustrating him. "Lying is bad."

This time, it's Ashtyn's turn to sigh. "You're right, I'm sorry. I'm just having a tough day."

Clarence looks up at her. "Are you sad?" He points to his chest, right above his heart. "In here?"

She has to bite her lip to keep the sob contained inside her, to keep all the sadness inside. She shouldn't be letting it interfere with her work, letting the kids see her like this. "I'm not sad," she says, but her voice cracks on the last word. She swallows, a single tear cascading down her cheek.

Clarence looks at her and places his tiny hand on her shoulder. "Don't cry, Miss King. I'm here."

"Thanks, buddy," she says, letting him lay his head on her shoulder. "You're a good kid."

"I hope you feel better," he says as the recess whistle signals the end of play time. He gets up, gives her one last smile, then heads to his teacher.

"Yeah, me too," Ashtyn says softly. "Me too."

* * *

It's Sunday, Ashtyn laying on the couch despite her protesting back, when Ava comes into the living room and slams a duffel bag on the ground. She starts stuffing Ashtyn's discarded clothes into it furiously.

"You're leaving," she says, voice firm and hard.

Ashtyn sits up, her back screaming. "Excuse me?"

"You heard me," Ava says, standing up straighter, seemingly mustering her courage. Shiloh is nowhere to be seen, even though Ashtyn knows he's home. "You need to leave."

She's only been here roughly two and a half weeks. She was too much of a coward to go pick up clothes from the apartment, so she'd made Shiloh go. He did it, but she could tell it upset him. She hates putting him in the middle of her and his best friend, but the thought of seeing Drew is too much. She just can't face him. "You're kicking me out?" she asks, voice like gravel. She's barely spoken to anyone, except for her kids at work. If she doesn't talk, her true feelings won't come tumbling out.

"Yes, because frankly, I've had it with you," Ava says, standing in front of her friend. "You're done sulking on the couch, rotting your life away. The pity party ends now." Ashtyn's not sure if she's ever heard Ava speak to her this way before. Of all the times Ashtyn has fallen down, Ava has always picked her up gently, with kind words and positive affirmations. Now, this seems like an entirely different Ava. One who's had enough of Ashtyn's shit. Not that she can necessarily blame her.

"Is that what you think this is?" Ashtyn asks, anger starting to stir in her veins. "A fucking pity party?" Her normal snarky tone is dead in the water. Instead, the words come out flat.

"I honestly don't know what this is, but we did this with Brandon, and I will be damned if we do this with Drew." Ava says, sharply. "I love you both too much to let you do this to yourselves."

"You're walking on some very thin ice, Ava Marshall."

"Good!" Ava exclaims. "I'm tired of playing it safe. Playing it safe means I wouldn't be with Shiloh. Playing it safe means you wallow on our couch for months on end, when you could be with Drew. Playing it safe means you don't get the happily ever after that I know you want."

Ashtyn's throat constricts. "Ava—"

"You seemed so happy before the reunion, Ash. You seemed like..." She sighs, unable to cross that line. So, Ashtyn does it for her.

"Someone in love," she answers for her friend, a dam bursting in her chest, flooding her system with feelings long repressed.

"Oh, Ash," Ava says, sinking onto the couch. She places a hand on her friend's shoulder. "Talk to me. Don't shut me out."

"But it's what I'm good at."

"Bullshit," Ava says, fiercely. "I am so tired of hearing you speak about yourself like you're not the most incredible person in my life. Why do you allow *me* to love you and not Drew? Why do you let Shiloh and all of our friends love you, but you won't accept Drew's love?"

The question rattles around in her brain. She's not sure how to articulate it, so she says softly, "Because romantic love feels different. Scarier."

"Is it really that different?" Ava asks. "All love is a *choice*. I choose to wake up every day and love you. To be your best friend, even on the worst of days. Even when you piss me off and make me want to tear my hair out. What's so different about waking up every day and choosing to love Drew as a partner? Wanting to share the most intimate parts of yourself with him?"

"Because what if he changes his mind? What if he decides he doesn't like every part of me?"

"I haven't changed *my* mind. I've seen every good and bad side of you, and I'm still here. Same with Shiloh. He's seen me at my worst, at my best, and he loves me through it all. That's what you do for the people you love."

"Bran—"

But Ava interrupts her before Ashtyn can even say his name. "You can't let *him* tell you how Drew feels. They're not the same, at all. Drew is so much better than him. He genuinely cares for you. I've seen the way he looks at you."

"I know," Ashtyn says, sniffling. "But I'm just so scared he'll change his mind."

"Love is scary," Ava says. "But it is worth it. You have to believe that. And you *know* Drew. You know he won't leave when things get tough. He showed you that night at the reunion that he wanted to stay."

"I thought that about Brandon," she whispers, feeling her resolve start to crumble again.

"Brandon is a gaslighting piece of shit, and if I ever see him again, I'm going to hit him with a shovel." Ava's response elicits a small laugh out of Ashtyn. "But, seriously. That was ten years ago. You are a different person now. Drew is *not* Brandon. He loves you so much. I've seen it. I just wish you could see it too."

Ashtyn knows Ava is right. She can feel it in her heart. She's let being scared hold her back for so long now. Her hands shake with the possibility. "I've fucked it all up," she admits. "There's no way Drew will take me back. He probably never wants to see me again."

Ava is about to say something when Shiloh steps into the room, clearing his throat. "You never know until you try."

Both girls look up at him in surprise. "Were you listening the whole time?" Ashtyn asks.

"Not the whole time, but I've been here, waiting to tell you to get off your ass and go tell my best friend how you feel about him."

Ashtyn stands on wobbly legs. "I'm scared."

"So was I," Shiloh says, nodding toward Ava. "I was terrified, but look how good it turned out. If you truly love each other, you will weather this storm. Together."

That word, *together*, has Ashtyn feeling a new sense of resolve wash over her. "Okay," she says. "Okay. I can do this. I can tell him how I feel."

"And how *do* you feel?" Ava asks, gently.

A smile tugs at Ashtyn's lips. "That I love him. That I'm scared to death he'll change his mind, but hoping beyond belief that he still loves me back, despite everything."

Ava squeezes her hand. "Go get him."

Ashtyn gathers her keys and heads toward the door, finger combing her matted hair as she goes, trying to look presentable before she loses her confidence.

"He's not at the apartment," Shiloh says, a small smile on his face as she wrenches open the front door.

She stops, foot just over the threshold, and looks up at her friend. "Where is he?"

Chapter 35

Drew stares at the shelf of movies, each one of them taunting him, laughing at him for losing her. He throws a tennis ball against the wall with a *thunk*. The TV isn't on, Drew's sad reflection staring back at him from the blank screen. He throws the tennis ball again and again and again. *Thunk. Thunk. Thunk.* He does this monotonous task every day now, unable to get up and do anything productive, unable to watch anything without thinking of Ashtyn.

His brain torments him, over and over again. Everything in the apartment reminds him of her. In every dusty corner, her presence haunts him. His sheets still smell like her, even after countless washes. Her things are still strewn across the apartment, a pair of shoes she left in the hallway, hair ties on the coffee table. So many little things that remind him she left.

His heart aches. Every beat reiterates, *she was too good to be true. You were too happy for it to be real.* He's never felt this empty and alone after a breakup, if you can even call it that. A breakup. Such a trivial word for what happened. No, it felt more like a severing of souls, something now missing from his life. He really thought he'd found his happily ever after. How fucking stupid.

She hasn't come by to get any of her stuff, despite being away for almost three weeks now. She sent Shiloh to pick up some clothes, but that's it. When Drew asked him how she was doing, he just looked sad and shrugged. "Not good."

The need to go to her, to make sure she's okay, is unbearable. Even if she hurt him. Even if she told him that he can't have her. *You can't fucking have me.* The words torture him. He hears it every time he closes his eyes. So instead, he stares at the blank TV, throwing the tennis ball back and forth... back and forth. The monotony lulls him into a state of vacancy.

He feels his phone buzz next to him, jolting him out of his stupor. He glances at it, not letting himself hope that it's Ashtyn. Still, disappointment washes over him when he sees Haley's name on the screen. He swipes open her text.

Hey, you still coming to family dinner tonight?

Ever since Haley's been back at home, they've implemented family dinner again every couple of weeks. Haley is slowly fixing her relation-ship with their parents, and Drew is happy for them. If family dinner helps, then he'll be there. But right now, he's dreading it. His parents will ask about Ashtyn, and he'll have to admit that they're not together anymore. Haley will have a million questions. He'll remember Ash at the table, looking like she belonged, and it will ache. God, he should skip. He shouldn't go. But he has to, if only for Haley.

He texts back with shaky fingers: *Yes.*

They burn with the urge to text Ashtyn. But then he remembers her words, and he balls his fists and presses them into his eyes until he sees spots. *You can't fucking have me.* Over and over again, it's all he hears.

He gets up off the couch in a rush, tugging on his jacket, trying to keep his hands busy so he doesn't text her, or call her, or yearn for her anymore. He doesn't look down the hall toward her room as he leaves, skipping down the stairs as fast as he can. Once in the parking garage, he takes a deep breath, letting the cool October air fill his lungs. He doesn't look in the passenger seat, where he knows her discarded cardigan sits. Everywhere. She's everywhere.

He turns the radio up as loud as it will go and rolls the windows down, not giving his brain a moment to think on the drive up to his parents' house. His hands drum a steady beat on the steering wheel, his non-driving leg jiggling anxiously. *Do not look at the cardigan*, he thinks. Do not look.

The drive ends way too soon, and his hands shake as he opens the front door. He instantly hears Haley talking a mile a minute, their father's big belly laugh echoing throughout the house. Not even that, or the smell of dinner, cheers him up. He enters the kitchen, where he sees his mother at the table, flipping through an old photo album.

"Ashtyn, I hope you're ready to see—" His mother stops when she looks up and sees only her son in the doorway. "Oh, honey, where's Ashtyn?" Hearing her name come out of his mother's mouth has him wanting to double over and cry.

"She's not coming," Drew forces himself to say, swallowing against the sadness.

"Is she sick?" Flora Mitchell asks, eyebrows furrowed in concern. "I can make her some soup and send it back with you—"

"No, Mom," Drew says, softly. "We, uh, decided to end things."

A loud clatter startles the room as Haley drops an entire baking sheet of potatoes on the ground. They scatter all over the floor in every direction. No one moves an inch to clean them up. "What do you mean you ended things?" Haley asks, her gaze laser focused on him. Her hair is dyed fully pink again, something he didn't even notice until now. It's a sign she's happy. That she's healing.

"Your hair is pink," he says, looking at her.

"And you're missing a redhead," she counters.

He sighs, running a hand through his hair. "I don't want to talk about it."

"Well, too bad," Haley says. "What the fuck happened?" Their mother doesn't even say anything about the swear jar. "You've been in love with this girl for over a year, and you just ended things?"

"Yes," Drew says simply, not bothering to correct her. No, *he* didn't end things. Ashtyn did. She left, and it hurt like hell.

"That's all you're going to say?"

"It's complicated, Haley," Drew growls, feeling his patience wearing thin.

"Then uncomplicate it! You two are supposed to be together."

"Yeah, well, sometimes things don't work out!" Drew exclaims.

"Bullshit," Haley says again. "That's a bullshit excuse, and you know it." Their parents are silent, watching the exchange with sad expressions on their faces. Drew can't stand it, the pity.

"I don't need anyone feeling sorry for me," he says, looking toward the ground.

"Oh, I'm not," Haley says. "I'm pissed."

"Oh, I'm sorry, do you think I'm not?" Drew asks, his voice starting to raise toward his sister. "Do you think I'm not miserable in my apartment, waiting for her to come back? Hoping that every little noise is her key in the lock? Praying that she changes her mind and decides to love me back? Do you think I don't fucking feel that?" His voice breaks on the last word, a tear escaping down his cheek.

"Oh, honey," his mother says, getting up and gathering her son into her arms. He feels like a child again, crying in his mother's arms, the smell of her perfume comforting him.

"Drew," Haley starts, shuffling her way through fallen potatoes to kneel in front of him, her hand on his knee. "I'm sorry."

He grips his sister's hand tightly. The unspoken love they have for each other passes between them. "I love her," he admits, quietly. "And I don't think I've ever felt that way before."

"What happened?"

"She left. She got scared, and she left. I told her I loved her, and she didn't say it back." It's easier to say this than the full story. Without having to repeat the awful things Brandon said to her.

"Then tell her again," Haley says, fiercely, tears in her eyes. "Fight for her."

"What if she doesn't want me to?" he asks, Ashtyn's words echoing in his heart, in his head, everywhere.

"Honey, you can't force someone to love you," Flora says gently, either to Drew or Haley, he's not sure.

"I've seen the way she looks at you," Haley says. "I know she loves you. I know it."

"Love can make even the bravest of people terrified," Sam Mitchell's deep voice echoes through the kitchen. Everyone looks up at him as he leans against the counter. "Lord knows I was terrified to admit I was in love with your mother. Took me a long time to pluck up the courage."

"She's been hurt in the past," Drew says, wiping his eyes on his shirt.

"Then she's probably scared to get hurt again," his father says. "All you can do is show her that you love her and hope she loves you more than she's scared. That she learns to lean on you in those scary times, rather than running."

Everyone's voices blur together in his head as he presses his hands to his eyes. "I need some air," he says, getting up from the table. There's nothing he can do right now anyway. "I'll be back in a bit." This time, it's him who's running.

The sky grumbles as he closes the front door, the beginning of a storm starting to brew, but he doesn't care. He trudges his way up to his favorite hill, the one he took Ashtyn to all those months ago. His legs burn as he makes his way up the steep slope, muscles not having worked this hard in weeks. He likes the burn. It distracts him from the pain in his heart.

As he crests the hill, the sun begins its descent, bathing the world in a golden amber that reminds him of Ashtyn's hair. He sits in the grass, the sky darkening minute by minute as the storm rolls in. A crack of thunder echoes across the sky, a flash of lightning illuminating the clouds. As the first few drops of rain begin to drop, Drew doesn't get up. He sits and lets the rain soak him to his bones.

<h1 style="text-align:center">Chapter 36</h1>

Ashtyn drives like a mad woman across the city toward Drew's parents' home. The sky rumbles with thunder, a downpour threatening to happen at any moment. She feels that thunder in herself, her body vibrating with the need to see Drew. To tell him everything. To apologize for her mistakes. The city flies by in a blur, fading from high rises to residential houses. That steady pace of home thumps in her heart, telling her to keep going, to not turn back. *Be brave*, she thinks.

She pulls up the driveway of the house, and her heart stutters at the sight of Drew's truck sitting there. She's out of the car and walking up the porch before she can change her mind. Her fist is poised to knock when the door suddenly swings open, Haley standing there, arms crossed over her chest.

"He's not here," she says. Ashtyn feels herself start to crumble, but then Haley tips her head toward the sloping hill, a small smile tugging on the corners of her lips. "He's up there. Go get him." Haley squeezes her arm before shutting the door in her face.

Ashtyn smiles. Then, she runs.

She regrets running about halfway up the hill. Her heart races so fast, she feels like it's going to burst out of her chest. Her legs ache and burn. She continues her trudge upward, albeit slowly, not letting anything stop her from her mission. As she crests the top of the hill, lightning flashes across the sky, illuminating the figure sitting at the edge of the grass, looking out across the city. Drops of water begin to plop from the sky, hard and fast, instantly soaking her.

She stops and stares at him for a moment, breathing heavily as the rain begins its downpour. Drew doesn't move, even as the water pelts his body. As she looks at him, she feels a hatred of herself start to stew, hating that she's upset him, that she's hurt him. Made him come to his favorite hill and sit in the rain. Hating everything she said to him. She just wants to take it back.

She tries to call out to him, but she's breathing so hard, her voice sticks in her throat, nothing coming out. She's not sure he'd be able to hear her over the rain anyway. Luckily, Drew decides to get up and head back at that moment. As he turns, he freezes in place when he sees her across the hill. She's bent over, still trying to catch her goddamn breath. She raises an arm to him in greeting, as if they're just two friends meeting up for dinner. "Hi," she breathes, chest rising and falling in quick succession. "I ran up that hill." She flails an arm behind her to point at said hill.

Drew takes a tentative step toward her, like he can't believe she's really here. Like he's imagining it. He raises an eyebrow at her. "You ran?" She can barely hear him over the storm.

She nods, hands on her hips, raising her voice. "Believe me, I'm just as surprised as you are. Sorry, can you give me a minute? I got a whole speech planned and just need to catch my breath."

"Ashtyn—"

"Please," she wheezes, stopping him in his tracks. She takes a few more deep breaths, finally getting her heartbeat steady again. She looks up at the sky, the rain splattering against her face. "I lied. When I said you can't have me, I lied." Drew crosses his arms across his chest as he stares at her. The rain soaks his hair to his forehead. She hates the distance between them. She wants to go to him, but she will wait.

She will tell him what she needs to tell him and wait.

She smiles at him, her face softening. She will be brave. "You have had me from the moment you dropped that box on my foot." Drew lets out a strangled breath, eyes going to the sky. "You have had me every moment of every day since. I may not have realized it, but I think I always knew. I knew that every road would somehow lead me back to you. That no matter where I ended up, you would always be there with me, because you are mine and I am yours. And the idea of losing you scares me to my very core. Scares me so bad that I thought leaving you would be easier, but I was wrong. I was so wrong."

Drew's gaze turns to her, and he takes a step forward, the rain now dumping buckets on both of them. But neither seem to care. "Ashtyn," he says. She steps into his embrace, her hands cupping his rain-soaked cheeks. She can't tell what is rain and what is tears. "You hurt me."

"I'm sorry," she says, her heart aching at his words. "I'm so sorry I hurt you. I'm sorry that I was scared and that I pushed you away when things got tough. I let a past relationship define me, when I should have talked to you, as my partner, and trusted you when you said you wouldn't leave. I'm so sorry. I'm so sorry I said things I won't ever be able to take back. I-I can't promise I won't make mistakes in this relationship. I can't promise I won't get scared again. But, I *can* promise that I will come to you when I get scared. That I will talk to you. I can promise that I will love you, for as long as you will have me. I love you, Drew. I love you."

They're soaking wet, the rain a steady downpour over them. Drew's forehead rests against hers, his thumbs stroking away the water from her face. "Please don't run from me again." His voice is pained. "I'm here, I promise. You have to trust me."

Ashtyn nods, fiercely. "I trust you."

"I have loved you from the moment I laid eyes on you," he breathes. A rush of relief and love courses through her as a clap of thunder strikes overhead, his grip tightening on her.

"I'm sorry it took me so long to realize," she whispers, their noses skimming each other, lips grazing. "I'm yours, if you'll have me."

"If you'll have me," Drew scoffs against her lips. "As if I could ever want anyone else in this world, sweetheart."

A small whimper escapes her. "I love you. I love you so much."

"I love you," Drew says, finally bringing his lips to hers. His kiss feels like coming home, like finally breathing fresh air after drowning, despite the rain around them. It feels like forever.

"Will you come home?" he asks.

"*You* are my home," she breathes. "I go where you go." She can feel his smile against her mouth.

"Then let's go," he says, grabbing her hand. They make their way down the hill carefully, but quickly, trying not to slip on the water.

"I brought my car," she says once they're at the bottom, facing both of their vehicles.

"We can get it tomorrow," he says, scooping her up in one swift movement and placing her in the passenger seat of the truck.

"And your parents?"

"Again, tomorrow. Right now, I just need you home with me."

The door to the apartment is barely closing before their lips are on each other again, their wet clothes falling to the floor with a loud smack. They're already completely naked by the time they reach the bathroom, Ashtyn shivering from her rain-soaked skin. Drew turns the shower on, rubbing her arms to keep her warm.

She shivers again as she steps under the hot water, letting it soak her bones. Drew joins her, his hands massaging her shoulders as they warm up under the water together. His lips caress the shell of her ear, and she feels a bolt of desire rush through her. She can't take her hands off of him, her body desperate to discover every inch of him. Desperate to discover everything he will give her.

"You know this means you're stuck with me, right?" Drew says, thumbs tracing the edge of her jaw. She smiles, as his hands travel down her neck, over her shoulders, and down her ribcage.

She hums in pleasure at the thought. "Mmm, I like the sound of that."

"Stay," he says, holding her tight.

"I promise," she replies, turning and placing a kiss on his chest. "I'm yours. Today, tomorrow, always. It will always be us."

"And I'm yours," Drew breathes into her hair. "I love you."

It feels like a vow, just the two of them under the spray of the shower. A promise they intend to keep, no matter the odds, no matter the obstacles. No matter how hard life gets, they will handle it together, as partners, like they were always meant to.

"You and me," she says.

"You and me," he repeats.

"Us."

NOVEMBER

Epilogue

It's warm for a November day, which means most of the animals are out, sunning themselves. A tiger lays lazily on the ground, his eyes closed in what Ashtyn can only assume is contentment. An arm wraps around her middle as she watches the tiger, Drew's face nuzzling into her neck. She smiles, leaning back into his embrace, a flush of color heating her cheeks as she revels in their love for each other.

"Happy Birthday, sweetheart," he says, pressing a kiss to her throat. She turns so she's facing him, his arms bracketing her as he places them on the railing. She grabs him by the shirt and pulls him into a deep kiss, one that has her wishing they weren't in public.

"I love you," she hums into his mouth. "Thanks for taking me to the zoo on my birthday."

"And I love you. You know, I can't even remember the last time I've been to the zoo," Drew replies, looking over her shoulder at the tiger. It continues its lay in the sun, unaware of the world around him.

"Do you think Jess descends from a line of tigers?" Ava asks, as she and Shiloh finally meander their way over to where Ashtyn and Drew have been waiting for them.

"No way," Ashtyn replies. "She's too little. And friendly."

"Hey, you don't know if that tiger is friendly or not!" Ava protests. "I bet he and Jess would be friends."

The tiger, as if sensing their conversation, huffs in his sleep and rolls over. There's a slight ache in Ashtyn's chest as she watches the ginormous cat. An ache that could be mended by a cat of her own. Even though she sees Jess all the time, it's not the same as having one that greets you when you come home and lays on your chest when you sleep. She's been trying to muster up the courage to ask Drew if he'd consider letting them get a cat. Hence the zoo trip for her birthday.

"That tiger would eat her for breakfast," Shiloh replies, kissing Ava's hand where it's intertwined with his. She harrumphs, then charges forward toward the next enclosure, dragging Shiloh along as he grins lazily at her. Ashtyn chuckles, then takes Drew's hand and begins to follow them.

"You know," she starts, biting her lip. "That tiger was pretty cute."

"Yeah," Drew replies, hands swinging between them. The sun is warm as it beats down on them, warm enough that they don't even need jackets. They pass the lion enclosure, seemingly empty. Maybe they're inside, hiding away for the day.

"Wouldn't it be cute? You know, having our own cat?" She doesn't look at him when she says it.

He coughs, loudly. "Uh, yeah, maybe. Oh look! Dang, that is one freaky looking bird." He points toward the next enclosure where a giant blue bird is staring right at Ava. She stares back with wide eyes, like she's never seen anything like it before.

Ashtyn pushes Drew's dismissal down as they join their friends. It was stupid to bring it up now, anyway. The plaque in front of the enclosure reads "Cassowary." The bird kind of looks like an ostrich, but smaller and with a blue neck and face. Its feet are like something out of *Jurassic Park*, the claws long and lethal.

"Okay, be honest. Me versus the cassowary. Who would win?" Drew asks.

"The cassowary," Ava, Ashtyn, and Shiloh answer in unison.

A zookeeper chuckles from where she stands off to the side. "That there is one of our more dangerous animals," she says. "Don't think anyone could win in a fight against that one."

"Oh my god, seriously?" Ava asks, turning toward the zookeeper.

She nods gravely. "See those claws? One swipe of those and you're gutted." Ava peppers the zookeeper with more questions as Ashtyn turns and heads down the path. She only makes it a few steps before Drew's arm wraps around her.

"You okay?" he asks, noticing her slight frown.

"Fine," she mutters.

"Hey." He steps in front of her, his hands coming up to her arms. She sighs and looks up at him. "What's wrong? You're not allowed to be upset on your birthday."

"I'm not upset," she says, biting her lip. "I just... miss Jess a lot, is all."

Drew pulls her into a hug, something she never thought she'd love as much as she does. His hugs feel like home, like she belongs exactly in the space between his chest and arms. He squeezes her gently, pressing a kiss to the top of her head. "I promise you," he says. "That we will get a cat when the time is right."

Ashtyn's eyes widen as she looks up at him. "Really?"

"Pinky promise." He holds up his pinky to her. She wraps her own around his, kissing her enclosed fist to seal the deal. He kisses his then moves their hands away and places a kiss to her lips.

"I'm holding you to that," she mumbles against his mouth.

He smiles. "Deal. Now, let's get going. I wanna see some snakes."

* * *

It's later in the afternoon when they arrive back at the apartment, sweaty and tired from a long day at the zoo. Drew can feel the anticipation of Ashtyn seeing her surprise tugging at his bones. He'd had such a difficult time keeping it from her, but he knew it would all be worth it. He can't wait to see her face.

As they approach the door, he can hear two distinct voices arguing from behind it. "What do you mean you lost her? She's tiny!" Mattie's voice is a hushed whisper.

"Well! She slipped out of my grasp! And this stupid apartment is ginormous," Haley grumbles.

Drew mentally slaps his forehead. He knew he shouldn't have enlisted these two for help. He should have asked Brooke and Jordan. He clears his throat, loudly, before opening the door to the apartment. Mattie and Haley are both on the floor, looking under various pieces of furniture for the misplaced surprise.

"We're back!" Drew announces, raising his voice so they can hear him. Both Mattie and Haley instantly jerk up, yelling their well wishes toward Ashtyn. She looks at them curiously.

"What are you two doing here?" she asks, accepting a hug from Haley.

"Uh, Drew enlisted our help with decorating!" Mattie says, eyes darting in every direction.

Ashtyn looks around at the undecorated apartment. "Really?"

"Well, we would have gotten more done if this one—" Haley jerks her thumb at Mattie, "—hadn't *lost* the most important decoration."

"I didn't lose her! You did!" Mattie exclaims, then slaps a hand over his mouth as he realizes his slip. Ashtyn looks between them with raised eyebrows.

Drew rubs his forehead in agitation. "Can I see you two in the bedroom, please?"

Mattie and Haley shuffle toward Drew's bedroom while Ava and Shiloh steer Ashtyn toward the living room. Once they're alone, Drew shuts the door. That's when he sees the half-assembled cat tree sitting in the corner. "You didn't even finish assembling the tree?"

"Again, Mattie's fault," Haley says, crossing her arms. "Apparently he doesn't know how to read instructions."

"Oh, you are so full of it!" Mattie replies.

Drew can't handle their bickering, so he holds up a hand to get them to stop. "Where exactly is the cat? That's the one thing you were supposed to keep track of."

Haley looks at the floor guiltily. "She's sneaky, that one! We were trying to assemble the cat tree, and she must have slipped away. We've been looking for her for like half an hour!"

Drew sighs, eyes going to the ceiling. Well, so much for the surprise. Now he's just worried where the kitten could have run off to.

"Andrew Mitchell!" Ashtyn exclaims from the living room. "Get your ass out here right now!"

Her tone isn't angry, but he still rushes out to the living room like someone lit a fire under his ass. "Ash—"

He stops as he sees her holding the tiny kitten in her hands, a ginormous smile on her face. "Did you lose something?"

"Oh, you found her!" Haley exclaims. "Perfect. Happy Birthday!"

The tiny black kitten meows, butting her head against Ashtyn's chin. The bell on her collar jingles, and Ashtyn looks down at the engraved plate that reads "Raisin."

She looks up at Drew with a wide smile and says in a perfect Winston impression, "As I live and breathe!? Raisin!?"

Drew laughs, remembering when he first saw that episode of *New Girl* with Ashtyn. He laughed so hard tears leaked out of the corners of his eyes. It was a gamble to name the kitten without asking her, but it looks like it paid off. "We can change her name if you don't like it—"

"She's ours?" Ashtyn asks, looking at the kitten in adoration. Raisin licks her cheek.

"Yes, she's ours. I picked her out at the shelter a few weeks ago. Haley picked her up for us today. Happy Birthday, Ash."

Ashtyn nuzzles the kitten, holding her close to her chest. "Raisin," she says. "She's perfect." Drew pets Raisin, the small kitten licking his finger in response. Ashtyn looks up at him. "Thank you. I love her. And I love you."

"Does this mean we can have cake now?" Haley asks.

Drew doesn't look away from Ashtyn as he says, "You and Mattie still have a cat tree to assemble. Get to it."

They both grumble but oblige, heading toward the room to finish their job. Ava smiles as she coos at Raisin from Ashtyn's arms. "We have to have kitty playdates!" she exclaims. "Oh, and we can get those backpacks for cats and take them out to the park!"

Drew's not sure if Ashtyn even hears what Ava says as she stares lovingly at Raisin. This, right here, is worth everything to Drew. Seeing her happy, seeing her loved and accepting of that love. It fills Drew's heart so much he feels it might burst. God, he loves her so much. He thinks he'd do anything to keep her this happy.

Raisin plops to the floor and proceeds to chase Ava's unbound shoelace. Ashtyn giggles, leaning into Drew's embrace, her laughter reverberating through his bloodstream. He squeezes her to him, leaning down to whisper in her ear. "That's not all. We have friends coming over soon."

* * *

Raisin is the absolute star of the party. Ashtyn doesn't really mind though, seeing how utterly enamored she is with the little kitten. She thinks this might be the best birthday she's ever had. Having all her friends shower her with love and celebration feels like a gift. And being here in her apartment with Drew, the love of her life, the partner of her dreams, feels like an actual dream come true. One she never wants to wake from.

Everyone ooh's and ahh's over Raisin, whose name is literally so perfect Ashtyn can't believe Drew knows her that well. The second she saw it, she knew what he was referencing. It's so perfect. Everyone wants a snuggle with the kitten, Raisin obliging everyone's kisses and pets.

"Hey, you," Drew says, finding Ashtyn in the kitchen refilling her wine glass. "I was wondering where you snuck off to. They're about to set up Blockbuster. Want to show them how good of a team we make?"

Ashtyn hums as she hops up on the counter, Drew coming to stand between her legs. "I think I'm getting déjà vu."

Drew play growls into her neck. "Are you gonna tell me not to touch you again?"

Ashtyn laughs breathily. "I don't think I could last a day without your hands on me anymore."

Drew presses a kiss to her collarbone, Ashtyn's hands running through his hair. She's about to suggest they should risk a quickie in the bathroom when she sees Mattie and Haley standing, shoulder to shoulder, on the balcony of their bedroom. "Hey," she whispers, pulling Drew's chin toward her gaze. "Look at them."

Drew sees the pair and groans, his forehead resting on Ashtyn's shoulder. "Those two."

She giggles, watching as Haley throws her head back in laughter, Mattie watching her with a small smile on his face. They pass a beer back and forth, arms leaning on the railing. "Is there a reason you needed *both* of them to help with my surprise?"

Drew smiles. "Now that you mention it, no there wasn't."

Ashtyn giggles again, fingers playing with the edges of Drew's hair. She pulls his face up to hers. "I love you, you know that right?"

"I do. I love you too."

They kiss deeply, getting lost in each other until Ava yells from the other room. "Time for Blockbuster!"

They pull apart, both smiling at each other like fools in love. "Should we tell them?" Drew asks, gesturing toward Mattie and Haley.

Ashtyn looks at them one last time, smiling as they bump each other's shoulders playfully. "Nah, let them have their moment. Come on," she says, jumping off the counter and pulling him toward the living room. "Let's go kick some ass."

Drew smiles. "You read my mind, sweetheart."

ACKNOWLEDGMENTS

Every time I get to this point, having a full novel sitting in front of me, I get an overwhelming sense of gratitude and amazement that I get to do this. I don't take a second of this for granted, and I am so thankful that I get to live my dreams. Thank you to everyone that makes this possible for me.

First, my husband, Isaac. Thank you for loving me on the days that I feel unlovable. I couldn't do what I do without your endless support and love. I love you, endlessly.

My parents, for showing me what a healthy relationship looks like. The love you have for each other inspires me everyday. I love you both so much.

My sisters, for always making sure the sibling dynamics in my books aren't ever too unrealistic! I love you both.

Emily, for keeping me on track and making sure I'm not using the same word three times in the same sentence. I can never thank you enough for all that you have done for me. Thank you again for designing the cover and doodles for this book.

My bananas, Katie, Nicole, Meredith, Rian, always and forever.

My book club girlies, Jenna, Mel, Brenna, Clarisa, and Danielle, for always cheering me on, no matter what. Your support never ceases to amaze me. A special thank you to Danielle for a certain name suggestion!

Grace, for helping make this book the best it can possibly be. I love your ideas, even when they're insane.

Mario, for being the kindest, sweetest person on this earth. Thank you for being my friend.

Lisa, for welcoming me into your home almost eleven years ago and letting me come and go still to this day. Thank you for everything.

Sumer, for always helping curate the best playlists known to man. You are essential to every book I write.

The incredible community I've curated online, thank you for always hyping me up and supporting me! It's such a joy to share this space with you all.

A special thank you to all my ARC readers. I appreciate your time, honesty, and feedback!

Finally, to the readers, old and new, a huge thank you to all of you. You are the reason I get to continue sharing these stories. Forever and ever, thank you. Truly.

About the Author

A.J. Woods is a native Texan where she participated in Girl Scouts, AYSO soccer, and German Club when she was a teenager. After high school, she attended Angelo State University where she majored in English with a specialization in Creative Writing and double minored in German and Gender Studies. She spent one semester studying abroad in Hannover, Germany. After graduation, she pursued her master's degree in English Literature and graduated December of 2020. She has dreamed of being a writer since the fourth grade.

You can connect with me on:

- https://ajwoodsauthor.com
- https://www.facebook.com/profile.php?id=61563303127340
- https://open.spotify.com/user/31mxwvmdvartl6nl23lvdcbhb62i

Also by A.J. Woods

Moving In

SHILOH BROOKS IS IN DESPERATE NEED OF A ROOMMATE. OR TWO.

Thankfully, Ava Marshall, and her best friend Ashtyn, are also in the market. When Shiloh moves in, divorced and down on his luck, it seems like a fresh start.

Ava, a head in the clouds romantic, knows she should keep things platonic with her new roommate. Unfortunately, her heart has other plans.

A year of boating, summer camping, and friendly soccer games bring Shiloh and Ava closer together, and a burning question arises: Can two, lonely roommates, find solace within each other? Or will they let their spark fizzle out, ruining everything they've worked so hard to build?

The Foreign Exchange

Marlee Adams is not looking for love. All she wants to do is not think about the fact that her mother is dead, hang out with her friends at the local diner, and drop out of school forever. She's definitely not looking to fall in love with the new, very hot, and very unavailable German exchange student, Maximilian Hoffman. But, love has a funny way of sneaking up on you when you least expect it. Spanning years and continents, Marlee finds herself inexplicably drawn toward Max for reasons she can't explain, all while dealing with grief, managing friendships, and most importantly, falling in love.

www.ingramcontent.com/pod-product-compliance
Lightning Source LLC
Chambersburg PA
CBHW071353300726
48976CB00006B/1861